PRAISE FOR BOOK 2: THE CONJURER

"Escape into a lush mysterious world with this paranormal treasure trove."

—SIONNACH WINTERGREEN, QUEER FANTASY/CRIME WRITER

"A seamless interweaving of myth & reality. She appeals to our intellect and our desire for vicarious adventure."

—THE OTTAWA REVIEW OF BOOKS

"The whole narrative plays out like an HBO show waiting to be developed, combining elements of LGBTQ+ and adult storytelling into a complex character study."

—ANTHONY AVINA, READER'S ENTERTAINMENT MAGAZINE

"A fascinating book brimming with tension. Briskly-paced, immersive adventure, gorgeous prose, dialogues that sparkle. Imaginative world-building and the realistic characters, and while this is the second entry in a series, it reads like a standalone novel."

—THE SERIAL READER

"Very enchanting story, with great characters and entwined mysteries. The book shows a lot of cultural understanding, and LGBT support and understanding."

—THERESA SAH

THE CONJURER

THE MAN IN BLACK 2

HARPER CARR

Blue Haven Press, Vancouver, Canada

http:bluehavenpress.com

ISBN: 978-1-998738-03-8 Paperback
ISBN: 978-1-998738-02-1 Electronic Book

Book Design: Wendy Hawkin, Blue Haven Press
Cover Image: Mythology Art

This book is a work of fiction. All names, characters, events, and incidents, other than those clearly in the public domain, are either products of the author's imagination or are used fictitiously. Some settings in British Columbia and Scotland are real. The author attempts to be as true to life as possible while remaining respectful, and is grateful for the opportunity to travel and experience the energy of such sites.

Cataloguing in Publication Information is available from Library and Archives Canada.

This book is for you, whoever you are.
Take courage, and be your own strong, beautiful self.

"True poetry (inspired by the Muse and her prime symbol, the moon) even today is a survival, or intuitive re-creation, of the ancient Goddess-worship." —Robert Graves, *The White Goddess: A Historical Grammar of Poetic Myth*

PRONUNCIATION GUIDE

Sorcha: Sore-sha
Kai Roskilde: Kigh Ros-kill-da
Dunchraigaig: Dun-crag-ag
Ballymeanoch: Bali-men-ock
Magus Dubh: Magus with a soft "g" as in magic. Dove.
Cernunnos: Ker-new-nos
Bhreachan, the Norwegian King: Vreckan
Bagh Gleann nam Muc: by glan nam moochk
Uamh Bhreacain: youve vreckan

1

Sorcha found it in the mud. A green-tinged, tangled mess. Pried it from beneath a thin flat stone with tenderness and a trowel, while Dylan watched, so entranced he forgot to breathe. When she popped the tool back in the faded caddy tied at her waist, he inhaled at last.

Peeling off one glove and then the other, she let them fall. As Sorcha cradled the object in her palm, her emerald eyes flickered as if it were speaking to her, and Dylan's mind flared again. Did she share his gift? When he touched a stone, it revealed its secrets. Perhaps, Sorcha had a talent for psychometry. Imagine holding a golden torque in your hand and seeing its tale unfold in cinematic brilliance. Imagine knowing whose neck it adorned, where all it had traveled, and how many lives it had seen saved or snuffed out.

Squatting, she dipped her treasure in a bucket of water and cleansed it with her bare fingers. Sorcha was a renegade archaeologist who didn't follow procedure or stick to the grid. Dylan usually admired that, but today it gave him shivers.

Kai stamped his foot like a nervous horse and shone the torch. "Gold," he murmured, and Dylan cringed, knowing he was considering the cash that could be made from the sale of such an artifact on the black market.

"Thank you, god." Sorcha held it to her breast.

It was just an expression. The only god she worshipped was fame. Sorcha O'Hallorhan was searching for archaeological connections between the Inner Hebrides of Scotland, where they currently stood, and a land twenty-five hundred miles southeast. Egypt. This artifact was quite possibly the connecting cord—the evidence she needed to prove a legend true and grasp that fame.

"Is it . . .?"

"Aye, lads." She fondled the turquoise beads. "Faience. Just like the beads that adorned the golden collar of King Tut. I knew we'd find her."

She was Meritaten, eldest daughter of Egyptian king, Akhenaten, and his queen, Nefertiti. It was the stuff of story, and to prove it true would change the way the world viewed prehistory.

Kai reached out his large, leathered hand. He wanted to touch it.

But Sorcha drew back, slipped it in her vest pocket and began to climb the rope ladder.

They'd dug down nearly eighteen feet into a pre-Celtic holy well because Sorcha had a theory. People offered gifts to the guardians of holy wells, and sometimes too, they used them to hide things. At this depth, the team had already traveled back in time three millenniums, and unearthed a scattering of bronze axe heads, obsidian arrowheads, jet beads and pottery shards; the skull of an extinct great auk with its long, curved bill still intact; the shed antlers of a stag, and sadly, a malformed infant. But that was nothing compared to this.

Kai followed her up the ladder, his nose way too close for Dylan's liking. Sorcha O'Hallorhan was the site boss, about to claim her PhD in archaeology, but Kai Roskilde was charged with old Viking blood and bent on booty. He'd have her, and anything she found, any way he could.

"Dylan, don't you want to see it?" Sorcha called, her voice fading as she skipped toward the artifact tent to examine her prize.

"I'm coming," Dylan said, rubbing his muscles into something pliant. He'd blown his right knee playing rugby and it was aching something fierce. But when he reached for the rope ladder, it jumped high, right up and out of the pit.

He heard Kai's crazy cackle and glanced up. Could see the sneer above the blond frizzled beard and just make out the long scar that split his right cheek from temple to chin. It was a switchblade—a souvenir from a bar fight in Eastside London. He'd killed the man in revenge and walked away, so he said. Logic told Dylan that was shite, but there was something malevolent lurking beneath those bloodshot eyes that gave it perverse possibility, and he didn't wish to try the man on.

"You're hilarious. Now toss her down." Dylan sniffed and scratched his nose. "Kai, come on."

But Kai was gone, and Dylan was left standing in the cold Argyll muck, cursing his decision to join this summer dig. He leaned back against the mucky shaft and steamed, as the faint clatter of camp filtered down. Kai would return but only when he was damn good and ready. When he'd made his point and embarrassed him in front of Sorcha. Dylan could wait him out. He'd done it before.

What am I doing here? he asked himself. He'd turned down a field school in Greece to come here this summer. He knew the answer. This land was home.

Argyll sprawled along the south-west coast of Scotland in the Inner Hebrides. Once the prehistoric center of the region, Kilmartin Glen was rife with chambered cairns, standing stone circles, and mysterious cup and ring marks—over one hundred and fifty documented prehistoric monuments. Dylan spent his youth here, walking the paths of his ancestors and living with his grandfather in Tarbert, a fishing village on the shore of Loch Fyne. Not some boy's cup of tea perhaps, but Dylan wasn't just any boy. This was where he'd first heard the stones speak, and it was those voices who called him home.

As time wore on, he was aching for a strong cup of tea, something warm to wrap his hands around. He heard scuffling and was just about to call out when Kelly Mackeras popped his head over the edge. Fine-featured and clean-shaven, Kelly looked like a kid.

"Dylan McBride. What're you doing down there all by yourself?"

Dylan scowled. "Kai."

Kelly rolled his eyes. He knew only too well the misery that Viking caused around camp. "Heads up," he yelled, and flung down the rope ladder.

"Do you believe in karma?" Dylan asked, as he crawled out of the pit.

"Aye, some days."

"Bawbag," Dylan muttered, slapping the dirt from his khaki pants.

"You know *why* he picks on you, don't you, McBride?"

As they followed the bacon and coffee trail to Sunday breakfast, Dylan's belly growled. "Because he's a giant arsehole?"

Kelly snorted softly. "It's because *she* likes you."

"Who?"

"Sorcha, you daftie."

"No way." A woman like her? Sorcha was a stunner. An Irish lioness with bright emerald eyes flecked in gold, skin like vanilla cream, and a mane of curly red hair that fell past her voluptuous breasts. Just thinking about her made him hard.

"Oh, aye. She wants you and he wants her." Kelly punched his shoulder. "So, mind. That bastard could sack a city single-handed."

Dylan rolled his eyes in agreement. "Thanks for this. But how did you know?"

He elbowed Dylan in the ribs. "Sorcha sent me."

Dylan gasped. "Do you really think . . .?"

Kelly noticed Dylan's bulging khakis and pinched his cheek. "Oh, aye, McBride. She'll soon drain the blood from these sweet apple cheeks."

Dylan shoved his arm away and they jostled.

"But it's no good," he said, catching his breath. Of course, he wanted her. She was bonnie and pure dead brilliant. But it would never work. Kai Roskilde spent nights in her tent whenever she left the flap ajar. Plus, she was his boss, the kind of archaeologist he dreamt of being and that was not a thing to mess with. Rumor had it, her mother was an archaeology professor, a lesbian who'd slept with her most handsome and promising male students, only long enough to conceive a child.

But there were worse things than antagonizing Kai Roskilde or ruining a career. Dylan knew if he so much as kissed Sorcha O'Hallorhan, he'd fall in love, and that would be the end of him. The only use Sorcha had for men was to feed her lust, and he wanted to be more than mere fodder for a woman, however pleasurable it might be. Hell, he was still recovering from Maggie Taylor, a Canadian girl who'd taken him for her own magical ride last fall.

"Nah. Even if you're right, I couldn't."

Kelly cocked his head. "She's watching you."

Sure enough, when Dylan glanced her way, Sorcha waved him over, flashing an open smile of bright white teeth, and he flushed, knowing he'd been bit.

"Just don't fall in love, McBride, and watch your back."

2

The lads were belly up to the Irish bar in Oban and the black stuff was flowing freely at Sorcha's expense. She'd taken the whole crew out for a Friday night piss-up to celebrate her dawn discovery. Oban was an hour's drive. They usually ended up somewhere close, but she'd insisted on an Irish night to honor her victory. Murphy's was packed with locals and spattered with summer tourists as the season was just beginning. A decent band rocked the stage.

Sorcha was tossing back whiskey shots like water, and Dylan figured he and Kelly would be hoisting her home. That's if Kai didn't get to her first.

"Remind you of anyone?" Kelly gestured to the great jolly Viking statue by the snugs.

"Aye, but that one's a damn sight more amiable than his cousin," Dylan said.

Sorcha caught him watching and danced her way across the black and white checkered tiles. Taking this as his cue to disappear, Dylan grabbed his pint and bolted up the stairs. He planned to avoid any interactions by taking refuge in the cool quiet of the beer garden. Liquored to the gills, she'd get distracted before she made it that far.

Spying an empty table in a far corner reasonably concealed by plants, Dylan hunkered down. As he sipped his pint, he stared up at the sky. It was a grand night—June twentieth, the eve of Summer Solstice. He couldn't believe six months had passed since Winter Solstice, when he'd watched the sun rise and gilt the six-thousand-year-old burial chamber at Newgrange in Ireland. Estrada had been there with his mate, Michael, and Dylan had been there with Maggie.

Dylan missed Estrada more than anyone else. He was a brilliant magician and a good mate. Last year, a maniac turned his life inside out, and Dylan feared he was broken still.

Leaning back, he stared at the stars. Those same stars shone over British Columbia where the coven would celebrate the solstice. He hoped Estrada was with them at Buntzen Lake. As their high priest, he was a key player in their ceremonies, and without him the magic wouldn't be the same. He hoped their high priestess, Sensara, had forgiven him for loving someone else so soon after loving her.

Of course, the folks here didn't know Dylan was involved in Wicca. It wasn't the kind of thing people shared on a dig. They didn't know he belonged to a coven in Canada called Hollystone, that he practiced his solitary magic while they were sleeping in their tents, or that he talked with stones.

He must have drifted off staring at the waning moon because he didn't know Sorcha was there until she draped herself around his shoulders and brushed her whiskey-stained lips across the back of his bare neck.

3

Summer Solstice at Buntzen Lake. Estrada absorbed the resinous smoke swirling from the braziers. Frankincense and myrrh. Fit for a king. Fit for a god. He felt him kick. The Green Man. Awakened, the summer god within his soul was desperate to dance.

As Daphne and Raine led him into the circle blindfolded, damp sand clung to the soles of his bare feet and stuck between his toes. Estrada heard their voices blend with the others in a slow chant of syllabic triplets. "Helios, Apollo. Hail our Lord, the Green Man." Rising in pitch, quickening in rhythm, it drove the witches as they began to dance.

Naked, but for a kilt of ferns, a scarf of hanging ivy, and a grapevine crown of oak leaves, Estrada stood before the bonfire—the front of his body toasted by flames, his back prickling in the cool night air. Laughing and chanting, they raced around him, raising power in their passionate frenzy, and filling him with power too, until Sensara signaled a halt, and their panting merged with the sough and songs of the lakeside night.

Estrada felt her move behind him, sensed her energy blending with his own, could smell her and taste her. Cedar and blood orange and, surprisingly, cinnamon. Had she finally forgiven him enough to wear cinnamon, his favorite spice? The tips of her fingers brushed his hair as she untied the silken blindfold. Did touching him rekindle intimate memories for her, as it did for him, or had she buried their affair in some cold coffin.

As she stood before him and spoke the ritual words, Estrada stared into her dark almond eyes. "Blessed be, Green Man. We welcome you. Celebrate with us this Summer Solstice when the sun reigns longest and brightest. It is your time."

"The time of the Green Man," echoed Daphne, Sylvia, and Raine.

"We honor you in all your guises." Lifting a large crystal bowl with both hands, Sensara offered it to him. "Join us in drinking the elixir of the sun. We've prepared it especially for you."

Cupping his palms over her hands, Estrada held the bowl to his lips and swallowed the sweet fiery elixir. Sparkling wine cut with Cointreau and absinthe, it swirled with strawberry slices and bright yellow blossoms. Protocol demanded he take only a sip, but the Green Man was a passionate god who soaked up liquor like summer rain. And, then there was Sensara. He absorbed her glamor along with the potion.

Draped in a flowing saffron gown, she wore garlands of the same bright yellow flowers draped around her neck and had woven them through her loose black hair—blossoms of St. John's Wort. Estrada tried to hold her gaze. He wanted her to see him in his godly guise. But she broke away and focused on the bowl, refusing to share this moment they'd shared so many times before. Had her love turned to hate? Or worse still, indifference?

Truly, all Estrada craved was her friendship—a relationship with Sensara was far too constricting for a man like him—but even that door remained closed since their brief entanglement eight months before.

Behind her, standing in their circle, was Sensara's new man, Yasu. He caught Estrada's glare and sneered. Why had she brought him here to ridicule their sacred rites? This was no place for skeptics. Did she want Yasu to see what he must accept to be her partner? Or was it something more? Did she intend for Yasu to replace him as her high priest? Estrada tilted the bowl higher and gulped.

"Save some for the rest of us," Sensara said.

Having finally caught her attention, Estrada grasped her hands firmly and guzzled half the bowl. Then, he held it to her lips. Sensara feigned a sip. She drank only on rare occasions and hated to let her guard down.

Estrada released her hands and stood watching as she carried the bowl around the circle, offering each witch a sip of the Green Man's nectar. He appraised Yasu. What did Sensara see in him? A delicate Japanese man, he looked enough like her to be her twin brother. When she offered Yasu the elixir, he leaned back and wrinkled his nose. Surely, she knew that Yasu could never take his place.

As the blessed wine had not been completely consumed, Sensara returned to Estrada and held out the bowl. He took it, tipped it, and drained it. After handing her the empty bowl, he wiped his mouth with the back of his arm and howled at the moon. Hearing giggling behind him, he winked and bowed. Their rituals weren't meant to be stern or grim. They conjured for power but also for pleasure, and he was, after all, the Green Man of the Wood.

Ignoring him, Sensara turned to the altar, where the ritual tools were laid out. Festooned in candles and draped in golden scarves, it shone like summer. She picked up a golden dagger and turned to face him. Estrada knew what was coming, had played this role a half dozen summer nights—though perhaps not quite so vividly.

"Green Man, we hold this vigil in your honor. For all the plant life growing on our planet we ask healing and sustenance. Without our partners, the plants, we cannot survive. Our forests are in peril. We ask that all humanity take into their hearts and minds the desire to protect our trees, flowers, fungi, and all sentient beings."

"Protect them," came the echo.

Circling him, Sensara stroked the knife lightly with her fingertips. "We understand an offering must be made, for there is no life without death, no resurrection without decay. For all life, we thank you Green Man and bless you for your sacrifice. The blood you spill this night will nourish the life to come."

"Blessed be the Green Man," came the echo.

"Let my blood nourish the soil," Estrada said.

Then, standing before him, Sensara plunged the knife into his heart. At the faint borders of his consciousness, Estrada heard Yasu cry out. Perhaps she'd prepared him for their theatrics. Perhaps not.

Clutching the knife at his breast, Estrada fell to his knees. The stage blood slithered down his belly and pooled in the sand. "So mote it be," he whispered, and falling sideways, he hit the ground hard, as a lone owl cut the silence with her screech.

The women covered him with a sheet. The stage knife and greenery were removed. Then, Daphne knelt by his head. He felt her hands against his scalp as she attached his headdress. Limbs hampered by liquor, he laid there a long time, entranced by the sound of the Earth's heart beating in his ear.

"All hail the Horned God, Cernunnos. Rise, Dark Lord. Rise and join us in the dance."

This was Estrada's cue. The Green Man was slain, but his twin the Horned God, who ruled the second half of the year, must rise in his place. And yet, he could not rise.

Sensara leaned down. "Going for an Oscar, Estrada?"

In his stupor, Estrada realized that if he did not rise as Cernunnos the Horned God, if he ruined the ceremony, his fate was sealed. Slowly, he pushed his drunken body up from the sand. He couldn't remember the scripted lines, but it didn't matter.

Standing naked before Sensara, he took a deep breath and allowed the god to speak. "I rise from the sleepy darkness of the earth. From this day until Winter Solstice may all sentient beings find love and joy under my reign." Tossing his head, he felt the deer antlers move as if they were part of his skull. "Dance. Celebrate my resurrection."

"Dance, dance, dance," they chanted, as the sun rose over the mountains. Daphne and Raine pounded their frame drums to set the beat. Moved by their rhythmic thunder, Estrada jumped into the circle and joined them. It was good to dance with his family on the beach this summer night, and it had been a long time since he'd felt good.

"Cernunnos. Cernunnos." His name resounded as they leapt and twisted around the bonfire.

Blood coursed through his body, empowering, hardening, every muscle.

"Cernunnos. Cernunnos."

Swaying with the beating drums, he yelled, "I am The Horned God. I am alive."

The women hoisted their long skirts and leapt over the bonfire. Daphne was the first to wrench the flower garland from her hair and toss it in the flames. She held up her fingers stained with the blood of St. John's Wort, whooped, and danced on. Raine followed, then Sylvia, and finally Sensara.

Estrada regarded the sway of her hips, remembering the slight curves beneath the saffron gown. He wanted to chase her down and throw her to the ground, rip off that flimsy fabric, and remind her how good it feels to love a god.

Grasping Sylvia's outstretched hand, he swung her around, then reached out to clutch Sensara—but in that moment, she linked arms with Yasu, and they jumped the fire together.

Ripping off the antler headdress, Estrada yowled, then hurled it in the sand, and ran.

Somehow, he found his Harley in the dark parking lot. Drunk and desperate, he pulled on a pair of black leather pants and a vest he kept stashed in the panniers. He turned the key and kick-started the bike.

Let her have Yasu. She'll find out soon enough that no one can take my place.

4

Dylan could smell Irish whiskey and women's sweat. Sorcha curled against his back like a ginger cat, her silky hair tickling his bare arms. Reaching up, he clutched the freckled hand that caressed his neck to keep from slipping out of his skin.

"Found you," she purred. When her lips brushed his earlobe, her warm breath flooded his body and sent him reeling. She stroked his cheek, then turned his jaw with her steel grip and kissed him full on the mouth. Dylan had never known a kiss like that. Sorcha was nothing like Maggie. Teasing him with her whiskey tongue, she swung down onto his lap and anchored herself with one leg on either side of his thighs.

When she took his hands and slipped them up inside her white tank, Dylan's breath caught in his throat. Startled by her low moan, he broke away and tried to remember all the reasons this was wrong.

"Relax, McBride," she whispered, holding his hands firmly. "No one can see."

"That's not it." Dylan bit his lip. "You're hammered. Tomorrow—"

"Feck tomorrow. I want you now." Her lips brushed his as she spoke. "How could I not want a fresh sweet peach of a lad who looks at me like I'm a goddess."

"Well, you are that. I'll no' lie to you."

"Lie *with* me. When we get home, come to my tent. I've need of you, Dylan McBride." She kissed him long and deep, and he felt the force of it right to the ends of his shuddering toes.

"But Sorcha . . ."

"You're about to bust your zipper. I'd like a wee taste of what's to come. Wouldn't you?"

Grinning like a Cheshire cat, she slid down between his knees and popped open his jeans.

Holy Christ. What could he do? Push her away? Confess it was his first? He was harder than he'd ever been, watching her red hair spill over his thighs and the flicker of her dreamy green eyes. Dylan told himself it was just a wee bit of sex, something Estrada enjoyed at least once a day, and likely more. And, then he closed his eyes.

There was nothing but her swirling heat and his fingers twining in her hair and for about twenty seconds he was fully Zen and then he was crying prayers to God. Head rolled back, he blinked to a fleeting shadow, but he didnae care for nothin'.

Sorcha was aching for a pint after that, but Dylan needed to clear his head, so he promised to take her up on her offer and staggered toward the street. It was just a wee bit of sex, and he was nineteen for Christ's sake. Like Estrada always said. *Carpe diem. Seize the day. Tomorrow may never come.* Still his head was humming, and the vision of her hair in his lap haunted him as he walked.

Most of the crew had come in the minibus parked out front. Dylan had already offered himself up as designated driver and pocketed the keys, as he had things to do under the solstice moon when they got home. Knowing the pub didn't close until two, he went searching for an all-night coffee shop where he could sober up and think.

He felt different somehow, more man than boy, like he'd experienced some coming-of-age ritual. And he hardened thinking of her offer. What if he did it wrong or couldn't please her? Would she compare him to Kai? Laugh at him? He craved her something fierce, and knew that even if she broke his heart, he'd crave her still. He was bit bad and swelling with her venom. Perhaps that's why he didn't see the man until he was right in his face.

"Spill, ya wee shite," he said.

Christ. The smell. Cigar smoke, whisky, and stale ale.

Brown eyes leered from behind dark-rimmed glasses. He had a long sharp nose, a drab mustache, and a straggly beard. Dylan recognized the face but couldn't place him.

"*She's* a looker. What'd that cost ye?"

Dylan knew he should punch this arsehole square in the face to defend Sorcha's honor, but he had no fighting skills, and the man was a good head taller and likely more experienced.

"Don't you be calling Sorcha—"

"Come on, lad. A burd like that didn't suck a shite like you—"

"Get away." Dylan tried to push past, but the man caught him by the arm and squeezed. "Look, I've no desire to fight you. Just let me by."

"Don't you want to see your picture?" The man waved his mobile and Dylan stood froze.

"Picture? You took pictures?"

"Ach aye, and a wee video too."

"Give it here." Dylan tried to grab the phone from the moving hand, but the man held it high in the air and snapped more shots.

"Easy, big man. I've a proposition."

"A proposition? Not bloody likely. I don't deal with blackmailers."

"I don't deal with blackmailers." The man mimicked him in a taunting tone. "Fine then. I'm sure Miss Sorcha O'Hallorhan will deal. She'll not be wanting her wild Irish curls—"

"How do you know her name?"

The man grinned. "Are you ready to listen or do I go below?"

"What do you want?"

"Rumor has it, the *lady* found an artifact. Get me the story and I'll press delete. Get me the treasure and I'll cut ye in."

"I won't tell you shite and you *will* delete it." Snatching the phone from his hand, Dylan jumped into the van and hit the auto lock. Ignoring the pounding on the window, he searched for the video.

"Some bastard ned's stole my phone," the man yelled.

Soon, there was tapping on the window and Dylan looked up into the dour face of a policeman. "Mr. Steele needs his phone. Give it over now."

Steele. That's why Dylan knew the face. Alastair Steele was a Glasgow journalist. He wrote a regular column and was known for breaking stories.

After surrendering the phone to the officer, Dylan was left to stand in the shamefaced position against the metal van. It gave him time to cool down, though his temper perked again when he heard the officer snigger. Steele had told him of Dylan's public indiscretion while leaving out his blackmail attempt. After producing his driver's license, Dylan was let off with a warning and slunk away from Murphy's dogged by their laughter.

Angry and humiliated, he wandered close to the sea, dodging scraps around the docks and remembering why he seldom came to town to socialize. After seeing a couple of drunks get tossed from one of the seedier bars, he grew worried for Sorcha. This was what he'd hoped to avoid—this concern for a woman who had no concern for him. Still, it was there, nagging at him, so he hastened back to Murphy's to make sure the bastard wasn't harassing her.

He found her on the dance floor, groping some stranger whose shaved head shone black. Wearing a wife-beater that revealed a bulky set of tattooed arms, the man held Sorcha upright by her arse. She wavered close to comatose, her face buried in his chest.

A shiver careened up Dylan's spine. He looked around for Kelly, not that he'd be much help if fists flew, but though his wee red mini was parked outside, he was nowhere to be seen. Then, Kai peered out of a snug looking about as pissed as Dylan had ever seen him and just this once, he was glad.

Kai did a double take on Sorcha and the stranger. Then he swaggered over and peeled her off the man, who narrowed his dark eyes but didn't argue with that drunken lug of a Viking. Throwing her over his shoulder like a sack of booty, Kai clomped up the stairs.

"Leaving now," Dylan shouted to the crew. He was relieved Sorcha was hammered. She likely wouldn't remember their earlier encounter and life could go back to normal.

5

When they were all tucked away in their tents—Kai in Sorcha's as usual—Dylan set out across the meadow toward the Ballymeanoch Stones. Visible from the highway, the standing stones were a testament to Argyll's past significance.

The silvery moon was near round and brightly patched in darkling blue valleys. It was a brilliant night. He'd scarcely seen one like it and mused that this was what his ancestors must have experienced—the spirit of the divine in each drop of dew, each fiery star, each stone, and breath of wind.

Since Summer Solstice was a fire celebration to honor the sun, Dylan would wait until dawn to cast his circle in its rising light. Given the clarity of the night sky, morning promised to be spectacular. He checked his mobile. It was just before three and sunrise wouldn't occur until half past four. Plenty of time to commune with the stones.

Drawn to one of the central stones in the parallel line of four, he sat on the earth and leaned back against the cool three-thousand-year-old rock. Feeling the indented cup marks against his ribs, he wondered at their significance. For thousands of years, humans had worshipped, as he did now, on this sacred landscape. Would the sun rise above a particular stone in this henge, if it was astronomically aligned as some scholars believed?

Dylan's practice had changed since coming to stay in the camp. He was now a solitary wizard, performing rituals alone with no support or comradery, subdued and requisitely silent. Yet, his ability to hear stories from the stones was growing daily. When Dylan McBride laid his palm against a stone it revealed its secrets. Sometimes, he heard voices. Sometimes, he saw visions. Of course, he dared not tell anyone what he experienced. They'd think him daft. Gifts such as his, used to get people hanged or burned, or both.

Dylan had discovered this ability just up the road in the cemetery at Kilmartin Glen when he was thirteen years old and laid his hand on a medieval stone slab carved with the effigy of a dead knight. The experience of that moment shocked and changed him.

Gravestones absorb aspects of a person's soul. Vivid details of their life and death. If a man was religious, the stone revealed that. And if a man was sadistic or mad or cold-hearted, the stone revealed that too. Though iron plates had saved the knight from being skewered, he'd tumbled from his horse, and that day in Kilmartin Glen, Dylan felt the final shudder of the man's body as his neck broke. It nearly knocked him senseless.

At first, he could only touch them for a moment—a person's life was difficult to digest—but gradually his tolerance deepened, and he could sit with his back braced by their solid weight. His visions grew. Sensory images flooded his mind, sometimes accompanied by the music of pipes or drums. And once, when he was confused and asked for clarity, the answer came immediately. That was the day he realized the stones could read his mind as clearly as he read theirs.

But too often, he was sickened by what he saw men do in the name of God and country. So, he left the carved slabs and worked with natural rock, developing a fondness for megaliths. He could feel each stone's unique energy, see flashes of its sculpting by nature, its weathering over millennia, the people who revered it, and lived and died in its shadow.

Like silent witnesses, these massive stones absorbed the essence of the land and the memories of its people. Limited by their inability to move, they could see, hear, and absorb, yet not act. Trapped by inertia, most were eager to speak, even the fiercest of them. Those who, like men, had seen too much evil and been turned by it. Also, like men, the stones longed to share their stories. So often, Dylan sat with them in the meadow, conjoined as he did this night, immersed in images, and listening to tongues so ancient he shouldn't comprehend, yet did.

Now, as he leaned back against the stone, Dylan could see a shaman. Dancing amidst decorated bell-shaped beakers brimming with mead, he wore a frayed buckskin breechclout and a red deer antler headdress, fashioned so the skeletal nose of the deer overshadowed his own.

Cernunnos. Dylan smiled, remembering Estrada's annual portrayal of the resurrected Horned God. "Dylan," he'd say, "you can't just *act* the god, you must *be* the god." And Estrada was—just like this dancing shaman.

A body was laid out ready for burning on a wooden pyre in the center of the circle. Each mourner dipped a hand in a mead pot and sipped its honeyed richness as they passed. When the shaman finished dancing, he lit the pyre, and the somber crowd stood watching as the smoke curled skywards. Fire released the spirit, while ash and bone fell to the earth.

The body on the pyre was an obese male. As the cloth burnt, Dylan grimaced. Half his belly had been ripped open.

Perhaps, he'd been gored by a wild boar. A polished copper axe and spear lay beside him, and a child sat nearby holding a metal object. Slender as a willow, she was tan skinned, her long brown hair plaited with the stems of plants. She sat apart from the others, looked different from them too, and Dylan felt her bond with the deceased. Perhaps, they were kin—travelers come to worship in the glen.

Then, a foreign group entered the stones, and a commotion erupted. At its center was a regal woman perched atop a litter, held aloft by four hefty men. The shaman flew into a rage and shook his rattle menacingly at the intruders.

Dylan stared, mesmerized by her beauty. He couldn't tell if her skull had been shaped in a peculiar way or if it was the jeweled headpiece, she wore that created such an alien visage. She didn't resemble the others gathered in the outer circle, though her enchanting eyes, edged thickly in kohl, seemed familiar. The flames from the pyre danced in the gleaming gold crescent-shaped broad collar she wore around her neck and shoulders. Inlaid with precious stones and faïence beads, golden strands hung from the bottom like rays of the sun, and at the end of each was an ankh, the Egyptian hieroglyph for life.

Dylan gasped. Was this Meritaten? Could her broad collar be the same green, tangled mess Sorcha pulled from the muck this morning? He knew this symbol from a course he'd taken on the Golden Age of Egypt. It was the sun disc, the Aten.

Once it was known only as a form of the sun god Ra. Then, around 1350 BCE, Meritaten's father banished the entire pantheon of gods and goddesses along with the priests of Amun and declared that the people could only worship the Aten. Of course, he proclaimed himself Son of the Aten—*Akhenaten*—so he too must be worshipped. It was a bold political move that infuriated the priests and people of

Egypt, angered the gods, and brought down plagues upon the land—a move that sparked the end of the king's reign.

Dylan flinched with the shock of it all and everything vanished. Wanting more, he edged back against the stone and waited. Seconds stretched into minutes, but nothing more came. That was the way of his capricious gift.

He wanted to run right back to camp, shake Sorcha awake, and tell her what he'd seen. If she shared his ability, she'd be thrilled. But, what if she didn't? Would she think him daft? Besides, she was likely still drunk. And there was Kai to consider.

But this was momentous. Meritaten had walked in this meadow wearing that gold, jeweled broad collar. He had to tell Sorcha. He'd wait for sunrise, get her alone, confess his gift, and tell her what he'd seen.

Stretching out on his back in the grass, Dylan covered himself with his cobalt blue cloak and considered what this could mean. Surely, if the stones had shared this vision, there was a reason.

6

"Christ, man. I've been out here banging for an hour." It was close to six a.m., but Estrada didn't care. He'd driven on autopilot straight to Michael Stryker's flat in the West End of Vancouver. "You never remember to stash a key. You should give me one."

"I believe I have once or twice," Michael said. "But why are you arriving now? And where's your shirt?" He glanced down. "And your boots? Don't tell me you drove here barefoot on your Harley."

Estrada raised his eyebrows and stared at Michael.

"You're lucky you weren't pulled over by the cops. And drunk too?"

"Not enough. Not yet."

"Death wish." Michael glanced around outside. Assured Estrada wasn't being followed by the cops, he grasped his hand and wrenched him in the door. "God, you're freezing. It's a good thing Zoey and Zara are here."

"The dancing twins?" Estrada said, as he followed Michael up the creaky stairs to his flat.

"Yes. We were just about to crash." Michael had slipped on his black silk kimono to answer the door, still wore the musky scent of love in his messy blond hair. For a moment, Estrada was jealous. Not of his sex life—he'd never hoarded that—but because nothing ever seemed to rattle the man. Believing he was the reincarnation of Lord Byron, Michael cruised through life on a sybaritic cloud.

"I'll take the couch and a bottle. You can go back to—"

"Nonsense. You must join us, compadre." Curling his upper lip, Michael flashed a fang. He'd been playing vampire, as usual. "When I told the girls that sounded like *your* Harley, they perked right up. We can all jump in the tub."

"I'm not in the mood."

"You're never in the mood."

Turning at the top of the landing, Michael shoved him up against the wall and kissed him. Leaning in, Estrada closed his eyes and returned the kiss. It was fierce, dark, and delicious.

"Feel how hard you are? I know what you need, compadre." Michael was a tease, but his kisses were real and his instincts dead-on.

Hands slid across Estrada's bare back and down his leathers. When their thighs touched, he was tempted.

"*Christ.* It's been six months. You've got to let it go. You haven't been the same since Ireland."

Estrada took a deep breath and turned away. They had a tacit understanding not to mention names that evoked raw memories, but they both knew what Ireland meant. *Primrose.* Her name hovered in the air like the final riff at a rock concert. She'd stripped away layers, leaving him open, vulnerable, and loving her. And then she was gone.

There had been moments like this. Estrada's brush with death had unmasked a tenderness in Michael, but he'd not been able to engage in his lover's legendary parties. His grief for Primrose couldn't be cured by casual sex, no matter how good it felt.

Michael stroked his cheek with one long nail, then opened the door.

Estrada tugged off his cold leather vest and flopped on the burgundy couch close to the window. "Fuck Ireland. And fuck Sensara and her clone."

"Problems in the pack?"

"We're witches, not wolves." Estrada rubbed his eyes. He was exhausted, but knew he'd never fall asleep feeling this way. "I need something. What have you got?" The alcohol was wearing thin, but Michael was a modern-day apothecary who stocked only the best. Known as the E-vamp, his Ecstasy was legendary and a prerequisite at his parties.

"Ah, let me see. Alcohol. Coke. Though I wouldn't recommend *that* right now. Some decent E. Some *unprecedented* weed. Valium."

"I'll take the E."

"Really? You don't think valium and weed might—"

"You asked me what I wanted."

Michael ran his hands through his hair and sighed. "That I did, but I know you, compadre. I quite enjoy you on E, as do others, but I know how far you plummet on the rebound. Considering how down you've been of late; I'd hate to see you hit the stars and then the skids."

A faint female voice interrupted from the other room, calling Michael by his nickname. "Mandragora? Come back to bed."

"And bring Estrada," another said.

Zoey and her twin sister, Zara, frequented Club Pegasus when they were in town. They loved the contrast between rigid discipline and frivolous debauchery. Both were beautiful ballerinas, but Estrada didn't want either of them. He wanted something else. He wanted—

"Do you want them gone, compadre?"

Estrada rubbed the back of his neck and blinked an inaudible *yes.*

Michael lit a joint and passed it over, then went into the bedroom to deliver the verdict. Estrada closed his eyes, sucked back the smoke, and felt like a prick. It was cruel to oust a woman from a warm bed at six a.m. and doubly cruel to oust twins. Add it to his growing list of transgressions.

"This *is* good weed," he said, when Michael returned. Vibrant traces swirled past his eyelids.

"I told you. The THC level's close to forty percent." Michael's hands were suddenly on his shoulders squeezing. "Man, you're tight." Running his hands up his neck, Michael scratched his scalp with long nails and ran his fingers through his hair. "Better?"

"Diverting."

"I have some incredible oil here somewhere," Michael said, searching the shelf. "Ah, here. Risqué. Vanessa says it's made with licorice, lavender, and ylang ylang. Guaranteed to turn a libido inside out."

"How's that been going for you?"

"No complaints, compadre." Michael lit another joint, took a long drag, and passed it to Estrada. "Finish this while I grab a towel."

"Grab the E while you're at it."

"You won't need it. Trust me."

The twins appeared flashing keen stares and slammed the door as they left.

"They hate me," Estrada said, when he returned.

"Quite the contrary. They're annoyed because you've been holding out for so long." Spreading a white bath towel over the dancing Persian rug, Michael created an oasis in the geometric sea of sculpted color.

"I didn't know you were a masseuse, amigo."

"Ah, well. Vanessa is studying Tantric massage and needs a willing subject. She taught me a few tricks." Michael caught his hair up in a band and uncorked a bright blue bottle. "Now, drop your leathers and lie face down."

"Listen man—"

"Compadre, smell this oil." After rubbing a few drops into his hands, Michael stood behind him and passed his palms in front of his face. He leaned in so close the heat from his lips warmed the back of Estrada's earlobe. "I will only touch what begs touching, and I promise to fill you with nothing but pleasure."

7

When Estrada awoke, he was still lying face down on the towel, but his naked body was covered with a silk sheet. The quiet clattering of kitchen things merged with the aromas of breakfast. He rolled onto his side and flicked on his cell phone. *Christ.* It was three p.m. His belly growled.

As if he'd heard it from the other room, Michael appeared carrying a tray. Hair still damp from a shower; he wore faded blue jeans and a black T-shirt and looked deceptively normal. When you're used to hanging out with an eccentric goth who pretends he's a vampire named Mandragora and considers himself the reincarnation of Lord Byron, your perception gets skewed.

"Man, that was the best sleep I've had in weeks. I need that weed."

"What you need is me." Michael grinned slyly, and he was right. What began as sensual massage morphed into carnality in no time. He set down the tray and squeezed Estrada's shoulders. "Ah, much better. Now you must eat. Feta cheese omelet, toast, black coffee, and a side of piquant salsa, I picked up at Granville Island. Sadie dragged me down there."

"Aren't you having any?"

Michael shook his head. "I grew ravenous hours ago and ate some sushi while I watched you sleep. I enjoy watching you sleep when I know you're going to wake up." Another veiled reference to Ireland. There, Estrada had fallen into a coma and almost did *not* wake up. Michael had flown over and sat by his bedside for days.

"Thanks man. This is perfect," Estrada said, between mouthfuls. "So was last night."

"Naturally. Now, are you going to tell me what got you so perturbed?" After lighting a joint, Michael leaned back on the sofa and put his feet up.

"Not a what, a who. Yasu. Sensara brought him to our ritual last night. There's something about him I don't like. He's cynical. A skeptic."

"So am I, but you accept me."

"Sensara isn't grooming you to take my place." Estrada smeared the last of his toast through the salsa and shoved it in his mouth. "Daphne says he's an environmental architect. Do you know what *that* means?"

Michael shook his head.

"He glues fucking Buddhas onto rocks."

"And you're sure Sensara wants this . . ."

"Yasu."

"And you're sure she wants him to become the high priest of your coven? Why? Did you do something to offend? Or . . ." Michael paused dramatically. "Is she in love with him?"

"I don't know. Maybe. She's obviously grooming him. Why else would she bring him to our private ritual?"

"Perhaps she wants to introduce him to her world." Michael lit another joint and passed it. "I hear that couples—"

"Couples?" Estrada scowled and rolled his eyes, then took a deep hit on the joint and fought to hold it in.

"You're not upset because Sensara's got a new boyfriend, are you? I thought you couldn't handle a relationship with Ms. Hetero Monogamy."

"I can't. But being High Priest of Hollystone Coven means more to me than anything in the world. If that ended . . . If I couldn't do that anymore . . ." Estrada shook his head. "No, I've lost too much of me already. This is a part I'm not willing to give up. Not for anything or anyone."

"God, that's intense. I had no idea—"

"*And* we were partners, Sensara and me."

"Really?"

"We used to do everything together. Laugh. Hang out. I could tell her anything. Christ, we were so tight, we could communicate telepathically." Estrada swallowed hard and shook his head. "Sensara's been my best friend for years, and now . . ."

"Yes, well, it's devastating when you lose your best friend. I used to have one myself. At least, I thought I did. Apparently, I was wrong. He was best friends with someone else all along."

"Oh, don't go all high school on me."

"So now I'm immature. Well, don't stop. What else is wrong with me?"

"Oh, I don't know. Self-centered? Narcissistic?" Estrada stood and pulled on his leather pants. "This isn't about you."

"Of course, it's not. How can it ever be about *me* when everything is always about *you*?"

"*Jesus*, Michael."

"I'm going to bed. Don't be here when I get up."

"Ah, don't be like that."

But Michael stomped into his bedroom and slammed the door.

Estrada heard the lock click and the sound of furniture being dragged across the hardwood floor.

He banged on the door. "I didn't mean it. I'm sorry."

But all Michael did was turn up the tunes.

Feeling friendless and misunderstood, Estrada slipped into a pair of Michael's boots, grabbed his vest and keys, and walked out.

8

Perched on the edge of a wooden bench in an iron-barred jail cell, Dylan sat with his head in his hands, the most mournful soul who'd ever lived. He'd driven by the Sheriff's Office in Lochgilphead many times as a teenager. He knew its medieval stonework and distinctive gray turret, but he'd never spent the night locked inside. It was late Sunday afternoon, and another night was fast approaching. Biting his lip, he forced back tears.

Murder. They'd arrested him for murder.

Billy Craddock was there, or rather, Constable Will Craddock as he now demanded to be called. Dylan knew him from school. His father used to beat him, so Billy beat other kids. Now he was a cop. It was Craddock who bagged Dylan's cobalt cloak after examining the silver elvish embroidery with rolling eyes. And it was Craddock, who dragged him from the field at Ballymeanoch, out through the fenced pathway toward the highway, handcuffed and pleading. "What's happening? What do they think I've done?"

"Shut it, you knob," was all he'd say.

When they reached Dunchraigaig Cairn, Dylan saw it was sealed off with crime scene tape and swarming with police, and he knew something dreadful had happened. The stones were weeping, tearing the air with mournful cries. Still, Craddock refused to explain why he was being dragged off in cuffs.

An inspector appeared at last and said it. "Dylan McBride. You are under arrest for suspicion of murder in the death of Alastair Steele."

Murder? Alastair Steele? That arsehole journalist from Oban?

Dylan had been stripped, searched, fingerprinted, photographed, and finally given the opportunity to call his granddad. He couldn't do it. How could he call and say he'd been arrested for murder? His granddad was an old man. News like that could kill him.

Finally, Craddock called and held out the receiver. Dylan's heart pounded when he heard his grandfather's voice. Words were uttered back and forth. The only thing he remembered from the conversation was telling his granddad to call Estrada. He'd rattled off the number.

Dylan didn't know what to do or how to act in a place like this. He wasn't one of the boys who stole or vandalized, or got drunk and fought, or cracked up their father's car, or beat up their girlfriend. He didn't do drugs. Christ, until last night, he'd never done more than let himself be kissed. Nineteen years old and he'd never made love to a woman. Now, he could spend the rest of his life locked up with men. Bad men.

He hung over the toilet and puked. After wiping his mouth, he tried to calm himself. It was a mistake. He was innocent and someone would prove it. The truth will set you free. Isn't that what people said? Estrada would find Steele's killer. Justice would prevail. If it didn't . . .

Dylan leaned back against the rock wall and tried to relax. But the stones flooded his brain with the intense despair of a thousand prisoners who, like himself, had crouched behind these bars and wondered what was to come. How had life come to this? Worse than a bloody beating was the despair of loneliness—the knowledge you might never again be free to walk with those you loved and who loved you. Mental torment far outweighed anything physical that might occur in a place like this.

Whoever said "if these walls could talk" hadn't heard their tales. One man tried to hang himself and failed miserably. Another anguished soul curled up in the corner and bit the stone walls until his teeth cracked. Both were innocent. Just like him.

Enough. Pulling back from the stones, Dylan perched on the edge of the bench. If he continued to allow the ghosts of this cell to speak, they would surely drive him mad.

9

When Estrada's phone rang at noon on Sunday, he hoped it was Michael. He knew he'd hurt his feelings, but he hadn't meant to. Best friends didn't do the things they did. Michael was more than a friend, so much more. Something indefinable. A part of him, like a second skin.

But the call wasn't from Michael. The man's raspy voice betrayed both his age and nation. Pausing between phrases to catch his breath, he sang his words and rolled his r's.

"This is Dermot McBride calling from Scotland. I'd like to speak with Mr. Estrada, please."

"This is Estrada."

"Aye. Good. Mr. Estrada, I'm calling about my grandson, Dylan."

Estrada's belly flipped. "Is he hurt?"

"No, no, he's fine. It's just that—" He coughed and then sighed. "Ach, there's no point beating about the bush. Dylan's been arrested."

"Arrested?"

A spasm of coughing erupted on the other end.

"Mr. McBride?"

"Just catching my breath."

"Why was Dylan arrested?" Estrada felt suddenly numb. He couldn't imagine Dylan ever doing anything illegal. The boy was pure innocence. He waited for the man to explain but the pause was so lengthy, he feared he was having a heart attack. "Mr. McBride? Are you alright?"

"Aye, lad."

"Why was Dylan arrested?"

"Murder."

The rolling r's sent shivers riveting up Estrada's arms. "Murder? That's impossible."

"I'm afraid you're wrong there, laddie. The polis arrested him yesterday morning. He's locked up in Lochgilphead."

"But Dylan could never . . . Who do they think he killed?"

"A journalist. Alastair Steele." He took a deep breath and tried to clear his throat. "Dylan needs your help. He said you were the only man he trusted. I know we're strangers and I wouldnae ask but . . . Ach, I don't know what else to do. Can you help us?"

"Of course. What can I do?"

"Dylan needs you here, laddie."

"Here? In Scotland?"

"Aye. We'll reimburse your ticket and any other expenses you incur."

"I'm sorry, but I can't—"

"I know it's too much to ask but please reconsider. This Steele is a dastardly newshound, the find-all, tell-all sort. There's likely cheers arising in pubs across the country due to his demise. But the polis arrested *my* grandson, and they're determined to convict him. Ach, I know Dylan could never—" Another coughing spasm seized him. When it subsided, he sighed. "Please, lad. Will you come?"

Why now? The timing couldn't be worse. Sensara was preparing Yasu to take his place in the coven. And Michael. If he left now, the way things were between them, Lord knows what *he'd* get up to. Still, Dylan was in jail, charged with murder.

"You know I'm not a private investigator."

"Aye lad, but Dylan says you're a damn good mate."

Estrada took a deep breath and exhaled. "Alright. I'll call when I've booked a flight."

"Aye, and you'll stay here with me. You'd best write this down. Piper's Dream, Pier Road in Tarbert. That's in Argyll. Everyone in the village knows my cottage. And dinnae fret about Dylan. He's a Scot and he's a McBride."

Estrada searched for flights. He needed a couple of days to organize his life and make peace with Michael. He chose a direct charter from Vancouver to Glasgow that flew on Wednesday and would allow him to avoid the chaos of Customs and Immigration at London Heathrow. Even with his Canadian passport, he drew constant suspicion from airport security and had been strip-searched more times than he cared to remember while crossing the American border. He wasn't sure if it was his Harley, his penchant for leather, his long black hair and swarthy complexion, or that certain combination, that made him a target. In their eyes, he was either a drug lord, a terrorist, or both.

10

By Tuesday evening, after several failed attempts at reconciliation, Estrada went to see Michael's grandfather, Nigel Stryker. A successful entrepreneur and owner of Club Pegasus, Nigel had employed him to perform a Friday night magic show for the past six years. A talented magician and escape artist, Estrada performed gothic theatrics, hypnosis, and the usual sleights. He drew a large crowd and appreciated the regular gig, which he did whenever he wasn't performing out of town.

But Nigel didn't just sign his pay cheques. He was the closest thing Estrada had to a father. So, he told him where he was going and why. Nigel had helped him before, and he knew he'd help him now. He was clever and connected and someone Estrada could rely on.

Business aside, Estrada took a deep breath and told him about Michael. He said they'd had a misunderstanding, and he was very sorry he'd hurt Michael's feelings. He was fishing really, looking for resolution to a distressing situation. Michael was so volatile, Estrada feared leaving things unsettled.

But Nigel knew nothing about it. Though Michael lived in a turreted tower flat in his grandfather's Queen Anne mansion, he'd been keeping to himself. He wasn't feeling well and hadn't come into the club the last couple of nights.

Nigel patted Estrada on the back. "It takes balls to say you're sorry, Sandolino. I respect that in a man. You know you're like a son to me. The patrons love you and obviously so does Michael. Don't worry. I'll check on him. He can be dramatic, but he'll come around."

Estrada wondered if Nigel understood the intricacies of their relationship or if he assumed they were having a lover's quarrel. He let it lie. Things that couldn't be explained were best left unsaid.

11

As the plane crossed the Atlantic, day morphed into night. Estrada slept fitfully, entombed by bodies, boredom, and bad air. He'd rather be cruising down the highway on his Harley with the wind in his face. Then he thought of Dylan locked in a musty old jail cell. Was there no justice in this world? Moments like this made him doubt his belief in karma. Of all people, Dylan was the least likely to kill a man for any reason. Why would this happen to him?

When the wheels touched the Scottish tarmac, bringing nine hours of cramped confinement to a screeching halt, Estrada was desperate to move. He'd packed light and brought only carry-on luggage, so dashed to the queue. Customs and security had recently been upgraded, said the businessman behind him, but black-suited police from the Anti-Terrorism Squad armed with MP5 submachine guns, did nothing to quell his anxiety. He hoped it wouldn't be apparent in his interview.

Waiting in the non-EU queue, he clutched his landing card and rubbed his chin. Perhaps, he should have run a razor over the twelve-hour stubble. His hair had grown three inches since his coercive head shave last fall, and now curled under the collar of his black leather jacket. It would take years to grow to its former length, but it was a start. He'd vowed never to cut it again.

He wore a black T-shirt, clean black jeans, and high soft leather boots—none of which was outlandish—and carried his jacket folded over his arm. He had multiple ear piercings but no visible tattoos, and he'd washed away all traces of eyeliner before leaving home. Men who wear makeup attract undue scrutiny.

Estrada wished he could conjure a glamor like Merlin did for Uther Pendragon and slip by unseen. Maybe someday. Taking a deep breath, he willed himself to ride the gray line between anxious and cocky. There was no cause for concern. He was just a Canadian visiting a friend in the U.K.

When he handed the immigration officer his passport, ticket, and landing card, he looked the man in the eye.

"What's the purpose of your visit to Scotland?"

"Visiting a friend."

"How long will you be staying?"

Estrada swallowed. "Two weeks." At least he'd bought his ticket with a two-week return.

Things were moving along without a glitch until the officer read something on the screen, narrowed his eyes, and called over one of the armed police officers. Turning their backs to him, they conferred in dull whispers for several seconds. Then, the cop walked a few feet away and made a call on his cell phone. Estrada broke out in a sweat, as visions of terrorist prisons flooded his brain. He could disappear. It happened. He'd seen it in the movies.

"Follow me." It was a wiry cop with an MP5.

Estrada took a deep breath and followed him into a cramped interview room. An older cop, also carrying a submachine gun, flanked him. Neither of them spoke and it turned into an awkward staring match—Estrada, seated in a plastic chair behind a table where he'd been placed, and the two of them standing guard by the door. They seemed stalled, were perhaps awaiting instructions.

"Is there a problem, officer?" he asked, anxious to break the tension.

The older cop sniffed, while the younger answered a call on his cell. "Aye," he said at last. "Will do, sir."

Sitting down in the chair, he stared across the table. "McBride." He waved Estrada's landing card in his face. "You've written here that you're staying in Tarbert with a man named Dermot McBride."

"Yeah?"

"What is your relationship with McBride?"

"I've never met him."

"Yet you're staying in his home?" He pressed his thin lips tightly together and then popped them open as if for emphasis.

"I know his grandson."

His eyebrows rose. "Name?"

"Dylan."

One eyebrow fell. "The Dylan McBride who is currently being detained on murder charges?"

"Yeah," he muttered. He crossed his arms over his chest and leaned back in the chair. What did it matter if he visited a friend in jail?

"What exactly is the purpose of your visit? I mean, considering your mate's in lockup and can't take you on a tour of the Highlands." Raising his eyebrows, he looked down his nose and grinned at his own bad joke.

"I came to support him and his family."

"The family you've never met." Another annoying pop was followed by a lengthy pause as the officer fiddled with his documents.

Estrada touched his forehead. Cold. Wet. Sweat.

"I see on your passport you entered the Republic of Ireland last November and stayed until Christmas. Do you have friends there too?"

"I did, yeah."

"Aye, so we heard."

"Sorry?" What the hell did that mean? Was he listed on some computer site as an unwelcome guest? *Do not allow this man into your country.*

"Are you Sandolino Estrada?"

"Yeah."

"The same Sandolino Estrada who was involved in three deaths in Ireland? One, a civilian, and the others, suspects in a serial murder case in Canada?"

"Yeah, but that—"

The cop took a deep breath, puffed out his chest, and launched into a rapid speech. "The Detective Chief Inspector of Police Scotland would like you to know that if you stick your nose into any murder investigations while you're here in *our* country, you just might lose it. If we suspect you of *anything,* you'll be joining your friend Dylan McBride in custody. Do you understand me, Mr. Estrada?"

"Yeah, but—"

"Good. You've been warned. Your name is on our radar, and we'll be watching you." He pointed his fingertips to his eyes in the universal gesture. "Comprender?"

Squeezing his fingers tightly into fists, Estrada remembered why he hated cops. If he ever got the chance, he'd take that MP5 and shove it right up his tight Scottish ass.

"Make sure you do, or you might just find yourself back in *Me-hi-co.*"

When he flung the passport, Estrada caught it in the air. "I'm a Canadian citizen."

"Aye, for now."

12

It was almost noon when the cab dropped Estrada off in front of West Coast Harley-Davidson at Charing Cross in Glasgow, but in no time at all, he was ripping up the A82 on a Heritage Classic, the color of merlot. It took a chunk out of his bank account, but he didn't care. Money could always be made, and that cop had taken a chunk out of his cool—something he intended to get back.

The sun was high in the sky and with Loch Lomond rippling to his right, he felt like cruising forever. But suddenly he saw the turnoff for A83, and he was veering left and climbing toward a stunning mountain pass and then all but flying down the other side. Following the rugged shoreline of Loch Fyne, he remembered Dylan once spoke of his grandfather gazing out over this lake.

He was just ingesting the green lure of the rolling Scottish landscape when he saw a sign for Lochgilphead and hit both brakes, sending gravel skittering in his wake. This was the place Dylan's grandfather had mentioned on the phone. Estrada sat for several seconds staring at the sign; the reality of the situation too much to comprehend.

Is Dylan really in there? Locked behind iron bars and charged with murder? Jesus Christ. Dylan would rather die than submit to sex with a man. He'll get himself killed.

No one answered the door at Piper's Dream, so Estrada locked up the bike and sauntered back down the street to a hotel pub he'd passed on his way through the village. His wolfish soul was crying for a bottle of tequila, but he wasn't fool enough for that. He'd need to restrict any drinking he did to a few pints. At least for now. When he drank tequila, he lost chunks of time, and he had no time to lose.

Tarbert was one of those quaint fishing villages where couples went for a romantic interlude. Fishers sold their fresh catch from boats moored in the harbor. It was late afternoon and the main thoroughfare, which curved around the sea, was bustling with tourists, some with children, most without. He tried to imagine Dylan spending his teen years here, living with his grandfather in the house up the road.

"Out touring?" The bartender struck up a conversation as Estrada sucked back his third pint. Perhaps, the ale had softened his edges.

"Touring?"

"Aye. Saw you cruise by earlier on that Harley. Fine-looking bike. Are you on a motorcycle tour? We get them through here. Tarbert being a ferry port."

"Oh, yeah. A Harley's a great bike for touring."

The man nodded once and went to deliver his pints. The place was filling, mostly with locals. A fresh copy of *The Evening Times* sat on a shelf nearby. Remembering what the cops had said about hearing the name McBride, Estrada picked it up. He didn't have far to look. It was right on the front page about mid-way down beside a stock photo of the murdered journalist. A narrow-featured villainous type, his dark-rimmed glasses did nothing to alter the malignancy bubbling beneath the surface.

MCBRIDE TRANSPORTED TO GREENOCK

Following his appearance today in Oban, alleged murderer, Dylan McBride, having made no plea or declaration, was taken into custody, and transported to Greenock prison. McBride, a former resident of Tarbert, is in Argyll working on an archaeological dig with the O'Hallorhan team at Kilmartin Glen. The body of investigative journalist, Alastair Steele, was discovered early Saturday morning, wedged inside Dunchraigaig cairn, mere feet from the A816. Witnesses report seeing the two men argue outside Murphy's Irish pub in Oban late Friday evening. Rumor has it O'Hallorhan unearthed an ancient Egyptian artifact Friday morning. The archaeologist was unavailable for comment.

"Jesus." Seeing the facts printed in text made it real.

"Ach, that's a hell of a mess." The bartender was back and wiping down the bar. "I know McBride. He lives up the street with his granddad. Good man. Good lad."

"What about this journalist? Is he as dirty as he looks?"

"Oh, aye. The last I heard of Steele, a young lass he worked with made accusations. Rape."

"Really? Did it go to trial?"

"Nah, they couldnae make a case. Steele claimed it was consensual. Ruined the poor girl's reputation."

"Do you remember her name?"

"Jane something. I remember cause it's my sister's name." He squeezed his eyes trying to force her name to surface, but nothing emerged. "Spike will know. He writes for our local rag."

Leaning over the bar, he yelled across the patrons to three men drinking at a far table. "Spike. What was the name of that burd Alastair Steele got tangled up with?"

"Janey Marshall," came the reply.

"Aye. Janey Marshall. I'll bet she was fair boilin' that Steele got off."

"Enough to kill him?"

"Ach, I don't think she could, not on her own. Just a wee thing. Still, 'hell hath no fury like a woman scorned.'"

Estrada raised his eyebrows. Rape was far from scorn. "This Janey Marshall, does she live around here?"

He shrugged. "In Glasgow, I imagine. Are you a journalist yourself, then?"

"No. Just touring." Estrada smiled. "Can I buy this paper?"

"You're alright," the bartender said and waved him off.

Estrada nodded gratefully, slapped a few pounds on the counter, and sauntered out.

The sun was setting over the sea and he felt guilty for appreciating the quiet beauty of the village. On the crest of a hill stood a grass-covered castle ruin guarded by a brown, shaggy-haired goat. The houses looked similar. It was the shade of trim that set them apart. All two-story and built of gray brick, they rose like sentinels from the harbor. There were no front porches, which seemed odd considering the ocean was right there on the other side of the road just begging to be admired. Perhaps, fishermen were so wearied by the sea, they didn't care to watch it from their homes. Some had pitched roofs and dormer windows, where an anxious wife or mother could scan the waves for signs of her man.

Though it was a postcard town, he wondered what secrets hid behind those brick façades.

When he arrived back at Piper's Dream, a white-haired man, much frailer than his voice, stood on the lawn with his hands behind his back, just staring at the sea.

"Let's sit out for a spell and have a wee dram," Dermot McBride said after introductions had been made. "I'm done in." He lit a well-worn bentwood pipe and puffed some.

As soon as Estrada breathed the heady tobacco, he thought of Michael. Was he still angry? He downed his whisky and placed the empty glass on the step.

The sight of a police cruiser on the road below interrupted his thoughts. "I don't want to alarm you, Mr. McBride, but that's the second time I've seen the police drive by and glance in. Are you under surveillance?"

"No, no. The press, though . . . Damn fools camped here for days." He puffed on his pipe as he spoke. "That lad in the cruiser is Billy Craddock. He'll keep an eye on Dylan. They were schoolmates. The polis here are fair and honest and protect them that need protecting."

Right. Estrada's introduction to the Scottish police force hadn't left him with that impression, but then, he was an outsider. They were intent on protecting Scotland from him.

"The people here know that Dylan's no killer."

"Yeah, I heard that said in the pub." Estrada sniffed the damp sea air. "I need to talk to him."

"If you can wait a day or two, I'll take you myself. I went to court today and then to the prison. I wanted Dylan to know he wasnae alone. It takes eight hours, there and back again, what with two ferry crossings. I only just arrived twenty minutes before they closed the visits room. I managed to leave £50 with the officer, though, so he can get what he needs."

Eight hours of travel for a twenty-minute visit? No wonder the old man was done in. "You should rest this weekend. There are things I can do here." Estrada was curious about the Egyptian artifact mentioned in the paper, the one found by O'Hallorhan, the archaeologist at Kilmartin Glen. It was likely connected and seemed a logical place to start.

"I wrote down the visiting times." Dermot pulled a scrap of paper from his pocket. "If we arrive by half-two on Monday, you can see him for thirty minutes. Tuesday and Wednesday, they only allow visits in the evenings."

"Let's go Monday then."

The old man pulled a flask from his pocket and refilled Estrada's glass.

This time he sipped. Late afternoon hugged the harbor town, eclipsing the chaos, and he sunk inside it.

"Can Dylan make phone calls?" Estrada asked at last.

"I don't know. I brought his mobile home." Dermot fished around in his pocket, pulled it out and stared at it. "It's nothing fancy, no web, but you can make local calls. You might as well use it. Then I can reach you if I need to. My number's in there under granddad." He handed Estrada the slim phone and smiled sadly. "Back door's always open and you're free to come and go as you please.

"Thanks. I appreciate that. I had so much on my mind, I left my own phone on my bedside table." He could use an internet café if he needed to contact anyone back home, but it would be good to have Dylan's phone for local calls.

Dermot downed his whiskey and hung his head in silence for several minutes while Estrada gazed at the lights reflected in the water. When at last the old man glanced up, his stormy eyes were thick with tears. "Ach, my boy's locked inside a prison cell. I still cannae believe it." He wiped them and sniffed. "Thank God his gran's nae here to see this day. It would break her heart."

It's broken yours, Estrada thought. "I'll get him out," he said. "I promise."

When the cruiser drove by a third time, Estrada considered what the cops had threatened at the airport. *Fuck 'em.* He'd do whatever it took to free Dylan from that prison, even if it meant ending up in there with him.

13

T he sun beating down against Sorcha's eyelids veiled the world in red. Red like the blood of kings. Red like a Galway sunset. The archaeologist was a little sun drunk that morning. It was the first hour she'd had to herself in weeks. Sick of the muck and the damp and the assaults by paparazzi on her camp at Kilmartin Glen, she'd stolen away to the western pasture. If they needed her, they'd call.

Stretched out on a vibrant Turkish sarong, she felt the hot sun caress her thighs. God, what she wouldn't do for more of that. Reaching behind her back, she unhooked her halter and slipped it off.

Sorcha believed a woman's body was beautiful, especially her own. At university, she'd explored the female form with other girls—even fallen in love. She'd learned what a woman liked and what she liked, learned to appreciate her body and use it to her advantage. Halters had their place, could accentuate and deepen, making mounds into mountains, but they'd surely been invented by men to tie down their women like their horses. And Sorcha was no horse, which was why she frequently let her breasts run wild.

She'd have to be mindful during this heatwave though. Bliss could turn to pain with skin so pale. She wished her mother had chosen a man without the Celtic gene. Someone swarthy like the man she'd danced with at Murphy's. *My Black Spaniard.* Her sigh took her back to the dance floor, and she remembered the feel of his hard muscles, the damp heat of his breath against her neck, his soft lips lingering on her flesh. *Spanish and Egyptian*, he'd said. His people must have come from somewhere south near the Sudan. She wished he'd taken her home that night instead of Kai. How grand it would have been to make love to an Egyptian with Meritaten's collar only a breath away. Ah, but so much for romance. That night had ended in disaster.

Feeling the sun's fire intensify, she rolled onto her belly and lay with her cheek pillowed against her arm. It had been one crazy week. She felt responsible for Dylan's predicament. Her plan to liberate his puritan soul with a little casual sex had backfired and cost him his freedom. She'd found and lost the Egyptian collar. She'd even dragged them all to Murphy's that night. If they'd gone somewhere else, anywhere else.

She flinched when her mobile rang and noted the caller ID. *Kilmartin Museum.* Likely another journalist was snooping around looking for dirt. The press had been buzzing like flies on a corpse since the news broke about Steele's murder and her discovery.

"O'Hallorhan."

"There's someone here asking to speak with you." It was Emma, a sweet girl who came to dig and stayed for the craic.

"Paparazzi?"

"Doubtful. His name's Estrada."

A flush swept through Sorcha's body beginning in her toes. *Estrada. Could it be him? My Black Spaniard?*

Emma breathed in the pause and then whispered, "You'll want to meet this one."

Holy Mary Mother of God. Her heart thumped loud and hard like the music at Murphy's, and she clapped a hand to her breast. "Did he say what he wants?"

"He's a friend of Dylan's. Just flown in from Canada."

Ah. Couldn't be him. She heaved a heavy breath as her dream collapsed. "Right so. I'll be along."

"Aye, Mr. O'Hallorhan. I'll let him know."

"Another one who assumes I'm Indiana Jones, is he?"

"Of course, sir." Emma giggled.

"Ah, you mad woman. I owe you a pint."

She combed out her crazy hair with her fingers and pinned it up, tied the sarong over her khaki shorts, and positioned the halter for maximum effect. Lord, it was hot. Not even a faint sea breeze. An hour before noon and the sheep were slow grazing under the shade trees. As she hiked up through the fields, sweat seeped between her breasts. Damn climate change. Northerners had lived without tropical adaptations for millennia. They weren't cut out for this.

Early Friday morning there were few strangers at the museum which made Estrada from Canada rather obvious. He was crouched in the graveyard by the church examining tombstones. He'd a lighter complexion than her man at Murphy's but was just as striking, and she was suddenly glad Kai had gone diving in the islands. The man could be intimidating. He claimed to be studying underwater archaeology, but Kai was a born pirate and the Hebridean coastline rich in sunken treasure.

She crept up behind the stranger and extended her hand. "Good morning. I'm Sorcha O'Hallorhan."

"Oh." He stood to his full height, easily six foot two, tilted his tanned face and grinned. "Estrada."

A Latin lilt and a voice like honey. When he took her hand in his, a twinge rippled through her belly and down her thighs. *Ancient genes.*

"I'm sorry to disturb you, but I wonder if I could have a word."

You can have more than a word. Take the feckin dictionary. Egyptian eyes nearly black, lined in kohl pencil and thickly lashed. *No, not Egyptian, closer to Spanish, and something else, something Indigenous.* Eyes wide, she appraised him. Hair as shiny and black as a raven's wing hung in his eyes. Ears riveted with turquoise studs. A long, angular nose, broken and reset, at least twice. *Is he a scrapper, then?* He'd shaved recently. She smelled musk mixed with sweat, but a scruff of beard crept like a sexy shadow across his chin and dimpled cheeks. Dark nipples pierced his pale blue tank. He had smooth brown shoulders and was well-muscled, athletic even, and well-packed into snug blue jeans. *And those lips.* Thick and heart-shaped, they begged to be kissed.

The looking continued for several seconds and then his gaze dropped to the significant cleavage threatening her halter-top.

"They're real," she said, with a little cheek. "Want to touch them?"

"Just one." Reaching out, he cupped her left breast in his palm and stroked the taut point with his thumb.

A quick gasp escaped before she could contain it, and she bounced back beyond his reach. "Shall we chat in the café? I need some real coffee." What she needed was real control.

From the outside, the café looked like an old barn, but the interior was all stonework and oak timbers. She watched him take it in and liked that he admired the rustic beauty. When he pulled out the chair for her, his hand brushed hers and sent a jolt up her arm.

He laughed, had felt it too. "I sing the body electric," he said.

"Are you a poet?"

"No. Walt Whitman's a poet. But who can ignore the charge of the soul?"

"Ah, you *are* a poet." Settling into the chair, she lost herself in those dark eyes. *Swarthy*, she thought, and smiled at the awkward sounding word that rocked her senses.

"No, a magician." His belly growled and he snorted. "A hungry one."

"Well, order lunch then. It's half eleven and I can vouch for the food." She passed him a menu. "A magician? Can you make a living at that?"

"I do about as well as an archaeologist," he said, pulling those delicious lips into a half-smile that nearly unseated her. How the hell was a man like this, friends with a lad like Dylan? Perhaps, he was an investigator sent by the McBride family.

"How is it you know Dylan?"

"We met through friends in Canada."

"Dylan's interested in magic, is he?"

"Actually, yes." When he leaned back and ran a hand down his neck, her hand moved unconsciously to her own. The skin was damp beneath her fingertips.

"Well, perhaps you can spirit him away from that blasted prison."

"The thought crossed my mind."

She'd been flirting, but his response was genuine. When his smoked salmon baguette arrived, he all but inhaled it. Then he polished off a bowl of roast tomato and pepper soup.

"Much better. I didn't realize I was—"

"Ravenous, like a wolf."

He cocked his head curiously.

"I don't know why I said that."

"Well, I *am* following a trail. I promised Dylan's grandfather I'd get him out of that prison, and I intend to do it. I thought perhaps you could help. You don't have to tag along for the jailbreak but anything you can tell me . . . "

"Aye, of course."

"I figure the only way to vindicate Dylan is to find the real killer. It could be dangerous."

"Ah, bring it on. Dylan didn't kill that fecker or have anything to do with stealing the artifact."

His eyes widened.

Was it wicked to speak ill of the dead or were Canadians not used to such terms?

"Right. I read something about that in the local paper. You found some treasure? Was it really stolen?"

"Aye, and not just *some* treasure. *Her* treasure."

"Her?"

"Meritaten, the daughter of Akhenaten and Nefertiti."

His brow furrowed. Was it concentration or confusion? Perhaps he needed educating.

"What I found confirms an Egyptian princess came to Scotland, just as the legend says."

"Legend?"

"Aye. In 1435, Walter Bower, the Abbot of Inchcolm Abbey, wrote what's now considered a historical document—*The Scotichronicon*. In it, he tells the story of an Egyptian princess who arrived in Scotland around 1350 BCE. Generally, we accept what religious people write as—"

"Gospel?"

His smile was compelling. "Aye, they wrote what had been passed down through the oral tradition along with Christian embellishments."

Estrada nodded as she spoke and looked her straight in the eye. She liked that about him. She liked everything about him.

She sipped her coffee, then said, "Bower called her Scotti."

"As in Scotland."

"I believe he was referring to her as a raider."

"But Egypt's got to be a couple of thousand miles south."

"Aye, but she didn't leave Egypt bound for Scotland. Bower claims her ships followed the River Constantine through Africa, and they stayed for some time in present-day Algeria. I've traveled her route. It's possible."

As she explained, she traced the path on the table as if it were a map.

"From Africa, they sailed to the island of Cadiz in Spain, and then to the northeast Spanish mainland, where they settled by the mouth of the River Ebro. The Indigenous People of Iberia didn't like being ruled by an Egyptian queen, so they were forced to flee again. With bridges burned in Egypt and Spain, they sailed north, past Cornwall, and on through the Irish Sea. After crossing the channel, they ventured into the sound."

"But how would they know where to go?"

"Ah, well. During the Bronze Age, traders from several nations were sailing through the channel regularly, trading goods from the Mediterranean and France with the people of Ireland and Scotland, even as far north as Skara Brae in Orkney. Everyone was after tin to smelt copper and the best place for tin was Cornwall. Three thousand years ago, the sea due west of us was a bustling thoroughfare, and this valley, a religious and cultural Mecca." She paused to sip her coffee. "I think she came here for the stones."

"The stones?"

"Aye, the standing stones."

He cocked his head.

"The megaliths?"

He still didn't seem to understand and paused with the thought.

Had he not seen them? The Ballymeanoch Stones stood in a field along the highway and were visible to anyone driving by.

"So, what did you find?" he said at last.

"Her broad collar."

Estrada narrowed his eyes.

"A neck and shoulder piece." She used her hands to illustrate how it sat against the woman's clavicle. "It was crafted in gold and decorated with precious stones and faience beads, just like the ones Carter discovered when he unearthed the tomb of her cousin, Tutankhamun. You've heard of him, I presume. King Tut?"

When he pursed his lips, his cheeks hollowed out in shadow. "Sure."

"Well, if she hadn't left Egypt, Meritaten would have ruled in his stead. Some say she didn't leave, but I know she did. And I'm sure the piece I found was hers."

"How can you be sure of something like that?"

Sorcha snorted. "Trust me. I'm sure." She wasn't about to tell him what she'd seen when she held that collar in her hand. He'd think she was mad. But her visions were revealing, and they never lied. She'd picked up images from metal objects since she was a girl. He didn't look like the type of man who required evidence but perhaps he did.

"In 1955, O'Riordain found a similar collar in Ireland at Tara with a corresponding date. The legend says, Meritaten's people fled there after the people of Scotland cast her out."

She sipped her coffee and watched him process what was second nature to her.

"Egyptians in Scotland." He tilted his head and narrowed one eye, an action that made him look, not just curious, but dangerous. "So, who do you think stole it?"

"Honestly, I'm baffled. I do know where it might surface though. There's a healthy black market for antiquities in the UK, if you know where to look. I'm heading to Glasgow tomorrow to do a little digging, pardon the pun. I know a wee fella."

"I have a Harley out front," he said, eyes brightening, "and I'm headed that way myself. There's a woman there with a grudge against Steele and I'd like to talk to her. Any enemy of Steele's . . ."

"It's a date." Her mobile rang then, and she slid it open. "O'Hallorhan."

"Sharesies?"

"What's the craic, Emma?"

"There's a Detective Erskine-Steele headed your way."

"Steele. As in Alastair Steele?" She felt a rush of something tantamount to dread.

"Aye, as in Mrs."

14

Estrada finally understood why Dylan had volunteered to dig in the dirt of the Scottish countryside surrounded by sheep shit all summer, rather than work in Greece. Sorcha O'Hallorhan was sexy and sagacious. She had a keen wit, and he liked her spirit. And on a more practical level, she made a fine ally. As partners, they stood a better chance of liberating Dylan. She knew her way around Scotland; something he did not. She also knew the people who worked at her camp. He was about to suggest forging a pact when a tall, willowy blonde flashed a police badge before his eyes.

"Detective Erskine-Steele. I have a few questions."

"Steele." Sorcha's eyes flickered. "You're not related to Alastair Steele, are you? The man who was murdered just up the road?"

"Neither a matter of consequence, nor your business."

Estrada wondered if the detective's eyes, hidden behind dark mirrored glasses, were as soulless as her voice. He wished to see them. Her platinum hair was bound severely in a low ponytail just above her collar. Having slipped her badge back in the pocket of her gray trousers, she stood stiffly, her pale hands braced against a thick leather belt from which were tethered several leather-cased items—a phone, a radio that emitted a dull hissing sound, what appeared to be a semi-automatic pistol, and an extra magazine.

"I think it is," Sorcha, said, recovering from the detective's curt response. "Both of consequence and my business. A friend of mine is in jail for Steele's murder. If you're related, I consider that a conflict of interest."

The detective lowered her gaze and stared down the archaeologist.

"Noted," she said, at last, her voice deadpan.

Sorcha took a deep breath and hissed. "Well, isn't she the bitch?"

The detective's lips rose in a slight sneer. Rachel Erskine-Steele was a woman who reveled in her power. If the archaeologist was fire, the detective was ice. Turning her back to Sorcha, she faced Estrada.

He gazed up at the lithe leaden form and wondered what it was she *really* wanted. Everyone has an agenda. If she was the victim's wife, perhaps it was justice, possibly vengeance. Then again, if the man was as vile as he seemed, she could be relieved, grateful even.

"Let's walk, Mr. Estrada." It wasn't a suggestion.

Recalling his experience at the airport, he stood and withdrew a few pounds from his wallet. He tossed them on the table. "I'll be right back," he promised Sorcha, then smiled and winked. He hoped to mollify the archaeologist. There was no point arguing with a grieving widow, especially one who was armed.

When he stood beside the detective, her height surprised him. He was six foot two and she was taller.

"After you," he said, and flashed his most captivating smile.

Though sinewy, she floated as fluidly as a dancer, her posture perfect. No panty lines, yet through the pale gray tailored blouse he perceived a lacy outline. A villain, yet oddly angelic. His mind reeled in the contradiction.

At her car, she turned and stood watching him. With a sudden breeze came the faint scent of feral sweat, and he breathed it in like a tonic. When she removed her glasses, her eyes, as icy gray as the North Sea, caught his and held them.

"*Fuck*," he said.

"Fuck you," she said. "We're watching you. We know what happened in Ireland last winter, and we know about your connection with the Stryker family in Vancouver. We know they're dirty and we know you're dirty. So, if you so much as breathe wrong, we'll jail you first and investigate later. If you value your freedom, Mr. Estrada, you'll catch the next plane back to Canada."

"Wait a—"

"Dylan McBride is a killer and will be convicted. This is the last courtesy you'll get."

Estrada wanted to protest, to scream corruption or threaten to expose her to the press, but as her hand strayed near her pistol, he felt a cold caress against his flesh. Turning, he padded into the restaurant where he'd left Sorcha. When he glanced back, Detective Erskine-Steele was sliding into her Prius.

"Did you give her a piece of your mind?" Sorcha asked.

Estrada felt slightly lightheaded. He glanced back, but the car had vanished. "She wants me gone. I don't get it. Why the intimidation? If *my* partner was murdered, I'd appreciate any help I could get. I'd want to know what happened."

"Ah, she's just a skinny bitch." Firmly planted in the chair, Sorcha crossed her arms beneath her breasts—a warrior queen poised and ready for battle.

"Was Steele's body found nearby?"

"Just down the road."

"Are you keen to solve a crime, Sorcha O'Hallorhan?"

"Aye, that I am, Estrada."

"Let's go then."

He sauntered out of the restaurant with Sorcha following behind. If the Scottish police were going to threaten him, he'd find out why.

"We could walk."

"I'd rather keep the bike close," he said, striding toward the Harley.

"How's about I drive, then? I know the way."

"You can drive a bike and you're legal?" The detective's threat harried him.

"Feck, yeah. Driven them all over the world."

Estrada wondered where Sorcha's license was. It wasn't in the pocket of those tiny khakis or tucked inside that halter. He handed her the extra helmet and waited. As she settled and started the engine, he slid up close behind and wrapped his arms around her waist. She took off fast, sending a spray of gravel sideways, obviously miffed that he'd questioned her ability. Within moments, she'd pulled off the A816 into a car park.

"It's just there." She pointed to the other side of the highway, where the remains of yellow police tape fluttered over a grassy rock-strewn hump.

"Is this the kind of thing you excavate?"

"Aye. It might not look like much but even Dunchraigaig Cairn can provide a stunning view into the past."

Standing amidst the rocks, a woman in her element, he watched her anger deflate like a balloon.

"The earliest burial we've found here occurred three thousand years ago. They laid a body on the earth and built a stone coffin over it. Must have been someone important to the community, someone they admired. Later, they left decorated pots with the ashes of people they'd cremated. Do you not find that the least bit intriguing?"

He shrugged. "What can you tell about people from bits of bone and broken pots?"

She flashed him an impassioned stare and he wished he could take that back. He'd belittled her profession, possibly her life's calling.

"I mean, how can you identify feelings and desires based on what they left behind?"

"We can tell they cared about each other. That they believed in an afterlife. They were as human as we are. Maybe more so." She scoffed. "What will future generations think of us two centuries from now when they sift through our landfills?"

He conceded. "Good point," he said, and examined the cairn more closely. One side of the large mound looked as if it had been pried open. A thick square stone hung over like a swollen lip. The inside was black with shadow.

"Where was Steele's body?"

"Just there." She pointed into the void. "He was lying on his right side."

"I suppose it's ironic his body was left in a burial cairn."

"Sardonic, I'd say, and personal. The killer bashed his skull in with a rock. At least, that's what Kai said."

"Kai?"

"Kai Roskilde. He's one of my crew. Kai was up early that morning, heard the commotion, and came to investigate. He saw them arrest Dylan. The poor lad was down in the other field sleeping by the standing stones when the police arrived."

"You're kidding. They think Dylan bashed Steele's head in and then went to sleep in an adjacent field." Estrada shook his head. "That's ludicrous. When did this murder take place?"

"Last Friday night. A week ago, today."

Summer Solstice. That explained what Dylan was doing out in the field by the stones. Without the coven, he was living as a solitary.

Estrada knelt and peered inside. "Not much room in there. Was Steele struck while he was underneath this thing or was the body placed there after the murder?"

"Killed right there." Sorcha squatted and peered inside the cairn. "A bloody rock was discovered beside his head."

"A rock with Dylan's prints on it?"

Sorcha shrugged.

"So, the killer somehow got Steele to crawl inside the cairn, bashed in his head with a rock, and then left everything for the police to find."

"What are you thinking, man?" She collapsed on the grass beside the cairn. The sun was scorching her pale Irish skin hot pink.

Estrada sat down beside her. "Someone lured him in there. Perhaps used your Egyptian collar as bait."

"High-priced bait."

"Yeah, but why Steele? What's the personal connection?" These things were rarely random.

"From what I hear, Steele courted enemies. He had a penchant for antiquities, collected artifacts and stories, and sold them worldwide to the highest bidder."

"I can't see Dylan getting involved with someone like that. What have they got on him? Other than finding him asleep in an adjoining field."

"Motive." Sorcha grinned. "And I'm afraid that's *my* fault."

He cocked his head. "Oh?"

"I had a fair bit o' whiskey that night. Kai's been giving Dylan a hard time lately and the fellas in camp tease him about being a virgin. So, I gave him a little *head* start if you get my meaning. Liked it too, he did. Caught him alone in the beer garden at Murphy's and had my way with him."

"Really?" Estrada chuckled. Dylan had no experience with women. This raunchy Irish woman *and* out in public. He couldn't imagine.

"Ah, it was all innocent and sweet to see his eyes roll. I think it was his first. Steele, the slimy shite, took photos and teased him. You can imagine how embarrassed poor Dylan was. He's so straight-laced. Anyway, he grabbed Steele's mobile and tried to delete the photos. I think he was protecting my honor. The police intervened. Kai heard them talking about it. They think Dylan lured Steele down here using the artifact to get his hands on that mobile. When things got rough, he killed him."

"Bashed his head in with a rock and then went to sleep in the next field?" Estrada scoffed. "Where's this phone now?"

"You want to see the photos?"

Estrada winked. "It could be useful."

"Ah, right. Taken into evidence or perhaps with the grieving widow?"

"There's a girl named Janey Marshall who accused Steele of rape. Apparently, the case got thrown out and it ruined her career. I think she might be more comfortable sharing her story with a woman."

"Right."

"How about I pick you up at the museum around nine tomorrow morning and we cruise into Glasgow?"

"Grand, but only if I can drive in the city. We should see the Wee Pict first, and you'll never find his shop, even with directions. It's a hole in the wall."

"Deal. Just be sure to bring your license." He was already under scrutiny.

Sorcha stood and stretched. "Hey, there's another one of my crew." She gestured with her chin.

Estrada looked across the rocky outcropping that topped the cairn and saw an angular young man perched on a rock beneath some strange-looking trees.

"Hey Kelly," Sorcha yelled and waved.

Kelly touched his sunken cheeks, smiled forlornly, and raised a hand.

"He looks upset," Estrada said.

"Aye. Kelly's a tad emo. Dylan introduced him to my crew and got him the job. They grew up together in Tarbert and he's taken it hard."

"He reminds me of someone," Estrada said. "Someone I need to call."

15

Daphne stood in the sun, towel-drying her chopped burgundy hair. It had been a long, rainy spring and British Columbia hadn't had many days like this—turquoise sky, sun-kissed ripples, and a hint of promise in the air. She smoothed out her towel and collapsed on her belly. After swimming across the lake and back, she was feeling delightfully exhausted. "I love this beach," she said.

"Me too." Sensara was stretched out on her back on a blanket soaking up the sun's rays after a leisurely float in the lake. "What's it called again?"

"The beach is White Pine. The lake is Sasamat. We only just discovered it. Raine and I love living out here. I know you're gonna love it too. There are so many places to play, and this lake is much warmer than Buntzen. It's too bad we can't use it for ceremonies."

"Why can't we? There must be a way in at night."

"There are trails over there," Daphne said, pointing across the water, "but they've blocked the parking along that road. And it's not as secluded as Buntzen. We might end up scaring someone."

Sensara snickered. "We've done *that* already."

Daphne flicked her arm. "You're terrible."

"I know, but it worked. The threat's been neutralized, and my mother will never set me up with one of her friend's sons again." She shook her head. "Did you see Yasu's face? I thought I might have to yank him out of the bonfire."

"Obviously never met the Green Man before."

"I think Cernunnos pushed him over the edge." Daphne's snort sent Sensara into hysterics. She had to lean up on her elbows to catch her breath. "When I grabbed his hand to jump the fire, he was vibrating."

Daphne opened her flask and gulped some water, then grew serious. "Did you talk to Estrada yet?"

When Sensara shook her head faint droplets flew from her long, dark hair.

"You're not still mad at him for what happened last fall? You know you'll never stop him from freestyling."

"I know."

"Besides, he was enchanted. We all were."

"We may have been reacting to a charm at first, but later it was real. At least, it was for me."

You still love him, Daphne thought. *That's why you can't let it go.* "Forgive him, Sensara. You saw how he acted at the ritual. Estrada acts tough but he's fragile."

"He's also unpredictable." Sensara sat up, squeezed some sunscreen on her palm and spread it on her arms, neck, and belly. "I can't believe he left his clothes on the beach—his new leather jacket and his boots. Do you think he drove home naked?"

"Naked and bootless. I wouldn't put it past him." Daphne's snort sent them into another reel of laughter. "At least he took off the antlers. Cernunnos naked on a Harley. That would be something to see coming at you in the middle of the night on the freeway." She turned onto her back. "Perhaps you should have warned him."

"My love life is none of his business."

And yet, you judge him for his, Daphne thought.

"Why should he care?" Sensara pulled a brush from her bag and jerked it through her hair. When she was annoyed, she could be just as intense as Estrada. "I don't comment on *his* love life."

Really? Daphne thought. *When you were a couple, you had plenty to say.* Estrada's sexual escapades were legendary. He was a romantic, who fell in love hard, fast, and frequently. Sensara was no prude, but she believed in serial monogamy. If he was going to be *her* man, he couldn't be lusting after other people. Especially this, Michael Stryker, who she detested and blamed for Estrada's lascivious behavior.

"No, but he doesn't bring his lovers to ceremonies either," Daphne said. She'd always had a soft spot for Estrada and hated to see him suffer.

"Good thing. They wouldn't all fit on the beach." Sensara rolled her eyes. "Besides, Yasu was *not* my lover."

"A point Estrada apparently missed. You know he still cares for you, Sensara."

"I know." Sensara sighed. "But you don't know him like I do. He's all about the drama. Drinking, drugs, sex . . ." She'd finished brushing her hair and was weaving it into a fishtail. "Anyway, he's not even here. He'll be in Scotland for who knows how long."

"I hope he can help Dylan. Sometimes, just before I drift off to sleep, I hear Dylan playing the bagpipes. Remember that melancholy tune he played last Mabon? It's still stuck in my head."

"Yeah." Sensara reached out and rubbed Daphne's shoulder. "I've been casting protection around Dylan but maybe we should gather for a ritual. Spin some positive energy and send it out."

"Sylvia would be into that. And Raine. And our high priest if he were here." Daphne reached into her bag, pulled out an apple, and passed it to Sensara. "Estrada may have his vices, but he's one of the good guys. Remember that."

16

Sorcha O'Hallorhan was deep in conversation with a brawny dwarf, she affectionately called The Wee Pict. His name was Magus Dubh—the last of which she pronounced *dove*. He'd welcomed her *la bise*, with a kiss on each cheek, and was now perched atop a cluttered desk cuddled up close to her cleavage. Sorcha really was a clever woman. The wee man was melting from the heat.

Working in a goth bar, Estrada had seen his share of eccentric individuals, but Dubh was a cut above. He wondered how he survived in a city like Glasgow. Perhaps, mingling amongst the hoard, he wandered the streets unnoticed. Or perhaps, he was more than he appeared.

Fully bearded, his long silver-streaked hair was drawn up in a high ponytail. Nothing outlandish about that; however, there was no air-conditioning in the shop, so he'd stripped off his shirt. All his exposed skin, including his face right down to the eyelids and earlobes, was tattooed in royal blue symbols—a beastly menagerie, interwoven with vines, spirals, crescents, and other abstract shapes. Estrada was reminded of Tyrion Lannister but cloaked in sapphire tats and sparse old leather. He belonged in Harry Dresden's *Nevernever*, yet here he was, a black-market mole.

Estrada scrutinized the tats, wondering how far the ink extended beneath the worn leather kilt and just how painful it would be to have your genitals tattooed. He knew about ink—wore the black lacy wings of an angel on his own back. The feathers extended across his shoulders and down his glutes, and that ink had broken more than his skin.

It was strange how memories were triggered by the oddest things. He'd seen plenty of tats and not thought of Alessandra. She was seventeen and extraordinary. He was thirteen and insatiable. They'd fallen in love, however crazy that seemed, and she'd refused to accept payment for her work. It was an act of adoration. She'd planned to immortalize him by painting his body in pictures, words, and love knots, only she hadn't had the chance.

Alessandra wasn't just his first lover—she was his first love. And, when he'd heard she'd been killed in a revenge shooting for something her younger brother did, Estrada discovered he truly was a black angel. Alessandra was the first girl to teach him that attachment causes the kind of pain that exacts vengeance. And he carried that corpse for years in the cracks of his soul. Until last fall when Primrose released his demons and set his heart free.

Catching himself wallowing in the past, Estrada turned away from the strange pair and wandered around Dubh's shop. Sorcha said The Wee Pict was a Druid who worshipped nature, particularly trees. Estrada felt a similar connection to the forest and assumed Druidry was something akin to Wicca. Dubh, she said, was a Gaelic word meaning *dark* or *black*, and Estrada wondered what black magic the wizard could spin.

The shop was dark too, eerily lit by the odd bare bulb, and cast its own enchantment. Just a cobalt blue door in a brick wall, it had no windows and no sign. No one would guess it ran so deep and was crammed with antiquities. It was a Dungeons and Dragons dream, embellished with shamanic relics from several continents, and a full catalogue of historic treasures.

The patrons at Club Pegasus expressed their fascination with Estrada's guillotine—a replica Sixteenth Century Scottish Maiden—by screaming madly or booing; sometimes even crying when the steel bar slammed down to slice off his head. So, to speak. Whenever life got stale, people yearned for the past. Medieval romance was in vogue and suited him, so the magician searched for paraphernalia he could weave into his act—escape artistry and illusion wrapped in a gothic cloak.

He'd just discovered a cache of torture devices from the witch craze and was considering how he might adapt a rack to illustrate the horror of the time, when a flash of light caught his eye. The shop door had opened.

Sorcha saw it too. She took one look at the customer and slipped behind a large wooden throne.

Following her cue, Estrada ducked behind an Iron Maiden and peered around to see who'd prompted such stealth.

Detective Rachel Erskine-Steele.

What was she doing here? Stalking him? Or had the woman drawn her own conclusion about the connection between the Egyptian broad collar and her husband's murder?

Dubh drew his tattooed arms across his chest and braced himself. He obviously knew the woman, or at least who she represented.

Conservatively dressed, in pressed gray trousers and a short-sleeved tailored shirt the shade of smoky quartz, she masked her considerable sexuality. Estrada wondered if she preferred women. Possibly, and yet she emitted an alluring pheromone that induced arousal, even at this distance.

After pushing her sunglasses up over her smooth platinum hair, the detective's hands came to rest on that well-equipped leather belt.

She sized up the shop, and flashed her badge. "Good day, Mr. Dubh."

"Detective." His voice rose curiously.

"I expect you've heard, an Egyptian artifact unearthed in Argyll has disappeared."

"Is that so?"

"Aye, it is."

"Huh," Dubh said from his desktop perch.

In one graceful movement, the detective slipped into a chair and swung her feet up on the desk beside him. To his credit, Dubh didn't flinch, even when her stiletto heel nearly punctured his thigh. Chic black slingbacks with a thin ankle strap—expensive, sexy, and not police issue.

"This artifact is possibly a neckpiece from the time of King Tut. A broad collar, I believe. It hasn't been authenticated yet, but it could be the real thing."

Her neck was long and slender, her flesh as pale as swan feathers. Estrada's skin prickled as he imagined her naked and draped in Egyptian jewels, a pearly Nefertiti. Catching himself, he wondered what the hell he was thinking. Steele was a spiteful cop. The widow of the man his friend had been imprisoned for murdering.

"The real thing you say?"

"Correct. Which makes it the property of the Crown and subject to the law of Treasure Trove."

"I am aware of that law, detective."

"Good. You wouldn't want to defraud the Queen and Lord Treasurer's Remembrancer."

"Hell, no. That would be treasonous."

"Criminal. Especially with the abundance of antiquities you have here." She glanced around the shop. "You wouldn't want me to suspect you of hoarding treasure, concealing artifacts belonging to the Crown, or arranging for the sale of such relics, would you Mr. Dubh.”

“I most certainly would not want *that*, detective. We dwarves gave up hoarding treasure when we crawled out of our caves. If it wasn’t for Professor Tolkien—”

“It doesn’t look that way to me.” Drawing up one side of her mouth in a smirk, her cheek flushed slightly. “So, what do you know about this Egyptian broad collar? Are you arranging a deal? Has it shipped? Or is it still around?”

As tenacious as she was beautiful, Estrada wondered what secrets hid beneath that prim demeanor.

“May I first extend my condolences, detective, on the loss of your husband. It’s a tragedy when a man is murdered in his prime. I pray you discover the identity of the perpetrator and bring them to justice.”

“I appreciate your candor, Mr. Dubh. Now, about the artifact.”

“In that regard, detective, I swear on my father’s grave, I cannot help you. I’d be lying if I said I wouldn’t like to see this piece myself. I am partial to Egyptian antiquities. But I’ve not heard a whisper as to its current whereabouts. I will call, if I do.”

“You do that sir, or when I return I’ll bring an army and a search warrant, and we’ll have a good look round your shop.” She stood and stomped a floorboard, and the opposite end popped up to reveal a tidy stash. “Even in those *secret* places.” Releasing it with a slap, she smiled smugly and sauntered out the door.

When Sorcha and Estrada emerged from their respective hiding places, her cheeks pulsed crimson.

“You handled that magnificently Magus. Don’t let that bitch get to you.”

Dubh held his palm to her cheek. "Don't let her get to *you*, my lovely Irish queen."

"Ah, I won't. She's just—"

The sound of the front door cut Sorcha's sentence short. Estrada grasped her arm and yanked her behind the throne in case the detective was returning. Anger wafted in scarlet streaks around Sorcha, and he was in no mood for a cat fight. Dubh skipped toward the front of the shop to put some space between them and whoever had entered.

"*Jesus.*" Sorcha clapped her hands across her mouth as a dark-skinned man swaggered toward Dubh.

"Can I help you?"

A few mumbled words from the man and then Dubh said emphatically, "No. I *really* don't."

Triggered by the distinctive click of a switchblade, Estrada leapt from behind the throne. But his elbow caught the edge of a suit of armor and sent it crashing to the ground. He fell forward, landed on his hands and knees, and yelped.

"Smooth," Sorcha said sarcastically.

The man cast him a death glance, then turned to Dubh, whispered something inaudible, and slashed the open blade in an upstroke across the wee man's naked belly. Dubh's cry ended in a gurgling groan as he buckled and hit the floor. The man bolted.

The spurting blood sent Estrada reeling back to Primrose and that night she laid in his arms with a knife in her chest. *Don't leave me, Primrose. I love you.* He saw her angel face. She'd opened his heart, and then—

Sorcha shoved him as she ran by. "Estrada. For feck's sake." Crouching over Dubh, she pressed a scarf to his belly to staunch the blood. "What's wrong with you, man? Move."

Estrada shook his head to erase the vision. Feeling compassion for Primrose's killer, he'd let him escape. This time he'd show no mercy.

He raced after the man and caught the edge of his jacket in his fist just as he opened the door. The switchblade skittered up the back of Estrada's hand, slicing the flesh between thumb and first finger all the way to his wrist. Blood sprayed up his arm. Surprised, Estrada released his grip, and, in that moment, the man lurched out the door.

"Go after him," Sorcha yelled.

When Estrada caught sight of the assailant less than a block away, he was running toward the river. And then, he vanished. A narrow, overgrown trail led to a blond sandstone tenement. He couldn't have made it into the building, but he likely knew the city and was hiding somewhere close.

For a moment, Estrada froze, caught his breath, and assessed his hand. The bastard had cut a vein. The slash ran deep and was bleeding profusely. He yanked off his leather jacket and then his T-shirt. After wrapping it hastily and tying it off, he put pressure on the wound to staunch the bleeding.

"I know you're here and I *will* find you." As he scanned each surface, he listened for sounds in the weeds. Estrada knew he was ramped up on adrenalin. He also knew he couldn't think straight in that condition. If he was to find this bastard, running blind and angry into the tenement would do him no good. He needed to calm himself and think past the panic.

Why had he suddenly thought of Primrose and the night she died? It must have been the blood. They'd both been covered in her blood. It was all he could see, and then she'd shown him the faeries. That night she'd taught him to see them, and then she'd taken the knife meant for him. Estrada sighed, as her voice echoed in his mind.

Calm yourself, Sorcerer. Focus on a peaceful thought.

Perching on a step, he took long deep breaths until his pulse slowed. *You are my most peaceful thought, Primrose. But I need to find this man. You told me if I ever needed you, you'd come. Well, I need you now. Please, help me.*

As he huddled in the alley, the sounds of the city night dimmed, and Estrada's eyes welled up with tears. Grief squeezed his chest. Grief for her and for Dylan, and now for Dubh who lay bleeding on the shop floor. It threatened to disable him, and there was nothing he could do but feel it. He snorted and sobbed, let it out, and then sniffed and wiped his face.

When Primrose's voice rose like birdsong on the wind, he caught it and held it.

Close your eyes and breathe. Find your own sweet heartbeat. I can feel it in my hand.

As if in a dream, Estrada felt her fingers drumming lightly against his breast as she kept the pulsing rhythm.

Now open your eyes just a flutter, just enough to let in the light. I'm with you, Sorcerer. Accept this gift with love.

The world slowed to a hush. The tenement, the laneway, even the bushes, appeared in varying shades of gray—a silent film of blurring lines and shifting mists. Light and shadow. Illusion.

As he scanned the passage, flushes of color emanated from the concrete like the dust of a Tibetan sand painting. One red footprint, and then another, moving down the sidewalk—a trail of heat prints left by the assailant. No need for night goggles when a man could see with faerie eyes. *Thermal imagining,* he thought, and smirked. *Thank you, my love.*

Following the tracks, he approached a rusted metal platform half-buried in the earth. It was cool bluish gray, but a smattering of red handprints clung to one hinged section. Carefully, he grasped the metal lid and lifted.

A rush of stale air burst from the hole below. Somewhere, in that darkness hid a knife-wielding killer.

He stashed his leather jacket behind a swath of weeds and wished he had the blade he carried in his boot back home. Oh well. The bastard had a switchblade and that would do.

He eased backward down the ladder and turned to find himself in what appeared to be an abandoned subway tunnel. The malingering odor of earth assaulted his senses, and something else—the unmistakable stench of death. Some rotting animal? A rat? He was in no mood to discover a body in the Glasgow underground.

Though dimly lit, he could make out a deep crack in the moldering tiles along the wall above the old train track, where trees thrust gnarly roots into the void. Unable to find an anchor, they twisted precariously and clung. Judging by the graffiti, this was a meeting place, possibly home to a Glasgow gang. Sorcha had warned him to ignore the *neds*—non-educated delinquents—who gathered in groups and harassed tourists. Was this their place? If so, where were they? And where was the man who'd cut Dubh? He was no ned.

Estrada heard water dripping and the odd clanging pipes but saw nothing to betray the man's whereabouts. Focusing on his breath, he waited until he could see the scattered patch of red that confirmed the assailant had been there. His tracks ran along the platform and disappeared over the side. Senses alert to enemies in the shadows, Estrada dropped onto the rocks surrounding the abandoned track.

17

Sorcha was sure that tight-assed detective was involved in this. Maybe not directly, but she'd led the Black Spaniard to the Wee Pict's shop. Why else would he suddenly appear wielding a switchblade? And why was he in Oban the night Steele was murdered? She shivered, remembering how much she'd desired him, drunk or not.

Placing her ear close to the Wee Pict's mouth, she listened to his ragged breathing. His skin was cold and clammy. He was in shock. Where was the feckin ambulance? She'd called ages ago. She lifted the scarf and peered beneath, then pressed a fist to her mouth to keep from gagging. Poor wee Magus. His guts were bulging out. What kind of man disembowels another in broad daylight?

Sorcha pressed her hand against the wound and sobbed. But it wasn't enough.

"If he dies," she yelled, "I'll hunt you down and kill you my feckin self."

18

The underground tunnel was a shadowy maze running nowhere; at least, nowhere Estrada could see from where he stood on the platform below the ladder. He searched the ashen ground for heat imprints, but there was nothing. The man had simply vanished.

Then, a slight sough overhead and he sprang like a panther.

Landing on his back, he caught Estrada's neck in the crook of his arm and squeezed to choke him out. Unbalanced, Estrada fell forward, sinking his teeth into the soft flesh and bone below the man's elbow. There was no etiquette to a life and death brawl. Shaking the arm viciously, he bit off a chunk of coppery flesh and spit it out.

The man seethed. "Animal."

An involuntarily jerk provided just enough space for Estrada to crawl out from beneath him and find his legs. The man rose too, shook his bleeding arm, and cursed as Estrada rammed his fist into his jaw with an uppercut.

Groaning, the man drew back and sucked in a breath, then careened forward. Fists flying, he caught Estrada with a succession of jabs to the gut.

As he curled over to catch his breath, Estrada heard a click and leapt back.

The blade reappeared. Right hand. Low. Estrada had seen plenty of this action on the L.A. streets and mirrored his opponent's moves. Fuming, the man searched for a way in.

Estrada kicked for the hand and missed. Taking swift advantage, the man drew up, going for his hamstring, but caught it low. The blade slashed across Estrada's calf, ripping through his jeans.

Feeling its bite, Estrada glanced down. He'd been passive too long, was out of practice, and anger was impeding his skills. If he didn't focus, he could lose to this bastard. And not just the fight.

The man leapt and lashed out again, slicing into his left shoulder and clean across his chest in a wide arc.

Estrada swayed, dizzy. Then, catching sight of the blood streaming down his bare breast, a surge of adrenalin spiked his rage.

The man glared. "You want more, muchacho? Maybe I cut your fucking heart out."

"Fuck you." Estrada's lips twisted into a sneer as the man lunged again.

This time he was ready and with all his energy focused on his right foot, he kicked up and out, smashing it into the man's gut.

Spiraling backwards, the body hit the tile wall with a thump and hung there for a second, breathless.

Estrada leapt and kicked the blade from the hand, then crushed his knuckles into the astonished face. Not bad for a guy using one hand. As he felt the bones in the nose break, he raised his palm for one last shot—a fatal smash to the bridge of the nose that would ram the bastard's nasal bones up into his brain. No mercy.

"Don't move Mr. Estrada." The steely barrel of a pistol kissed the back of his neck, and his stomach flipped. *Rachel Erskine-Steele.* What the fuck was she doing here?

Holding his hand to his nose, the man spit bloody snot, then turned and squeezed through a dark hole in the wall like a rat.

"He's getting away."

The muzzle of her pistol pressed harder. "He won't get far."

"He sliced Dubh."

"It appears he sliced you too."

Estrada felt her step back though the pistol didn't move.

"Raise your hands and turn around."

He hesitated.

She pressed harder. "Do it."

Out of choices, Estrada turned. Both her hands were wrapped around a Glock aimed at his heart. Would she kill him? Usually, he could read people, but this woman was a mystery.

"Aren't you supposed to protect the innocent, detective?"

"Do you see someone innocent? I just stopped you from murdering a man." She rolled her eyes. "Vigilante. I knew you couldn't leave it alone." She motioned toward the ladder with her gun. "Now move."

"Listen. That bastard assaulted Dubh and just tried to kill me. Christ, he probably killed your husband." His breath was off. Too shallow, too fast.

"Don't talk."

"At least call someone to—"

"The police and ambulance are on site. It's under control."

Feeling suddenly lightheaded, he swayed and bounced off the wall.

Reaching out, she touched two fingers to his carotid. "You need medical attention, Mr. Estrada."

"Stop calling me that."

"It's your name."

"Estrada. Just Estrada."

"Fine. Let's climb out of this hole, Estrada, so I can assess your injuries."

Holstering her pistol, she hooked her arm around his waist. He was surprised when she took his weight on her shoulder. She was stronger than she looked. "Watch yourself," she said, as together they shuffled along the track.

"It's just a graze. Why are you—?"

"You've lost a great deal of blood and you're in shock."

Shock. Right.

"Up you go," she said.

Grasping the rungs of the rusted ladder with his good hand, he climbed from darkness into sunlight that was near blinding. Feeling nauseous, he turned and retched, then dropped onto a cement step and wiped his mouth with a fist.

The detective emerged into the sunlit passage unruffled and peered at his chest wound. "Needs sutures. Your leg and hand do too."

"Nothing Crazy Glue can't fix."

"Perhaps, if we were camping in the Canadian wilderness, but Glasgow has emergency services. Let's go. I'll take you."

"Nope. Not into it." She'd ruined his chance at redemption and now she was holding him hostage. First, she'd take him to the hospital and then to the airport. He wouldn't go willingly no matter how bad he felt.

"Desperado." For several seconds, she stood and stared at him, calculating her next move. Then she shook her head. "How about a deal?"

"A deal?"

"Yes. I have a first aid kit in my flat."

"Your flat?" Why the sudden change of heart? Looking quizzically into those mercurial eyes, Estrada saw a spark of something perilous. "Then what? The airport? Jail?"

She almost smiled. "Is *that* what you're afraid of? You can relax. I'm just concerned with your welfare. Trust me."

"*Trust* you." Trusting police was out of his comfort zone. Especially this one.

"I did warn you to stay out of it." She picked up his jacket and tossed it to him.

He narrowed his eyes and caught it.

"Now you've involved yourself in a rather complex issue."

"Just how complex? International incident? Police corruption? The Mob?"

"You'll just have to trust me."

There were those words again. But what choice did he have? She was a Glock-wielding detective in a foreign country, whose husband had been killed *allegedly* by his friend. It was an intriguing game and he had just enough bravado left to play. Hell, he'd even play by her rules for a while. She knew things. Had connections. Held a Glock he wouldn't mind getting his hands on.

He stared into her eyes until she flipped her shades down and he saw his pale face reflected in the black mirrors. "Explain."

"Either you come with me or I call for a patrol car."

"That's not a deal."

She holstered her gun, then held out her hand. "It's the only one I'm offering."

19

Michael couldn't sleep. How many nights had passed? Six? Seven? Estrada still hadn't contacted him. Of course, that was nothing new. Once, he'd disappeared for weeks and not returned his calls. Michael was, it would seem, as superfluous as last night's wine.

He rolled the small wooden ball between his fingers, then held it to his nose and inhaled the pungent cedar scent. Estrada had slipped it in his pocket when they were in Ireland last December. It was supposed to bring him luck. *Bullshit.* All he felt was empty. Desolate. Abandoned. Again. As usual, he was stuck in Vancouver, while Estrada flew off to Scotland to play hero. *Fuck him and his witchy friends.* He flicked the cedar ball across the bedroom, watched it ricochet off a crystal bong, and fall to the carpet.

After gulping another mouthful of wine, he lit a cigarette and gazed down at the young man sprawled across the bed beside him. Raven tresses. Exquisite bone structure, sharpness, and shadow in perfect proportion, and not a line or crease. Of course, Christophe was years younger than Estrada, just a teenager really.

Michael took another drag and blew a smoke ring while he watched his lover sleep. So young and beautiful. If he'd been an artist, Michael would have painted him. At the very least, he must write a poem to immortalize Christophe's flawless symmetry as Byron would have done.

Sensing Michael's gaze upon him, Christophe reached over and stroked his belly with long, sharp fingernails. Whitened tips from a French manicure, a faint trace of cocaine trapped in the creases.

"What do you need, Mandragora?"

Michael loved being called by his nickname. It made him feel distinctly dangerous.

"Nothing you can provide." He blew another smoke ring and punctured the circle with his finger. "Can you cure this anguish? Quell this madness of the heart?"

"So dramatic. You come from another time, *n'est-ce pas*?" The fingers danced, reawakening a sensual hunger in Michael's weary body. "But perhaps I *can* cure your madness, chéri."

"How?"

"With love."

"Love." Michael scoffed, his tone carrying a certain contempt disregarded by the young man.

"Oui, *amour*."

A long sigh. "What do you have in mind?"

"Whatever you desire. I live only to please you."

"Ah, Christophe." His lover was a budding actor, a sought-after model, and almost as beautiful as Estrada. In fact, his appeal grew when Michael noticed how much he resembled the Estrada he'd met years ago—the one who'd been infatuated with him and his parties. "Whatever I desire? Anything?" Raising his upper lip, Michael exposed one of his fangs.

Propping himself up on his elbow, the young man held out his hand and took the cigarette from Michael's fingers. "Anything and everything." He paused for an elaborate French inhale, then dropped the cigarette into the ashtray. "It is whispered Mandragora has developed an exotic taste of late."

"Is it?"

"In circles as intimate as ours there are few secrets, *mon ami*, and you are a legend."

Michael ran a fingertip down the sculpted cheek and across the lips. "Anything and everything," he echoed.

They kissed feverishly for several moments. Then catching an edge of the swollen lip between his teeth, Michael bit down hard with his fang.

The boy inhaled sharply.

He tasted Christophe's coppery blood. "Even if it hurts?"

"Can there be pleasure without pain?"

Picking up a small mirror, Michael offered his lover another long line of white powder. Then, dipping his fingertip into the cocaine, he dabbed it on the puncture. With a razor blade, he cut out a portion for himself and snorted it all. After setting the mirror back on the dark glass table beside his bed, he held out the dusty blade. "Such a keen edge makes this an instrument of both pain and pleasure. Do you agree, Christophe?"

"Both the pain and pleasure are mine, chéri, but you must sip from somewhere the camera cannot see." He tossed the soft white sheet to the floor and offered his inner thigh.

"Ah, Christophe. I hate to mar your beauty, but I do so want to hear you moan."

20

Lions perched above the arched entrance to the Steele's ornate Victorian apartment building, though the flat itself was a showcase for contemporary Scandinavian design. A blatant contradiction, like the woman.

If Alastair Steele had lived here, there was no trace of him now. Had the detective obliterated every suggestion of the man since his death nine days ago? The lingering odor of chlorine suggested he'd been scrubbed from her life.

"Chic," Estrada said, glancing at the white walls, polished wood floors, plump gray leather sofas, and gleaming French doors.

Rachel beamed. She'd dropped the first line of her defense and appeared hospitable. Excited, even. He wondered how long it would last.

He suspected her curt exterior was something she'd cultivated to survive the Scottish police force. She couldn't be over thirty and to make detective at such a young age showed ambition. He could imagine the woman fighting off a passel of sexist pigs. Any females in the force would hate her on principle. Her beauty was daunting. But why go through that? Why police work when she could easily be a cover girl.

"You're bleeding on my floor," she said, and for a moment, they both stared at the red drops by his feet.

"Oh, sorry." Estrada readjusted the balled-up towel she'd pulled from her gym bag in the car and pressed it harder against his shoulder.

"It's coming from your calf." She gestured to a spiral staircase. "The shower room is downstairs. Can you manage?"

Estrada nodded, but then, feeling suddenly faint, literally bounced off the wall.

She caught his shoulders and settled him on a bench. "You're still in shock."

He watched her slink toward an oak cabinet in the dining area. He'd never seen a woman move like that.

Returning with a bottle of Cognac, she half-filled a brandy snifter and offered it to him. "Here, sip."

Estrada cupped his hand around its warm belly and inhaled the heady nectar, then tipped it to his lips and downed it all, exhaling with a shiver as the heavenly spirit surged through his body. Cognac was something he savored with Michael on damp winter nights by the fire during the Vancouver rains. It made him remarkably poetic and superbly horny.

He sighed aloud. "Refill?"

Rachel made a tisking sound as she shook her head. "That was a good four ounces."

"Ah, come on. Don't St. Bernards carry brandy through the mountains for the lost and injured?"

She almost laughed, and he felt encouraged. "Go clean those wounds," she said, pointing downstairs to the shower. "Hold the handrail and I'll join you shortly."

"Join me?"

Her stern look said it all. He'd overstepped some invisible boundary.

Estrada glanced again at the pistol packaged so neatly around her slender waist. "Sorry, detective. It's post-traumatic stress."

"Aye, of course it is." Tipping the bottle, she sent another splash that filled his glass.

"Why, detective . . ."

"I'll get my kit." She pointed one long gleaming fingernail. "Sip."

Estrada gulped. Ironically, the brandy made him feel grounded; leastways, his feet felt weighted. Balancing the snifter and his leather jacket, he leaned against the wooden bannister and thumped downstairs. The doors to all but one room were slightly ajar, and he peered inside each one.

The largest bedroom—he assumed it was the master—adjoined the shower room and was decorated in the same contemporary style as the rest of the suite. An immense bed with slate gray leather headboard and footboard dominated the room. Apart from a crisp white duvet and pillows, there were no things—no photos, plants, books, or keepsakes—nothing to reveal the woman's story. Was this how she lived? With all details trapped behind stiff white walls in an Ikea catalogue. Another set of French doors led from the bedroom onto a terrace, and he paused to relish the afternoon sunlight streaming through the sheers.

"Lost?"

Estrada stirred at the sound of her voice. "I was just thinking how wonderful it must be to have a terrace off the bedroom, a place to relax on moonlit nights and—"

"I've never used it," Rachel said curtly, then disappeared into a large walk-in closet and shut the door.

Taking this as his cue to hit the shower, Estrada dropped his leather jacket on the floor, sucked back the remaining brandy and set the empty snifter down gingerly on the vanity. The shower stall was twice the size of his Commercial Drive bathroom. He turned on the faucet and hot water cascaded down in a misty waterfall. Stepping beneath the massive rain head, he delighted in the sensation, until his legs gave way and he collapsed on the wooden bench. Slumped against the wall, he closed his eyes to curb the spin while the water streamed down. The next thing he heard was Rachel's voice.

"You're drunk."

"You did feed me liquor."

"You didn't even take your clothes off."

He opened his eyes and gasped. She posed in a white sleeveless mini dress, her long legs and feet bare, her toenails pearlescent in the steam.

"*Jesus,* woman. I could fall in love with you."

When she smiled, the shower stall glowed.

"Did I say that out loud?"

"You should have gone to hospital, Estrada. I'm going to check your vitals." She shut off the water, then gripped his wrist and stood silently for several seconds.

"Will I live, nurse?"

"Too soon to tell."

Her pale hair was still upswept and caught water droplets like dew in a spider's web, while the mist curled tendrils round her ears.

"A silver swan caught in winter's ice."

"What?" She giggled in a girlish way that made him grin.

"When you laugh, I hear bells."

"No more brandy for you. Not until you've regained your senses."

"My senses are perfect." Everything about her appealed.

She pulled off his bloodstained tank, then grasped the handheld shower and rinsed his shoulders and chest with warm, clear water. Despite the pain, it was divine. She was divine.

"You pretend you're tough, but you're really an angel."

"I see you have wings of your own." She ran the stream down each angel wing on his back from shoulder to gluts. "This is quite the tattoo."

Her fingers danced on his skin. Then she squirted soap on the wound, and he yelled. "Ow. What the fuck."

"Come now, Estrada. It's only antibacterial soap. I can see from your scars you've endured far worse."

"Sadist."

She rinsed off the soap and placed a clean linen towel over the wound. Taking his good hand, she pressed it against the towel. "Keep pressing until it's sutured."

His other hand was still bleeding, so she washed it and wrapped a clean towel around it. Then, she pulled a pair of silver scissors from her kit.

"Can you stand? I need to cut off your jeans."

"No way. I need my jeans. Unless you're planning to hold me hostage." He winked to no response. "Come on. I'm attached to my jeans."

"That you are. I suppose they can be mended, if you can get them off, that is. They're skin-tight and now that they're wet—"

"Don't talk like that, detective, or I'll never get them off."

Rachel flashed him another scathing look which he ignored.

When he stood and unzipped his jeans, he was ready for love. Hadn't been with a woman for months. After Primrose he'd lost the urge. But now it was back. Months of apathy caught in one shameless erection.

A pink cloud rose on her cheeks.

"If you can hold the towel, detective, I'll just . . ." He shimmied out of his jeans, boxer briefs, and socks, and kicked them all aside.

Placing his good hand over hers, he caressed the soft flesh between her fingers. When their eyes met, her pupils dilated. Noting her desire, he leaned in for a kiss, then feeling suddenly woozy, he wavered.

She pushed him down on the bench and tossed a towel over the offending item. "Whatever blood was left in your brain all rushed south." Stooping, she rinsed his leg with the handheld, and peered at his calf. "This looks bad. You're fortunate nothing vital was nicked."

"They'd better catch that bastard. If they don't, I will."

She shut off the water. "Ms. O'Hallorhan gave a detailed description and a bulletin's been issued. There's no need for more vigilante threats."

When she dried her hands and slipped on a pair of latex gloves, he feared he'd pushed some invisible button. "You don't need gloves. I've been tested and I'm clean." He wanted that made clear.

"Perhaps you are. Perhaps you're not." She sniffed. "I don't know you well enough to take your word for it. Besides, I'd get retested if I were you."

"Why?"

"Well, even if you're clean, how clean is Mr. Dubh?"

"What?" Estrada shook his head. She wasn't making sense.

"The assailant cut you right after he cut Dubh, yeah? Did he clean and sterilize the knife in between?" Still wearing her gloves, she patted dry the wound.

Estrada glanced at his hand and remembered how the man had slashed up his thumb with the knife while he held him at the door. The blade had been covered in Dubh's blood. Was it possible to transfer a virus like that?

Rachel opened a package of butterfly sutures and began applying them to the wound on his calf. "From what I hear, Magus Dubh has a penchant for boys—the kind that don't always look after themselves."

"Dubh's a pedophile?" He hoped not. He liked the guy.

"Perhaps not *that* young."

"You mean he's gay." Estrada didn't believe that for a second, not the way he was fawning over Sorcha. Perhaps like himself, Dubh didn't discriminate.

Rachel straightened. "Scotland is a conservative country."

A low growl escaped Estrada's throat and ended in a question. Where was she going with this? She stood and began applying sutures to the long diagonal slash along his chest and shoulder. But Estrada had lost his buzz. Now he just felt drunk and defensive. What kind of information traveled between borders? *Warning: bisexual magician. Admit at your own risk.* Was that written in a file too?

Rachel was still talking. "Of course, it happens here. We even allow same sex marriages now. Things are just done discretely."

"Like in closets." She was either naïve or in denial. He was sure Glasgow was as proud of its queer community as any other European city. She didn't comment and the room felt suddenly cold and silent. He leaned back as she finished suturing the slash across his hand.

"There. Now all you need is a sling."

"No sling, detective. I need my arms. I'm riding a Harley, remember?"

"Suit yourself, but you won't heal properly." She frowned, and a spot of color appeared in those pale cheeks. "Pig-headed too."

"As long as it's only the one part."

She snapped off her gloves and tossed them in the wastebasket. This was the most emotion he'd seen her display, and he wondered what had triggered it. Was she homophobic or just cautious? What was her game?

Then, as she slipped through the door, he caught a mumbled invitation. "There's coffee in the kitchen."

His jeans were destroyed so he wrapped a white towel around his waist and gathered the rest of his wet things.

He leaned out the bathroom door and glanced at the spiral staircase. Maybe he needed to show Rachel Erskine-Steele just how much he could enjoy a woman.

When The Proclaimers sang from the pocket of his leather jacket, Estrada recognized the ring tone, but not as something he should be answering. He'd forgotten Dermot had given him Dylan's phone. He pulled it out of the pocket and slid it open.

"Yeah."

"Estrada? Where the hell are you?"

"Sorcha." He'd forgotten about her.

"Who were you expecting? The bloody queen?"

"How's Dubh?"

"Still in surgery. Look, if you're wondering where your bike is, I drove it to the hospital—the Royal Infirmary on Castle Street. Where are you?"

"I'm . . . I'm at a walk-in clinic." He hoped there were such things in Glasgow and paused. When she didn't object, he continued. "I caught up with the bastard, but he cut me and disappeared."

"He cut you. *Jaysus*. How bad is it? Where are you? I'll come get you."

"It's my turn soon. I'll call you after I've seen the doctor."

"Alright."

And that was that. The only doctor he wanted to see was the one who'd just sutured his wounds. He slipped the phone back in his jacket pocket, folded it over his arm, and crept upstairs. When he saw her he dropped everything.

She stood facing the stainless-steel counter in her perfect kitchen. She'd strapped some high silvery heels on those slender ankles. Her skintight dress was backless, the shoulder straps merging into a long V at the base of her spine and hugged the curves of her ass. It ended about two inches later—an effect that made her legs seem six feet long. With her hair pinned up in a French roll, she looked exquisite. High class. Perfection. A woman did not dress like this for herself.

Edging in close behind her, he dropped the towel from his hips and laid his hands over hers on the counter.

She took a quick breath, though she must have heard him coming. He could hear her heart thrumming from across the room. She was leaning slightly forward, her weight on her palms, gazing out the window at the terrace. Her scent, as intoxicating as old brandy, rekindled his buzz.

For several seconds, they stood locked in this embrace. His bare chest edging her bare back. His fingers caressing the sensitive skin between her knuckles. His lips brushing the back of her neck. And like a drug, he breathed her in.

"You found me." She purred like a sultry Siamese.

Merging into her silhouette, he teased her shoulders, smelling almonds and spring flowers, as the tiny hairs at the back of her neck prickled beneath his lips. Reaching up, he pulled the pins from her hair, let it spill, and ran his fingers through it.

Her sigh was barely audible, but she leaned back, and the weight of her head filled his hands.

"Can't do this wearing a sling," he said.

"Can't do a lot of things."

He kissed her long pale neck and meandered slowly down her back, tasting her, savoring her, tracing her form with his fingers. At the base of her spine, he unzipped the dress and slipped it off her naked hips. Burying his face in her flesh, he inhaled her musky scent. God, she was savory.

Rising, he swept her hair aside and kissed the soft flesh behind her ear. Blood rushed through her veins like a spring creek flooding its banks.

"This is why you brought me here, isn't it, Rachel? You want me." Catching her cheek in his hand, he turned her face and stared into her silvery eyes. "I want you too. I want to kiss every inch of you."

"No. I can't." Breaking away, she scooped up her dress and used it for cover as she darted across the room. "I just can't."

"I know you feel it. This thing between us is strong. It's—"

"You should go."

"Rachel, I—"

"No, Estrada. No. This can't happen."

21

S orcha was fuming by the time she slid off the back of the bike in front of the Kilmartin Hotel. Estrada had insisted on driving the Harley all the way back, and he was surly too, in one hell of a mood. Didn't want to talk. Didn't want to eat. Didn't even want a pint.

She'd hoped to spend some quality time with him and get to know him better. Maybe even get him in the sack. She craved tangibles like food and flesh, after spending hours in the infirmary worrying about whether The Wee Pict would live or die.

Ah, feck it. A woman on her own in a pub never stays alone for long.

Several pints later, she stumbled home through the sheep trails using the tiny torch she kept in her bag to find her way. Almost midnight, and the sky above Kilmartin Glen was studded with stars. She wondered what the ancient ones, whose shattered bones and shards she painstakingly dug from the earth, thought of these glittering diamonds in the sky. Were their cup and ring marks in the rocks really maps of constellations or something else? She'd give anything to understand them, to go back in time and live among them. It was one thing to imagine. It was another to live it.

The broad collar had revealed some of its owner's secrets when Sorcha had placed it around her neck that day in the privacy of her tent. Meritaten *had* walked these fields, had lived here, and loved here, and almost died here. But the thief had stolen it before she'd seen it all. That's why she needed it back. Not for money or fame—those were just perks—but to know its secrets.

She slipped inside her tent and stripped off. After downing one last shot of whiskey, she opened her bed chamber and knelt. She couldn't wait to stretch out inside her down bag. And that's when she heard it. Breathing. She wasn't alone.

"Who's here?"

"Who were you expecting?" The voice was deep and rough and tinged with northern timbre.

"Kai? Not you. You said you'd be gone all weekend."

"Did I spoil your plans, boss?"

"No. I just had a shite day and wasn't expecting a Viking in my sack."

"We were never expected."

"Right so."

She felt his large rough hand touch her shoulder. Imagined him running wild, raping and killing, women, monks, anyone too weak to escape those long, violent strides. Yet, Kai had a tender side that brought her comfort, and that was why, on nights like this she laid in his arms spooned against his chest and slept soundly with his breath warming her neck.

"Come on, Irish, lie back and tell me about your shite day."

There was no point resisting. Half-drunk and exhausted, Sorcha melted into his flesh.

"I went to Glasgow this morning to see if The Wee Pict had heard anything about the collar."

"And?"

"While I was talking to him a man burst in. Slashed his belly wide open. *Jaysus*. I knew him." She still couldn't get that image out of her mind.

"Yeah? Did he—?"

"Kill him? He's not dead yet. But *Christ*. Poor Magus. His guts were hanging out, Kai. It was like something from a movie." She shivered, and he rubbed the bumps from her bare arms. "He was still in surgery when I left."

"And this man . . . You say you knew him?"

"Oh, aye. I danced with him at Murphy's. Dark-skinned. Shaved head. Did you see him that night?" Though she didn't remember coming home she'd never forget The Black Spaniard.

Sorcha felt Kai tense. Then he took a deep breath and sniffed. "Sounds like the man you were dancing with just before I carried you out."

"Aye. That's him. Half Spanish, half Egyptian, so he said."

"I don't remember his face. Do you?"

"I'll never forget his eyes." The way he'd stared into her soul when he plucked her off the bar stool.

"Did they catch him?"

"Estrada went after him, but the bastard cut him too and then vanished."

"Estrada?"

"Oh right. You haven't met him. Estrada's from Canada. He's a friend of Dylan's come here to help."

"Help how?"

"He intends to exonerate Dylan by finding out who really killed Steele."

All went quiet in the tent.

"And you went to Glasgow with this Estrada?"

"Aye. We both had business in the city, so we went together. Drove in on his Harley, went to see Magus, and then that bastard walked in and sliced him. Gutted him like a fish."

By then she was ranting, needing to vent. "Something's going on and Meritaten's collar is involved. Estrada will figure it out. He's cunning and knows more than he lets on." The more she ruminated, the more she wanted revenge. "You know, if Magus Dubh dies, it's murder."

"Your man won't die, Irish. He's a tough wee prick."

"Aye. Well, if he does, it's cold-blooded murder. I saw it all and I can identify him."

"Jesus, boss. You did have a shite day." She felt him shift and lean over her in the dark, felt his whiskers brush her cheek, smelled the faint odor of whiskey on his breath. "Shall I put you to sleep?" Kai Roskilde was rugged, like the land of his ancestors, a man of mountains and fjords, a real man's man, but he never took without asking and often gave without taking.

"Aye, Kai. Put me to sleep." Reaching out, she caught him behind the neck and brought his mouth to hers. It was this remarkable mouth that gained him passage night after night.

"Lie back and close your eyes, Irish. I'll take you where you need to go."

22

Vicious voices. Searing steel. "Confess, witch. Confess, and this will end." Vague shadows. Round men in dark robes. Estrada smelled the putrid stench of burning hair, burning meat. His head lolled and the sight of his breasts, naked and flayed, triggered another spasming pain.

Gasping, he bolted upright. *Breasts?* His throat was parched, his shoulder throbbing. Another one of *those* dreams, likely triggered by Dubh's torture chamber and the trauma of his recent injuries. In the night, he'd rolled onto his slashed shoulder and wedged it beneath him.

Easing onto his back, he took a deep breath and sighed it out, then rubbed his eyes open with his fists. In the dim light of the bedroom, he fumbled for Dylan's cell phone and turned it on. It was 10:10. Sunday, June 29. He *could* smell burning meat—back bacon to be exact—but there were other scents too: strong coffee, potato scones, eggs and mushrooms frying in butter, baked beans, and something that involved the sweetly spiced and blended organs of a sheep. Was that cinnamon? His empty gut growled, triggered by the strong aromas.

Hallelujah. He was in Scotland, and Dermot McBride was cooking a traditional fry-up. But how did he know the details? And, more importantly, was it polite to turn down a national dish? He was almost sure, the sheep organs comprised something called haggis. Then again, if cinnamon was involved, how bad could it be?

He turned on the bedside lamp to assess the damage to his body. There were russet smears on the sheet along with fresher, redder streaks. *Damn.* He'd have to launder it somehow. Blood still seeped through the gauze crazy Rachel had used to swath his chest and shoulder. The ten-inch gash ran down his breast almost to his nipple. Had the bastard struck any lower or deeper, he could be dead.

And Rachel *was* crazy, as capricious as the bobcat Michael once tried to tame, and just as beautiful. Why bring him to her lair, seduce him, and then reject him? Getting close to a desirable woman had triggered all kinds of stuff he'd locked away. It suffused his mind as he slept, merging with memories of Michael.

Primrose was there too. She'd once told him she'd always be there to help—*in every breath of wind*—and she *had* helped him in the alley. She'd gifted him with fey sight. It was a strange comfort to know she was only a sigh away, even if she'd transformed into something beyond human.

And Michael. Estrada couldn't stop thinking about him, and that meant something was wrong. As Michael, the world was relatively safe, but as Mandragora, his deviant nature intensified to the detriment of himself and anyone else he might beguile. Estrada didn't want to come off like a stalker, but if the man had caught him across the throat, he'd have bled out in that stinking hole without ever having said what he needed to say. This quest could very well get him killed and there was no backing out, not until Dylan was free.

He needed to talk to Michael. He could phone from Dylan's cell or use the landline, but Michael screened all calls. That left email. Unfortunately, Dylan, the ever-frugal student, didn't have data on his phone. Estrada berated himself. How had he managed to forget his phone? He could clearly see it in his addled mind, sitting on his bedside table. He'd awoken to its alarm, then showered, dressed, grabbed his bag, and dashed out without it. It was stupid and thoughtless. He'd had too much on his mind.

After pulling on a pair of black jeans, he splashed water on his face and fixed the bandages. He'd need to get fresh ones today and redress the wound. He slipped on a black cotton button-down shirt and descended the carpeted stairs. There was no point telling Dermot what had happened in Dubh's shop or the abandoned tunnel. The poor man was stressed enough. The bandaged hand he couldn't hide, but he could say he'd stumbled at the archaeology site and smashed it on a rock. And that's exactly what he did.

After breakfast, they sat on the front steps sipping second and third rounds of coffee. Estrada had a pain in his gut, and not from the haggis.

"I need to check my email. Is there an internet café in town?"

Dermot shook his head. "The wee library has computers, but it's closed until Tuesday. I cannae think of anywhere else. I dinnae use it myself but Dylan frequents the library. You can see it just there." Dermot pointed across the water to the other side of the horseshoe-shaped bay.

As Estrada strolled through town, he relaxed into a sense of hope-filled calm. Sunshine glinted off white masts of sailboats in the harbor and transformed the small sleepy village into a postcard. Idyllic. Magical. Surely, they'd find a way to prove Dylan's innocence and bring him home.

The library was closed, but the pharmacy had just opened. After picking up gauze, tape, and antibiotic ointment, he asked the pharmacist if he knew of any place with internet access.

"You're that lad who's staying with Dermot McBride. Dylan's mate from Canada." It was a statement, though not accusatory, and Estrada was reminded that secrets and anonymity didn't exist in a village the size of Tarbert.

Estrada nodded amiably,

"There's the library just there, but it's Sunday and—"

"Sorry to interrupt, Mr. Brechin."

Estrada turned as a gaunt young man held out his hand. "I'm Kelly Mackeras. Dylan and I are mates."

Grinning, Estrada shook his hand. *Kelly.* This was the guy Sorcha pointed out yesterday by the cairn where they'd discovered Steele's body. *Emo,* she'd called him. He couldn't be more than nineteen.

"I work at the Kilmartin dig with Dylan, at least I did until—"

"He got arrested. Yeah, I'm trying to remedy that."

A nervous grin spread across Kelly's face. "Dylan's cheap. The cheapest lad I know."

"As in, too cheap to buy a data plan?"

"Aye. Exactly. But he's no killer."

Sometimes, Estrada could pick up colors around people, energy flowing through their aura in differing hues, depending on their feelings and state of mind. Anger was bright red, as was passion. Kelly was swathed in a dreary blue haze slightly deeper than the shade of his eyes. He was thin, fragile, pretty, and wounded. Shaggy brown hair edged his gaunt face, highlighting strong bones over hollow cheeks, long lashes, and pouty lips. If Michael had been there, he'd have seduced Kelly Mackeras in a second. Estrada thought back to what Rachel had said about homosexuality in Scotland. What would life be like for a gay boy growing up in a village like this?

The shadowy veil shrouding Kelly's face lifted slightly. "I've got Wi-Fi at my flat and you're welcome to use my laptop."

"Yeah?"

"Aye, sure. If you don't mind waiting while I get Mum's pills."

"If your mother's sick . . ."

"Oh, Mum won't mind. She keeps to her room." He lowered his voice to a whisper and glanced around the shop. "Mr. Brechin knows, but Mum doesn't want everyone in town taking pity on us." He gave Estrada a look he didn't comprehend. "Cancer." He mouthed the word.

"Oh. I'm sorry."

Kelly's eyes glassed over.

A mother sick with cancer. That explained a lot. Sorcha must not know. If she did, she surely would have mentioned it when they saw him at the cairn. Sometimes it was easier to confide in a stranger than someone you had to face every day.

"She fought it a few years back. I just keep praying she'll win again."

"Maybe I shouldn't . . ."

"Oh, aye, you should. Once Mum's had her pills, she'll sleep for a while, and she'll rest easier knowing I have a visitor. She says I keep to myself too much. You know how mothers are."

He didn't. It'd been a long time since a mother worried over him.

Twenty minutes later, they stood in an old Victorian house by the sea, where Kelly and his mother shared an upstairs flat. Though tiny, it was decorated in shades of pink and gray. It had snug dormer window seats, comfy armchairs strewn with knitted throws, and walls lined with books. A framed painting of pale poppies dominated the wall above the sofa.

Estrada took a deep breath. "Man, it smells good in here."

"I baked this morning."

"Yeah?"

"Oh aye. I lived a wee while in Edinburgh and worked part-time in a bakery while I was in acting school. I came home when Mum got sick."

"You're a good son."

"An only son."

"That makes it hard."

"It's been that way forever." He walked into the kitchen, and then popped his head around the corner. "Can I offer you coffee and cinnamon toast?"

"Are you serious, man? I love cinnamon."

"It's Mum's favorite too. The aroma cheers her up."

His sad smile was a heartbreaker and Estrada considered seducing Kelly himself. What if he never knew, never experienced, a lover? No, he'd been to acting school in Edinburgh. Regardless of what crazy Rachel said, the capital of Scotland was a modern, vibrant city. Surely, Kelly'd had a boyfriend.

When he finally got logged on, Estrada was surprised to see a reply from Michael. It was brief.

Forget me. I've found someone who loves me and will not abandon me. Someone who'll do anything I desire. I don't care if you ever come back.

Christ. When Michael was in one of his moods, he was so melodramatic. Though he'd never allowed himself to be diagnosed, Estrada suspected Michael was bipolar, a kind of Jekyll and Hyde. Self-medicating did little to stabilize his erratic mood shifts, and Estrada spent considerable time and energy playing the equalizer.

Once, Michael had one of the new Sentries—the club's version of bouncers—publicly flogged on the stage at Club Pegasus until he begged for mercy. Then, he took him to bed with two of his favorite ladies. Dell still worked for him, and that, Michael said, was loyalty. Estrada could only imagine what he'd get up to with this new lover. Male or female, it wouldn't matter.

Now he had the opportunity, Estrada didn't know what to say or how to say it. The written word could be interpreted in too many ways. He sat for several seconds, eyes closed, seeking inspiration. He decided to be brief and honest, hit reply and typed.

Dylan is in prison for murder. If it was you, amigo, you know I'd do anything to free you and bring you home. Please understand and be careful. I'll be back soon. E

"I don't mean to pry, but is it girl trouble?"

Estrada sniffed back his sorrow. He wasn't sure why he felt like weeping, but he did. "Boy trouble," he said.

"Oh, really?"

Kelly seemed empathetic and Estrada felt a kinship forming. He imagined if he returned to Edinburgh, Kelly could be himself, but here in this village he'd never be able to come out.

"Yeah, my friend Michael is pissed at me."

"Are you a couple, then?"

"Not exactly, but we're solid, you know. At least we were." He shrugged and sighed. "It's complicated."

Kelly sighed too, as if a solid relationship with a man hovered beyond his reach. "I'm sure things will be alright now you've written and explained. Sometimes, we just need to know we're loved. We need to hear it."

I hope someday you hear it, and from somebody decent, who means it.

23

The trip to Greenock Prison took over three hours and involved the crossing of two lochs by ferry. Estrada was relieved he wasn't driving. Despite fresh dressings, his shoulder throbbed. He'd need to rest for a couple of days and let it heal, or he'd end up having to see a doctor. He couldn't risk an infection with so much at stake. The charming scenery he'd marveled at on his way into Argyll took on a dull tarnish as Dermot described Her Majesty's Prison.

With over two hundred and fifty inmates, the crowded prison was famous for having once housed a Libyan terrorist dubbed *The Lockerbie Bomber*. Megrahi was convicted in the bombing of Pan Am Flight 103. The bomb exploded over the Scottish town of Lockerbie on December 21, 1988, killing everyone on board and several people on the ground. Total fatalities: 270. Megrahi was sentenced to life but granted a transfer to Libya on compassionate grounds in August 2009. Diagnosed with terminal prostate cancer, he'd been given three months to live. Dermot knew all the details and was still furious. Three months had stretched into two and half years.

"The man never should have been released. Ach, my grandson is locked in that damn Ailsa Hall with murderers and terrorists."

"We'll get him out, sir."

"The Crown has one hundred and one days to prepare their case. They'll hold him until his trial in the high court."

"What about bail?"

"I cannae see it. We'd need to give them a good reason—the real killer or a name and evidence that points to him."

Or her, Estrada thought. He hadn't pursued Janey Marshall after what happened to Dubh, but there could be several women angry enough to kill a rapist. Perhaps even his crazy wife.

The prison complex was a mass of brown bricks, concrete, and barbed wire. Estrada made it through the ID screening with his passport and drivers license and was allocated a table in the visits room. Then he had to pass through a metal detector and endure a pat down. He sat in the waiting area for what seemed like ages wondering how Dylan could cope in this place.

When he was finally allowed into the room, he sat nervously at the table, remembering the warnings he'd been issued by the police at the airport.

At last, Dylan was brought in. When he started talking, Estrada was more concerned about his headspace than legalities. Normally even-tempered, the kid had spoken with his lawyer earlier and was frantic.

"He wants to plea bargain with my life. Wants me to plead guilty to culpable homicide."

"Manslaughter?"

"Aye. He wants me to stand up in court and confess that I killed the man *accidentally*. Says it will reduce the sentence. I'll only get five years and be out in three. Three years. This is his *good* news. Tell me you've got better news than that,

Estrada. Tell me you've got some way to prove my innocence and get me out of this place."

An officer hovered in the corner but seemed oblivious to their conversation. "Is he listening?"

Dylan emitted a long, low hiss. "Nothing we can do about it if he is." When he slumped in the chair and crossed his arms over his chest, Estrada's heart broke.

"Tell me what happened."

"I apologize man. Here, you've come all this way to help me and I'm acting daft. I wish I smoked. Most of the men smoke and it seems to help."

"It doesn't." Estrada thought of Michael and his chain smoking. "You remember what we do back home to calm down and focus, right?"

"Aye. Breathe. Meditate."

"Better than smoking." Estrada was worried. He'd never seen Dylan quite this agitated. "Tell me what you remember. Why did they arrest you?"

"I scuffled with Steele in Oban. That's the only time I ever saw the man. I swear."

"I believe you. Run me through the details."

"Aye. Sorcha took us all to Murphy's to celebrate. She'd found a three-thousand-year-old Egyptian collar." He smiled at the memory lagging in his brain. "She got drunk, really drunk, and she . . . she . . ."

"Gave you a blow job." Estrada grinned, and Dylan turned scarlet.

"How do you know that?"

"She told me."

"She *told* you. Christ. What did she say?"

"Just that."

Dylan covered his face with his hands, but Estrada could still see the red blaze that burned the tips of his ears. He could imagine how embarrassed he'd been when Steele told him about the pictures.

"Is nothing private?" Dylan whispered at last.

"Not when you do it in public." Estrada winked to lessen the tension. "What happened after?"

"After, aye." Dylan took a deep breath. "She went downstairs to the bar, and I went for a walk to clear my head."

"And . . ."

"And that's when I ran into Alastair Steele. I didn't know who he was. Just some wanker. He said filthy things about Sorcha. He'd taken a video and photos of us in the beer garden. I told him to delete them. He agreed to *if* I told him about the collar. He said he'd cut me in if I got it for him. I couldn't believe it. I was so pissed, I grabbed his phone and locked myself in the van. Then the polis appeared and made me give it back."

"And then?"

"I went walking."

"Anywhere special?"

Dylan shook his head. "Just around the docks. When I got back to Murphy's, it was near closing." He rolled his eyes. "Sorcha was near comatose and draped over some black man. A hard man, I'd say." He cleared his throat. "Kai carried her to the van, and I drove us home."

A black man? Estrada had seen very few black men since he'd left Glasgow and none he considered tough. He thought of Dubh's assailant and Sorcha's reaction when he first appeared in the shop. Could it be the same man? Had Sorcha recognized him from the pub that night? He'd been so upset by his experience with Rachel, they hadn't talked after. Nor had they since.

He glanced at Dylan. "You ended up sleeping in a field, I hear."

"Aye, by the Ballymeanoch Stones. It was Summer Solstice, and well, I miss being with you all."

Estrada eyed the guard and lowered his voice. His dream still haunted him, and he didn't want the guard to know anything about their activities. Though times had changed, witches were still suspect. "Yeah, it's hard to be on your own, especially for Sabbats. Did you hear anything? See anything?"

"I saw—" Dylan stopped talking.

"What?"

"Just a vision." Reaching up, Dylan rubbed his neck and shoulders to relax the taut muscles. "I never saw the sunrise. I fell asleep with the stones. That's where Billy Craddock found me in the morning."

"So, what have they got on you? Your lawyer must know."

"My lawyer thinks I'm guilty. I'm sure of it. They're saying I lured Steele down to the cairn with offers of the collar, and then cracked his head open with a rock when he refused to delete the photos of Sorcha. That police officer from Oban is a witness."

"Sexy photos? So what? Neither of you are married."

"Opportunity? They found me sleeping in a field near Steele's body."

"Which makes *no* sense. You don't bash a man's head in and go sleep in the adjoining field. Do they have any evidence?"

"One of my hankies . . . smeared with Steele's blood."

"What? How do they know it's yours?"

"My granddad gives me a box every Christmas. He gets them monogrammed. DDM."

Estrada huffed. "Where'd they find that?"

"Just outside the cairn. They think I used it to clean up."

"And tossed it?"

"No, it was stuffed in a hole behind a rock. They brought in a dog."

"Did you lend a hanky to someone?"

Dylan shook his head.

"You know what that means."

"Aye, sure. Someone is framing me. Someone from the dig."

"Look Dylan. Something else is going on here. I don't know what yet, but it involves that Egyptian collar."

Estrada rubbed the stubble on his chin. He wanted to tell Dylan about Magus Dubh and the man who'd cut him. And he wanted to warn him that if Dubh died, the man could be charged with murder. If it was the same man Sorcha danced with in Oban, all three of them could be in danger. They could all identify him. But he was leery of the guard who'd just glanced over and pointed to the clock.

"He just gave us the five-minute sign. Tell me. How are you doing in here?"

"Surviving. My cellmate is decent enough. He's innocent too."

Sure, he is, Estrada thought. *As innocent as every other guy in prison.* Knowing how awkward Dylan could be around the subject of sex, he didn't know how to bring it up, but he had to say something.

"Listen Dylan, if your cellmate, or anyone else, tries to get *friendly* with you—"

"Ah jeez, don't talk about *that.*"

"Listen to me."

Dylan hung his head, couldn't look him in the eye.

"I know how you feel about *that*, but it's not worth dying over. You hear me? If someone corners you, it's best not to fight back, just relax and—"

"Take it up the arse?" His voice was low and emphatic, muffled by his hand. "Is that what you're saying? I should take it up the arse."

"If you get caught, the more you resist . . ."

Dylan shaded his eyes.

"There are worse things."

"Worse than being buggered?"

"Yes. You could get the shit kicked out of you, or get cut, or maimed, or killed. If you don't fight back, they don't have to show their power."

"*They? Jesus Christ.*" Dylan crossed his arms over his chest and stared at the floor.

"I'm going to get you out of here, man, but I need you to stay alive."

"I'm done talking about this."

"You want to see Sorcha again, right?" Estrada winked and Dylan's cheeks flushed crimson. "Christ, man. You've got it bad for her, don't you? Are you *in love* with her?" He said it in a teasing tone, to lighten things up, but Dylan's flushed ears revealed the truth. "Whoa. You are. You're in love with Sorcha."

Dylan's chin dipped when he cleared his throat. "What if I am?"

"Hey, she's a gorgeous, sexy woman. I get it."

"Estrada, you can't tell her. She'll laugh at me."

"No, she won't."

Dylan seethed through clenched teeth.

"Okay. I promise. I won't say a word."

"And don't *sleep* with her. I can't think about you out there with her while I'm locked up in here."

"Listen man, I flew across the ocean to get you out of this. Trust me."

"I do. I trust you. At least, to set me free."

"Oh, but not when it comes to Sorcha."

Dylan pressed his lips together in a pale thin line and stared into Estrada's eyes.

"Fine. I won't sleep with Sorcha. You have my word."

Dylan seemed content with that, and they both glanced up at the clock. It was time to change the subject.

"Listen, I've been thinking about something." Dylan lowered his voice to a whisper and the guard shuffled a step closer. "You told me once you connected with Sensara telepathically."

"Sort of," Estrada said.

"Do you think you could—"

"Connect with you?"

"Aye. Try it now. Can you tell what I'm thinking?"

Estrada rested his forehead in his hand and closed his eyes. Immediately shapes appeared in the darkness. The speed and clarity surprised him. He was shocked they shared such a strong connection. Perhaps it was because they'd played out so many rituals together with the coven.

"Tree branch," Estrada said.

"Aye."

"Letters." Estrada spelled them out. "O A K. Oak."

"Magic." The guard moved in and signaled for Dylan to stand. "I go to sleep early. Ten o'clock. Can we try it then?"

"Absolutely," Estrada said. "Stay safe." His eyes stung as he watched the guard lead Dylan back into the prison.

24

That night, Estrada excused himself early and went upstairs. Dermot seemed relieved. After the long drive and stressful news from the lawyer, he'd spent the evening sipping scotch and quietly clutching his heart. Dylan's incarceration was weighing on the poor, old man. Estrada needed to fix this before anything else occurred. That bloody hanky bothered him. Knowing that someone from Sorcha's camp was intent on framing Dylan, narrowed his list of suspects but also raised the stakes. He needed intervention of the divine kind.

Now, sitting in a steaming bath, he carefully removed all the dressings and examined the wounds. His hand and calf were healing rapidly but his shoulder and pec looked grim. The sutures held it closed, but the skin around the edge was raw and oozing pus. *Infected. Damn.* He had no time for injuries. He laid a compress against the wound. Draw out the infection and give it air. That was what his abuela had always told them as kids. Back in Mexico she'd used leaves and roots to heal. He had nothing but antibiotic ointment. He left the bandages off. He'd have to cover the wounds again before he went to bed. Dermot had discovered the blood stain and changed the sheets. He hadn't asked and Estrada hadn't offered. Some things were best left unsaid.

After gathering his tools, Estrada stood naked in the center of the room and cast a circle around himself by chanting the ritual words:

> *"I conjure this circle as sacred space*
> *I conjure containment within this place*
> *Thrice do I conjure the Sacred Divine*
> *Powerful goodness and mystery mine*
> *From the East to theWest*
> *From the South to the North,*
> *I cast this circle and call magic forth."*

Then, beginning in the east, he raised his hands to the sky and thanked the gods and goddesses of all creation for the element of air that sustains life through breath.

Turning to the south, he imagined the sun and blessed the element of fire for its light and heat and protection, even from the earliest times.

Facing west, he stared into a basin of water until he envisioned a waterfall. Cupping the water in his hands, he sipped and touched it to his face, then said, "Blessed be the precious water that cleanses and heals us."

Turning north, he sipped from a glass of deep, red wine, and imagined Dionysus walking barefoot through a warm vineyard. He thanked the earth for nurturing such bountiful grapes and drank again.

Finally, he stood in the center. "Blessed be the sacred spirit within me and around me. I am grateful for the ability to move and bend and shape energy. For this is Wicca."

Then he sat and observed his breath. For breath was life. A man could survive being buried beneath the earth, or trapped underwater, or even in fire, if he had air. Oxygen. Watching his breath flow into his nose and lungs, and out again, Estrada calmed and focused his mind. Thoughts slipped away. There was nothing but breath—a pale pink mist surrounding his body, flowing in and out, warming every cell.

Dylan's unexpected entrance into the circle startled him. Appearing as a swift shadow, he swooped in, hovered in the air for several seconds, as if ascertaining that he was in the right location, and then settled into a similar seated position across the circle. With Sensara, it had been different. They'd passed images between them while still both in corporeal form, and once he'd entered her mind and body, even felt what she was feeling. But it had never been like this. Dylan was here in spirit, a shimmering astral traveler, having left his body behind in prison. "Stone walls do not a prison make," Lovelace wrote. Perhaps, he too, had learned to free his soul.

Dylan didn't need to speak. His thoughts appeared directly in Estrada's mind.

We need to cast a spell.

The last time we did that, it didn't turn out so well, Dylan.

It stopped the man.

And four people died.

This time we're more aware, Estrada. I know what to do. I dreamed it. It was so vivid.

Tell me.

There's an oak forest at a nature reserve called Taynish. Go there and cut a wand. You'll know the branch when you see it. Best go alone and . . . Well, do it right. Bring an offering.

And then?

One week from tonight at midnight, cast a circle among the standing stones at Ballymeanoch and conjure the Oak King.

The Oak King? I don't know—

The Celtic Oak King. This is his territory. Ask for protection and aid in unveiling the true killer. I'll come too, as I am now, but you must be there in body. You must bring the tools, cast the circle, raise the power, and conjure him. Find out everything you can about the Oak King and bring him something precious, something to please him.

I can do that, Dylan.

And Estrada, Taynish is an unusual place. You might see things you've never seen before.

25

Christophe heard the ping of Mandragora's laptop as he dozed on the soft leather couch. Curious, he flicked the long dark hair out of his eyes. His lover was such a trusting soul. As usual, he'd left his email open. Even as he focused on the print, Christophe knew he was breaking some tacit boyfriend agreement. He didn't care. This Estrada was a stalker. Some ex-lover who couldn't let go, and who Mandragora fretted about incessantly.

He's already left several emails, and Christophe had deleted them all. Finally, out of sheer frustration, he'd responded. He told Estrada he'd found someone else, and they were done.

Now, as he read Estrada's response, he thought of a harsh reply—something that would end it completely. He typed a few letters, then reconsidered. What if he got it wrong? Added too little or too much? Used words Mandragora would never use? He stared at the words *if it was you, I'd do anything*, bit a nail, and exhaled. Then, just as he had done with all the others, he hit delete.

Mandragora was still soaking in the tub, had likely passed out. He opened the deleted folder. There it was again.

Permanently delete? *Yes.* There were no more precise words in the English language for what he wished for this magician.

Rising from the couch, Christophe slipped off his silk robe and slunk into the bathroom. It was time to up the ante.

26

Estrada wiped the steam from the bathroom mirror and examined his shoulder. The wound was inflamed, the gash crusted with pus. He slathered it with antibiotic ointment and popped some pain pills, then covered it with clean gauze. He'd do anything but go to a hospital. They'd want to know things, like how it happened.

He dressed and walked over to the tiny Tarbert library. It was open only two days out of seven: Tuesday and Thursday. He sauntered in mid-afternoon. There were two other people there—a young woman and her daughter. The elderly librarian offered him the remaining laptop and he set to work.

The first thing he did was scan his email. Several newsletters and adverts that he deleted without reading; an email from his agent with some intriguing gigs—a week headlining in Las Vegas that provoked a snort (like he'd ever play Vegas); a private gig in Los Angeles that made him wince (too many memories there); a ski lodge/spa in Colorado that sounded promising; several corporate gigs in various East Coast American cities that were offering big bucks; and a

Hawaiian cruise. Check. He replied and told his agent to arrange the last three.

There was no message from Michael. A nervous wave passed through his gut, and he swallowed to choke back his trepidation. Who the hell was this new lover? And what could they offer Michael that would turn his head so completely?

When he closed his eyes and conjured Michael, he saw a nebulous silhouette shrouded in darkness. He hoped he didn't return to find Michael obsessed with some junkie. Addiction took many guises, and what he felt inside Michael was the languid stasis of opium. It pissed him off because there was nothing he could do about it. If Michael chose to morph permanently into Mandragora and dwell on the dark side, he'd have to walk that road alone.

Realizing he was slipping into a black place of his own, Estrada determined to focus on the task at hand. Dylan wanted him to conjure the Oak King. Appealing to gods and goddesses was integral to their ritual magic but before he went that far he wanted to know more about him. Spirits from the supernatural realm tended to be tricky.

Cernunnos was a fearless and lusty hunter, the quintessential fertility god. With his killing spear, he provided protection and meat for the tribe; while with his fleshy spear, he fertilized the goddess. Wearing the horns and skins of his freshly killed stag, Cernunnos was bloody, erotic, violent, and ecstatically charged. But the Oak King? This was someone Estrada had never encountered.

After scrolling through a few pagan websites, he gleaned a cursory understanding of the mythology surrounding the Celtic Oak King. He was engaged in a life and death struggle with his shadow aspect, the Holly King, over the affection of the goddess. It was a love triangle. That was nothing new. And they followed a yearly ritual.

At Winter Solstice, the Oak King killed the Holly King, usurped his power, and began his reign over the waxing year. At his peak on May first, he mated with the fertile Goddess at the Beltane fire. Then, at Midsummer—the time just past—the Holly King killed the Oak King . . . burned him alive. The Holly King then ruled the waning year. He, too, mated with the Goddess before the Oak King regenerated to slay him. And so, the circle of birth, sex, and death continued eternally.

Though it sounded complex, it was no different from the ritual drama the coven had just performed at Summer Solstice when the Goddess (played by Sensara) sacrificed the Green Man (played by him), and he revived as Cernunnos. They too were twin aspects. One symbolizing the plant world, and the other, the animal kingdom.

When the librarian placed a large book on the desk in front of him, Estrada startled. The white embossed cover showed a triad of golden oak leaves.

"The White Goddess," he read aloud.

"Aye. I noticed you've been searching the internet for knowledge of the Oak King. The web serves its purpose, but to appreciate the old ways, a book's what you need, a divinely inspired book. Robert Graves. He's the one. Mind, I've read this tome several times myself and cannae grasp all the man is saying. It's akin to the Bible in that respect. But there's parts that might help you, especially if you've the soul of a poet, which I think you have. You certainly have the broodiness." She rolled her r comically and winked. "I'm closing the library for today, but you can take it with you. I know you'll bring it back."

"Thank you. But don't I need a card or something?"

"I know who you are, and I know Dylan. Take it and help the lad and blessed be."

"Blessed be," Estrada echoed, surprised this tiny white-haired woman was spouting Wiccan phrases.

Back at Piper's Dream, Estrada sipped coffee and leafed through the book. Wicca followed a yearly round of Sabbats tied to the seasonal landscape, but Robert Graves revealed a calendar based on thirteen lunar months. The Celts understood that nature pulsed with spiritual energy. Each calendar month was dedicated to a sacred tree, for the energy of trees was a source of divine healing. Still more amazing, each tree stood for a letter in the ancient Druid alphabet. Graves theorized that the tree alphabet was a secret code created by Druids to preserve pagan culture during the onslaught of Christianity, when witches and oak groves had been burned alive.

The seventh tree in the calendar was *duir*. The Oak. *Duir* meant door in many languages. People built doors from oak because of its strength and endurance. Estrada believed a door was a portal and he wondered what waited on the other side. The moon began June 10 and ended July 7, which was, coincidentally, the day Dylan had chosen for their midnight rendezvous with the Oak King. Had the librarian introduced Dylan to *The White Goddess* too?

Cernunnos was closely related to the Oak King though these two wore different masks—one animal, the other botanical. Still, the storyline was universal: birth, regeneration through the sexual act, and finally death. Three elements spiraling in a continuous cycle. The land must be fertilized to ensure a harvest, just as the goddess must be impregnated to ensure the continuation of the tribe.

There is no life without death, no death without life, and no perpetuation of life without sex. This was the sacred dance of the god and goddess, and *this* he understood.

27

Perhaps it was the remnants of the circle he'd cast with Dylan, or perhaps it was the land itself, but the trees at Taynish whispered at every turn, their voices merging into a mesmerizing chant the farther Estrada wandered. He loved the fecund odor of the forest, the primeval scent of damp earth, especially after a rain. Elemental and enchanting, it was something he relished about the Pacific Northwest, and this was like that, only different.

Taynish was ancient deciduous woodland, whereas most of the Pacific Northwest was densely evergreen. Ash, holly, hawthorn, rowan, birch, and oak—all the trees in the Celtic calendar grew here, their skins shrouded with mosses, lichens, liverworts, and ferns. Gnarly wooden faces noted his passing, as did dragonflies and tawny saffron butterflies that danced on slight sea breezes like Shakespeare's faeries.

For hours, Estrada wandered entranced. He passed the shoreline of Loch Sween and the salt marshes, then walked on and on through woodland trails; watching, as Dylan had said, for a sign from the tree who would offer a branch for his wand. Before leaving Tarbert, he'd stopped at the ironmonger's shop and purchased a new hunting knife. It was safely sheathed in his boot. He wouldn't be caught short again; though, ironically, its first taste of blood would be his own. For only a blood offering would suffice.

Sorcerer. The voice was faint at first, evanescent, a lilting on the breeze, and he thought he'd imagined it. *Sorcerer.* He heard it again. Higher, louder, clearer, the tone teasing. And he whirled around, searching for *her*. There was only one woman who called him by that name; whose cadences were flecked with old Irish. But where was she?

Later, Estrada realized he'd walked past her several times without seeing her. With skin so summer-tanned, and draped in verdant gossamer rags, she merged into the bush, her tiny nut-brown face concealed by shadowy bark. It was her eyes that finally gave her away. Golden yellow, they glittered like cat's eyes when she smiled.

"Primrose."

"Ah, Sorcerer. You found me."

Her cinnamon voice sent a shiver through his soul. Remembering the feel of her faerie flesh, he held out his hands. "Can I touch you, Primrose?"

"Only if I can touch you back."

Estrada smiled. He'd missed her wit.

"I thought I'd never see you again." Grasping her hands, he kissed them and touched them to his cheek. "You feel so real. I thought I'd never feel you again or hear your voice. Never—"

"Make love to me again?"

"Again? But we never—"

"Ah." She sighed. "You didn't bring back your memories. More's the pity. Well, no matter. You *will* remember this." Running her fingers along his jaw, she caught his lips with hers and kissed him, filling his mouth with the taste of spiced apples.

Stepping back, she eyed him curiously, her shaved and tattooed head cocked to one side like a songbird. The tattoo had always amazed him. A Celtic mandala—three intertwining violet trees infused with vivid green spirals and lightning bolts—it ran from forehead to spine and ended in a serpent's tail.

"You've changed, sure, though I can't fathom how."

"*You* changed me," he said.

"All I did was free you from your burdens. But this is something else. Something in your essence, in your cells, in your . . ." Running her tongue along his throat and neck, she tasted his flesh. "In your *blood*."

"My blood?"

"No matter." She wrapped her hands around the back of his neck, stretched up on her bare toes and kissed him again.

Wanting nothing else, Estrada swept her up and cradled her in his arms, their bodies dancing with memories. When at last he broke away, it was only to whisper *I love you* with his eyes, staggering as if an arrow had pierced his heart.

"And I love you," she echoed aloud. "Now take me to some mossy bank and ravage me."

"Primrose," he whispered, feeling Cernunnos stir within, "you are a goddess."

"Have you only just figured that out?"

He walked a while with her in his arms, searching for a fitting bed for his fey lover, and when at last he laid her down, it was beside a rivulet swathed in wildflowers. Standing over her, he tugged off his jacket and shirt.

"What's this now?" Sitting up, she stared at the bandages. "Are you hurt?"

"It's nothing. Just a scratch."

"Ah, go on. Show me."

Estrada sat down beside her and watched as she unwrapped the yards of gauze.

Her eyes narrowed as she examined the gash in his shoulder. "How'd you get this?"

He winched when she touched it. "Asshole with a switchblade."

"Tell me now and tell me all."

"Can't it wait?"

"No."

Estrada sighed, clutched, and kissed her hands again. It felt like a lifetime since he'd been near her.

"It happened in a weird little shop in Glasgow. I was with an Irish woman like yourself, an archaeologist. An Egyptian collar she'd dug up in Kilmartin Glen was stolen and she thought this antiquities dealer might know something."

"Did this lad have a name?" Primrose asked.

"Sorcha calls him The Wee Pict. He's a dwarf, all tattooed in blue symbols."

"Magus Dubh."

"Yeah. You know him?"

"Aye. I know him. What earned you this?"

"While we were talking, some bastard barged in and gutted Dubh. I went after him. Chased him into an abandoned tunnel."

"Underground, like?"

"Yeah, like an old subway system." He cupped her cheek and kissed her lightly on the mouth. "You came to me. You helped me."

"Did I?" she asked, with a hint of teasing in her voice.

"You know you did."

When she giggled, her eyes twinkled. "Lie back, Sorcerer. Rest against the earth and let me heal you."

Remembering her skill as a healer, Estrada closed his eyes and hoped it wouldn't hurt too much. The last time was agonizing. But the soft moss cradled him like a cool velvet blanket as her warm hands moved over the wound. When he felt her fingers unclasp his jeans, he opened his eyes only to discover her kneeling naked beside him.

"Did you drift off?"

"Away with the faeries." He slid out of his jeans, his grin spreading, and caught her in his arms. And in the late afternoon stillness, he made love to her slowly with his whole body and soul. It was the first time he'd loved a woman since her death last December, and he didn't want the moment to end.

"In the old days, *that* would have made us a baby," he said, afterward, surprised by his own thought.

Primrose nuzzled beside him with her head tucked under his chin, her soft lips brushing his throat. "Aye, in the old days." The sorrow in her voice rent his heart in two.

"Can we be together, Primrose?" Estrada had never imagined himself as a married man with a family. Not until her. But now, that was all he wanted. The woman had unleashed some desire in his soul that eclipsed sex.

"Like wed, you mean?"

Estrada grinned and kissed her. "Yeah, married with a family."

"Ah, Sorcerer. You can love me till the cows come home, but you're a flesh and blood man with a hefty desire for physical pleasure. I'd never hold you to loving only me. You need your freedom, always have."

"I don't know. Since I met you, I've thought about marriage and children a lot. Maybe it's time. Maybe we can find a way to—"

"Hush now," Primrose said, and sitting up, she stared deep into his eyes. "You must let me go. Pledging your life to me will only bring you pain. Keep you locked in a kind of limbo. And I love you too much to see you suffer like that." Touching his cheek, she said the words he didn't want to hear. "Sorcerer, I'm dead. I died there on that faerie rath in Ireland."

"Don't say that."

"I must. You need to hear it and accept it. I'm dead as a doornail dead. I'll never be human again. I'm not the one for you. Not now. Not like this. You've got to let me go and move on."

Estrada's eyes burned and he turned his face away.

"Ah, don't cry, beloved. You'll be a father one day."

"I will?"

"Aye, my love."

"But how do you know?"

Pulling him against her shoulder, Primrose stroked his hair. "Trust me. You'll be a father and a grand one. But it won't be me by your side. We fey can't conceive, you know that."

"Right. Faeries steal a baby from the human world and leave a changeling in its place." Estrada rolled on his side. Even in his grief, perhaps because of it, he was desperate to make love to her again.

"That's one tale. But Sorcerer, what's that on the back of your leg?"

"Another gash. The son-of-a-bitch tried to hamstring me."

"You're fortunate he missed. Show me."

When he peeled off the adhesive bandage, she ran her fingers over the wound. Estrada watched her face. "What's wrong? Is it infected? It doesn't hurt."

"Look yourself."

Sitting up, he crossed his legs and pulled the skin of his calf forward. "It's healed."

"Look closer."

"There's a thin line of shiny gold dots, kind of like the chrysalis of a monarch butterfly."

"Aye."

"What does that mean?"

"You remember when I said you'd changed, like there was something different in your blood?"

"Yeah?"

"Have you felt or experienced anything strange since this happened?"

"Besides making love to a faerie in the woods?" Estrada winked, and she looked annoyed. "I had a weird experience with my friend Dylan in our circle the night before last. He's incarcerated, and yet it was like he was right there in the room talking to me. It was Dylan who sent me here." Estrada wondered if he would have met Primrose at all if he hadn't come to this place.

"Well, Sorcerer, I think you may have a few more of those experiences."

"Because?" He waited, barely breathing, while she gathered her words.

"Your leg was cut with the same knife that cut Magus Dubh, yeah?"

"Yeah."

"Well, that wee lad is as fey as he is human. His mother was born in the Highlands, but his father is fey."

"That really happens?" Estrada's eyes widened.

"Oh aye. Not so much now, but in the old days, ofttimes a fey man would steal himself a bride if he wanted children of his own."

"So, making love to faeries in the woods isn't particularly weird?"

"It happens. It happened to Moira. Her ancestors were Picts, but her lover was of Danu, one of the Sidhe."

"The *shee*. They're the Tuatha de Danaan," he said, remembering what she'd told him months ago. The tribes of the goddess Danu were Neolithic farmers defeated by the invading Milesians in Ireland. Only they didn't die. They fled underground and survived as faeries, the Sidhe. Primrose was now one of them. "Does Dubh know?"

"Oh aye, and uses his powers, sure, and not always for good. Magus Dubh is not his real name. It's a moniker he gave himself when he became a Druid. Magus means priest in the ancient tongue, and he is a priest, of sorts, something like yourself."

"A dark priest."

"Aye. Now this gold dust embedded in your scar tells me you've been touched by the fey. The dark priest's blood runs through your veins. By the time that man cut your shoulder, the magic must have been spent. But that healing I just gave you will amplify it, sure."

"*Jesus.*"

"Sorcerer, you're walking between the veils now, straddling the edge of two worlds. My own entry into living with the fey was years long, and I had my ma and gran to help me understand. I waded in slow-like. But you've jumped in hard and fast. I haven't had that experience, but I can tell you this. You'll need to keep your balance lest you trip. A fall, when you've a foot in two worlds, can land you in the breach."

"What do you mean? Like purgatory? Oblivion?"

"Hush now. Make love to me again." Catching his mouth with hers, Primrose climbed on top of him and danced a sultry dance that left him spent.

As darkness fell on the forest at Taynish, Estrada fell into a dreamless sleep cradled in her arms. It was the deep sleep of a man who fights a long hard battle, and then, for one moment feels utterly safe. Her healer's hands could do that to him.

"Sorcerer, wake up." Her voice, as soft as milkweed silk, played at the edges of his awareness and he feigned sleep just to hear her speak again. Only Primrose could get away with calling him sorcerer—a term with evil connotations—and he loved it like he loved her. "Wake up." Loud and insistent, she shook him vigorously.

"Kiss me and tell me this is no dream." Stubborn as she was, Estrada felt her refusal in the silence and reluctantly opened one eye to her sweet, somber face. "What's the matter?"

"You may be touched by the fey, but your belly's growling like a hungry bear. It's dusk. It's time."

"No, not yet. Please. I don't care about food. We can stay here forever and live on love."

"Or on that cheese you're spouting. Romantic poets. Holy God."

He leaned up on his elbows. "Well, I *am* thirsty. Is there a faerie well about?"

"Aye, but you know better than to eat and drink in the company of faeries, I presume?"

"Yeats mentioned that. But does it matter now that I'm—"

"Sorcerer. You're not invincible. That blood may enhance your senses and help your body heal quickly. But you're not one of us. You're still human as we both can see by that saber you're sporting between your legs. Holy God, man. You're insatiable."

Estrada rolled on top of her. "It's you, Primrose. You do this to me. I'm going to keep you captive here forever."

But when his cell phone sang, he jumped and reached out automatically to retrieve it from his jacket pocket.

"Saved from another ravaging by modern technology."

"Not yet you're not." Estrada checked the screen. "It's only Sorcha. I won't take it."

"Ah, go one with you," she said, and vanished in a kind of rushing mist.

"Primrose." Estrada stood and searched the trees to no avail. *"And what seemed corporal melted as breath into the wind."* The phone continued to sing, insistent and demanding like Sorcha, until finally, he slid it open.

"Estrada. Is that you?"

"Yep."

"Are you busy? Did I catch you in the middle of something?"

"Yep."

"Well, I'm sorry. But I've just spoken with the hospital in Glasgow. It's bad news."

"Tell me."

"Magus is dying." Sorcha's voice caught.

"I'm sorry, Sorcha."

"Sorry? Is that all you can say? He's been moved to Intensive Care. The poor Wee Pict's in critical condition."

Rachel's threat of AIDS sprang to mind, and Estrada grew suddenly wary. If Dubh's faerie blood had filtered through, what else now percolated in his veins?

"What happened? Infection? What?"

"Ah, the buggers won't tell me. They only talk to family."

"So, say you're family."

"They'll want proof. The only way we're going to find out anything is if we sneak into the hospital and—"

"We?"

"Aye, you and me. You've got to help me, Estrada. I'm sure Magus knows something about Steele's murder. Something he's not even aware of. Why else would that bastard from the bar in Oban try to kill him? The Wee Pict is the only lead we've got."

So, there it was. Dubh's assailant was in the bar in Oban the night Sorcha found the artifact and Steele was murdered. It was all connected.

"Let me think about this. I'll get back to you tomorrow."

"Promise?"

"What?"

"Promise you'll call tomorrow morning."

"I'll call." He pushed the button. *Damn her.* She'd interrupted his time with Primrose and that was precious time he'd never reclaim. Who knew when Primrose would suddenly reappear, if ever?

Sorcha was right about Magus Dubh though. He knew something—something worth his life. And whatever it was, it was tied to Steele's murder. Saving Dylan was reason enough to sneak into a Glasgow hospital.

Estrada dressed and sat on a log ensconced in dusky shadows willing Primrose to return. She didn't. Even when he called her name. Apparently, this was no scenario in which he could invoke her or command her to appear. The woman was no genie. She was, he decided, something akin to a ghost. Though no ghost could ever please him like she just did.

Cold and hungry, he finally accepted that she wasn't returning and started the long trudge back to the car park. About halfway there, he paused. Off in the east, one tree glowed with a radiant mist. As he moved closer, he saw it was an oak tree. *An Oak Tree.* Bemused by Primrose, he'd forgotten the very reason he'd come to Taynish.

Kneeling by the base of the tree, Estrada bowed his head and took several deep breaths. Finally, feeling calm and centered, he reached his palms toward the tree's trunk. Several inches away, he could feel its energy, a kind of sweet heat emanating in deep pulses from its core. He'd always known trees were alive, but this was something miraculous. Life vibrating in the palm of his hand.

"I'm Estrada, High Priest of Hollystone Coven, and I've come to you for help. My friend, Dylan McBride, is wrongly imprisoned. Please give me one of your branches to use as a wand. Your power will aid us in our quest for truth and justice. I offer my blood."

Pulling the knife from his boot, he cut across his left palm and drizzled the blood on the earth beside the tree's roots. For several moments, he knelt, listening. Wind rustled the branches, a pair of owls called out to each other, and small creatures crept through the grasses. When rain began to fall, Estrada raised his face and tasted its freshness against his parched tongue. And when he lowered his gaze again, he saw it. Lying on the ground beside him was a solid oak branch twisted at the end in the shape of a serpent, and it was shining gold.

"Thank you. I'll use it well."

As he rose and backed away, the storm worsened. After picking up the golden branch, he held it to his side and loped along the path. He was perhaps a mile from the car park when he realized he was following a trail no human ever could. Though stratus clouds concealed the waxing moon, he could see everything. Estrada could see in the dark.

28

Estrada was perched on the front steps of Piper's Dream sipping coffee with Dermot in the Friday morning sunshine, when the gray Prius pulled up.

Detective Rachel Erskine-Steele.

When she stepped out, the first thing Estrada noticed was her missing cop belt. Minus her battle gear, Rachel looked deceptively casual, benign even. In tight white capris and a skinny tank, she aroused more than his interest. Whatever unseen force drove his libido had multiplied exponentially since their last meeting—something he attributed to the infusion of faerie blood. Rather than climb the steps to join them, she leaned against the car and motioned for him to come down. Estrada admired her audacity but held his ground, refusing to be summoned.

"Do you have a date?" Dermot asked.

"No, I do not." Estrada set down his coffee.

"She's a beauty." The old man stroked his chin.

"She's a cop, and a little crazy." Estrada stood and ran his fingers through his hair. "I suppose I should find out what she wants."

"I'm curious myself."

As Estrada approached the car, Rachel retrieved a parcel wrapped in plain brown paper from the passenger seat.

"Detective," he said.

"Good morning, Estrada. I brought your jeans. The laundry patched them."

She'd drawn her platinum hair up into a high ponytail and he grew transfixed watching an ivory vein throb in the soft flesh of her neck. The woman was mesmerizing, and he wondered if she'd somehow cast a spell of her own.

"I know you're attached to them," she added flirtatiously.

He stepped closer and accepted the package. "Well, thank you, detective. I'll just go and get the pair I borrowed from you."

"No, don't worry about that. Not now."

They stared at each other until it felt awkward, and she glanced away.

"I'm impressed you took the time to find out where I was staying, and then drove all the way from Glasgow," he said, facetiously. They both knew he'd been flagged in the police system. "Was there something else you wanted?"

Her lip trembled and settled into a half-smile. "It's a beautiful day."

"It is that, detective."

"Call me Rachel."

"If you insist."

"Since the weather's so grand, I wondered if you'd come for a wee drive with me."

"A drive."

"Aye, our last meeting ended abruptly. I'd like a chance to make it up to you. Perhaps explain."

"No need, detective. You just lost your husband. I understand."

"I'd consider it a personal favor if you'd come." Leaning back against the car, she smiled and crossed her arms. "I promise to be pleasant."

Estrada could smell the almond-scented soap she'd used that morning and, beneath it, all the subtle odors of a woman's body on a warm day. As he breathed her in, his wolfish senses quivered, and he realized she was ovulating. Was this another effect of faerie blood?

"Pleasant," he repeated, caught up in his thoughts.

"Aye." She slid into the driver's seat and pushed up her shades, a sense of desperation creeping into her smoky eyes. "Will you come?"

"Give me a minute." He turned and sprinted up the steps.

Dermot was in the kitchen pouring another cup of coffee. He raised his bushy white brows when Estrada bounded through the door.

"That, sir, is Rachel Erskine-Steele. Alastair Steele's widow. She's a police detective."

Dermot's chin sunk against his chest. "Aye?"

"She wants me to go for a drive with her."

"She's nae arrestin' you."

"No, I think she has other ideas." Half-grinning, Estrada raised his brows.

"Oh. Oh, aye," Dermot said, with sudden understanding. "Well, surely you're nae askin' my permission."

"No, but I'd like your opinion."

"I see." Dermot stroked his whiskers and sniffed. "Well, first off, you should know how much I appreciate all you've done for my grandson. You've put yourself in harm's way and you're a good mate."

"It's nothing Dylan wouldn't do for me."

Dermot nodded. "But that one. She's the look of a vixen. Whatever you do, be careful." Dermot paused to sip his coffee.

"Do you think a woman like that could help or hinder my boy?"

Estrada ran his fingers through his hair. "That's the question I asked myself. She knows things we don't, has access to police records, and frankly, I'd rather work with her than against her. She could be a bridge to the other side."

"Bridges can be dangerous. Some water's deceptively deep and some's an undertow."

And some harbor trolls, Estrada thought, turning away from the old man. Dylan had been lucky to wind up living with his granddad. The more time Estrada spent with Dermot, the more he saw their similarities and was determined to reunite them, whatever it cost.

As he closed the kitchen door, he heard Dermot quip, "And make sure she buys you a decent breakfast, laddie."

29

"Where are you taking me, detective?" A few miles south of Tarbert, Rachel had turned east off the main highway onto a single-track road that wound around steep green hills and haphazard rocks by way of treacherous hairpin turns. She drove like a maniac, and after just missing a couple of straggling sheep, Estrada was gripping the edges of the seat.

"The beach," she said.

"There's a beach?"

A truck appeared on the road directly ahead and, as the track was simply too narrow to accommodate two vehicles, Rachel swerved into the closest pull-off, braked, and waited for it to pass. The driver sped by without so much as a nod.

"Aye, sure. We used to come here when I was a child," she explained, as she pulled the car back onto the road.

"You and your family?"

Rachel bit her bottom lip. "This part of Scotland reminded my mother of her childhood home in Sweden."

It was pastoral, picturesque, and largely untouched by progress. Estrada felt as if they were traveling back through time. As they turned south, the verdant hills and valleys gave way to ocean cliffs and sparkling blue vistas.

Rachel rolled down the window and took a deep breath.

"Your mother was Swedish." That explained the platinum blonde hair blowing back from her shoulders in a silken veil.

"My mother *is* Swedish and quite famous. She was a dancer and model when she was young. Now she's an actor. Perhaps you've heard of her. Her name is Magdalena."

"Sorry, no. But if you look anything like her, I can see why she's a star." He bit his bottom lip, wishing he could take that back. Sitting next to her was unnerving. The sea breeze wafting through the open window washed him in her scent and set his body tingling. It was indescribable. A sensual picnic that galvanized his heart.

Reaching her left hand across the seat, she stroked the inside of his thigh. "You don't have to romance me, Estrada. You were naked in my shower. Remember?"

And you were naked in your kitchen. Right before you threw me out.

There was something about Rachel that left him unhinged. Whether it was her bravado, or the fact she was a police detective, or something else entirely, he didn't know, but when he was with her, he felt like she was driving him the way she drove her car. Her fingers had found their way to his zipper. Any second now, she'd be gearing down.

"How much farther to this beach?" He jammed his hand on top of hers to halt its roaming.

Truthfully, he was conflicted. Rachel Erskine-Steele was the first woman in months he'd been sexually attracted to, and yet, his heart ached for Primrose. A woman who existed in another realm. A woman who could never be human again. A woman who'd told him to forget her and move on. Still, their lovemaking in the forest at Taynish was so real, so vibrant, so fresh, so raw, he felt guilty to be careening down a seaside highway on a drive that would invariably end in sex.

Stranger still, what if *this* woman was *the* woman Primrose alluded to? *You'll be a father*, she'd said. That haunted him still.

When he glanced at Rachel, she smiled and bit her bottom lip. "There's nothing but beaches along this coastline." She moved her roaming hand to the wheel as they sped around another curve. "And there's a gorgeous little hotel in Port Righ at the road's end. I thought I'd treat you to lunch there."

"You don't have to do that."

"It's the least I can do after what you've been through. You only came here to help your mate, yeah?"

My mate. Exactly. He remembered what she'd said the day they'd met at Kilmartin Glen—the day she was ready to hang Dylan from the nearest tree.

"Do you still think he's guilty?" Estrada asked.

"It doesn't matter what I think."

"Sure it does."

"Guilt is a matter for the court to decide."

"But don't you want to know the truth? Don't you want the real killer brought to justice? If it was me . . . If someone killed my partner—"

"You'd track them down and skin them alive." Rachel glanced at him and grinned. "We're similar in that regard."

"Then you need to know the truth."

"Truth is a matter of perspective."

That just pissed him off. "Listen. Dylan had nothing to do with this." She raised one pale shoulder and cocked her head. "Your husband's death is linked to the theft of the Egyptian collar."

Rachel stiffened and her eyes narrowed beneath the shades. "Why do you say that?"

"Why else would Magus Dubh be attacked?"

"You're making assumptions. There's no evidence to suggest the two incidents are related. Dubh's been involved in illicit activities for years. Anything could have precipitated that attack. A deal gone wrong, a vengeful client."

"Except, the bastard who cut Dubh was in the Irish bar in Oban the night Sorcha found the collar—the same night your husband was there and ended up dead just down the road."

"How do you know that?" She geared down, braking so hard the tires squealed.

Gasping, Estrada fought to keep his cool. "Sorcha remembers dancing with him at the—"

"*Sorcha? Christ.* I thought you had something *real.* Not O'Hallorhan. She was hammered." Regaining her equilibrium, Rachel eased the car onto the shoulder beside a pale sandy beach. "I'm a detective, remember? I've interviewed countless witnesses. And the one thing I know is the stories drunks tell are not credible. They don't hold up in or out of court."

She mumbled something incomprehensible and shut off the engine, then opened the door, and stepped out.

Estrada sat staring at the sign ahead. *Grogport.* Rachel was right. Sorcha liked her grog, and she was wasted that night. She'd been carried out of the bar and remembered nothing except the man. And she'd only glimpsed him for a few seconds before he ran out of Dubh's shop. Sorcha was an unreliable witness. He hung his head, feeling suddenly defeated, like all his investigating had come to naught.

When he glanced up again, Rachel was standing by the edge of the road, gazing out over the sea. Against the sparkling azure water, strands of her silvery hair caught in the morning breeze like filaments of a spider's web.

Leaning in the window, she flashed an apologetic smile. "I'm sorry, Estrada. I've been stressed lately but I've no right to take it out on you." The hollows of her cheeks flushed pink with emotion. "Can we take a break from all this? Just for a wee while? Will you walk with me by the sea?"

Dermot's comment echoed in his head. Estrada didn't much like deep water anymore. When he was a boy, they used to visit his mother's home near Mérida in the Yucatan, and swim in a deep cenoté the color of cyan. An underground river exposed by the collapsing limestone shelf, blood red stalactites hung like spears from the ceiling amid slick tree roots and caught the sunlight filtering through a hole in the ceiling. He remembered diving, splashing, and laughing in the warm water. It was a good memory—one he'd not recalled in years. They were happy then and life was simple. Perhaps, like Rachel had been when she'd come to this place with her family.

Estrada opened the door and stepped out.

"I feel somewhat disadvantaged," he said. "You know all about me, and I know nothing about you."

She'd slipped off her high-heels and was strolling through the wet sand bare foot. Against the blue of the sky, her skin glowed like alabaster. Even her toenails were ivory.

"I don't know *all* about you."

"You know where I work, what I do for a living, and who my friends are. You've searched my criminal record. Christ, you probably know how much I paid in income tax last year."

"Negative. I don't care about your financial situation." She turned and stroked his cheek. "You're incredibly sexy. I like that."

Catching her hand, Estrada held it firmly in his fist. "What do you want from me, Rachel?"

She broke free, picked up a handful of smooth stones, and began tossing them into the waves one by one. "Let's play truth or dare," she said.

"Truth or dare? How old are you?"

"Come on. Can't we just have some fun?"

Estrada rolled his neck from side to side and heard its telltale clicking. He was stiff and it seemed like a long time since he'd had fun.

Rachel took this as a sign. "I'll start. I dare you—"

"Wait. You can't start with a dare."

"Aye, sure you can. I dare you to wade into the sea with me."

"*No es problema*. The sea and I are old friends." Leaning against a rock, he pulled off his boots and socks and rolled up his jeans.

"Your wound healed quickly," Rachel said, staring at the pale gold threads woven through his flesh. "How's your shoulder?"

"Is that one of your questions, detective? Because I believe it's my turn," he said, stepping into the waves.

Estrada had forgotten about his shoulder. Primrose had healed it completely with her faerie hands only yesterday. Not even a scar remained. He'd need to keep this inexplicable phenomenon hidden.

"What do you want from me?" he asked.

"This," she said, and caught his mouth with hers. Her kiss was titillating and slightly wicked, as he imagined it would be. Not like Primrose or Michael. Something altogether new, and it left him breathless.

He flung his boots across the sand and stroked the back of her neck, let loose her hair, and tangled his fingers in the silken strands.

As her lips brushed his ear, he heard her answer. "I want to make love with you. No commitments, no promises, no complications."

"No complications?" He released her and stepped back. "I'm here to help free the man accused of murdering your husband."

"*Christ,* Estrada. Can't we just live in the moment. I thought you wanted me. Last week—"

"Last week, I made a mistake and I'm sorry for that. I was drunk and you were vulnerable. I shouldn't have taken advantage of that."

"Did you ever lose somebody, Estrada?" A tear slipped down her cheek. Taking off her dark glasses, she wiped her eyes, and his heart shuddered.

"Yes." Estrada touched her face, then wrapped her in his arms and held her, feeling the beating of her heart against his. "Yes, I have."

"I lost my baby two years ago and Alastair never forgave me."

This confession was unexpected. "That wasn't your fault."

They strolled in silence, her arm pressed against his, waves lapping at their feet. Estrada thought of all the things he might say, but nothing seemed right. At least she'd stopped crying.

"How do you feel about me?" she asked, at last. "I know I can be cold."

Estrada stopped walking and took her in his arms. "I don't think you're cold," he lied. "I think you're beautiful and sexy and I could tear up this beach making love to you. But if I did, I'd fall in love. I know I would. And that would be complicated because I'd want more than sex. I'd want promises, commitment. I'd want it all." He touched her cheek with his finger and felt skin as soft as a flower petal. Stepping back, he stood amazed by the string of sentiment that had flown from his mouth.

"Really?" She clutched her chest. "Thank God." Like a delighted child, Rachel danced around, the water swirling beneath her feet. "I was lying."

"What?"

"Aye. Your reputation. I—"

"My reputation? How the hell did you hear—?"

"The Pegasus chat room. They're quite explicit."

"What are you saying?"

"I want to fall in love with you too."

Estrada was still reeling from the idea people were describing his sexual exploits in a chat room.

"Well, if that's true . . . If we're contemplating a relationship, we can't start with sex," he said, finally.

"But, last week—"

"Last week was different. If we want something beyond sex, we need to learn to trust each other, with our clothes on."

Rachel took his hand and kissed it tenderly. "If that's what you want."

Estrada brushed his thumb across her lips. "I want to do it right." Leaning in, he kissed her gently in a way that said, *I want you bad, just not here and now.* And it was no lie. "If we're going to trust each other, we must be open and honest. We must be allies."

"Allies, sure." She locked her arm in his as they began to walk.

Estrada chewed his bottom lip and decided to take a risk. "I don't want to get you in trouble, but perhaps we could help each other by sharing information about the case." He figured calling it "the case" made it sound more benign. It wasn't about Dylan or Steele. It was just something they were both enmeshed in.

"What do you want to know?" They'd come to the end of the beach, turned around, and were ambling back toward the car, their bare feet catching the edge of the surf. Her eyes were fixed on the horizon.

"Sorcha's worried about Dubh. He's in intensive care. She thinks he's dying."

"Aye. Dubh's condition is deteriorating."

"Do you know why?"

"Blood. He lost too much blood."

"Can't they give him a transfusion?"

"They've tried. All the blood is incompatible. He has some rare blood type."

"So, it's not AIDS complications or—"

"Oh. No, I shouldn't have said that." She stopped and grasped his arm. "It's just when I heard about you and Michael Stryker."

"*Fuck*." He shook his head.

"Exactly," she said, smugly.

Estrada let that one go, and they walked again in silence. He didn't intend to defend his bisexual nature or his need for freedom. Until recently, he'd indulged in sex whenever and with whomever he felt a mutual attraction. Gender didn't matter to him. It never had. Nor had love or romance, though both could enhance the experience. He'd lived that way for years and could easily revive his libertine passions. If things got serious between them, then he'd share everything—his dreams, fantasies, preferences, even proclivities. She likely had her own. Everyone does.

When Rachel unlocked the Prius, they both slid inside. He watched her fiddle with the seatbelt and put the key in the ignition, then touched her hand to stop her from turning on the engine.

"You said Dubh has some rare blood type. Does that mean they can't find a match?"

"They've tried. That's what the report said."

Two thoughts struck him then. The first was logical. If Rachel was reading hospital reports on the condition of Magus Dubh, she was working the case. The second was incredible. Dubh had fey blood. He just didn't have enough. Estrada had an infusion of Dubh's fey blood. He might not be fully fey, but his own healing had been miraculous due to this potent fluid. He could save Dubh's life.

"How much time do they think he has?"

"From what I hear, it would take a miracle."

30

Sorcha didn't hear a word from Estrada until Friday evening when he called her mobile and asked her to meet him across the street from the museum at the Kilmartin Hotel. When she walked into the pub, she could tell right off something was different about him. He'd been with someone. She suspected a woman. Softened like butter when you leave it sitting out on the counter in a warm pantry, his smile lit up the dark contours beneath his cheekbones. She was infinitely jealous.

"Listen Sorcha. I'm sorry I didn't call you earlier, but I know what to do about Dubh." He shoved a pint across the table in her direction.

"Well, out with it."

He glanced around the room surreptitiously and lowered his voice. "You're an archaeologist. You must have read and seen some bizarre things in your travels, right? Things most people would consider impossible simply because they're so incredible?"

"Aye, sure. Humanity's bursting with peculiarities. That's what makes my work so fascinating." She took a long haul on her pint and leaned forward. His eyes were brighter too.

"What I'm about to tell you, you can't tell anyone. Understand? I'm trusting you with this information because it might save your friend's life."

Sorcha nodded. "Go on, then. Cut the drama."

"I know what's wrong with Dubh."

"How do you—?"

Estrada shook his head. "That's not important. Listen. It's his blood. The doctors gave him several transfusions but nothing's working." He paused a moment. "They can't find the right match."

"You're saying Magus has some rare blood type?"

"The rarest. Now, this is the incredible part." Estrada took a deep breath and leaned in close to her ear. "Dubh is half human and half . . . faerie."

"Faerie?" Sorcha giggled. "Ah, now you're having me on, man."

"No, I'm not." His face was dead serious. "His mother's name was Moira, and she was a Pict, but his father . . . His father was fey. I know it's hard to believe but—"

"You do recall I'm Irish?"

"How could I forget?"

"Well, we Irish are faerie spawn. Why wouldn't I believe?"

"That makes it so much easier."

While he tipped his glass and finished his pint, Sorcha signaled the server for another round.

"So, The Wee Pict's half fey. I can't say I'm surprised. It's fey blood, he's needing then."

"Exactly." When the server came by to drop off two fresh pints, Estrada hushed up.

"So, where the hell are we supposed to get—"

"Me." Estrada grinned. "Remember when I fought with that bastard who slashed Dubh?"

"Aye."

"Well, he cut my hand, and the wound healed overnight because Dubh's blood was still on the knife. And when he tried to hamstring me and sliced open the back of my calf, that wound healed in two days." Estrada pulled up his pant leg and showed her the faint line of gold dots. "My shoulder needed a little more magic, but it's healed now too."

"So, you.

"Yeah, me. My blood will work."

Oh, Sorcha thought suddenly. *Perhaps it's not a woman who's transformed Estrada at all. Perhaps this fey blood is the catalyst.* What effect would it have on the human mind and body? Could it heighten his senses? Fine tune his powers of perception? Enable him to appear and disappear at will?

Faeries were known for sudden appearances and just as sudden vanishings. As a child, she'd seen a horse drawn carriage driven by faeries in the forest near Galway where her grandmother lived. The woman was dressed in a beautiful violet gown and the man wore a crown. The woman smiled and gave her a wild rose. But when she told her mother, she didn't believe her, even mocked her. She said they were travelers playing a prank on a gullible child. Sorcha squashed that rose with her boot and never mentioned them again. She stopped believing and made science her god, just like her mam.

But Jaysus. Now he's saying they're real.

"Sorcha?"

"Aye?"

"What are you thinking?"

"We need to get some of your blood into Magus." When Estrada reached across the table, took her hand, and kissed it, the shiver ran right up her arm. "Drink up," she said, and took a big swig of her ale.

"You've seen them, haven't you?"

"Aye. Once upon a time in a land across the sea. Now, how are we going to go about this caper? I mean, do you know *how* to get your blood into his veins?"

"I haven't quite figured that out yet. You don't know a doctor or nurse you can trust, do you?"

"No. But I've taken forensic archaeology classes and carved my way through a few cadavers. I know my way around a body. More or less."

"A corpse, you mean."

She flung up her hands.

"Well, that'll have to do. We can do a direct transfusion. I looked it up at the library yesterday."

"Internet directions? *Christ*, man."

"Why not? Between the two of us, we can do this, Sorcha."

"Aye. We'll do it for Magus."

Sorcha raised her glass, as he raised his.

"For Dubh," he chimed, and they struck their glasses together.

31

It was half ten when Estrada parked the Harley outside the Glasgow infirmary. Sorcha waited while he swaggered in and engaged in a flirtatious conversation with the night receptionist. In tight black jeans and leather, he looked like a rock star. He'd lined his eyes in black and was emitting sexual energy she attributed to this new fey blood. She'd not seen him quite like this before and the whole package sent lusty shivers down her spine. When he sauntered out, he was whistling.

"I gather you found out where the ICU is."

"Yes, ma'am."

"And what did you tell her to make her smile so?"

"I'm planning to surprise my girlfriend with a proposal after she finishes work. She's new here, an ICU nurse. I needed to know when she'd be off and what door she'd exit from, so I could be out front on my knees when she did."

"And she bought that?"

Estrada winked and pulled those hearts-shaped lips into a lopsided grin.

"Of course, she did."

"There's a shift change at 10:50. They'll be coming out that door right there. Estrada gestured with those sultry eyes.

"Exactly how does this help us?"

"I figure there'll be fewer nurses on the floor after eleven, and if we wait until midnight, most of the patients will be asleep. They'll all have had their bedtime meds. Don't you agree?"

"Actually, I think we should enter just before eleven," Sorcha said. "When they do their shift change, they'll chat for a while at the main station, to pass on anything vital and catch up on the gossip. Those leaving will be tired and thinking of bed, and those arriving won't be settled in yet. They'll all be preoccupied. If we're stealthy, they won't notice us at all."

"Brilliant."

While they waited, Estrada explained what he'd read about the procedure for a direct blood transfusion. It made some sense, but Sorcha figured they were way out of their league. Still, they slipped in as planned and split up to search for Magus Dubh.

Sorcha couldn't find him in the ICU. At first, she panicked, thinking he'd passed on and been moved to the morgue. Frantically, she searched nearby rooms. Finally, she found him, sleeping like a baby; in fact, they had him in a child-sized bed. Fortunately, though it was a semi-private room, the other bed was empty. The poor Wee Pict was hooked up to several machines and an I.V.

She texted Estrada the room number and then assessed the equipment. She could leave the syringe attached to the vein in Dubh's arm, but they needed another syringe to connect the other end to Estrada's artery. They were apparently thinking in synch because when Estrada appeared, he pulled one out of his pocket along with a handful of other instruments.

"Stealthy," she said.

"Naturally."

She motioned for him to help her move the other bed beside Dubh's. The two fellas would need to lie adjacent for this to work. They set everything up and Estrada had just stepped into the bathroom, when a custodian popped his head into the room. Then the rest of him emerged. A rather large, bald man, he carried a broom. The name *Marek* was written on a badge attached to his uniform.

"What you do here?" His accent was thick.

Sorcha stood in a pair of faded blue jeans and a tight gold T-shirt, biting her lip. Momentarily stunned, she couldn't even concoct an appropriate lie. "He's my father," she blurted out, then cleared her throat.

"Father?"

It threw him. Perhaps, Marek was trying to comprehend how a dwarf could have a daughter anything like her. Since a mutated gene causes dwarfism, it was entirely possible, but this wasn't the time to explain.

"What? You don't believe me?"

"You go," he said. He leaned his broom against the wall and pointed at his watch. "No visit now."

Sorcha was suddenly afraid he was either going to accost her or report her.

"But, Marek," she said, all pouty and seductive, "if it was *your* father . . ." Leaning forward on the side of the bed, she pushed up her breasts with her arms. It was an exaggerated move, an invitation no man could mistake. "*Please* let me stay."

Marek's gaze fell to the deep cleft between her breasts, and he took a step forward, a sly smile stretching across his face. Estrada opened the bathroom door, but Marek didn't notice. He was much too focused on the midnight opportunity that had befallen him.

She saw Estrada pull something from the pocket of his jeans and raise his hand. A twirling crystal suspended from a silver chain dangled from his fingertips.

"Hey man."

When Marek turned, Estrada held the crystal directly in front of his eyes, where he couldn't help but see it.

"Watch it now. Watch it turn. This crystal is your whole world, turning and shining like the North Star. It's making you sleepy. Your eyelids are so heavy, you can't keep them open. You must sleep. Lie down on the floor and sleep. Stay asleep until I wake you."

Sorcha watched in amazement as Marek laid down on the floor and closed his eyes.

"How did you do that?"

Estrada shrugged. "I'm a magician. Hypnosis is part of my shtick."

"You've got to teach me how to do that."

"You have your own mesmerizing tricks," he said, thrusting out his chest.

Sorcha punched him in the arm and giggled. It eased the tension and they both took a breath.

Estrada winked, and then closed the door before anyone else could wander in. "Help me drag him over here. If we're lucky, no one will notice he's missing."

"Are we ready to do this?"

"I am," he said.

"Grand. Lie here," she said, gesturing to the bed, "and relax your right arm. I'll need to make an incision to expose the artery. How are you with blood?"

Estrada shook his head. "No problem. Do it."

She put several gauze pads underneath his arm to absorb any blood spill. Then, she disconnected the cord running from the I.V. down to the Wee Pict's vein and attached one of the fresh syringes from the tray. Following the line of the thumb on the underside of Estrada's wrist, she felt the area where she believed the radial artery to be. After swabbing the skin with a gauze pad and disinfectant, she picked up a small scalpel and made a tiny lengthwise incision, being careful not to cut so deep as to nick the artery itself.

With a sharp intake of breath, Estrada grimaced, but made no sound.

Blood leached from the wound and Sorcha covered it with a fresh gauze pad.

"*Christ.* I can see the artery, but I need another hand. Can you hold the incision open while I insert the syringe?"

Leaning over, he used his thumb and pointer finger to spread the incision. "Piece o' cake."

"Right." But just as she was about to insert the needle, Marek moaned, and she flinched.

"Steady woman. He's probably dreaming of some buxom damosel."

"Be careful, Estrada. You're in no position to make lascivious remarks." By the time she'd finished her sentence, she'd inserted the syringe. "There, it's in."

"It doesn't feel like it's in."

"Be still, mad man. If indeed you have a heart, it should pump your fey blood right into The Wee Pict's vein."

Straight away, Sorcha could see blood moving through the tubing. "How amazing, that in this moment we're saving a life, and not just any life, but the life of a half-fey dwarf."

"How do you know when to stop?" Estrada asked.

She considered. "Either when he perks up or you pass out."

When Estrada closed his eyes, Sorcha sat on the edge of the bed and stared at him. He was exceptionally beautiful, and she wondered again if someone had melted his heart. She hadn't seen him for a few days. Perhaps he'd met someone.

Moments passed. Sorcha should probably have been timing the procedure, but she hadn't thought to do that. She glanced over at Magus. If his skin grew pinker, surely that would be a sign. But through all the blue ink, she couldn't tell the difference. There must be at least one part of Magus Dubh that wasn't tattooed.

Curious, she drew the sheet aside and gasped. The Wee Pict's penis was tattooed in turquoise snake scales. The artist had filled the scales in silver to give it the appearance of armor.

"Eager to meet the mighty dragon?" With a voice like sandpaper Magus spoke and the dragon began to grow. "Like what you see, my Irish queen?"

"I like what I hear," she said, dropping the sheet. "Are you better? Have you had enough?"

"Enough what?" He turned his head toward Estrada. "Is he giving me his blood?"

"He is."

"Why?"

"Just lie still now, Magus. I'm going to remove this syringe and ligature Estrada's artery. I think he's passed out."

Indeed, he had. After cleaning his incision with saline, Sorcha closed it with butterfly sutures and wrapped it in gauze. Still, Estrada slept on.

"Magus, I'm going to reattach your I.V. I think you'll rally now."

"How long have I been here?"

"Seven days."

Dubh's eyes widened.

"The bastard tried to gut you. It was bad."

"I remember. Did they catch him?"

"Not yet. Your belly is stitched and bandaged. But they couldn't find a donor to match your blood. You were dying until Estrada discovered he was a match. You owe the man your life."

"Saints alive."

"Aye. He's that." Sorcha cleaned up everything as best she could, and then went into the bathroom and washed her hands.

When she returned, Magus was staring at Estrada. "He must have extraordinary blood. I feel like dancing a jig."

"Aye, he's extraordinary and so are you." Sorcha brought him a glass of water and set in a bendy straw. "But there'll be no jigging. Sip this."

She wiped Estrada's face with a cool cloth. When the water touched his lips, his eyelids fluttered.

"Hello, beautiful man."

"Hey. How'd it go?"

"See for yourself."

Estrada glanced over at Magus, who nodded. "Much obliged kind sir. I am indebted, and a Pict always pays his debts."

"I'll be coming to collect," Estrada said. "We've a few things to discuss."

"Aye, you've made me most curious."

Marek groaned.

"Estrada, if you can walk, I think we'd best be off. We've been here over an hour. Our luck must be running thin."

32

"The damn pub's closed," Estrada said. "We should have stopped somewhere." With Sorcha driving the Harley, they'd cruised from Glasgow to Kilmartin Glen in just over two hours.

"Ah, well. I've a fine old bottle of Irish whiskey in my tent that's been waiting for an occasion," Sorcha said. "Come back to camp and we'll hoist a few to The Wee Pict."

"Only if you promise not to seduce me," Estrada said, in as grave a tone as he could muster. Something had unleashed his wolfish soul. Whether it was the faerie blood that stirred in his veins, his magical time with Primrose, or the possibility of romance with Rachel, he didn't know. But he felt alive and free and potent, despite the blood loss.

"I can't promise that, you being a handsome hero and all. Whiskey's after waking my inner harlot. It's both a blessing and a curse."

"Then I can't come," Estrada said, in all seriousness. "I made a promise to a friend, and I can't break it."

"A promise concerning me?"

They were parked in front of the Kilmartin Hotel. Sorcha was stretching after the long drive, and he was leaning heavily against the bike. The woman was growing on him. He was impressed by the way she'd handled herself at the hospital, and the more secrets they shared, the more he admired her.

"Yes, a promise concerning you. And since I also promised *not* to discuss it with you, the subject is closed."

"Dylan McBride." She shook her head. "Holy Mary, Mother of God. Why do they always have to fall in love? Can a man not just enjoy a woman and let it go at that?"

"I agree." Estrada had enjoyed countless men and women without falling in love. "But a promise is a promise."

"Fine then. I'll *try* not to seduce you." Tossing back her head, she ran her fingers through her long red curls. "In the condition you're in, I don't think you could take it."

"Taunting me will get you nowhere."

"I'm serious, man. You look as if you're going to keel over."

"I am feeling a little lightheaded."

"Ah, it was only blood, and you saved a man's life."

"We saved a man's life. I couldn't have done it without you."

"Aye. We're a good team, you and me. Shall we celebrate our victory over Death?"

"I can taste that whiskey now."

Sorcha parked the Harley in behind the museum, and they headed out across the field on foot. Wisps of cloud partially covered the silvery half-moon hanging in the sky and the earthy smell of dew-stained soil was thick.

Estrada ambled through the grassy fields, breathing the wet salt-rich air, and felt energized. "It must be after two. Won't everyone be asleep?"

"On a night like this?" Sorcha strutted ahead as regal as any Irish queen. She took a deep breath and sighed. "Who wants to sleep? Ah, it's grand here. Reminds me of home." She slipped off her leather jacket and slung it over her arm. "Don't worry about my crew. Archaeologists are a special breed. Only a handful stay here, and most of them are locals who go home on weekends."

As they drew near the camp, Estrada could smell the distinctive scents of wood smoke and weed. In the distance, bodies lounged on blankets and deck chairs in front of a blazing bonfire. He watched a banjo player pick a tune, his fingers a blur, while two girls banged out guitar chords.

"Ah, see. They're having a wee session. Joel there is from the States. He's been teaching Gina and Shelly how to play his style of bluegrass."

"Bluegrass? In Scotland?"

"Sure. Down Home America is all the rage here. You know, this is one of the best parts of a camp like this. People come from all over the world and the craic is ninety."

Estrada eyed her curiously.

"The camaraderie," she explained. "Join them if you like. I'll just nip into my tent and fill a couple of glasses with the good stuff."

"That's a tent?" Sorcha was walking toward a huge green fabric structure that looked more like a space capsule. He estimated it to be six yards long. It had windows and even a front porch.

She unzipped the door and turned to him. "Curious? Come in, then, and I'll give you the official tour."

Estrada slipped off his boots, following her lead, and stepped inside. He expected to see sleeping bags on the floor. He'd camped once with friends in British Columbia, and they'd all piled into one crammed square like a crate of drunk puppies. But, when she turned on the lamp, he saw a scene from *Arabian Nights*. Patterned fabric hung from the walls and rich Persian rugs covered a floor strewn with large sleeping mats, vibrant pillows, and blankets. An engraved brass table served as a central gathering area, and several shelves along the far wall housed books, maps, pottery pieces, and various other treasures. It was much like a yurt he'd been in once.

"Very cool." He strolled toward the shelves.

"Welcome to my home. When you spend your life living at a dig, comfort is key." Kneeling before a heavy metal trunk, she fiddled with a combination lock.

"Treasure chest?"

"Aye. Some things can't be left lying about. Great craic, but not everyone can be trusted."

Estrada wondered how valuable an item had to be to make it into the chest. "Was your Egyptian collar locked in there the night it went missing?"

"No, I kept her close to me that night. That was my mistake." She'd lowered her voice, so he crouched down close to hear. "You see, sometimes I see images in my mind when I touch certain artifacts. Wood, not at all, but there's something about bronze, copper, silver, especially gold. It's like watching a play. I can see where the piece has been and who it's been with."

"That must be advantageous to an archaeologist."

"Aye. It's one of the reasons I went into this field. That, and . . ."

Her thought drifted but Estrada's curiosity was peaked. "Go on."

Sorcha stood suddenly as if her story was too much to tell from a crouch. Catching her arm, he rose with her. Her face took on that of a faraway dream.

"When I was fourteen, a body was unearthed in a bog near Dublin. It was the second body they'd dug from the peat in three months. Both were noblemen during the Celtic Iron Age, and both had been ritually killed."

"Sacrificed?"

"Aye. My mother knew the team at the National Museum, so she took me to see the bodies. Old Croghan Man was a young king. He'd been skewered, stabbed, decapitated, and cut in half."

"*Jesus.*"

"Though just a headless torso, he was still wearing a leather-braided armband with a bronze amulet covered in copper mounts. Even through surgical gloves, the moment I touched that ancient metal, I saw him, and Lord, he was beautiful. A tall, beautiful man. I'll never forget his face." Her eyes glazed over at the memory. "That was the moment I knew I had to know them . . . my ancestors . . . how they lived and how they died."

"Psychometry."

"Aye. I've heard it called that. I'll tell you; I nearly fell on my arse when it happened."

"That's quite a gift."

"One I can't explain." When Sorcha grinned, her eyes sparkled. "I don't even know why I'm telling you this, except I think you'll understand and we're sharing secrets tonight."

Estrada thought of Dylan's ability to communicate with stones. These two really should talk. They had more in common than they could imagine. But Dylan's gift was not his to share.

"That must be quite a boon for an archaeologist . . . like traveling through time."

"Aye, and that's why I need Meritaten's collar back. There's a wealth of knowledge trapped inside that artifact I've yet to discover."

"We'll find it," he promised. "And don't worry, your secret's safe with me."

"Good. You see those bones there on the shelf?"

Estrada glanced at what appeared to be the skeleton of some reptilian bird flanked by several spiked antlers and cattle horns.

"That's all that remains of the last man who crossed me. Now then." Leaning over, she pulled a green bottle from the open chest and brushed her hand over it, as if it were made of diamond.

She presented it to him, and he read the label aloud. "Connemara Peated Single Malt Irish Whiskey." He made a clicking sound with his lips. "Sounds serious."

"Sixty percent serious and twelve years old. The barley's dried over peat fires in Connemara—that's my childhood home. It tastes like the smoke of heaven."

"You continue to impress me, Ms. O'Hallorhan."

Sorcha smiled and winked. "I've been saving it for a special occasion." Accepting the bottle back, she opened it, then sniffed and groaned. "Ah, go on then. Have a whiff yourself."

Estrada breathed it in. "Gorgeous. May I?"

"You may." She set two glasses on the table. He poured both and handed her one. "To Magus Dubh, a ballsy wee man with a heart of gold. And to you, Estrada, a magician who could charm the knickers off a nun."

"Guilty."

"Ah, get out."

"Just one or two. I *was* Roman Catholic." He winked. "But you've forgotten to toast the most important person here and that's you." He held the glass high. "To Sorcha O'Hallorhan because she cares about people."

"That's it? That's all I get? She cares about people. How about, to Sorcha O'Hallorhan for her bravery in the face of eejits, her surgical audacity, and her incredible breasts?"

"They are beautiful," he said, and they clinked glasses.

"*Sláinte.*"

The first swallow rushed through Estrada's body like a stream of liquid gold.

Sorcha refilled their glasses and they each downed a second shot.

"*Jesus*," he said, collapsing into a heap of pillows. What was wrong with him lately? He used to party all night. This whiskey went straight to his head and kicked out his legs.

Laughing, she set another full glass on the table in front of him. "Ah, we're just warming up, man."

When Sorcha flopped down beside him and brushed out her long red curls, Estrada suddenly wished he hadn't made that promise to Dylan. The woman was brave, beautiful, intelligent, tough, sexy, and charming. And he was a free man.

"I can see why Dylan's fallen in love with you." Estrada gasped. "Shit. I wasn't supposed to say that."

"Too late, and I must advise you to be careful." She threw back her head and drained the glass, then crashed it down on the table. "Saying things like that could get you in trouble."

"What kind of trouble?"

"You could wake up naked and spent and wondering what transpired."

"I promised not to sleep with you," he said, in all seriousness.

"Ah, well, there'd be no sleeping." She leaned in so their cheeks touched. "I've been wanting to kiss those perfect lips since I met you. Would it break your promise to share a kiss?"

Estrada turned to look into her eyes, then touched her cheek with his palm, and she moved her mouth against the soft flesh of his hand.

"Just a kiss, to celebrate our victory," she said. "No dishonor in that."

Estrada drew in close and caught her other cheek with his palm. "I think a kiss would be—"

But before he could finish, Sorcha covered his lips with hers and pushed him back into the pillows. Their mouths joined in a sensual dance that traveled the length of their merging forms. Catching his hands in hers, she held his arms back against the blankets and rocked against him. The alluring rhythm sent his senses reeling. Somewhere in the recesses of his whiskey-stained mind, he wondered just how far he could push the promise line. *This is still just a kiss*, he told himself.

"Who the fuck are you?" A man was suddenly in the doorway. Ducking his head, he sauntered inside stinking of sweat and alcohol.

Releasing Estrada, Sorcha sat up, swung around, and yelled, "Jesus, Kai. Get out of my tent."

"Shut up, bitch." The man spat the word so vehemently, spit flew.

Estrada sat up, downed the rest of his whiskey, and tossed the glass into the pillows. The pair rose simultaneously, and Estrada shoved Sorcha behind him, just in time to catch a sucker punch to the gut.

Winded, Estrada reeled back to catch his breath and assess his opponent. So, *this* was Kai Roskilde. He was only slightly taller, but a good fifty pounds heavier. Russet beard and blond hair that fell long and loose around his face. That was something Estrada could use to his advantage. No rules, no mercy. A long scar ran down the man's cheek, which meant he didn't know how to protect his face. And he was stumbling drunk.

Grasping Sorcha by the shoulders, Kai shook her. "Everything I do for you, Irish, and you bring this dick into my camp?"

"It's not *your* camp, Kai. It's mine, and this is *my* tent. Now, get out before I fire your arse."

"Ungrateful bitch." Kai spat, and backhanded Sorcha across the face.

When a man gets mean with a woman, there's nothing to do but take him down. Estrada approached from behind, grabbed a handful of Kai's frizzled hair and yanked. Cursing, the man leaned backwards, then turned to grapple him. But before he could, Estrada brought his knee up high and caught the bastard in the nose. Heard the bones break. Saw the blood.

Letting go of his hair, Estrada pushed off, took a couple of deep breaths, and waited to see the result.

The man had no moves. He'd likely bullied his way through life using intimidation to avoid any real physical altercations, except for perhaps the man or woman who'd wielded the knife. Emitting a stream of foreign curses, he lurched forward.

Estrada blocked his punch and countered with a hard, quick kick to the groin.

Down went Kai, gibbering.

"Enough." Sorcha stood in a corner, hand to her cheek.

Maybe, Estrada thought, *but maybe not.*

Kai stood grimacing and staggered around like a wounded bull. Had he left it there, Estrada would have too. But he didn't. Turning to Sorcha, he spat a bloody gob that landed on her breast. "You'll pay for this," he said.

Estrada set up his kick and deftly lifted the man's kneecap.

Kai went down then, threats and blood flying from his face.

Just to be sure, Estrada hoisted the brass table and bashed him over the head with it until the noise stopped.

Sorcha stopped him. "Jesus Christ. Don't kill him." Kai was still breathing but had no fight left.

"Kai," she said. "I know you can hear me. I'll make a call and get you out to the highway, so the ambulance can pick you up. But after that you're on your own. Don't come back here."

Pivoting, she turned to Estrada and shook her finger in his face. "For future reference, I can take care of my fecking self."

Several faces peered in through the tent door, some petrified, some shocked, but most with broad smiles on their faces. "Somebody get the tractor and cart," she said.

She turned to Estrada and shook her head. "You just made yourself one feck of an enemy."

33

Dylan was relieved to see Estrada sitting in the visiting area on Sunday afternoon. He needed that protection ritual, and he needed it now. Wiley, his *innocent* cellmate, had offered him a deal. He'd shield Dylan from other men in the prison, but in return he wanted favors—sexual favors Dylan was not prepared to give. It was only a matter of time before Wiley stopped asking and started taking.

This was what his life had come to. He existed in a world of men—bad men whose lust for power knew no bounds, and the only power he knew lay in magic.

"Did you get to Taynish?" Dylan wrung his trembling hands to keep Estrada from seeing how bad things were.

"Yeah, a couple of days ago. You won't believe who I saw there."

He rubbed his eyes, hadn't slept in days and was feeling woozy.

Estrada's eyes lit up. "Primrose."

"Primrose?" Dylan thought back to Estrada's experience in Ireland. When he'd slipped into a coma, Maggie's gran had said he was "off with the faeries." Was it possible? Were faeries real? Had Estrada somehow slipped between the veils again?

"I mean it, man. Primrose was there and as real as me or you. I could feel her, smell her. We made love. It was amazing."

Dylan played the bagpipes at her funeral. Saw her laid out in a casket festooned in flowers. "And you were awake? It wasn't a dream. Or a trip?"

"A trip?" Estrada snorted. "It was real, man. I was walking through the woods, and she called out to me. She was there."

"I'm gobsmacked. How did you—?"

"I don't know. But thank you for sending me there. If I hadn't gone to that place, maybe it never would have happened." Estrada reached across the table, grasped Dylan's hand, and squeezed. "She helped me sort things out. I feel like I can move on now."

Dylan could see from his friend's face, he was telling the truth, not that he ever considered Estrada would lie to him about anything.

"But enough about me. You're edgy. What's—"

So much for pretending everything was alright. He'd forgotten Estrada could read other things besides facial expressions. "You need to do it right away. Tonight."

"Did someone—?"

Dylan shook his head. Had no words for it. "Are you ready? Did you get what you need?"

"Yeah, and I'm making progress. A friend of Sorcha's remembered something—something that almost got him killed. A woman came to his shop looking to sell the broad collar."

"A woman?"

"A young woman. She didn't have the piece on her, but she described it. She was likely sent by the thief. Now, this dealer owes me, so I'm going to get him to give the police that information, and maybe that will be enough to get you out on bail. It's worth a try, right? Your granddad says, if we can give them enough evidence you can be released."

Dylan stared down at his hands. Hearsay wasn't evidence and even if they caught the thief who stole the artifact, that didn't make him or her Steele's killer. He rubbed his face with both hands. His lips felt dry and tight like they were stretched over his teeth. "How's Sorcha?" Dylan asked at last. He didn't want to mention her but couldn't help himself.

"She's good. She's helping me."

"Is she." It wasn't a question.

"Look. I need someone who knows their way around here—someone I can trust. I'm positive whoever killed Steele also took the artifact and is connected to the dig, and those are *her* people."

Dylan hoped Estrada had kept his promise. But it didn't matter now. Sorcha was just an image he conjured at night when he lay stiff in his bunk.

"Oh, and I met your friend Kai last night."

Dylan snorted. "Kai Roskilde is no friend of mine."

"Yeah, I thought you'd like to know. He took a beating. He's a terrible fighter and he's suffering. Dislocated kneecap, busted nose . . ."

Dylan glanced down at Estrada's bruised knuckles. "Jesus."

"And he no longer works at the dig. Sorcha fired him. So, when you get out of here, no more Kai. That's good news, right?"

Dylan forced a smile. He was thrilled to hear Estrada had taken a piece out of Kai but was beginning to think the only way he'd get out of Greenock was in a body bag. "Aye. That's the best news I've heard since . . . Christ, I don't even know how long it's been. He'd seen scratches on the stone walls in Lochgilphead. Now he knew why. The days just blended.

"Two weeks and two days." Estrada's lip flattened in sympathy.

"Sixteen days. It feels like years."

"Don't give up, Dylan. After tonight, things will accelerate. Look, the guard's giving me the nod. I'll go prepare, and catch you later, right?"

"Aye. Later."

Dylan couldn't explain this latest threat to Estrada. Speaking it aloud would make it only too real and he knew what the response would be. It was Wiley's thirtieth birthday next Friday, and Dylan was to give him a very special gift. If he didn't agree, Wiley was going to trade him to Ezekiel. This "Big Zeke" as they called him, wasn't just a rapist, he was a sadistic killer.

Estrada would say give your cellmate what he wants.

Only Dylan couldn't do that. He'd rather die.

34

When Estrada left Greenock Prison that afternoon, he knew if he didn't get Dylan out soon, his friend wouldn't survive. If he could trade places with him, he would. Dylan had been threatened. He could smell the fear. But there was nothing he could do about what went on inside a prison.

He considered calling Rachel to ask if there was something she could do but decided that a Glasgow detective would be just as powerless inside one of Her Majesty's prisons as anyone else. If Dylan had given him something concrete, perhaps, but he wasn't talking, and he never would. It wasn't something Dylan *could* talk about and he'd fight to the death before he'd allow a man to molest him.

All Estrada could do was spin as strong a protective cocoon around Dylan as possible and find the true killer. If he failed in his quest, Dylan would die.

35

Leaning over the railing of the yacht, Michael surveyed myriad flickering lights in the distance. They'd embarked from Vancouver four nights ago. The first two days were heaven. The last two, hell. The crew had rigged the sails and under sun and azure skies, they'd scuttled up the coast as far as Lund. Michael partied hard those first two days, relishing the freedom of the sea, and Christophe, high as a soaring eagle, had surprised him with delicacies, aged champagne, and a plethora of good drugs.

But after a sunset supper on a cedar-shaked patio, Michael was done. His appetite for adventure sated, he was ready for home. He missed his lair, Pegasus. And though still annoyed at Estrada for leaving him behind, and for something else he couldn't remember, he missed the magician most of all. Christophe had smiled and said, "Of course, chéri," but when Michael arose the next afternoon, the yacht was headed northwest across the strait, and they were fighting the westerlies.

The gray rain sunk into Michael's bones and curdled his soul. He cried like a child. "I want to go home." And when he searched his pockets for his cell phone, he discovered it was gone. "Where's my phone? What have you done?" he yelled, between bouts of puking. But Christophe only held back his hair as the boat surged on, and said, "It must have slipped overboard, chéri."

When the yacht tucked into a marina somewhere on the west side of the strait that night, Michael stayed below, surly, and dank, his belly heaving with each quaking wave. He'd been on boats before and wasn't prone to seasickness. This was something else. Anxiety. He hated the lack of control and felt imprisoned.

The next morning, under clear skies they chugged up a blind channel. Trees, rocks, and sea. Lonely, desolate islands. And always Christophe, clinging and whispering, "Trust me, chéri. We're almost there, and then you'll know the secret of the ultimate gift."

Michael had smoked his weed and drank his wine and sprawled on a deck chair, longing for escape.

And now, at last, they were here.

As their yacht docked, Michael observed others. Monstrous white powerboats reeking of corporate money, several sailboats, and two antique vessels trimmed in wood. Most bore American tags, and all had been emptied by the raging bash whose beats eclipsed the night.

"You're so grave, chéri. Laugh. Enjoy the party." Catching him against the railing, Christophe kissed him. "I give you this gift because I love you, Mandragora."

Love. That word was bandied about much too casually. Michael gazed into eyes craving praise with canine desperation, and when they kissed again, behind his closed lids he saw a black spaniel. His stomach lurched.

Club Pegasus was Michael's domain, and he rarely ventured outside those walls. It was one thing to frolic in fantasy—reality was another thing entirely. No one understood this, but Estrada. The two men shared an uncommon intimacy that couldn't be duplicated, which was why it hurt so much to be abandoned and ignored at the magician's whim yet again.

"What is this ultimate gift?" Michael asked. Christophe was completely in control of this escapade and Michael didn't like it.

"Come. I'll show you."

"Just tell me."

"It cannot be said. It must be experienced. But you'll love it, Mandragora. Trust me."

The full moon cast silvery shadows through the trees lending the whole scene an eerie ambience, and always in the distance, the tumultuous beats throbbed as if the island itself were alive.

"How did you ever find this place?"

"The Earth has much magnificence. A man need only ask the right questions."

"A man must also know the right people to ask." Michael opened his silver zippo and lit a cigarette. Then, with a flick of his wrist, he clicked it shut. "Was this place built as a movie set?"

"No. It was a gift from a nobleman to his lover long ago."

"A nobleman? How long ago?"

"It's said, the builder sailed these waters in 1775 aboard *La Sonora* with Juan Francisco de la Bodega y Quadra."

Michael snorted and blew a smoke ring.

"It's true. We passed Quadra Island this morning when you were ill."

Michael mulled this over as they left the dock and followed a crushed stone pathway. Lit by flickering lamps, it meandered through dense pine and cedar forests.

"Are you really trying to tell me this resort has been here, hidden away on an island for over three centuries?" he said at last.

"Le Château is not really a resort, although people do come here to play."

"I dislike your riddles." Michael disliked much of what was happening, however glamorous it sounded. Days of imprisonment. A lack of control. A lover who tried too desperately to please. Yet, a sense of nervous excitement mingled with trepidation and made his fingers tremble.

When at last they turned a corner, Michael stopped and stared. An exotic palace loomed before him.

"My god." Michael knew little of architecture, but he could appreciate antique symmetry. Floodlights emphasized the deep carmine walls and polished mahogany double doors ensconced in their carved stone façade. Byron journeyed to palaces such as this in the Mediterranean. "I feel like I've traveled through time."

Christophe exhaled. "Ah, chéri, I knew you'd love it. And this is just the *hors-d'oeuvre*."

Michael had never seen Christophe smile like this. The pleasure, erupting from somewhere deep inside, illuminated his entire face.

But there was something infinitely dark about the scene Michael encountered when he walked through those double doors. A magnificent gold cathedral, whose lavishly frescoed walls rose into a soaring coffered ceiling, played host to a writhing debauchery of bodies engaged in deviant play, most of which had a sado-masochistic bend. Beats blasted from hanging speakers in the paneled dome, as strobe lights flashed through a smoldering dope haze. Is this what Christophe thought he wanted?

"Come," Christophe said, and taking Michael's hand, he led him through the throng. Stopping before a stone archway, words were exchanged with two burly guards, and then the thick oak doors swung wide. They stepped into a cool tiled passageway that ran several yards before ending at another oak door.

For the first time since arriving on the island, Michael couldn't hear the beats. "That looked like a scene from the Spanish Inquisition. Just to be clear. That is *not* what I want."

"Of course, chéri. I know you are not like *them*. This is an antechamber to cut off *this* from *that*. But someone must pay the bills, no?" Christophe grimaced.

They stopped beside a candle in the stone wall and Christophe used its glow to assess Michael. Fussing, he combed out his long blond hair with his fingers and then glancing down, he frowned. "You are not dressed quite right, I think. Remove your shirt."

"My shirt?"

"The black trousers are chic. But you must reveal your perfect neck and chest." With quick fingers, Christophe unbuttoned Michael's shirt. Running his hand across the smooth breast, he smiled. "Your flesh is like alabaster. So pale and perfect."

Feeling a sudden rush of anxiety, Michael grasped his hand. "Who are these people you're taking me to meet?"

"Do not be afraid. They are the ones you revere. *Authentique.*"

"Authentic what?" Michael took a quick breath. "What do you mean? Where are we?"

"Le Château des Vampires, chéri. I have arranged it all."

36

Passing through a fine mist, Estrada skirted Dunchraigaig Cairn. Steele's ghost hovered in the pitch, and Estrada's rippling flesh warned him to stand back. He hadn't felt this presence the first time he'd been here, but he could feel it now, even see it—a shapeless, shimmer over the cairn like rising heat on a summer's day. The man, as vile as he was, had been bludgeoned unexpectedly and left to bleed out. Perhaps, like King Hamlet he awaited justice.

He padded along the fence line and opened the gate into the fertile pathway separating field from field. The six remaining Ballymeanoch Stones stood in two parallel lines in a verdant sheep pasture to the southwest. It was the first time Estrada had stood amid the towering stones and feeling humbled, he marveled at their stature and the men who'd erected them. Running his flashlight beam over the cool gray surface, he examined the lichen and sunken rings that signified, he knew not what.

From his pack, Estrada pulled a white scarf, unfolded it, and set it on the grass in the center of the stones. On it, he placed candles, a vile of creek water, a quartz crystal, and a golden eagle feather—each object symbolizing a different element, and all necessary to achieve a sense of unified balance. After stripping off his clothes, he picked up the oak wand he'd created from the Taynish branch. Drawing it close, he inhaled the sweet fragrance of the wood. Tipped in an amethyst dragon's tooth, it was a simple, potent tool for directing energy and, he prayed, enough to invoke Dylan's Oak King.

As he walked toward the stones in the east, the moist night breeze swept across his skin stirring his tactile senses. He was just about to cast the sacred circle when he heard a shout.

"Wait, Estrada. Wait for us."

Coming out of the north, a jagged beam of light skittered haphazardly from the hand of . . .

"Sorcha. What are you doing here?" She arrived panting, chest heaving.

"We're here to help."

"We?"

And from out of her shadow emerged a winded Magus Dubh.

"How did you know where I was?"

"You have powerful blood, Estrada. I healed straightaway, and when I did, I knew what you were up to here tonight. Don't be alarmed but I seem to have gained some knowledge of your thoughts along with your blood. We're now blood brothers in the most intimate of ways."

This news left Estrada speechless. He stared into Dubh's eyes and thought loudly: *If you ever fuck with me, Dubh . . .*

"Don't be alarmed. I'm discrete and trustworthy and aware of the importance of what we're about to do. Please, don't fret, my friend." Dubh reached out a hand which Estrada accepted. "I've conducted many of my own rituals over the years and I'd be honored if you'd allow me to lend my power to the proceedings."

"Me too," Sorcha said. "Better three than one, yeah?"

"Magnifies the power. That's why we work as a coven." Estrada glanced again at the dwarf. Just how many of his thoughts traversed the dark wizard's mind?

Dubh winked. "I'm sure this effect will fade with time."

"It better," Estrada said. "I was just about to cast the circle."

"Ah, do I need to . . .?" Sorcha appraised Estrada's naked body and then pointed at her clothes.

"Aye. Everything, my Irish Queen." Then, turning to Estrada, Dubh quipped, "Ah, to glimpse the breasts of the goddess."

Estrada rolled his eyes. "Get it over with now Dubh, because once we begin, I need your complete concentration on the task at hand."

"And you'll have it," Dubh said, doffing his clothes to reveal the full extent of his tattoos.

"The same goes for you," he said to Sorcha. "This is Dylan's life we're here to save."

Sorcha's usual smile turned grave. "My appraisal is complete."

Estrada held the serpentine oak wand aloft with both hands and called down the gods of protection and light in the East. The oak wand released a golden glow as he worked. Walking clockwise, he continued casting an enormous circle to encompass the standing stones. At each compass point, he invoked and summoned the gods, asking for aid in their endeavor.

Dubh stood in the center with a blackthorn wand casting a violet light from a quartz crystal embedded in the tip. Estrada heard him banish all negative energy and call the spirits of the ancient Druids and Fey to join them in the circle.

When Estrada walked back to join him in the center, he was thrilled to find Primrose standing skyclad between them.

"You're really needing four. Right, Sorcerer?"

"Four is perfect," Estrada said, taking her in his arms. "As are you."

"Ah." Sorcha smiled. "Here's the butter. Is she . . .?"

"Aye. Primrose is Fey," Dubh said.

Estrada glanced at Sorcha and furled his brow. "Butter?"

But the archaeologist just shook her head and grinned at them both. And so, introductions aside, Estrada took a deep breath and began.

"Our circle is cast. We are between the worlds. In this protected space, we raise our power." Estrada opened a bottle of absinthe and poured several ounces into a deep brandy snifter. Then, he held a sugar cube over the mouth and drizzled cold water over it. A few swirls with his wand and the greenish liquid transformed into a creamy white louche.

He offered the concoction to Sorcha, who looked hesitant for the first time since he'd met her. "It's absinthe. Seventy percent alcohol but diluted. The main herbs are fennel, anise, lemon balm, and wormwood, and none will harm you."

Sorcha sipped and passed it to Dubh, who took several swallows and offered it to Primrose. Clutching the snifter with both hands, she took a long drink, and then passed it back to Estrada who finished it off and set the glass back with the rest of his tools.

"Join hands to seal the energy." Estrada and Dubh stood across from each other with Sorcha and Primrose between them. The moment they all clasped hands; Estrada's fingers tingled. He'd never experienced a circle with anyone who wasn't human, let alone a faerie and a half-fey Druid priest.

When he glanced again across the circle, a shadowy Dylan sat cross-legged in the center. Eyes half-closed, he'd come in spirit, leaving his dense body back in Greenock Prison.

Estrada took a deep breath and felt their strength multiplied. Where he'd first stood alone, now there were five.

"This night, here among these sacred stones, we call upon the ancient Oak King to aid us in our quest. Known by some in his animal guise as the Horned God Cernunnos, the Oak King holds sway in this land over life and death. He is the god of endurance and triumph and bestows protection on those in need. And so, we bid the Oak King join us in our circle. Hail Oak King. Hail Cernunnos. Hail Oak King. Hail Cernunnos."

As they continued to chant, Estrada bent his knees in the pose of the mountain for the earth quaked beneath his feet.

Releasing hands, they all took a few steps back. A fresh breeze swirled through the treetops, scuttling clouds, and exposing the half moon, as the sound of shifting leaves and branches grew to a near-deafening roar.

Estrada didn't know what he expected to see but when the Oak King appeared it was like nothing he could have imagined. Towering above them, he filled the circle, an enormous tree creature like Tolkien's Ent. Birds flitted around the oak leaves and mistletoe that garlanded his gnarly face. Primrose leapt high to embrace him and clung to his bark like a tree frog. Sorcha stood stunned and speechless; her jaw dropped. Estrada had lost sight of Dubh and Dylan entirely.

"Hail Oak King. We welcome you to our circle." When the wind diminished, a sudden eerie silence descended, and Estrada held his breath. Then, great booming laughter filled his ears.

"Hah. It's been a long time, a very long time," the Oak King said.

"Gracious Lord," Estrada said, "I thank you for coming to us tonight. We call you to right a wrong. Our friend, Dylan, is in danger. A man was killed here, and Dylan was blamed for his death. He's in prison but he's innocent. We ask for justice and protection in his name. And we ask you to aid us in our quest to find the true killer."

"That is much to ask. You say this man is in prison?"

"I'm here," Dylan said.

"Ah, I see you, young sprout." He stared at the shifting image to his right. "You fall to shadow, as do I. A prison is a terrible place. There is neither earth, nor sun, nor rain, nor wind. Without freedom, we fall dormant. It is a living death." The Oak King shivered, and the rustling leaves echoed like a wind chime. "So much of this land is dead. Desecrated. It began when they felled and burned my sacred groves. I feel your innocence and I will honor your request for protection and justice."

Dylan eyes glazed with tears. "Thank you, Lord."

"Do you require recompense?" Estrada asked.

When one of the Oak King's branches descended beside Primrose, she climbed on, and he raised her gently to his face. "Your embrace pleases me, fey child." As she touched his cheek, her hand shimmered gold and he laughed joyously.

He glanced down at Estrada. "People have forgotten the old gods. It's enough that you remember. I am honored by your calling. I wonder though . . . You summoned my brother, the Horned One. His visceral nature may require something more substantial."

"We'll give him whatever he desires," Estrada said, wondering if a blood sacrifice would be demanded. If it was, he would comply. He'd done so in the past and bore the scars proudly.

"The earth reeks of blood." This was a new voice, a sultry voice, and it flowed from lips like ripe mulberries, from a face that could only be described as something merging man and deer."

"Cernunnos," Estrada whispered. How many years had he worshiped the Horned God, and now here he was.

Above the elongated nose, the god's eyes were vibrant and human, a shade like ripe chestnuts. His mustache and feathery beard were amber, a shade darker than his long, loose mane. Tall, youthful, and well-muscled, animal skins adorned his body, and he wore the rack of a red deer on his head.

"Once a sacrifice came willingly to show reverence and devotion," Cernunnos said. "Now blood is drawn only in greed. It sickens me." He sashayed around them on cloven hooves, and then his eyes settled on Sorcha. "You *will* need my help," he said, never shifting his gaze from her. Reaching out, he touched her temple with a fingertip and cocked his head as if listening to her thoughts. Then he ran his fingers slowly down her cheek, her neck, her breast, and her belly, finally settling on her hip.

Sorcha's silence surprised Estrada. What was she thinking?

"Aye, you will need my help, and you will have it. But for this, I exact a mate."

"A mate?" Estrada narrowed his eyes.

"When the Earth turns and streams run wild with spring rain and life rekindles. Then, I will come." Taking Sorcha's hand in his, he brought it to his dark lips and kissed it. "I will come for *you*."

Beguiled, she appraised him in much the same way he did her. Then, taking a step closer, Cernunnos inhaled her scent and danced around her body, touching her hair and her soft pale skin. When the hide hanging from his hips rose and parted, she gasped.

"You're on," she said.

"Sorcha, are you sure?" Estrada didn't understand the terms. Did Cernunnos want her only for a night, say for Beltane? Or did he intend to take her away somewhere?

"I've never been more sure. I'm honored to be chosen as your mate. Whatever that entails."

"Then it is settled. I will come for you on Beltane. We will walk together, and we will merge."

"Hah. Splendid," the Oak King said. "There was a time long ago when we worked alongside the humans and the fey. Perhaps, that time will come again. It is sorely needed." And with that, the wind grew blustery, the earth quivered and quaked, and they all fell to the ground.

When Estrada glanced up, they'd both disappeared.

"Close the circle," Primrose said. "Trouble's coming. Pack up and hide yourselves."

In the distance, Estrada saw headlights in the lot across the road from Dunchraigaig Cairn. He couldn't make out who it was, but that mystery was soon solved when two cops sauntered down the passageway between the cairn and the Ballymeanoch Stones. He recognized their white and black checkered hatbands in the swinging beam of their flashlights. Trees ran along the hedgerow, and they all hunkered down out of sight. As the cops drew closer, he could hear their conversation.

"Ach, there's no one here. It was probably just kids again. Since that reporter was killed, this place has become *the* place to hang out."

"Aye, everyone wants to find a body. It's the new drug. If they *were* here, they probably saw us coming and lit out."

"I hear they do fertility rights here."

"What'd you mean?"

"You know . . ." And with that he feigned rutting gestures.

Estrada heard Dubh suppress a giggle with a kind of soft snort.

"That would liven up the night."

"Aye, well they're nae at it now, so let's go back. This place gives me the willies. All those stones standing here for eons."

"Ah, piss on it," his partner said. And then, he did.

Having just experienced the power of the gods, it was all Estrada could do to remain ensconced in the shadows while the idiot desecrated the stone. When he finished, they wandered off.

Sorcha laid her hand on Estrada's shoulder. "It's no different than sheep's piss and the rain will wash it clean."

37

"**I** thought they were both aspects of one entity but they're individuals. One plant, one animal." Estrada body was buzzing, his mind racing. "I didn't expect that."

"You conjured them." She stared at him adoringly as did Dubh. "That's something to add to your resume."

"I owe you my life." Dubh swallowed another mouthful of absinthe. "Whatever happens now, I'm in."

The three of them huddled around the brass table in Sorcha's tent. It was near daybreak and her tapers had melted into tepid wax pools. Whether it was his fey blood, or the absinthe, or sheer adrenaline, Estrada didn't know, but the shadowy world was etched in trails of shooting stars. Magic was energy. To create it, to resist it, to use its power, all demanded a price. Together, they'd experienced something awesome, in the true sense of the word, something they weren't ready to part with for mere sleep.

"Me too." Sorcha sprawled among the pillows, her long, red hair braided, her head wrapped in gypsy scarves.

Estrada smiled and toasted them both, then wondered again what Cernunnos would demand of her at the fertility festival of Beltane.

"Aren't you afraid?"

"Of him?" Sorcha shook her head. "I'm an anthropological archaeologist. I live my life sifting through ancient waste because I need to know and understand prehistoric cultures. It's my vocation and something of an obsession. A find like Meritaten's collar is rare. Most of the time, I'm picking through middens, man. Trying to imagine what life was like from bone fragments and refuse. And now, along comes this stunning mythic god, who wants to *merge* with me."

"What if he wants more than sex?"

"Hell, man. You're in love with a faerie. And you're half-faerie," she said, turning to Dubh. "So, let me have my moment. Whether it's sex or something else entirely, I don't care. I want it. I want to know him. I want to experience him."

Estrada raised his hands in the gesture of surrender. Sorcha could take care of herself. Dylan might not be pleased the woman he loved was planning to merge with a god, but Estrada felt comforted they'd at least secured him some spiritual muscle—though he had no idea what the Oak King or Cernunnos could do to help.

"We should go over what we know and make a plan. Truthfully, I'm not sure how to proceed from here." They had yet to find Steele's killer or the artifact thief, if by some chance they weren't the same person.

"Well, I told you about the woman who visited my shop. Not everyone knows its location, so this lovely must have been sent by someone familiar with Glasgow and antiquities."

"I wish you'd had the chance to tell us about her that morning we came to Glasgow. We might be one step closer," Estrada said.

"Yeah, well that skinny bitch interrupted our plans, didn't she?" Sorcha took another swig from the bottle of absinthe, was still carrying a grudge.

Whatever it was Estrada had started with Rachel Erskine-Steele must remain his secret.

"And you'd never seen this woman before she came into your shop?" he asked.

Dubh shook his head. "Nor have I since."

"Too bad you didn't snap her picture," Sorcha said. "What did she look like?"

"Well, she was *slightly* taller than me," Dubh said sarcastically, and Sorcha smacked him.

Dubh was growing on Estrada. He was savvy and charismatic, and so far, hadn't revealed anything resembling a dark side. He grinned as he conjured the woman behind closed eyelids.

"Aye, I remember now. Five nine or ten and stacked, much like yourself, Miss O'Hallorhan. She was wearing a skin-tight mini dress with a high neckline, scarlet, I believe. It hugged her firm bottom. Long bare legs. Oh, and fancy brown cowboy boots, high heeled with a pointy toe and burnished floral pattern."

"Apparently he did take her picture," Estrada said to Sorcha.

"At least from the neck down. What about her face, her hair?"

"Long, straight, shiny black, with a blunt fringe. Cleopatra style. Could have been a wig, I suppose."

"A Cleo wig to sell an Egyptian artifact? Someone has a sense of humor," Estrada said. "And her eyes?"

"Sunglasses."

"Naturally. Can you remember anything else about her? Tattoos? Piercings? Jewelry? A particular way of speaking?"

"Sorry."

"Ah, you've done well, Magus. That's more than we had before." Reaching over, Sorcha clutched him to her breasts and he burst into giggles.

"True enough." Estrada crossed his hands behind his head and leaned back against a stack of pillows. The adrenalin was wearing thin. His body craved sleep, but his soul longed to solve the murder. "So, two days after the theft, a mysterious woman—let's call her Cleo—calls on Dubh at . . . Does your shop have a name?"

"Certainly. It's The Blue Door."

"Of course, it is." Estrada remembered the blue door in the brick wall.

Sorcha giggled. "Aye, it is. I've seen receipts. The man's legit. Even does paperwork."

"So, how did you leave things with Cleo?"

"I told her I could move anything she could produce."

"And?"

"I assumed she'd return with the merchandise."

"But she didn't," Estrada said. "I wonder why not."

"Perhaps the thief's plans changed. I doubt our Cleo is working alone," Dubh said.

"It must be someone connected with this camp. Whoever killed Steele had one of Dylan's handkerchiefs. They wiped Steele's blood on it and stuck it where it could be found. Whoever framed Dylan likely knew he was sleeping in the field that night too. How many women work here?"

"Three full-time and a handful who work occasionally. They're all volunteers, in it for the experience and the craic. The full-time girls are all studying archaeology at uni. But I can't imagine any of them doing something like this. Kai, though. He could have enlisted some woman to help him."

Enlisted was too kind a word for Kai's methods. *Coerced, blackmailed, forced, paid,* all came to mind.

"Was he with you that night? Here, in your tent, I mean?" Estrada was a little surprised Sorcha was involved with Kai Roskilde, but then again, he'd never understood why women chose the men they did.

Sorcha shook her head. "I honestly don't know. I passed out in the van and don't remember a thing."

Rachel was right. Sorcha was an unreliable witness. Dubh's assailant may have been in Oban that night, and she may have danced with him, but it would never stand up in court. Too many witnesses could testify to her inebriated state.

"Except . . . Kai was at the cairn early Saturday morning when Dylan was arrested."

"Like maybe he knew it was going to happen," Estrada said.

"Kai's an arse. I can't defend him." Sorcha was fidgety despite the late hour. She slipped off her scarf and unbraided her hair, scraped her fingers through it and gathered it up, then tied it in a knot. "It all leads back to the broad collar."

"Steele tried to bribe Dylan for information about the artifact. Perhaps, someone else took the payoff and things escalated." Estrada thought of Janey Marshall. "Did he talk to any women at the pub? Perhaps Cleo?"

Sorcha shook her head. "I don't remember seeing Steele that night at all."

"Ah, but you remember that bastard who tried to disembowel me." Dubh winked.

"Well, *he* was hard to forget. We danced." Sorcha cleared her throat. "I'll tell you another thing that bothers me. This woman comes into The Blue Door on Monday afternoon looking to barter, and then it's a full five days before *he* appears and accuses Magus of being the fence. Why so long?"

Estrada shook his head. "Just before he cut you, he said something, didn't he, Dubh?"

"Aye. I'd forgotten that. It was something like . . . *If you've brokered a deal, kill it. The piece is not for sale.* The bastard paused and looked at me like he was debating something. Then there was a loud bang, and he said, *what the hell*, and cut me."

Sorcha wrapped her arms around Dubh and hugged him.

"*What the hell*, like, why not eviscerate the dwarf?"

"Why wouldn't he want you to sell it?" Estrada asked.

Dubh shook his head. "In this business, you hear bizarre things. Artifacts have more than monetary value. Some people fancy them as objects of status and power."

"We need to find that woman," Sorcha said. "Maybe these two aren't working together at all. Maybe, The Black Spaniard was just trying to stop you from selling the broad collar because he wanted it himself."

"By killing me?"

"That *would* stop you," Estrada said. "I agree with Sorcha. We need to find the woman, find out who sent her, and how they're connected. She must know something."

"Oban is an out-of-the-way place. I mean, a Glaswegian wouldn't go to Oban just to drink. So, if Cleo or her accomplice met up with Steele at the Irish bar in Oban two weeks ago, there's a good chance she's local. Maybe even a regular," Dubh said. "If we described her to the bartender?"

"Murphy's is the place where all these people intersect," Sorcha said. "The scene of the crime, so to speak."

"Well, then," Estrada said. "What do you say to hoisting a few pints at the Irish bar?"

38

Estrada awoke with a Wiccan hangover. Parched, queasy, and peevish. He heard music. The Proclaimers were singing again. It must have been the absinthe. Sorcha had wanted him to stay with her and Dubh in the tent, but he'd needed time to think, so cruised back to Tarbert on the bike.

He checked the screen. *Rachel.* He flipped it to silent and tried to recall their conversation three days ago on the beach. They'd agreed to meet Tuesday evening in Glasgow. He checked the time and date: Monday, 7 July, 3:52 p.m. Was she calling to confirm or cancel?

What does she want from me? Love?

The word conjured only pain. He'd loved three women so far in his short twenty-eight-year life, and each brought him grief. Whenever he opened his heart to a woman, it closed in tragedy.

Alessandra, his first love, murdered in a vendetta he'd been honor-bound to avenge.

Sensara, first his friend, then his spiritual partner, and finally his lover. Now, he feared, hating him with the same passion she'd once loved him.

And Primrose, so sweet and precious. Dead because of him. Or at least, forever fey.

Love was a villain that could not be trusted.

39

"You must trust me, chéri." Christophe shoved open the heavy door. Michael felt his lover's hand at the small of his back, steadying him and urging him on. "Behold."

Le Château des Vampires? This resembled a behind-the-scenes glimpse into a risqué Euro fashion show. Gorgeous young men in varying states of dress and arousal, lounged on rugs, cushions, and couches, touching and embracing, talking and drinking, flirting and pouting, smoking and imbibing. Several were somber faced, some elated, others wasted. A pungent hashish haze drifted through the scarlet and gold chamber and clung in the hollows of its lobed Moorish arches along with the salty scent of love. Michael breathed deeply of the ethers and sighed. It wasn't the horror show he feared, though tension hung in the fog like a fiend.

He reached for the gunmetal case in his trouser pocket. After extracting a slender, gold-banded cigarette, he lit it with a flick of his monogrammed lighter, inhaled the Turkish smoke, and leaned back against the young Frenchman.

Christophe brushed Michael's hair to one side and kissed the back of his neck. "You see? Here, there is only love. Come, we must meet and mingle."

Before any introductions had been made, however, the two men settled into a swank crimson couch in the central courtyard. Tiled in terracotta, ivory, and sapphire, a coffered ceiling protected guests from the elements. Gilt-edged paintings stood out from deep scarlet walls. A dense wooden balcony ran around the square, its many closed doors offering a haven to those guests preferring seclusion.

"Was it worth the journey?" Christophe asked.

Michael cocked his head, assessing his surroundings. "I haven't decided yet. But if we ever come here again, we're taking a float plane." Now they'd arrived, he'd forgiven Christophe for kidnapping him.

Christophe sighed. "I thought you would enjoy the yacht. I'm sorry you were so ill, chéri."

"I'm sure we can find an airport on the mainland. I'm not spending another four days on that bloody boat."

A vintage bottle of red wine was proffered by an alluring young man in a tuxedo, and a smoking hookah by another. As the wine and hashish made their mark in Michael's brain, he sank into the opulence and gazed at Christophe.

"Le Château des Vampires. You're playing with me, my charming boy. There are no vampires here. They do not exist."

Christophe's eyes were so deep brown, there was no difference between iris and pupil save a faint circle of flecked gold. With a soft smile, he winked. "Do you like my play, chéri?"

"It's unorthodox and extravagant. Of course, I do."

"Such a scene would enhance Club Pegasus, no? A private room for artful play?"

"Perhaps. It's rather like an elite gay club for only the young and beautiful. Very *Dorian Gray*. I'm curious though. Why are there no women here?" Michael had seen several in the outer chamber, the one where the *beasts* played.

"Women are mere fodder to Don Diego. He lost interest in them long ago."

"Don Diego?"

"Oui, this is his home. All of this belongs to him, and yet, he is gracious and shares his good fortune. But I must tell you his story, for soon he comes."

Michael leaned forward and took several long hauls on the hookah. He didn't care to hear the man's story, even if he was rich and powerful. As the smoke billowed, he sank into the cushions and his imagination soared. Was this Mecca anything like Lord Byron encountered when he journeyed through Ottoman Turkey? Exotic and carnal, it was a pleasure palace straight out of *Arabian Nights*. He must write about it as Byron did with "Childe Harold." What would Estrada think of it? He must exaggerate his homoerotic adventure just to make him jealous.

Michael stared at the couple lounging on the chaise across the way. A black man, whose long hair twisted into a mass of beaded dreadlocks, kissed his lover's neck; then, a trickle of blood escaped and dripped down the pale flesh. Sensing eyes on him, the man turned, curled back his upper lip, and exposed a fang, as Michael often did himself. But this man's fang dripped blood.

A shiver rippled through Michael's flesh. He'd been entombed with Christophe for days and was bored. A man needed variety and could only endure so much bootlicking. When every hunger is fed, there's nothing to crave but freedom. Intrigued, Michael ran his tongue across his lips flirtatiously.

"Mandragora? Are you listening?" Christophe motioned to the man with the hookah. "Indulge, chéri. You must let go."

"Let go of what?" His body felt like stone. He could barely lift his hand to grasp the pipe stem. Exhaling a cloud of smoke, his eyelids fluttered, and the spectral patterns in the carpet wavered and danced. The hashish was potent, headier than anything he'd smoked before. Close to passing out, he leaned into Christophe.

"Let go of your beliefs. Of everything you judge real or unreal." Christophe found his mouth and kissed him.

As Michael closed his eyes, time and space merged into a swirling sea of color. When at last, their lips parted, his lover's eyes remained locked on his.

"Listen, Mandragora. Listen and believe."

"Very well, Christophe. If that's what you want."

"It *is* what I want." He poured a tall glass of red wine and placed it between Michael's fingers. "Drink and listen."

Michael drank.

"Don Diego was born in Madrid. He became a Spanish naval officer when he was young, crossed the ocean, and married a woman in Peru."

"Don Diego. The man who sailed with Quadra in the late 1700s."

"Don't mock, Mandragora. Believe. If only for me."

"Fine. For you, I will suspend disbelief."

"Come, lie down."

Grateful for the invitation, Michael gulped the rest of his wine and swung his legs up on the couch. Stretching out, he dropped his head in Christophe's lap.

"Where was I? Ah, oui. Don Diego sired a son and named him Salvador . . . *Savior*. But, on his many sea voyages, he missed his son. And so, when Salvador reached the age of twelve, Don Diego took him on his first voyage."

Michael closed his eyes and imagined the tableaus. Fingertips massaged his temples. He opened his mouth to speak, and then closed it again, luxuriating at last, in a moment of total abandon.

"Salvador voyaged with his father for three years, and then one night while they were exploring the Alaskan coast, a tempest struck. The sea covered the deck and Don Diego found his only son clinging to the railing. Crying out, he raced toward him through the sleet, but his boot caught in a rope which had blown free of the mast. Entangled, he fell to the deck."

"And then?"

"The boat dipped, and a great wave swept over the railing. When it receded, Salvador was gone."

"Gone." Michael sighed.

"Don't look so sad, Mandragora. There's a happy end to this tale."

"How can there be? The man's son drowned at sea."

"True. Don Diego grieved for many years. But then, one night, he met a man who offered him salvation—a way to immortalize his Salvador, to make him the savior he was intended to be."

Michael's confusion must have shown on his face, for Christophe touched his pursed lips with his fingertip. Leaning over, he kissed him again, slowly, and deeply, and his fingers slipped inside his trousers.

"I want to make love to you, Mandragora. These sharp bones in your face, these dark hollows in your cheeks, they thicken my blood. Each scarlet drop belongs only to you." Christophe's wandering hand had found its mark. Each kiss, each rhythmic caress, brought Michael closer to the edge. "Ah, but we must wait, for soon he comes."

"God, Christophe, you're a tease. Don't leave me aching."

"Chéri, there will be time for play."

"You don't play fair."

Sighing, Christophe slipped to his knees and unzipped Michael's trousers. Michael gave the dreadlocked man a lingering glance and to his delight, he dropped his lover on the couch and appeared above him. Kneeling beside Christophe, he gave Michael a slow, deep, coppery kiss. Michael's heart thrummed, and when the man pierced his neck and guzzled his blood, he swooned.

Christophe shoved the man away while Michael lay dazed. "I felt the sharp kiss of the blade in my neck. How did he—?"

"You make me jealous, chéri. Am I not enough?"

Basking in the lingering glow, Michael didn't reply. Of course, Christophe wasn't enough. Michael was a libertine who satiated his appetites with whomever he desired. Surely, the boy knew their relationship wasn't exclusive. They'd never discussed such things, but *this* was not the time and place for melodrama.

Touching his neck, Michael felt the warm stickiness of blood. How had the man punctured his skin? It was more authentic than razor blades. It felt real and fired his libido. Scanning the room, he searched for him.

In the ensuing silence, Christophe sipped wine from a golden goblet and pouted. "These scars you have given me. I cherish each one."

"As do I." Catching Christophe in his arms, Michael pulled him close. "Don't be jealous. I came here with you, didn't I? Though I still don't understand your ultimate love."

"That's because I did not finish the tale." Christophe refilled their wineglasses and sipped. "The young men who come here, those you see all around you, they are waiting."

"Waiting for what?"

"For Don Diego to make his selection."

Michael squinted in confusion.

"Each hope to become El Salvador, the chosen son. When it happens, they are filled with such joy, they renounce their old life and give everything they own to their new father—their inheritances, their businesses, their yachts. What need have they for these mundane things when every desire is met? It is a great honor to become one of Les Vampires."

Michael slowly applauded. "Vampire Paradise. Great story. I suppose you're waiting to be chosen too."

Christophe's lips twisted down. "Once that was my hope. But I came to accept that I would never be chosen. To be Vampire is not my destiny."

Michael looked at the young Frenchman quizzically as his dulled awareness grew. "Then we are here . . .?"

"For you, chéri. I am the procurer."

"Procurer? As in pimp? You're a vampire pimp?"

"Do not be base. It is an honor to discover the man who will become the next Salvador. It is a joy beyond imagining to *be* the next Salvador. Don Diego pours all his love into the creation of his sons."

"Creation? Listen, Christophe—"

"Ah, he comes." Excitedly, he hauled Michael to his feet.

Throughout the room, the young men stopped whatever they were doing and stood respectfully for Don Diego. Short, slender, and middle-aged, a high, starched, white collar sprung from his waist-length black jacket. His dark hair was combed straight back, and a widow's peak emphasized sharp cheekbones, a handlebar mustache and goatee.

Michael followed his gaze around the room as he appraised the young men gathered in his courtyard. And when it fell on him, the dark eyes melted into gold. No breath, no motion, shook the silent room. Then Don Diego raised his hands in welcome and the young men bowed.

"He likes you," Christophe whispered. "I think you will be—"

"I think I will *not* be. *Fuck,* man. How could you?"

"Come on Estrada, tell me your secrets. I told you mine." Rachel was back to playing games. Estrada fondled the strands of flaxen hair veiling her pale breast. Talking was the last thing on his mind. Ducking under the silken sheet lying askew across their bodies, he searched for the one thing that could avert conversation.

Rachel rolled onto her side. "You can't get out of it that easily."

"Really?" he asked, cuddling up behind her. So far, it had worked perfectly. No more talk of love or relationships had sullied their tryst.

Springing irately from the bed, Rachel disappeared into the bathroom. A few moments later, she appeared in a short white robe, rubbing her hands with lotion.

"Listen, Rachel—"

"I want to *know* you, Estrada, not just fuck you."

He had to agree there'd been little talk since they'd arrived at her flat after an Asian fusion feast in downtown Glasgow. He possessed unusual stamina. Perhaps, it was the faerie blood brewing in his veins that heightened his senses and quadrupled his energy. It was now nearing morning, and he feared their date was about to end with showers and coffee. Having not yet segued into his current challenge—that of securing police files—he reasoned revealing a few of his less dangerous secrets might prove opportune, perhaps even sway her fidelity.

"Alright." He cleared his throat. "What do you want to know?"

"Why not start with your past, your family? Everyone comes from somewhere."

"Will you accept an abridged version?"

"If it's true."

"As true as I remember."

Satisfied, she uncorked another bottle of wine and refilled their glasses, then cuddled up facing him on the bed, still wrapped in her robe.

He clutched her hand and brushed his swollen lips across her almond-scented flesh. "I never tell my story. I don't believe in dredging up the past. But, this one time, and only because you asked, I will. Then we won't speak of it again. Deal, detective?"

Rachel stared into his eyes. "Deal."

Estrada took a deep breath. He wasn't playing up the pain. It hurt to speak of such things.

"Where are your parents from?"

"You want a genealogy?"

"I'm curious, that's all."

"My mother's Mayan and my father's Mexican."

"Ah." She placed her pale hand beside his dark hand. "Go on."

"Is this how you conduct your police interviews?"

Rachel smiled. "Estrada, I want to know you—"

"Yeah, yeah."

"Where were you born?"

"*Jeez*, woman." He breathed deeply and exhaled. "You know the answer to that."

The past was the past. Michael always said *to live a life of pleasure, one must revel in the moment.* Even he didn't know all of Estrada's secrets.

"Mexico's a big place," Rachel said.

"Mérida. In the Yucatán."

"And you grew up there?"

"No. First we moved to Mexico City, so my father could work in commercials. Then, when I was nine, he landed a movie deal, so we moved to L.A."

"*Christ.* I wasn't expecting that."

Estrada shook his head. "You wanted the story."

"A movie deal in L.A. Your father must be a handsome man."

Estrada crossed and uncrossed his legs. Why couldn't they just have sex again? Why did he have to talk about his family?

"What happened? I can tell by your face."

"Yeah, well. A few years later my handsome father disappeared. Just didn't come home one day. The same day my baby sister was hit by a car." There. He'd said it.

"*Oh my God.* Did she—?"

"Yes."

"I'm so sorry. I wouldn't have asked if I'd known."

"Well, you didn't."

Rachel cupped his cheek in her palm and kissed him sweetly, then slipped out of her robe and cuddled in the bed beside him. She was warm and soft and smelled like heaven.

"Were the incidents connected?" she asked.

"You really are a cop, aren't you?"

"Hazard of the job. I was thinking about your poor mother. What happened to her?"

"She lost it. Couldn't cope," Estrada said.

"That's understandable."

"My Uncle Eduardo and his wife had immigrated to Canada. He felt bad his little brother's family was messed up, so he came to L.A. and offered to take us all back to Vancouver. My mother refused. She took my sister, Ana, and went home to her village."

"And you?"

"Me, she sent to Canada. Figured I needed my uncle's strong arm. At thirteen, I was already too much for her to handle."

"And were you?"

"I'd been recruited by a street gang," Estrada said, sniffing back the memory of Allesandra.

"At thirteen? I don't believe it."

"You're a Glasgow detective. How can you *not* believe it?"

"Oh, I know it happens. It's just hard to believe it happened to you."

"Well, it did. One minute, I'm the son of an actor living in paradise, and the next, *poof*, I'm a kid running dope to stay alive. Then, with another wave of the wand, I've lost my family and I'm living in another country with a Catholic tyrant who believes in corporal punishment. I picked up a wand and learned to use it."

"You became a magician." Rachel kissed him with a fierce intensity that left tears in her eyes.

"I understand pain and anger. I lost my parents too."

"Tell me." Estrada kissed her gently, keen to shift the focus from himself. There were too many things he couldn't say.

"When I was about the same age you were, my mother left us to live in Sweden. It's weird we both had celebrity parents who abandoned us."

She cuddled into the crook of his arm where he couldn't see her face.

"My dad looked after me as best he could until he was . . ." Her voice drifted off, and he waited in silence for her to find the words and the courage to say them. "My father was shot in the line of duty," she said at last.

"Your old man was a cop? So, that's why."

"Why what?"

"Why you're a cop. When I first saw you, I wondered why a woman with your grace and beauty hadn't become a model."

"A model? That's why she left us. She didn't want me ruining her career. After my dad died, I ended up in the system."

"I'm sorry, Rachel. So, you're righting wrongs like your dad."

"I'm not half the man he was."

"You're perfect just the way you are." He pulled her close and held her face between his hands. "Though if you were a man, I'd still seduce you." He winked, and she slapped him, just hard enough to provoke a wrestling match.

When they calmed down, they'd passed through some portal into a new level of intimacy. Sharing secrets had that kind of power. When she kissed him, his heart heaved with her breath, and he felt himself falling.

"I know we live oceans apart, but perhaps there's a way we can work this out, Estrada. People do it all the time."

"This as in . . . this *relationship*?"

"If that's what you want."

"You know I have to see this through, Rachel. I made a promise to a friend."

"Of course. I understand that's your priority."

"Will you help me?" Estrada asked.

Rachel paused, perhaps considering how much of a conflict of interest she could dodge. "I said, I'd be your ally, and I meant it."

"There are things I need to know."

"Like?" Sitting up, she leaned against the gray headboard and wrapped her arms around her knees.

"Like the evidence the Crown has against Dylan. Other leads the police are following. Details in the files." He pulled himself up to sit beside her.

"His solicitor should have all that information."

Estrada shook his head. "He wants Dylan to cop a plea."

"Hmmm. Well, tell me what you know, and I'll try to fill in the blanks."

"Alright. I know a bloody handkerchief was found near the body." As soon as he said it, he froze. It was her husband's body. How insensitive. He flung his arm around her shoulders.

"It's in evidence. I haven't seen the findings, but I can locate them." She sounded surprisingly detached. Perhaps that's how a cop stayed sane.

He kept his arm there and gave her a little squeeze. "And I know Sorcha's stolen artifact is connected. It disappeared that night and a woman came into Dubh's shop a few days later asking about buyers."

"That's news to me."

"Yeah. Dubh forgot about her when he was attacked." Estrada took a deep breath and exhaled. "Sorcha still maintains that The Black Spaniard—"

She coughed. "Who?"

"Sorcha calls him that. We don't know his name."

Rachel cocked her head and his arm fell.

"The man who attacked Dubh."

Her eyes narrowed and she nodded.

"Well, before he gutted Dubh, the guy told him *not* to sell the artifact."

"Perhaps, he was looking to buy it himself or worked for a buyer."

"But why kill the broker?"

"Maybe he didn't intend to kill him. Maybe it was a warning."

"He gutted him. That's some warning." Estrada sipped his wine and thought for a moment. "I also know Kai Roskilde had access to the artifact that night. He put Sorcha to bed in her tent. What I *don't* know is why the Crown has Dylan McBride locked up in prison when none of this has anything to do with him."

"They have enough to hold him." Rachel wrung her hands, and he wondered why she was distressed. "My leave is almost over. When I go back to work next week, I can find out more. Would that help?"

Estrada kissed her. "Absolutely."

"You know a part of me doesn't want to help you."

"I understand. I keep forgetting it was *your* husband who was killed. It must be hard for you to be involved in this."

"Alastair and I were finished long ago." She took his hand. "What I'm afraid of is losing you. When this is over, you'll go back to Canada, to your work and your friends."

"Rachel. All we can do is take one day at a time. I'm here now and this thing between us, whatever it is, feels good." He grinned. "You were right. Talking helps."

Sharing his story and hearing her own had opened Estrada's heart and deepened his understanding. The woman was just trying to cope. Mother a star who didn't want her, father killed, time in the foster system, husband a brute, workmates who were cops. She had plenty to deal with. Estrada felt like he'd cracked her hard shell and freed the angel inside. He was afraid to say the words, *I'm falling in love with you*, but surely, she could feel what was simmering between them.

From behind her ear, Estrada produced a white rosebud. "A gift for a white goddess."

"*Christ.* Where did that come from?"

He answered with a kiss that propelled them halfway through Thursday.

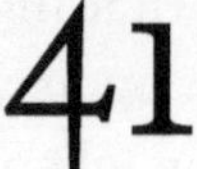

41

Michael's thoughts raced as he bolted from the room. To exist forever enslaved to bloodlust and this Don Diego. Did Christophe really think that was his ultimate desire? Had their dalliance been nothing but a ruse to ensnare him? Another victim for this fiend who exploited young men for their assets. It was nothing but a cult.

Michael touched his neck and felt two holes. Twin punctures. Blood drizzled down his skin. He thought of the dreadlocked man, his fangs, that thrilling bite, and the sensations it caused in his body. Was it possible? Did vampires *really* exist? What had Christophe said? *The women are mere fodder.* Was this all an elaborate ruse to lure potential victims to a vampire nest?

After clearing the candlelit hallway and S&M gallery, he ran. There was only one way to escape this lunacy. Find his way back to the dock and hijack a boat. But he'd never been physical, and with a body tempered by too much wine, hash, and tobacco, he could barely walk. Still, his life depended on it. And so, Michael ran. Eight, perhaps twelve, steps until his stomach revolted. Slipping behind some shrubs, he sank to his knees and vomited. The vile liquid burned his throat, fumes caught in his nose. Coughing and gasping, he wiped his mouth, then peered through the trees. Had they seen him? Were they following?

Christophe had chartered the boat they'd arrived on. Even if the crew had remained on board, he had little cash to buy them, and they couldn't be trusted. But tied to the dock some ten yards distant was a power yacht. Sleek, white, and luxurious, pale foam gurgled at her stern. She was off on her own, and she was running. Standing nearby, smoking a fat joint, was a kid. Not one of the pretty boys, just a regular sun-bleached, tanned-skinned, beach bum wearing a white T-shirt and shorts. Most likely, a deckhand left to guard the yacht while his rich employer slipped inside for some novel entertainment.

The kid's feet were bare. Michael remembered that detail because when he charged the wasted deckhand and rammed him off the dock, a pale foot flipping through the air was the last thing he saw. He untied the lines and slipped them from their rings, then pushed the boat as far from the dock as possible and leapt aboard. He could only hope no one was downstairs.

The kid, foolishly zealous, grasped a dangling line and attempted to swing aboard.

Grabbing a boat hook, Michael swung it like a baseball bat and caught him across the cheekbone.

Howling, the kid released the rope and grabbed his face. "*Motherfucker*." He sneered, then sobbing, he pulled out his cell phone.

Michael peered inside the empty yacht.

And then suddenly, Christophe was racing down the dock. "Mandragora. Let me explain."

Driven by the current, the boat was drifting back. The kid Michael hit was bleeding and cursing. Voices filtered down from the château.

Go. Now. Dashing from the stern, Michael flew downstairs passing white leather couches and a wooden galley decked out for a party. Sliding into one of the leather captain's chairs, he shoved the throttle lever forward and the engine surged.

When Christophe appeared beside him, dripping, shivering, and garbling in French, Michael froze.

"Mandragora."

"Shut up." Michael couldn't think. Couldn't take his hands off the wheel, though he wanted to wring Christophe's bloody neck. Couldn't do a damn thing until he cleared the harbor. And then what? Cast his lover into the sea? He sure as hell couldn't take him along.

"Forgive, chéri, forgive. I thought—"

"Don't think, Christophe. Go see if anyone else is on board."

"Oui, I will help."

Help? Help what? Help me escape the vampire? Michael had read plenty of vampire stories over the years. As a kid, he'd been obsessed. *Dracula, Salem's Lot,* and Anne Rice's *Vampire Chronicles* kept him spellbound for hours. But they were just stories. Weren't they?

Could Diego really be a vampire or was he simply a charade? An elaborate hoax created to entertain and defraud the rich and powerful? But myths had to come from somewhere. Was Diego cruel and heartless? Did he drink blood? Sire progeny? Fly like a bat? Could he drain humans of more than their assets?

As he cleared the harbor, Michael searched the sky, wondering if some winged creature would descend suddenly, pierce his jugular, and transform him into some hideous leather-winged monster.

Glancing over his shoulder, he saw Christophe emerge from the aft cabin, a white towel draped around his slender hips. With another, he was drying his long dark hair.

Angrily, Michael shoved the throttle full out and the yacht surged ahead. Steering into the night, he turned off the running lights and prayed there were no submerged rocks or deadheads in the channel. They would surely follow. A posse.

He needed a place to hole up, a place to think. He studied the map on the console. None of the names were familiar. He'd just stolen a yacht easily worth a million dollars, probably two. That was grand theft. Add to that the assault on the deckhand. If he didn't figure this out, he was going to jail. That's if *they* didn't catch him first.

He switched off the radio and the GPS. Did the yacht have a tracking device? He was almost sure if he didn't activate a distress beacon the boat couldn't be tracked by satellite. Almost sure.

When he felt Christophe's cool hands clutch his shoulders, Michael's stomach churned again.

"Chéri, I thought you wanted this. You crave the blood. I thought—"

"You thought wrong, Christophe. But don't worry about it. You made a mistake." The error was not in thinking Michael wanted to become a vampire, but in the treachery, the betrayal. *Procurer. Vampire pimp.* What gratuities did Christophe receive for his services? How many men had the cloying Frenchman lured to their deaths with promises of the *ultimate love?*

"Ah, chéri."

Michael felt kisses on the back of his neck, fingers in his hair, tender caresses along his ears, his throat, his chest.

"*Je t'aime.*" I love you. Christophe wanted sex. He assumed once past *that* barrier; forgiveness was assured, and all would be forgotten.

Michael pulled back on the throttle and let the boat idle. Catching Christophe's face in his hands, he kissed him. *Let him think he's safe, loved, forgiven.*

Grasping the towel, Michael flung it aside and pressed against Christophe's naked body. His lover kissed him back, and then dropped to his knees. Aroused by the familiar touch, Michael gasped as hungry lips engulfed him—the force of a lover's desperation. Dark wet hair caressed his thighs as fingers flickered across his flesh.

Michael waited. Caught the damp head in his hand and held it. Then, reaching across to the champagne bucket on the nearby table, he yanked a full bottle out of the tinkling ice and brought it crashing down.

Careening sideways, Christophe's body lay still.

Michael picked up the frail wrist and felt a faint pulse. He dragged the body into the first cabin and laid it on the bed, being careful to place Christophe on his side facing the wall in recovery position. He didn't want the *procurer* to awaken with a concussion and choke to death on his own puke. No one deserved to die like that. Not even the man who'd lured him to what was to be his own death. Or worse.

Searching through the drawers, Michael discovered several scarves which he used to bind the limp wrists and ankles behind the body. He considered a gag, then decided against it. Even if Christophe screamed, there was no one to hear him. Finally, Michael ripped the blankets from another bed and covered him. In case of shock, keep the body warm. Managing a nightclub had taught him a few things.

I don't hate you, Christophe, but you should have asked me, not just served me up like the main course at a dinner party. How dare you presume to know me like that? There's only one man who really knows me, and he'd never do a thing like that.

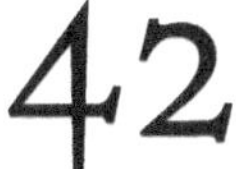

Rachel Erskine-Steele could spin a charm better than any witch Estrada had ever known. For two days, the amorous pair hadn't left her sandstone flat, except to christen the moonlit patio. If any vestige of Alastair had lingered in those Scandinavian ethers, it had been exorcized by their coupling. Estrada's flesh was scraped raw, while sparks literally flew from his fingertips, amid whispered promises and intimate confessions. She'd never known love, she said, and now she couldn't live without it, without him. In his delirium, Estrada confessed how much he wanted to have a child, surprising himself with shivers of truth. She wanted a child too. A dark-haired, dark-eyed child.

On Thursday afternoon, when Sorcha rang to remind him about their meeting that night in Oban, Estrada didn't even consider going alone. With Rachel on the back of his Harley, he felt strong and complete, like a man cruising through the past, present, and future collapsed in a single breath. And he knew something else. They were on their way to saving Dylan. With Rachel, he felt renewed. Fearless, unstoppable, and hopeful.

Estrada was in love.

And two hours late.

They were hit by Sorcha's anger as they descended the stairs at Murphy's Irish Bar. Surging scarlet rays shot across the room. In no mood to watch the two women fight, Estrada deflected with swirling turquoise waves created from memories of the cenoté, his childhood refuge.

For a moment, Rachel hesitated, struck by the heat, and then recovering, she entwined her fingers in his, straightened, and walked tall beside him.

"Why did you bring that skinny bitch?" Sorcha downed the glass of whiskey clenched in her fist and slammed it on the table. It was obviously not her first.

Everyone turned to see the skinny bitch and Rachel cast a stone-cold glare at the red-haired archaeologist that left her spitting fire. You don't have to be Wiccan to be a witch. Rachel, he'd discovered, was a natural at manipulating energy and power.

Dubh perched on the edge of the bar stool, his short legs dangling above the floor. He nodded to Rachel. "Detective," he said, grinning—whether apologetically, with nerves, or simple delight, Estrada didn't know.

"Call me Rachel, please. I'm not on duty, Mr. Dubh."

"We're all grateful for *that*, detective. You may call me Magus."

"A feckin word, Estrada." Sorcha hopped off her stool and stood stiffly against the bar. Braless, and poured into a copper tank and leather jeans, he suddenly realized the root of her fury. She'd dressed for *him*, had come expecting to extend that kiss they'd shared before Kai burst into her tent.

Estrada glanced at Rachel. She was flushed from the wind and a quick brush up against an outside wall. After teasing him all the way from Glasgow, he couldn't help himself. In her tight white mini, ankle boots, and leather jacket, she sent him reeling. Her platinum hair hung long and loose around her face. Her lips burned red with kisses.

"*Jesus, Mary, and Joseph.* Is the bitch in charge now?"

Estrada grasped Sorcha by the wrist and led her across the bar and into a snug. Rachel could manage with Dubh.

"What's wrong with you? This," he said, gesturing between him and Rachel, "is not your concern."

"Ah, you're wrong there. Herself is married to the man your mate is accused of killing *and* she's a detective. We can't trust her, and if you're tied to her, we can't trust you."

"You think I don't know that? I haven't considered the implications?"

"Frankly, no. I think you're thinking with this." Reaching down, she grabbed his crotch.

Estrada caught her hand and held it.

"Probably think you're in love."

Releasing her hand, he lowered his voice. "Listen to me. Rachel can help us. She—"

"*She* has never helped anyone but herself. Any idea what she's done to Dubh over the years?"

Estrada cleared his throat and swallowed. He hadn't thought of that. He knew they'd met, but he never considered their history. Glancing across the bar, he saw the two of them sitting side by side at the bar ignoring each other. "They seem to have sorted it out."

Sorcha shook her head. "Did you at least consider your woman?"

"My woman?"

"Aye. Primrose? Our fourth? The love of your life? Have you forgotten her so soon?"

The women had forged a bond that night at the ceremony. Conjuring magic in a closed circle could do that.

"Primrose won't mind. She told me to forget her and move on because of the way things are. She'll be happy that I—"

"Shhhh." Sorcha stared at something over his shoulder.

Estrada turned. With a flick of his head, Dubh motioned to a woman who'd just come down the stairs. Medium build, her long black hair was cut in layers. She had full bangs, just as Dubh described, and overkill eyes. Slithering in a tight black dress, she looked like a cobra slipping out of its sack.

Sitting back, Estrada scanned her aura. A pale bluish haze whispered only of sadness. The woman was in pain, had been abused somehow.

"Cleo," Sorcha said, in a low breath.

"I'll talk to her." Estrada tried to stand but Sorcha's hand came out, caught the edge of his belt, and yanked him back down.

"Some detective you are. Never hear of surveillance. Let's see what she's up to. Perhaps, she's here to meet someone."

Estrada could see Sorcha's point, but the woman looked so sad, he thought if he spoke to her, maybe she'd tell him what she knew. Perhaps all she needed was a comforting touch and a gentle ear.

Dubh appeared and scuttled into the snug beside Sorcha. "I thought it best to disappear in case she recognized me."

"Ah Magus. Always thinking. Not like Romeo here."

Seeing an opportunity to ditch Sorcha and her foul mood, Estrada stood.

"Just keep Juliet away from me," she said, as he walked away. "And remember how *that* play ended."

Rachel perched on the barstool; her long legs crossed at the knee. She sipped a gin and tonic. Estrada came up behind her and placed his hands over hers as he had that first day in her kitchen. The band kicked up, loud, meaty, and with a Celtic edge, and he leaned in close.

"Dubh pointed out the woman who came into his shop."

When she turned, he caught her mouth with his. God, she was gorgeous. No matter what Sorcha said. No matter what anyone said.

With his eyes, Estrada gestured to Cleo.

Rachel smiled. "Now what?"

"Watch and wait."

"Loo." Slipping her leather bag over her shoulder, Rachel kissed him and sauntered off to the ladies' room, her departure followed by sundry, hungry eyes.

Catching the bartender's attention, Estrada ordered a pint of amber ale and a glass of whiskey. He chugged the whiskey as he watched Cleo navigate the room. It burned its way down his throat, and he extinguished the fire with half the pint. Then he ordered another round of the same.

Why did Sorcha have to mention Primrose? She'd healed him and he'd always love her. But Rachel? Surely, *she* was the woman Primrose alluded to. The one to settle with, to make babies with.

Estrada's thoughts were interrupted by the sight of the serpentine woman mounting the stairs with a tall, angular man. He downed the rest of his ale and followed. Rachel hadn't returned from the bathroom, but he couldn't let this chance go by. He had to see where they'd end up. Likely the back seat of a car, but perhaps not.

At street level, they turned right, and he saw the man reach down and squeeze her ass. Leaning into him, she laughed invitingly, and Estrada considered she might just be a working girl. If so, she might have been hired. He needed to talk to her and find out who—

Brass knuckles caught Estrada in the throat. Concentrating so acutely on the couple in front, he hadn't seen it coming from the side. The force of the blow knocked him into the wall. He gasped as a knee landed in his crotch. The voice, the laugh. In a daze, he recognized his assailant. Kai Roskilde.

"How do you like it?"

Frantic, Estrada tried to think past the pain, to cobble a defense. Doubled over, it was easy enough to reach into his right boot and extract the knife he'd hidden there for this very reason. The cold metal gave him courage. Consciously, Estrada braced himself and found his balance. Then he began the upward spiral that would end in him stabbing the Viking bastard in the gut.

In the periphery, Estrada glimpsed Rachel's spectral form and heard her scream. Fingers grasped her pale hair. A knife kissed her throat.

"Drop it," Kai said.

Estrada stood his ground. Did the son-of-a-bitch have the guts?

"Drop the knife or I'll cut her. You don't believe me?"

With a grizzled smile, Kai drew the knife across her white skin. Blood burst along the blade and dripped down her neck. "Don't try it, hero," he said, and backed away, still clutching Rachel.

Estrada stood helpless, unable to make a move without endangering her.

It wasn't until Kai stopped beside a camper van that Estrada understood. He was taking her with him.

"Too bad we don't have a set of your handcuffs, detective. It would save your lovely face."

For a second, Estrada wondered what Kai meant, and then, still clutching her by the hair, he cracked her head viciously against the side of the van.

"No," Estrada cried.

The blow knocked Rachel senseless.

Estrada rushed him then, but Kai yanked a pistol from inside his belt and fired.

"Oops. Missed."

But Kai had *not* missed. The bullet pierced Estrada's thigh. He hit the ground grasping his bloody leg, fighting pain that seared the edges of his brain. Where the hell were Sorcha and Dubh?

Kai opened the back door of the campervan, thrust Rachel inside and slammed it shut.

"Don't take her. Please."

"The bitch is mine. You want her? Come and get her. If you still want what's left when I'm done." Kai opened the driver's door and swung one leg into the cab, then stopped, and came limping back. "I almost forgot," he said, and lifting a boot, he planted the heel firmly in Estrada's face.

Fuck." Estrada snarled, as the bones in his nose shattered. Choking on the blood, coughing, and snorting, he came up ready to block. But another boot to the side of the head landed him on the pavement.

"Night, night, asshole."

Whether they were kicks or punches, Estrada didn't know, but they rained down on him, and, within seconds, he lost consciousness.

43

Fear. People talk about how humans fight, flee, or freeze when faced with fear, but there's another type too—a slow, monopolizing fear that trickles like syrup on a warm spring day. Sometimes, people feel it percolating, incapacitating, but don't know what it is. Some demean it by calling it anxiety. But Dylan knew it for its true nature and was no stranger to it. This fear was one reason he'd made Wicca his refuge.

Nights, as he lay shivering and sweating on his prison bunk at Greenock, he remembered those times he'd met Fear. It dogged him through childhood in the guise of bullies—boys who were bigger, stronger, and meaner. Boys who took his fair skin and high flush, his quiet nature and love of books and music to mean gay. Boys who called him homo or fag-bag, and who persisted in trying to stick things up his arse, and sometimes did—claiming it was for his pleasure and not their own.

Home was no refuge once his dad had been sucked down by the sea, taking his mother with him in an alcoholic spume. Dylan had loved his dad. Bobbie McBride was a fisherman who'd crossed the Atlantic from old to new Scotland dreaming of a better life.

But sometimes dreams mean nothing, and sometimes dreams are obscured, like the bloated bodies of foundered fishermen.

When the late spring storm took Bobbie's trawler down off the coast of Yarmouth, it left Dylan with one more fear. The sea. Over the years, living in the Maritimes with an alcoholic mother, Dylan's fear grew into a phobia that sent him digging underground to rocks and stones for comfort, and skyward to Wicca for inspiration.

This fear rippled through him now, and no amount of meditation or calling for protection brought him peace. His psychic cries to Estrada unanswered, Dylan realized it was just a matter of time before his childhood bully struck again.

Today was Friday, his cellmate's birthday, and there was nowhere to run. Wiley's revelation, that he was no rapist, provided little consolation. He wanted consensual sex. It would benefit them both, he explained, and if Dylan refused, there was always Big Zeke.

Dylan smelled Wiley's fetid breath before opening his eyes.

"Wish me Happy Birthday, Dylan. I'm thirty today." A clammy hand meandered under the blanket.

Scooting sideways, Dylan wedged his back against the wall.

"Come on, boy. Let me have a pull."

Dylan had no words for Wiley's desire but blinked. Afraid to close his eyes. Afraid to keep them open. His insides burned and shook.

Wiley stepped back and dropped his boxers. "Observe McBride. In ready mode, it's no bigger than a bratwurst. 'Twas made for a novice, darlin'."

"Shut up."

"It'll fit any orifice you please. Front-side. Back-side. Top or bottom. What's your pleasure?"

Dylan leapt off the bunk. It was nothing he'd planned. Days of lurid looks and sickening innuendos and suddenly he was on the little weasel, his hands twisting the bony throat and shaking and shaking and the little prick hanging gurgling, his eyes bulging, and then his bad knee busting that scrawny sack. Finally, Dylan flung the body against the bars so hard it pissed as it fell.

The guards were on him then, and Dylan knew he was done for. After dragging him out, they locked him in an isolation cell. Neither said a word, but he saw their thin smiles as they turned.

"Rachel." Every cell in Estrada's body screamed for her. Kissing her caused a cataclysmic pain through his head, face, and jaw. His heart ached. He couldn't breathe. Couldn't move his legs. Couldn't make love but wanted her more than he'd ever wanted anyone in his life. Holding her in his arms, he crawled through those gray eyes and then her body shattered into a billion particles and vanished into a swirling vortex.

"Rachel."

"Estrada." A voice pierced the edges.

Insistent shaking hastened her disappearance and heightened the painful sensations in his desperate body. He'd only just found her. He couldn't lose her now.

"Estrada, wake up, man. You're having a nightmare."

He couldn't focus. Rubbed his eyes. "What? Where . . .?" Raw throat. Pain. *Rachel.* All he could remember was her perfect face striking the side of the van and that look of shock.

"You're in hospital, mate. You've had surgery. I think you need more pain meds. I'll call the nurse."

"No, no. I need to think." He couldn't afford to addle his brain with drugs. *Rachel.* He must find her before Kai hurt her anymore.

"All you've been doing is thinking. Thinking and talking and moaning."

Estrada glanced at the edge of the bed. Magus Dubh stood there, his blue-etched hands clutching the blanket by his side.

"Your throat must be dry. Sip some water."

Dubh placed a straw to his lips and Estrada sipped. The cool water soothed his throat.

"I'd ask how you are, but I have a damn good idea already."

"Where?"

"Oban. Lorn and Islands District Hospital."

"No. Rachel. Where's Rachel?"

Dubh shook his head. "Sorry, man. The polis are on it. There's one standing outside the door."

"Am I under arrest?"

"Not yet, but you're something of a celebrity. Two polis: a DCI from Glasgow and a sergeant to *protect* you."

"Protect me? They should be searching for her."

"They are."

"I have to get out of here. Kai—"

"Listen to me. That bastard beat the daylights out of you. Busted your nose, bruised your throat, cracked a couple of ribs, and shot you in the thigh. You can't go just yet."

Estrada growled. "I'll kill him." Once he heard the extent of his injuries, everything throbbed. He slid his hand down his leg and felt bandages.

"You're one lucky son-of-a-bitch. The pretty nurse said the bullet just nicked the femoral artery and missed the bone. A fraction of an inch more and you'd have bled out."

"Where were you, Dubh? You and Sorcha?"

"I'm sorry, mate. I was trying to calm her down. Neither of us noticed the woman had disappeared or that you'd gone after her. We ran upstairs when we heard the shot. Roskilde was taking off in the van and you were on the ground."

Estrada rolled his eyes. "Some team."

"I *am* sorry. If there's *anything* I can do to make it up to you, I will. I already owe you my life."

"There is. I need an infusion of fey blood so I can find Rachel and plant that Viking's head on a stick."

"That could be difficult with the sergeant posted right outside the door. Besides, how would we get the blood from me to you? It's mid-day."

Estrada thought for a few seconds. Initially, Dubh's blood had entered his body through cuts in his hand and his calf. Blood to blood. Those wounds had healed almost overnight. But, with the extent of these injuries, he'd need more than a few drops. If they couldn't rig up a transfusion, he'd have to ingest it another way.

"Cut a vein. I'll suck it."

"Like a vampire?"

"Mr. Estrada. I see you've regained consciousness."

A flashing badge. They'd snuck up on him and he didn't like it.

"I'm Detective Chief Inspector Lyon, Glasgow CID. He gestured to the uniform beside him. "This is Sergeant Cruickshank."

Damned if it wasn't the same racist pig who'd threatened him with deportation to Mexico the day he'd arrived at Glasgow airport. Why was *he* here now? Surely, Oban was out of his jurisdiction.

"We've met," Estrada said.

"That we have."

He'd traded his MP5 for a Taser, but Estrada still wanted to shove it up his ass.

"We have a few questions," Lyon said.

"Did you find her?"

"Off you go, now," the sergeant said, shooing Dubh out the door. "You can come back and visit your boyfriend later."

Racist and homophobic.

Dubh smiled and gave him the finger. "Oh, I will sergeant, and I'll bring something special for you."

"Mr. Estrada." The velvety bass voice belonged to Lyon. Dressed in a tan suit, white shirt, and chocolate striped tie, the man exuded competence, and Estrada was glad of it. His thick auburn hair, buzzed short on the sides, receded into a widow's peak.

Catching his gaze with piercing brown eyes, Estrada found it hard to look away. The man had a mesmerizing charm, was handsome, and Estrada supposed, young for a chief inspector. He must be smart or connected, or both. He extended his hand.

"It's just Estrada." Lyon's handshake was strong, and he caught himself respecting the man despite his profession.

"We've lost one of our own and we need your help to find her."

"I want what you want."

"Good. We understand each other. This is a complex situation, as you can imagine. And it's perplexing, as some aspects don't quite make sense. For example, we're having a hard time understanding what you were doing with a detective whose husband was so recently murdered, allegedly by *your* friend." Lyon bit his bottom lip. "It's odd. Some might say, unethical. You understand our need for clarification."

"It confused me at first too." Estrada wondered why they hadn't brought the question of this unethical tryst to Rachel. Of course, it had only just occurred, and she was still on leave.

"Could you explain your relationship with Detective Erskine-Steele?"

"Rachel and I met a couple of weeks ago when she came to Kilmartin Glen to investigate her husband's murder. One thing led to another, and we fell in love."

"In love?"

Cruickshank snorted.

"It happens, Inspector. Do you not believe in love at first sight?"

"Since Mrs. Lyon isn't present, I can confess that no, I do not." His lips flattened. "What were you two doing in Oban at Murphy's Irish Bar last night? Out on a date?"

Estrada wondered just how much he could say without implicating Sorcha and Dubh. Of course, the police already knew Dubh was connected. That's why he'd been banished from the room. He decided to tell the truth; after all, they both wanted to rescue Rachel.

"Well, as you know, my friend, Dylan McBride, is in prison for killing Alastair Steele. I came here to help him."

"We warned him at the airport as you instructed, sir," Cruickshank said.

"Aye, sergeant."

Estrada choked in surprise. Was it really Lyon who'd given the order to threaten him that day on the phone?

"Easy now. Take your time." Lyon picked up the glass of water from the bedside table and handed it to him.

Estrada sucked on the straw and the cool water soothed his throat. He nodded his appreciation and took a deep breath, while he scrambled to put together the right words to convey the least amount of information.

"You were just about to tell me why you and Detective Erskine-Steele were in Oban last night."

"Right." He cleared his throat. It still hurt like hell. "Magus Dubh remembered a woman who came into his shop to inquire about buyers for an artifact unearthed the day before Steele was killed. We thought this woman might lead us to Steele's killer."

"Why the Irish bar?"

"Sir, you and I both know a man of your intelligence already knows the answer to that."

"Perhaps our thoughts differ."

"Steele was at Murphy's the night he was killed. He was interested in the artifact and later ended up dead near the site where it was discovered." Estrada left out the part about Sorcha's Black Spaniard. That would lead them down trails he'd rather remain closed.

"Did you discover the identity of this woman?"

Estrada shook his head as he sipped more water. "No, but she was there last night. I was following her when Kai Roskilde ambushed me." His throat ached almost as much as everything else. He needed Dubh's blood inside him. Needed to heal enough to get out of this place and away from these people. Needed to find Rachel.

"And this Kai Roskilde, the man who assaulted you and kidnapped Detective Erskine-Steele. How does he figure into this?"

"Just an asshole that hates me."

"Shocking," Cruickshank said, sarcastically. He punctuated the close of his remark by sucking in his thin lips and releasing them with a pop.

Estrada wanted to choke him with his checkered hat band. Instead, he winked.

Cruickshank narrowed his eyes and lifted his right nostril like a lizard might.

The Inspector cast the sergeant an disapproving look and intervened. "I understand Kai Roskilde also works at the Kilmartin dig."

Estrada's eyes widened. Of course, they knew about Kai. He was about to say that Kai didn't work there anymore but that would only generate more questions.

"Do you think Roskilde had anything to do with the theft of the artifact or Steele's death?"

"Like I said, he's an asshole that hates me."

"You must have an opinion. A suspicion."

"Since you're in bed with a police detective." Cruickshank smirked.

Estrada ignored him. It was either that or get into something he had no chance of winning. "Honestly Inspector, I don't know who's behind this but if Kai Roskilde is Steele's killer, I'll be thrilled. For what he's done to Rachel, I hope you send him to prison for life."

"Estrada, you've done nothing illegal. You're a victim in last night's incident, and I encourage you to press charges. However, I must direct you to stay out of the investigation. You are *not* to go after Detective Erskine-Steele. Not under any circumstances. You must leave the policing to us. Do you understand?"

Estrada nodded once.

"If you're contacted by Kai Roskilde or anyone else, you're to call me immediately." He took out his card and laid it on the table. "Otherwise, we'll charge you with obstruction. We take abduction of our officers seriously. Rest assured, we will find her and bring to justice all who are responsible."

"I hope so, sir."

"I've assigned Sergeant Cruickshank to guard you."

"You said I wasn't under arrest."

"It's strictly for reasons of security."

Whose? His or theirs? Clearly, this was his punishment for messing in things he'd been warned to stay out of. Estrada rolled his eyes. Lyon was putting him under hospital arrest.

Cruickshank stroked his Taser. "My pleasure," he said, punctuating the finality of his statement with another one of his annoying pops.

Business concluded; Lyon left. Estrada knew his answers meant nothing to the man. This disingenuous interview was orchestrated to feel him out and warn him politely to mind his own business. It was something Estrada had no intention of doing and they both knew it. Still, Lyon had done his duty. Cruickshank was his guard dog—a dog Estrada must now distract, so he could get some fey blood percolating in his system.

His mind was inordinately fuzzy, a lingering effect of surgery, no doubt. He was plagued by fragments of last night's fiasco. Sorcha's rage. Dubh's mysterious woman. Kai's brass knuckles. The knife at Rachel's throat. Her pale swanlike neck stained red with blood. Her head crashing against the metal van. Christ, what had Kai done to her? What was he doing even now? And why? Was it just to get him alone, so he could vent his insane jealousy? Or was there more to it?

Estrada was still reflecting when Dubh walked back into the room and said, "Sorcha just called. She sends her love."

Cruickshank snorted and hovered by the door.

"Shouldn't you be standing guard outside." Estrada said.

The cop sent him a scathing look and hunkered down in a chair just to annoy him.

"She said the Harley's safe. She rode it home last night, but she'll be along with it later. Not that you're in any shape to ride."

"That could be remedied." The threads of a plan to distract Cruickshank were drawing together in Estrada's muddled mind. If his thoughts still intertwined with those of The Wee Pict, they might just pull it off. "I'm curious about something,

Dubh," Estrada said softly, intimacy teasing the edges of his voice.

"What's that, mate?"

The sergeant sat up straighter and tilted his head like a sheepdog. Stealth was not his forte.

"I'm curious why you came here with me last night when you could have gone back to Kilmartin Glen and spent the night with Sorcha." Estrada winked an eye only to Dubh. "I know you like cuddling with your Irish queen."

"I do, most certainly. But we Picts take our debts seriously, as I mentioned before."

"Is that the *only* reason?" Estrada batted his eyelids flirtatiously. It was campy, but Cruickshank was dull enough to need an iron skillet over the head before he'd understand.

Dubh closed in on the bed. "Ah, now you've found me out." Laying his hand along Estrada's cheek, Dubh brushed his lips with the edge of his thumb. "I confess, Sorcha was jealous of Rachel, but not nearly as jealous as me. You are tantalizing, my sweet, even when broken."

"Queers." Cruickshank scoffed. "You lot make me sick."

"That sounds offensive, officer. Don't you undergo sensitivity training in Scotland?"

Dubh spoke up. "Aye, but homosexuality is still disparaged by some Scots—men in particular. It was a criminal offense until 1980. They didn't pass a bill to outlaw gay discrimination until 2009, and it was nigh onto 2015 before same sex marriage became legal."

"Seriously?"

"Oh, aye. Trust me. I know a wee bit about discrimination."

"I imagine you do. Perhaps, the sergeant here could use some sensitizing." Estrada patted the space beside him and, a moment later, Dubh climbed up on the bed and cuddled against his chest.

"Easy on the ribs." Estrada winced. "I have to admit, I've never been with anyone quite so—"

"Small?"

"I was going to say *blue*. I know small is inaccurate. I've heard about the mighty dragon."

"He's a shy bugger but emerges on occasion. You two should meet." Dubh lifted his worn leather kilt. "Spits molten fire, he does."

"Incredible? How painful was that?"

"*Ah, jeez,*" Cruickshank said, his cheeks pulsing through his flush. "Don't be doing that in here."

"Considering this is *my* room and homosexuality is no longer a criminal offence, we can do whatever we want in here. If you're offended by it, sergeant, I suggest you step outside."

Estrada turned to Dubh. "I think he's a peeper."

"Likely watches gay porn with his hand on his Taser."

Cruickshank wavered for a moment, caught between disgust and duty. "This is a public place," he said at last. "Ach, but you're nae worth it." Shaking his oversized head, he stepped out the door and shut it.

"I wonder what he'd do if he knew what we're about to do now?" Dubh produced a pocketknife and deftly slit a small vein in his wrist. "Stop when I say and don't spill a drop."

Holding the wizard's blue-etched wrist to his mouth, Estrada gripped his hand and swallowed the precious fey blood.

45

For the past three hours, Michael had driven from the flybridge atop the yacht. His eyes adjusted rapidly to steering by moon and stars, after turning off everything that might betray his, not so stealthy, exit from the island. His plan was to find a city with an airport. He'd left his wallet aboard the sailing yacht, but he could call Nigel collect, get him to wire money, and grab a flight back to Vancouver. He traveled slowly, watching the compass and shoreline, while fighting to stay alert to hazards. The quiet sough of the propeller was soothing and combined with distance and the churning sea, drowned out Christophe's moans.

Michael was still contemplating the disposal of his lover. He didn't relish complicating the situation, so murder was out of the question. Abandonment was not. Christophe's intentions may have been pure, but Michael felt deeply betrayed. This journey up the strait was no *ultimate gift*. Christophe intended him never to return; at least, not alive, and wasn't that tantamount to murder?

Somehow, Michael had steered through the tangle of islands in the sound and fought the westerlies through the passage into Johnstone Strait. When they'd sailed in, he'd been drunk, fighting with Christophe, and begging to go home, yet there were flashes of things he recognized—a village ruin, a logging operation, a rustic lodge. Things he'd passed before.

A *phoof* of exhaled breath roused him from his revery. Turning, he watched an enormous pod of orcas surface on his starboard side, their jagged white markings reflected in the scant moonlight. Killer whales. Traveling west up the strait, they must be hunting salmon caught in the flood tide. Michael steered in a meandering sort of way, carried along by the tide like the salmon, skirting bouncing whales, and buoys that alerted him to the presence of submerged rocks.

An impenetrable wall of evergreens swathed the land on both sides, and behind him, in the northwest, massive roiling clouds obliterated the stars. Mountains loomed to the north, feeding a fear he could follow the shoreline to the end of a blind inlet, break a prop or hit a reef, and end up marooned.

He stared at the compass. He must continue sailing east, follow the strait and find the lighthouse on the point. From there, he could make his way to the more populated south coast. It had taken the better part of the day to travel from their last mooring to Le Château des Vampires, so the lighthouse was hours off. Still, he had a plan.

Michael lit a cigarette. He'd been such a fool. Just before they'd arrived, Christophe had the crew anchor in some bay and plied him with champagne, oysters, and sex long enough to convince him this really was the *ultimate gift.* The Frenchman wanted him calm and receptive. His allegiance was to Diego, whoever or whatever he was, and he wanted no fights or scenes, nothing to mar his big surprise.

Huddling in the chair, Michael fumed. He'd never felt so cold and alone. Even after ransacking the cabins and appropriating a long-sleeved white T-shirt, he couldn't get the chill from his bones. He checked the time: 3:47 a.m. The witching hour when the world folds in on itself. Anyone still conscious is only aware of immediate concerns or mired in an introspective stupor. Even night creatures like himself. Dawn was imminent, though the sun would take some time to reach him as it was blocked by mountains. Still, with the dawn, his greatest fear—that Diego would swoop down from the sky and attack—might dissipate.

If the stories were true.

Captivated by the moon-slick sea, Michael's mind drifted back through time to a summer sixteen years ago. Though just a boy, that summer he'd driven a yacht much like this one, but twice the size. He was grateful in this moment that his grandfather had sent him away that summer to work aboard his godfather's yacht near Baja, California. He'd learned to drive a yacht. But he'd never told Nigel, or anyone else, what happened out there.

Victor Carvello owned several nightclubs in California, a mediocre hotel in Vegas, and *Deception,* a 120-foot yacht that exuded swank. No one ever boarded with someone they knew, unless it was the partner of someone they knew too well. In this floating circus of chicanery, strangers signed a pre-boarding confidentiality contract that forbade them, under threat of death, from ever divulging anything about the experience. Carvello could back the threat and had. Michael had seen the photographs.

Headless bloated corpses.

He boarded the yacht an innocent boy not quite thirteen and disembarked a man. Carvello came for Michael himself that first night, took him to his cabin, and showed him what some men crave and will sell their souls to possess.

Michael hated it. But he was good at it, and what choice did he have? Soon, they all wanted him. He remembered the bloated corpses and did as he was told. He took no money. Though tokens often appeared in his cabin after a stopover in port—chocolate, a bottle of fine wine or some exotic liqueur, a pair of butter soft leather boots or jacket, silky shirts and cashmere sweaters, designer jeans, and once an emerald the size of his thumbnail, that was said to match his eyes. Grown up gifts for a grown-up boy. Carvello called him *Peter Fucking Pan*.

While his friends back home were playing Dungeons & Dragons, Michael was playing sex games. He became a chameleon, using what he learned to his advantage, just as he now used the knowledge of how to navigate and pilot a yacht.

After lighting another cigarette, Michael blew smoke at the cursed moon. He lingered over the last few puffs of Turkish tobacco and tossed it overboard. He needed coffee.

When he cut the engine, his ears rang with the silence. He descended the stairs silently and then, just at the foot, he stopped. *Voices.*

Christophe was talking to someone and that someone was talking back.

46

After several hours in solitary, the guards opened Dylan's cell, shackled his wrists, and led him down the hall. He didn't know if it was day or night. He'd slept fitfully, silently crying out for Estrada, even sending his spirit home to Tarbert. But his mate wasn't there. Leastways, he couldn't rouse him. Couldn't rouse a soul. When the guards stopped in front of Big Zeke's cell, Dylan's lip trembled. It was over. He was being offered up to the devil.

47

Estrada's eyes were closed, but even before Sorcha spoke, he knew she was there. He could smell her. The feral scent of leather and sweat, damp earth and denim, the mint in her cheek, the green apples in her fiery hair, and something else. Coffee and whiskey. He grinned and her heartbeat quickened.

"Let's see," she said. "How's your Scottish sojourn been so far, man? You've fallen in love with a skinny bitch copper who's been kidnapped. Beaten a man near senseless. Been beaten near senseless yourself. Been punched, cut, and shot. Himself is still in the clinker, and you're no closer to solving the mystery of who murdered the shitemonger."

Estrada adored her. Opening his eyes, he recalled the first time they'd met in the cemetery at Kilmartin Glen, when he'd touched Sorcha's breast and called her bluff.

She'd slipped off her short leather jacket and her ivory skin shimmered with sweat. Her white tank was split almost to the buckle of her jeans and her nipples made dark stiff points in the fabric.

"Must be hot out."

"Global feckin warming." Leaning over, she kissed him on the lips, opening her mouth, inviting him in.

He accepted, sucked the mint off her tongue, and felt a stir. He was feeling infinitely better.

Sorcha smiled. "I'm sorry, Estrada. Forgive me for being such an eejit."

"We're good."

"I brought you an Irish coffee, made as my gran would've done. If it won't heal you, it will at least distract you."

"I must confess. Dubh had a go at me already and it's worked like a charm." He accepted the coffee. "But thanks for this. Did you make it with that Connemara peat?"

"Peat's what we burn in our fires, but you're close. It's the least I can do since your entanglement with me has brought this misery down upon you. So, tell me. What's the craic?"

"Is that cop still outside the door?"

"Aye. Ginger-haired goon. Buff, but not lovely like you."

Cruickshank was wiry and dark. They must have changed shifts. The news gave him some relief.

"There's something I need you to do, Sorcha."

"Name it."

"Go to Greenock Prison and see Dylan. I mean *see* him. I had a terrible dream earlier. I feel like he was trying to contact me when I was unconscious. I think he's in trouble."

"You think he's been scrappin'?"

"Not willingly. And if someone's been *at him*—you know what I mean—tell the guards. Demand to see the warden. Dylan will never tell them himself."

"Holy God. It was me that got him in there and you in here. I'm worse than a feckin hex."

Estrada shook his head. "No, you're not."

"Well, I'm here to make amends. I'll go tomorrow and use my feminine wiles to get in and see your man."

"Remember, he loves you, Sorcha, and remember you're not supposed to know."

"Aye sure. I won't let on." She raked her fingers through her curls. "Anything else I can do for you while you're lying here in bed looking so helpless and needy?"

One thing he could say for Sorcha. She never gave up trying.

"Can you unwrap the dressing on my leg. I want to see how it's healing. Dubh gave me some of his magic juice, and I'm feeling mighty spry for someone who just took a bullet in the thigh."

"Ah, jeez, Estrada. I'm sorry Kai's such an arse."

He watched as she lifted the sheet and carefully removed the gauze. The skin, though pinkish, was almost healed.

"That's amazing," she said.

"Yeah, but how am I going to explain it?"

"Miracle? Holy Spirit? Perhaps, the Blessed Virgin herself?"

"Or maybe, it would be best if I left now, before the nurse comes to change the dressing and Cruickshank returns."

"Cruickshank?"

"Yeah, you wouldn't much like him." Estrada shook his head. "It's time this magician pulled a vanishing act."

"Are you feelin' that good?"

"Good enough to sit on the back of a Harley."

While Sorcha worked her magic on the ginger cop, Estrada dressed and wrapped himself up in a blanket. She packed him into a wheelchair, and they started off down the corridor. Two nurses smiled as they passed by.

"What did you tell the cop?" he asked.

She pulled a card from the pocket of her jeans and flashed it before his eyes. "I promised to have you back in ten and join him for coffee in fifteen."

Estrada laughed. "Vixen."

Sorcha continued to push him casually around the hallways until it seemed no one was paying them any attention, then slipped right out the door. It was late afternoon, and he had to shield his eyes from the bright July sunshine.

They'd almost reached the bike when Kelly Mackeras sauntered out of the parking lot. They saw him right about the same time he saw them, so there was no avoiding a conversation. His shaggy hair needed washing and dark smudges ringed his bloodshot eyes. The hollows of his cheeks had deepened as if he'd been starving himself. Still, he was pretty, his blue eyes as intense as a summer sky.

Estrada wanted to hold him, to brighten the dreary slate clouds shrouding his heart. He liked Kelly. He liked him a lot, and he pitied him. Kelly was trapped in a world that didn't understand him, didn't even try. When all of this was over, he'd invite him to Vancouver, introduce him to Michael, and let nature take its course. Michael sought pleasure, but like himself, valued freedom above all else. He'd sort Kelly out in no time, and he'd do it tenderly.

"Kelly, hey. What's the craic?"

His cheeks turned scarlet. "Sorcha. I didn't expect to see you here. Estrada, is that you?"

"Yeah, man."

"He got into a scrap with Kai on Thursday night at Murphy's," Sorcha said.

Kelly paused for a moment as if imagining the fight. "I'd like to have seen that. What does Kai look like? Worse, I hope, than you."

"Afraid not. He got the jump on me with a pair of brass knuckles and a gun."

"*Christ.* If anyone deserves an arse-kicking, it's Kai."

"Well, the truth is, Thursday night was payback for what I did to him last week."

Kelly's lip curled into a half-smile.

"What brings you here, Kelly? Everything alright?" Sorcha asked.

After seeing the sickly vibes streaming off him, Estrada hoped to avoid the question. Leave it to her.

"It's my mum. The doctors admitted her yesterday into palliative."

"Sorry, man," Estrada said.

"I'm staying here in Oban until . . ."

"If there's anything I can do, you'll call, yeah?" Sorcha said.

Estrada grasped Kelly's hand. "Same goes for me. Call anytime. I've got Dylan's phone."

"Dylan," Kelly muttered, his voice breaking.

"I'm going to see him tomorrow," Sorcha said.

Kelly averted her eyes. "Well, I should get back. The doctors say it's just days, maybe hours. If I wasn't there when she . . ." He crossed his arms over his chest.

Kelly had one of the saddest smiles Estrada had ever seen. "Listen man, I'll see you back in Tarbert." He didn't want to talk about Rachel or what he was about to do. The kid had enough to worry about.

"Sure. Come by for tea." Kelly smiled. "Hey, wait." Reaching into his pocket, he pulled out a key. "Take this, Estrada. Just leave it under a flowerpot outside and use the flat whenever you like. You can even stay there. The net's working and my laptop's there. You should use it."

"Are you sure?"

"Aye. I'd feel good to know you're there."

When Kelly turned to go, Estrada got out of the wheelchair, spun him around, and hugged him.

Kelly rested his head on Estrada's shoulder and sighed.

Estrada could feel the beating of his heart through his chest, the quiet sough of his quivering breath against his neck. His hair smelled of whiskey and cigarettes. Kelly was tired. Exhausted from weeks of caring for an ailing parent.

Estrada stroked his hair, and when Kelly glanced up, he kissed him. His lips were soft and full, his mouth open and welcoming, his kiss lingering and affectionate.

"We'll talk in a few days, okay?"

Tears glazed Kelly's eyes. Then, he turned and walked on without saying another word.

As they mounted the Harley, Sorcha said, "So, Kelly's gay, is he?"

"Gay. Straight. Who cares?" He cleared his throat and spit. "Kelly needed that. We both needed that."

48

"**A**lright, big man." Big Zeke had been staring across the cell at Dylan for several moments and finally spoken. His voice was as harsh as a bear after hibernation. "Heard ye play the pipes."

Dylan swallowed and prepared to defend himself. "Is that what you call it? Well, I don't—"

"Aye, ye do. Heard ye. In Glasgow."

"In Glasgow?" Just how far did these sick rumors travel?

"Half a dozen years back at the World Pipe Championships. You was just a kid. Competed against my brother, Jerry. You won fair and square."

Dylan leaned back on his heels. He hadn't thought of that day in ages. After living with his granddad in Tarbert for two years and playing the bagpipes for hours every day, he'd entered the competition and placed first. He was fourteen.

"Oh, the bagpipes." He took a long, deep breath. "Your brother plays the bagpipes."

A month ago, if a man had asked Dylan if he played the pipes, he would have known exactly what he meant. Strange, how fear could wipe a man's mind of all the saner thoughts.

The big man's muted weeping filled the small, confined space and sparked a shiver.

Dylan stared at the floor and waited.

"Played," he said at last.

"Oh, I'm sorry."

"That's why I'm here." Not a muscle moved in that grim, chiseled face. Then one tear rolled down his cheek and Zeke wiped it away with the back of a fist. "Yous could be twins, and he was *like* you too."

Dylan cocked his head, not understanding what he meant.

"G A Y," he spelled. "His pals used to call him Jerry the Fairy."

"Yeah, I'm not gay."

"Listen, laddie. I don't care if ye are or ye aren't. All I know is ye remind me of Jerry and he was killed for it."

Gay bashing? Dylan had read plenty of news stories about gay bashing in the UK. Bullies everywhere concocted their own excuses.

"So, that weasel is nae touching you, McBride, unless . . . unless it's what ye want."

Dylan stared in disbelief and then shook his head. "It's not. I hate Wiley. It's not what I want at all."

"I couldnae protect Jerry, but I *can* protect you."

"I don't know what to say."

"Say what ye want done with Wiley. Weasel tried to fuck with ye. Someone should fuck with him. Guards are saying ye beat him. You're a hero, mate."

"Hero?" Suddenly the fear was gone, and Dylan could think again. "Wiley's just trying to survive like the rest of us."

"Well, you're bunked in here with me now." He gestured to the empty upper bunk and Dylan raised his eyebrows. "No one will fuck with ye. No one fucks with me." Zeke's deep belly laugh broke the pressure in the room. "Hah. They'll think you're my bitch, when really ye'll be my new wee brother."

Dylan smiled for the first time in weeks. He wished he could remember Jerry from all the pipers who competed at that championship years ago. Wished he could say something wonderful about him. Wished Jerry would have won that day instead of him. Dylan had his own thoughts on homosexuality. It wasn't his thing, but no one deserved to be harassed, beaten, or killed because of their sexual preferences. He thought about the boys who used to assault him, and then about Estrada, his liberal lifestyle, and his advice.

"I'm sorry about your brother."

"Aye." Zeke sniffed and rubbed his eyes with giant crusty mitts. "If we really were the prophets Mum named us for, we'd have known."

"Prophets?"

"Ezekiel and Jeremiah."

"Aye, of course."

"If I'd known . . ."

Zeke's voice drifted off, and Dylan didn't ask. For the first time in many days, he felt so relieved, he was overcome with the need to sleep.

Michael braced to turn but before he had the chance, Diego approached. How had the vampire made it to the yacht undetected? Michael stared transfixed. Dressed in a black cassock with red satin buttons, the vampire floated several inches above the floor.

"You wonder why I wear the vestments of the Catholic church," Diego said, reading Michael's mind. His head sank to the right and one eye narrowed. "I took this from an English bishop, who condemned me to Hell right before I drained him of his life's blood." Diego shook his head. "I never liked the English." His dark hair blew back from his face, and he pursed his lips. "Unfortunately, I overindulged and spilled. There is a small stain, here. You, see?"

Michael glanced at the red piping that trimmed the black cape falling from Diego's shoulders. He crossed his trembling hands across his chest. Couldn't swallow. Couldn't breathe. A razor-edged fingernail caught the cleft of his chin and forced him to confront that mesmerizing gaze. Rancid breath, sallow skin, and eyes like smoldering coal.

"Be calm. It is not your time, yet." He ran a fingernail through Michael's messy hair. "First, I must know why,

Mandragora? Christophe never falls in love. I would have chosen you, if only for him."

"I don't want to be your chosen one." Michael whimpered and hated himself for it.

"*That* is a lie. To be vampire excites you beyond any pornography you might conjure in that lurid mind of yours. For years, you have impersonated us, lived the romance. You taste the blood and dream. Yet now, when offered the chance to live your fantasy, you cower and run like a frightened girl, steal a yacht, *my* yacht, and assault my—"

"Pimp?"

"Agent. Procurer." The clawed finger trailed down Michael's neck and chest, tracing blood rich veins, and came to rest upon his throbbing heart. Leaning in, Diego inhaled sharply, and the rasping air caught in his throat. Then, lifting the edge of his thin lip, he exposed a fang.

"He kindles my thirst, Christophe. The flesh smells French. Château Margaux. Is this what draws you to him?"

Michael had forgotten about Christophe. He emerged from the shadow of the cabin, dressed in a pair of skinny black tights that clung to his pelvis. His hair had dried as he slept, and hung straight and black, cloaking his ribcage. But his face was tear-stained, one side swollen and bruised from the bottle.

"I don't know why I love him, Padrino."

"Even *now*? After his abuse, his insults?"

"Mandragora is my world."

Michael trembled. When had his lover's fascination turned to obsession? They'd only been seeing each other a few weeks.

"What would you have me do, Christophe?"

Michael stood staring, unable to speak, though words raged in his mind. Diego was preparing to bite him, perhaps drain him. If Christophe loved him, could he persuade the vampire to let him go unharmed? It was the only way out.

"Christophe, please," Michael whispered at last. "You know I love you. I just . . . I just—"

"I just, I just." Diego mimicked him. "Say what you mean, Mandragora. You want to be Vampire, but on your terms. What you cannot abide is losing control."

"No man should decide another man's fate."

"There. You see Christophe? It is neither you, nor Vampire, that Mandragora spurns. He simply feels he was not given a choice. He worries he is no longer in control of his destiny. Like other insolent children of his era, he must decide for himself and, if he cannot, he will have none of it. Such arrogant volatility. Do you really want such a creature?"

"Christophe, please—"

The slap hit Michael's face like lightning and spun him across the cabin. He crashed into a table and fell to the floor.

"Enough theatrics."

But the hand that caught Michael's arm and helped him up was tender. Leaning into Christophe's shoulder, the coppery taste of his own blood filled his mouth, and he watched Diego disappear into the cabin.

"Please help me," Michael begged. "I'm sorry. I shouldn't have hit you and tied you up. I was just so scared."

"I forgive you, chéri." Christophe kissed him gently on the lips. "This is the first time I have tasted your blood. Now we have sipped of each other."

Diego reappeared carrying a slim red oak coffin by its two brass handles and set it down before the men. On the lid, a gold plate was engraved with a blooming rose. In its center, was a calligraphic *D*.

Michael's breath caught in his chest.

"Sunrise comes," Diego said. "It is time."

Michael exhaled. If Diego feared the sun, he must retire to the coffin as the legends claimed. Surely, Christophe would choose him over the monster. And, when Diego slept, what couldn't he and his lover do to the vampire? A wooden stake? Fire? He tried to remember all the ways to destroy a vampire.

"Christophe, you have served me faithfully. For your fidelity, I give you this *man*." He said the word with a twist of contempt. "Tonight, you shall be joined."

"Oh, Padrino." Falling prostrate before the vampire, Christophe clasped his hand and kissed it.

Michael glowered. *Given? Joined? What new threat is this?*

"As you see by the insignia, this coffin belongs to my family. When my sons travel, some prefer to rest during the day, and so we store them on board. Now, Mandragora, you will experience another aspect of Vampire." When Diego lifted the lid, Michael stared at the shimmering scarlet satin lining the coffin. "Lie down."

"What? You want me to—"

"Lie down in the coffin. Am I so difficult to understand? You will rest. I will rest. Christophe will pilot the yacht back to my palacio, and later we three shall meet again for the joining."

"Joining? What do you—?" But before Michael could say another word, the vampire scooped him up and flung him onto his back in the coffin. The lid clamped down and Michael could hear nothing save his own cries ringing in his ears. Pounding his fists against the lid, he begged and pleaded, but to no avail. The coffin lid stayed shut.

50

Christophe watched as Don Diego padlocked Mandragora's coffin and slipped the key into his inner suit pocket. "I will keep the key, so your obsession with this man does not cloud your judgment."

Christophe hunched over and held his aching gut. He'd never intended for any of this to happen. His plan had been simple and perfect. Take Mandragora to the island, where Don Diego would choose him as his next son. He'd confessed his love and assurances had been made. Mandragora would be thrilled to live out his fantasy, and Christophe would become his personal blood doll, supplying his lover with all the pleasure he could ever desire. Mandragora's melancholy would disappear, and once he lived in the palacio, he would forget this *Estrada* ever existed.

Never once did Christophe consider Mandragora would refuse this coveted gift or steal a yacht. Though once he had, Christophe knew Don Diego would come after him. Offended and dishonored, he would pursue Mandragora until appeased. The vampire stood beside him now pointing to the sky. Dawn was moments away, yet dense gray clouds obscured the heavens like a thick, churning blanket.

"A storm threatens," Diego said. "Come inside. The yacht drifts in the flood."

Glancing up, Christophe noticed the moon had disappeared. He shivered, remembering how once, centuries ago, Don Diego had lost his only son to a storm at sea.

"You must not fear the storm, Christophe."

"But I've never driven the yacht. And alone? And in a storm?"

"Follow the coastline north. Keep close to the shoreline. If the storm breaks, unleash the anchor, and steer the bow into the wind. You will learn because you must. You will pilot the ship because you must. There is no one else."

Christophe glanced at the dark red coffin. "But I'm frightened, Padrino."

"You must be brave, Christophe." A cold hand caressed his shoulder. "Tonight, I honor you."

"You honor *me*? Do you mean . . .?"

"Why do you look so shocked? Do you not believe yourself worthy of being the next Salvador?"

"But you never choose me."

"Because I am greedy. The young men you bring me are always perfect."

"And I am not."

"You are wrong, my son. You surpass perfection. Both exquisite and the best procurer I have known in two centuries. The others do not have your talents. Still, tonight I will reward your devotion. You are my son, and you will become my Salvador."

"Oh, Padrino."

"As for your lover," he said, pointing to the coffin. "I leave it to you to decide his fate. You may turn him, or you may keep him as a human captive—a blood slave to quench your desires. Mandragora is my gift to you. But now, I must depart, for I am old and tired and need to rest."

51

Christophe stood on the deck, hair flying like Medusa's snakes in the burgeoning wind. First rain, and then hail, erupted from the black sky, decreasing visibility, and increasing his anxiety. He'd come outside to see how close he was to the shoreline. Very close. Too close. On his way back, he passed the red oak coffin that imprisoned Mandragora.

Gripping the controls, Christophe tried to maneuver the yacht away from the rocks and into the oncoming wind. The problem was, the westerlies kept blowing it into shore, and he was driving so slowly the yacht could gain no momentum. Yet, he was afraid to drive any faster. Perhaps, he should stop and let down the anchor? The roaring of the wind and waves assaulted his ears. He trembled. Mandragora knew how to drive a yacht. If only Don Diego hadn't padlocked the coffin. A flash of lightning illuminated the vampire's coffin in the master cabin as if to say, *I know what you are thinking*. Could Don Diego perceive a man's thoughts even when he was at rest?

Suddenly the wind caught the yacht broadside. It lurched sideways and water surged over the deck. Christophe screamed. What to do? Was it dark enough in the cabin to open Don Diego's coffin and extract the key? Could he free Mandragora without waking his padrino? Liquor bottles hurtled from the bar smashing against walls and windows. Cupboards opened, casting out their contents, as glass and china shattered in the chaos. And then, the boat tilted.

Mandragora's coffin slid across the floor.

Running, clutching, Christophe sprawled across the red oak lid.

"I will get the key," he cried.

But getting there was impossible. The boat pitched so far sideways, he could only reach the cabin by grasping furniture and hauling his body up, and alas, Christophe had no upper body strength. When finally, he fought and won and hung against the doorway of the stateroom, he glanced back to see Mandragora's coffin afloat. The sliding door at the back of the yacht had come ajar and water gushed in. The posh salon was flooded.

When the realization struck him, Christophe laughed at the absurdity of it. He was going to drown alone, while the two men he loved most in the world floated in sealed coffins.

After releasing the door frame, he staggered back across the salon through frigid water and grasped the brass handles of Mandragora's coffin. Clinging to it with all his strength, his body trembled. The water was so cold, so deep. Laying his head against the wet wood, he heard the pounding fists, the terrified cries, but could do nothing.

"I will not leave you, chéri," Christophe cried.

And then the boat flipped.

Everything was underwater. The will to live overcame Christophe's fear, and he fought his way to the surface. He was so cold, so tired, fighting desperately to remain afloat in water that churned around him, when all he wanted was for it all to end.

When a coffin hit him in the back, he used what little strength he had left to hoist himself on top and cling there—chest flat against the wood, heart slowing, numb fingers clutching the handles at either side, and drifting like debris in the storm.

But Christophe would not leave his lover, would not abandon him to die alone.

It was an hour before he realized the coffin, he clung to was black. Don Diego slept below him, not Mandragora. The man he loved was somewhere lost in the tempest.

When the truth of this sunk into his heart, the young Frenchman bit through his lip until he tasted his own blood. And then, prying his stiff frozen fingers from the brass handles, Christophe slid off the coffin and into the sea.

52

Sunday afternoon. Three days and nights had passed since Kai Roskilde kidnapped Rachel Erskine-Steele outside Murphy's Irish Bar, and Estrada still hadn't received a call. What kind of game was he playing? Kai's words repeated over and over in Estrada's mind. *You want her? Come and get her. That's if you still want what's left when I'm done.* Rachel was a cop, but Roskilde was a violent bully. Estrada had seen him bash her head against the door of that van. And, when you're dealing with flawed souls, as he'd learned last fall, sometimes you lose. The waiting was driving him mad.

He could have gone with Sorcha to Greenock Prison, but he wanted Dylan to have some alone-time with the woman he loved. He also wanted to give Dylan time to mend from whatever had ensued. Estrada felt a sense of peace with him he hadn't felt before, so he assumed the crisis had abated, at least for the moment. However, if he spent any time with Dylan, he'd know if he'd been raped, and Dylan would know he knew, and that would make things worse. Having a secret shame is one thing; having it discovered by a friend is quite another. Let Sorcha go and distract Dylan with her Irish charm. She owed him that and his friend deserved to dream.

Stretching out on the carpet, he obsessed about his beautiful white goddess. Determined to prevent another woman from dying because a man was obsessed with *him*, he decided to call in divine guidance. If he could just focus, the gods might show him where she was or how she was, at least proffer a clue. He felt she was still alive. Even though they'd only met a couple of weeks ago, they'd bonded in the most intimate of ways. He could feel her energy and like a flame, it flickered still.

Kai Roskilde was intensifying his sadistic game by making him wait. Of course, Kai didn't know Estrada was healed. With the beating he'd inflicted, Kai would assume he'd be incapacitated for weeks, not days. He'd want his opponent weak but healthy enough to break again. That's how bullies worked.

Closing his eyes, Estrada observed his breath. *Breathe in. Breathe out.* It was the simplest way to engage his mind. The counting technique, he'd learned years ago from a Buddhist monk at a Vancouver temple. He'd put his own spin on it by adding visuals on a patina of gold.

1 2 3

He watched the numerals form in the darkened theatre of his mind. Shimmering. Calligraphic.

4 5 6

He switched to letters, changing with each breath in and out.

A B C

Then he sketched them on blank vellum with a quill, imagining he was some medieval monk, like those who illustrated the *Book of Kells*.

A B C

D D D

He took a deep breath, focused, thought *E F G* and saw only *D*. Curling in gold, it rose from the center of a blossom.

When for seven successive breaths it stayed static, Estrada rubbed his eyes, then got up and searched Dylan's desk for a pencil and something to write on. Returning to his meditative position, he drew the vision from memory— a calligraphic *D* in the center of a multi-petalled rose. This was a message, but what did it mean? Was it a tattoo? A logo? An initial? *D*, but *D* for what?

He closed his eyes and the *D* reappeared—this time embossed on a gold metal plate. He lifted the edges of the vision, zooming out to deepen and widen, but saw only a rich shade of vermillion beyond the gold borders. The sensation that enveloped him then, came not from Rachel or Dylan, but from Michael. He shivered as if chilled by winter rain, and with it came a knowing: Michael was imprisoned. Entombed somewhere so dark, Estrada could see only the outline of his supine form.

"Michael." When Estrada called his name aloud, Michael's head jerked, as if he'd heard his voice. And, then the vision vanished.

Using the phone in the upstairs hall, he tapped in Michael's number. *Answer. Come on.* But even as he listened to it ring and ring, he sensed the futility. His voicemail wasn't even kicking in.

Swiftly, he lit Dylan's candles in a circle around the room and laid down in the center. He took several breaths and begged his guides for help. His mind swept into a swirling vortex of crashing waves and floating debris. It took everything he had to remain calm. Eventually he saw within the waves the golden plate. It was attached to the lid of a blood red wooden coffin.

A floating coffin? What the fuck. Don't tell me he's trapped inside. But even as the thought occurred, he knew it was so. Michael was trapped inside a coffin floating in the sea.

He grabbed the phone again and dialed Nigel. *Come on, man, pick up.*

Nigel answered on the fourth ring. "Stryker."

"Sir. It's Estrada."

"Sandolino. Are you back?"

"No, and I won't be for a while yet but . . . Where's Michael? Have you seen him? He's not answering his phone."

"It's strange you should call. I haven't seen him since Monday. He went sailing in the Gulf Islands with a friend." Estrada's guts churned. "I expected him back Friday, and frankly, I'm concerned. He didn't show up for work and that's not like him."

"I think you should call the police, sir, and the Coast Guard. I think he's been kidnapped."

"Kidnapped? Has someone contacted you?"

"No, but please, trust me. I know this will sound weird, but I think . . . I'm pretty sure that Michael is locked in a coffin that's floating somewhere in the sea."

"*Good God.* Why would someone—?"

"I don't know. I didn't want to believe it myself, but now that you tell me he went sailing in the Gulf Islands, and hasn't returned . . ."

"*Goddamn it.*" Nigel paused and took a deep breath to regain his composure. He wasn't a man to emote. "We had a vicious storm here last night."

"He needs us, sir."

"I know you're involved in some strange things, Sandolino, but how can I tell the police something like this?"

Estrada's mind spun. "Tell them he called you from the boat and thought he was being stalked. Now he's been missing a few days and he's not picking up his phone. You'll know what to say."

"I'll call Mowbray, and I'll ring you back at this number when I hear something."

Seconds later, Dylan's cell phone rang. It was Sorcha.

"I thought you'd want to know this. Angus ran into Kelly last night in Oban. His mum's passed on."

"*Shit.* How is he?"

"No one's heard from him. Can you go by the house? Him giving you a key and all?"

He was sure the "and all" referred to the kiss they'd shared in the parking lot. "Yeah, sure."

"Grand. Now listen. About what happened back at the hospital. I want you to know that I've been with my share of fellas and girls. I wasn't judging Kelly. I was just surprised. *Christ,* I don't even know the people I work with. I mean, I saw him, but I didn't really *see* him. You know what I'm saying?"

"I do."

"It pisses me off, yeah?"

"I get it."

"Oh, and I almost forgot. Dylan said the Oak King came through."

"Really."

"Aye, and it wasn't just for my benefit either. Dylan looked grand today."

"Grand?"

"Aye. Relaxed, confident, happy even. I was almost after applying for a conjugal visit."

"Well, if you do, make sure you mean it."

"You're one to talk about meaning it."

"Later Sorcha."

Estrada put the phone down and stared at the circle of candles still flickering around the room.

Should I stay here, rescue Rachel and free Dylan? Or catch the next flight home and find Michael?

53

The question hounded him as he walked to Kelly's house. An old woman was cutting flowers in the garden when he arrived.

"Good day, lad. Name's Mrs. Rose. Can I help you?"

"I'm here to see Kelly."

She pulled a hanky from her folded sleeve and dabbed her eyes. "Ach, he could use a mate. The poor lad is cursed. I've been renting this flat to Ann and Kelly for years. I just can't believe she's gone." She wandered as she talked. "That lad's endured tragedy upon tragedy. First, his father disappears, and then Ann gets sick with the cancer, and now she's gone and left him an orphan."

Mrs. Rose had trapped him in an awkward conversation Estrada couldn't politely disengage from as she didn't stop talking long enough for him to get a word in.

"Did he ever tell you about his father? I suppose he doesn't like to talk about it. The poor lad never knew him. Ann was still carrying him when it happened."

Estrada raised his eyebrows, and she took it as sign.

"It was during one of those terrible wars. I can never keep them straight. Alan and Ann had just married. Well, they'd no money, so he joined the army. The next thing you know he's been shipped off to Africa." She shook her head. "Africa. Can you imagine? Well, he never came home and there was the poor wee thing widowed and with child. That was nigh twenty years ago, but I remember it like it was yesterday." She cut another flower. "Even as a bairn, wee Kelly was special."

"Special?" She'd finally piqued his interest.

"Ach, you know, he dressed like a girl, and such. Ann indulged it. She'd really wanted a girl. Bought him wee pumps and dresses at the thrift shop. He was such a sweet child with his big blue eyes. And those curls." She smiled as she shook her head. "I volunteered at the shop some days, and that's when she'd come, on the sly-like, so no one would know. Of course, they all knew. You know how it is in a small town."

Estrada followed her around to the other side of the flower bed where she continued to add to her bouquet.

"Some were right gobsmacked by it. Ann carrying on like that, pretending he was a girl. Well, Kelly'd had enough of it by the time he went to high school—you'd nae get away with a thing like that around here—and then he trotted off to Edinburgh to become an actor. Well, wasn't he a natural? The lad had been acting all his life."

He certainly had. A picture appeared in Estrada's mind of a pretty boy in a wig and heels who cruised the local bars leaving no one the wiser. Still, Estrada had to smile at the explanation Mrs. Rose had created to explain Kelly's passion for crossdressing.

Remembering why he'd come, Estrada asked again. "Is he home?"

"Poor soul came home late last night. I don't think he slept well though. I heard noises into the morning. You know, pacing and furniture being shoved about. I was going to knock on the door and say something, but then I thought,

Mary Rose, the lad just lost his mum. You let him be. Must have been looking through her things, rummaging through memories. He's been quiet as a church mouse today. Must be exhausted. Shall I let you in?"

"Yes, please." There was no point telling her that Kelly had given him a key. It would just be one more bit of gossip to add to the tragic tale of Kelly Mackeras.

After she unlocked the door, Mrs. Rose handed him the bouquet she'd been collecting as they talked, and Estrada felt a twinge of guilt for branding her an old busybody, even if that's what she was.

"Kelly likes daisies. Helped me plant these when he was just a wean. And poppies. Ach, he loves the deep pinks. Of course, poppies don't last once you cut them. No matter," she said, and after cutting several pink poppies, she added them to the daisies she'd already gathered. "Take these upstairs now, and tell him, if there's anything he needs Mrs. Rose is right here."

"I'm sure he'll appreciate that."

When Estrada's foot touched the bottom step, his flesh broke out in goosebumps and his throat went dry. Something was wrong. With each creak of each step the sensations deepened. At the top of the stairs, he stood on the landing, faced the door, and touched the doorknob. He turned it slightly, and then stopped. Perhaps Kelly was asleep, and it was just his unfathomable grief Estrada could feel. He knocked and waited. Then he called out, "Kelly?" and knocked again. When there was still no answer, he turned the knob and shoved open the door.

"Jesus, Kelly."

His body hung from a beam in the front room. Tongue swollen and purple, jutting from a face as pale as a lily—a noose wound tightly around his neck.

Estrada dropped the flowers and ran to him, righted the wooden chair, and climbed on it. Lifting Kelly, he hugged his cold, stiff body. He knew it was too late. Still, he clung to him, unable to let him go. His throat ached with words unsaid, his nose dripped, snot and tears dampening Kelly's shirt.

Why? I know it's hard, but why? Your grief would've passed. You could have left this town, gone back to Edinburgh or anywhere in the world. Gone to a place where you could be yourself without hiding and live your life without fear. Jesus, Kelly. You could have come to Vancouver with me. You could have been free.

After a while the rant ended. The shell that had held Kelly Mackeras was empty and lifeless, and Estrada shivered to hold it. His soul was gone. He climbed down from the chair and took out Dylan's phone. He should call someone. But who? Sorcha. Sorcha would know.

She answered on the second ring, almost as if she'd been waiting.

"What's wrong, Estrada?"

"It's Kelly. He's . . ."

"He's what? Say it, man."

"Dead. Hanging in the flat."

"*Holy God.* Are you there now? Have you called the police?"

"I don't know who to call."

"I'll call. Have you checked his pulse? Are you sure?"

"He's gone, Sorcha. He's pale and cold and stiff and . . . *Christ*, he's been here a while."

"Right so. Just wait there. And don't touch a feckin thing."

"I can't leave him hanging here like this."

"Oh aye, you can. Go wait outside if you must. But do *not* cut him down. They'll want to investigate."

"Sorcha, he looks so—"

"Estrada. Stop looking at him. *Jesus, Mary, and Joseph.* Are you after having more trouble? Let the police handle it. Promise me you won't touch a thing."

He turned his face away, closed his eyes, and took a deep breath. "You come too, eh?"

"Aye, I'll be right there. Just wait and—"

"I know. I know."

He ended the call and glanced around the room trying to shift his focus from the lifeless body dangling from the beam. And that's when he saw it. On the coffee table, where they'd shared a cup of tea only last week, lay an envelope with *his* name on it. Estrada touched the key in his pocket. Kelly had planned this.

He wanted me to find him.

Collapsing on the couch, Estrada picked up the envelope and held it in his hands. After a while, he slid it open and pulled out the letter. It was handwritten on plain lined paper with a gel tip pen, the ink smudged in several places.

Dear Estrada. I'm sorry you had to find me like this, but when you read this letter, you'll understand. This morning I realized we were kindred spirits, and they are few in this world. More than a mate to me, you're a mate to Dylan. You must give this letter to the polis, for it's my confession and Dylan's ticket to freedom. You might ask why I've waited this long. The answer is simple. I'm a selfish prick. I couldn't put Mum through anymore shame in this town. She protected me from the time I was born. It was my turn to protect her. But now she's gone, and I can tell the truth.

I KILLED ALASTAIR STEELE.

What? Kelly killed Steele. It was written all in caps and underlined so no one could miss it. Paper trembling in his hand, Estrada read on.

On Friday, June 30, I drove to Murphy's Irish Bar in Oban to meet up with our team and celebrate Sorcha's find. After Dylan went outside, I got my things from the car and changed, as I've done many times before. I've left everything I wore that night on my bed. The pink sweater in the plastic bag is stained with Steele's blood.

In Edinburgh, I started going out to bars dressed as a woman. I can't tell you how good it felt to be myself in public. Once I returned to Tarbert to look after mum, things got tricky. Still, I managed. Sometimes I even found men who didn't care what lurked beneath my skirt. By the time we got down to it, they were either drunk or wasted or willing to do anything to get off. Many of them were thrilled by it too.

Alastair Steele was not one of them. He was right keen on me as a woman and wanted to know all about the Egyptian collar he'd heard about in the bar. I told him I worked at the dig and could get my hands on it. Lord, that thrilled him. Thought he'd get it off and get the artifact. So, we got in his van and started driving. He bragged about taking photos and a video of my boss sucking the bejesus out of some lad in the beer garden. When I saw them and realized it was Dylan and Sorcha, I just thought, what an arsehole.

By the time we got to Dunchraigaig Cairn, Steele was so into me, I thought he wouldn't care. He kept saying he had a morbid fascination with cemeteries and dead things. It was his idea to crawl inside the cairn and do it there. So, we started up and Steele right away stuck his hand up my skirt. Well, he started cursing. Called me things I'd never heard before, described the horrible things he was gonna do to me. I got scared. He ripped off my bra, yanked it so hard it cut clear across my back. And then he grabbed my balls. Said, he was gonna get a knife and make me a girl. He spat on me. And then he said he was gonna kill me, slow and painful-like because that's what fags deserved.

Sometimes it's just talk, but I heard the hate in his voice. He meant it.

I reached out and grabbed a rock and hit him in the head. I just meant to knock him out so I could escape, but he grabbed my throat with both hands and choked me. I kept bashing until he fell over and went quiet.

I never meant to kill him. Please believe me. Then I thought of Dylan and how those pictures would go viral once Steele's body was discovered, so I took the phone. I erased the photos and video. His mobile is in the bag with my clothes.

Estrada stopped reading. His guts churned. He stood over the toilet waiting to hurl, then opened the window and took several deep breaths. Clearly, Kelly killed Steele in self-defense. The bastard had attacked him and threatened to kill him. And so what if he was a gay crossdresser? Wouldn't his mother have accepted that? She must have known. If only he'd said something. He glanced at the body dangling from the rope and shuddered. *"Jesus, man."* He picked up the letter and read on.

I'd just crawled out of the cairn and was heading toward the van when I heard a voice. Kai Roskilde.

"Where do you think you're going? I saw you," he says. "I saw it all."

He grabbed me and my wig came off. Well, he laughed when he recognized me. Said he'd always known I was a little fag and now I was a murdering little fag. Said he owned me. Said I'd do whatever he wanted from now on, and the first thing I was gonna do was steal Sorcha's artifact and fence it for him. Said if I didn't, I was going to jail for murder and the men there would whore me.

I couldn't refuse. It would have killed Mum, broke her heart.

I took the collar from underneath Sorcha's cot. It was right where he said it would be. She was passed out and didn't hear a thing. I took it back to Kai. We got in Steele's van and drove back to Oban. We left the van near Murphy's and I drove us both back to camp in my mini.

A few days later, Kai sent me to Glasgow to see Magus Dubh at The Blue Door and ask about buyers. I don't know where the collar is now, and I feel terrible for betraying Sorcha. Please tell her I'm sorry. I didn't have a choice.

When Dylan was arrested for Steele's murder, I felt trapped. Mum was dying and I couldn't let her die alone worrying about me in jail for murder.

All my life I just wanted to be accepted, and you did that, Estrada. Thank you. I'm truly sorry you had to find me like this. Please forgive me.

I ask the Crown to free Dylan McBride and make things right for him. He's innocent, the most innocent man I know.

And Dylan, I beg you to forgive me for putting you through the hell that should have been my own.

This is God's truth, and I swear it on the Bible.

Kelvin Mackeras

Estrada folded the letter, slipped it back into the envelope, and dropped it on the table where he found it. Then, he considered a few things. Kelly might have hit Steele in the head with a rock to defend himself, but Kai Roskilde sat back and witnessed it, could have stopped it, and didn't. Instead, he blackmailed Kelly into stealing the collar. And what did Kai have to do with framing Dylan for Steele's murder? In all his details, Kelly never mentioned stashing Dylan's bloody hanky. He suspected Roskilde was to blame for that, and if that was the case, he'd gone back to the cairn without Kelly to do it.

Kai Roskilde had Sorcha's Egyptian artifact stashed somewhere. And he had Rachel.

Estrada stood and walked into the bedroom. There on the white bedspread was Kelly's wardrobe. Dresses, wigs, shoes, lingerie, makeup—all neatly laid out on a garbage bag. And off to the side was a large clear freezer bag, inside of which was a cell phone and a bloodstained sweater—two pieces of evidence that would exonerate Dylan and free him from a life in prison.

Hearing sounds outside, he wandered over to the window and peered into the back garden. Mrs. Rose was gone, but someone else was there. A dark-haired woman laughed and danced around the flower garden. Estrada watched her pluck an armful of pink poppies and hold them out. Goosebumps raced up his arms. Kelly stood in the middle of the garden. He took the poppies from his mother, and tossed them high in the air. Then, laughing, they joined hands and danced in circles beneath the falling petals.

Once Estrada started sobbing, he couldn't stop, not even when he heard sirens and the thud of police boots on the stairs.

54

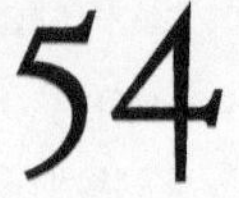

I ronically, though Michael Stryker had played at being a vampire for several years at Club Pegasus, he didn't believe in the existence of such creatures. Unlike Estrada, he was too practical for such romantic drivel. For him, Vampire was an elaborate charade, a delicious hoax. As Michael, he was just a man, but as Mandragora, he was liberated, coveted, celebrated. A shadowy character who reveled in pleasure.

Michael knew several eccentrics who claimed to be sanguinarians because of their penchant for blood. A nest of them lived together in a West Vancouver flat and frequented Club Pegasus. It was there Michael had first seen bloodletting and tasting, tried it, and savored it. Now, he mused, Christophe must have been there too, lurking in the shadows, waiting, and watching.

But the undead—immortals who morphed from human to animal, who ignited in sunlight and slept in coffins—in this, Michael could not believe. Vampires were merely an erotic creature of myth and story. Even now. Especially now. For to believe in the existence of Don Diego, a Spaniard who'd sailed the Pacific with Quadra in the late 1700s, was to believe in his own imminent death or worse. Eternal torment.

Still, it rattled him. How had Diego traveled unseen from his palace to the yacht? As much as he fought to deny it, as he lay locked in the coffin, Michael came to accept the truth.

When Diego had lifted him, as easily as if he were a child, Michael glimpsed the telltale canines, ocher-stained with age and blood in the reeking copper mouth, the flaring amber eyes, the pallid, waxy flesh. He'd seen it and smelled it, and he knew. Diego was real. With this acceptance, came a panic far greater than he'd felt when the lid closed over him, and it sent him into a paralytic stupor.

He lay shivering, wondering how he could escape what would surely be death, by one means or another. What had that vile creature said to Christophe? You decide? Surely, Christophe, who loved him desperately, would turn him into a vampire, rather than drain him in one orgasmic moment of exsanguination. But then what? As a vampire, would he lose all sense of morality and become an evil killer like Diego? Would he stalk Estrada one black night and bite him? Turn him into a monster too, so they could spend eternity driving each other mad like Louie and Lestat?

Despair descended like a linen sheath when Michael realized Estrada was the only man he'd ever truly loved. He'd known myriad lovers but none of them mattered. Now his life was ending, and the last thing he'd said to the man he truly loved was something mean and petty. He couldn't even remember what it was or why they'd fought, but he'd thrown Estrada out of his flat and refused to take his calls. Then he stopped calling. Now it was too late.

Wedged in his scarlet tomb, Michael remembered intimate moments with Estrada, so rare he could count them on his fingers. Moments, when just the two of them made love as if no one else existed. Crossing his hands over his chest, Michael felt the throbbing beneath his breast. He must cling to these fragments of humanity—this obsessive mind, this beating blood-soaked heart.

His intellect warned him to stay still and ration the oxygen. There were no air holes in this box. It was as black as soot. What did the dead need with ventilation? Somewhere, he'd heard that a man buried alive in a coffin could live between one and two hours.

The coffin shifted suddenly, and Michael's right shoulder smashed against the wood beneath the slick satin cover. He banged on the lid with the heel of his hand and yelled: "Christophe. You son-of-a-bitch. Let me out."

And then, a jolt back to the left, so fast his head hit. He wedged his hands and feet against the sides of the box. What the hell was happening out there? He had to keep calm. The more excited he became, the more oxygen he would consume and the faster he would die. No. He would *not* die. They were just messing with him, trying to scare him, punishing him for ruining their party—Christophe and that horrible creature.

Michael rubbed his neck. It was a rigid rope of muscles. *I need a cigarette. Just a drag to take the edge—*

Sliding, Crashing. Battering. Bruising. And then the coffin was rising, and though the motion continued, it was different, cushioned somehow, the swaying still intense, but less aggressive. Chaos tossed his body against the sides of the wooden box. His head pounded. His guts turned.

Seasick. He was seasick. The coffin was floating.

Another jarring sensation. Michael turned his head and puked. Then the box keeled over and down, forcing all his weight against one end, wedging his head, and finally flipped several times.

Motherfucker. They've tossed me overboard.

"If I ever get out of here, Christophe, I will kill you. I will slit your pretty throat."

55

It was late Sunday night before the cops released Estrada. DCI Lyon had been there with Cruickshank. It seemed, anytime Estrada's name came up, this duo appeared. They were thorough—he'd give them that. Had he said too much? Forgotten something key? Estrada sat near the harbor with the conversation playing over and over in his mind. They'd taken the letter into evidence, but he couldn't forget the image of that smudged ink or Kelly's dangling body.

When he returned to Piper's Dream, Dermot was waiting up and they shared a bottle of scotch. Both men were overjoyed about Dylan's release, but also shocked and saddened by Kelly's suicide. Drunk and exhausted, Estrada finally staggered upstairs to shower and sleep.

Afterward, when he scooped his jeans up off the floor, Kelly's key fell out of his pocket and clattered on the wooden floor. He picked it up and squeezed it, and then the tears came. All Kelly wanted was the freedom to be himself, to fulfill his desires. Why must the cost be so high? Still clutching the key, Estrada collapsed on the bed and struggled to erase the image from his mind.

He jumped when his cell phone rang, adrenalin surging through his body. Rachel's number flashed across the screen, and he bolted upright, suddenly sober.

"Rachel?"

"Still in the game, hero? I hear your boyfriend's getting out of jail."

Kai Roskilde. "Of course, I am. But how do *you* know?"

"Blondie had her police radio in her purse." Kai coughed, then sniffed. "So, the little queer confessed to murdering Steele."

Kai was fishing. He wanted to know what Kelly had said in the confession and Estrada was damned if he'd tell him anything.

"Let me talk to Rachel." He glanced at his trembling hand and the impression Kelly's key had made in his palm. He squeezed it again.

"She's busy. Let me put the phone down so you can hear."

"Just give her the phone." Estrada heard her cry out as if he'd grabbed her.

"Rachel?"

"Estrada?"

"Are you hurt?"

"Do what he says. Please."

Estrada's mind flashed on the pain that crossed her face when Kai smashed her against the metal door.

"I love you, Rachel."

"I love you, Rachel," Kai mocked.

Estrada clenched his shaking fist around his rage until his knuckles went white. "Now what?"

"Now you wait."

"I've *been* waiting—" The call ended.

"You son-of-a-bitch."

56

Like a deadhead, Michael's crimson coffin careened through wave after wave, as all around him the tempest raged. The ungodly wail of the wind joined the driving rain on the roof of his prison to create one deafening assault. And then some new horror amplified the cacophony—the cannon crash of surf against rock.

He lay on his right side, wedged against the scarlet satin, knees and chin drawn up tight to his chest, like some fetus in an unholy womb. His throat and gut ached from relentless vomiting. Grasping the back of his neck to calm his throbbing head, he envisioned a mountain stream, a fountain, a backyard hose, a running tap, a tall glass of water, *God,* even a toilet. Dehydrated and suffering with oxygen deprivation, he licked his parched lips and wanted to die; and then, when he realized he *was* dying, wanted only to live.

The coffin had somehow righted itself in what he now realized was one hell of a storm. Percy Shelley's body washed ashore after his boat sank off the coast of Italy in a storm like this, and it was said Byron couldn't look at his friend's decomposing body when they burned it on a beach pyre. Two years later, Byron died while a devilish storm raged over

Greece. Had he thought of Shelley in those last few hours? Died broken-hearted?

Too young. They were both too young. And he was too young.

How ironic that a fake vampire, a fraud, a pretender, should meet Death locked in a coffin. Still, it was prudent he should die alone this way. Had Don Diego or Christophe embraced him with a vampiric kiss, he would most surely have hunted Estrada and turned him too, because, honestly, he couldn't live in a world without him. Estrada was his Shelley. If only he could tell him.

"I love you Estrada. I've always loved you," he murmured.

But there would be no last words.

The first thrust came with such force Michael bit through his tongue and tasted blood—the vibration passing through his back teeth like a dentist's drill. Holding his breath, he waited as the coffin was drawn back by the waves, and then exhaled as it hurled forward again. A rhythmic crash of wood and rock. Understanding came in the next reprise. The coffin was caught in breakers. This was it, then. His body would be dashed on the rocks and wash up someday, somewhere, a pale, bloated mass of pulpy flesh.

With the third collision came the siren shriek of splintering wood. He batted his eyes to a narrow crack of light, rolled onto his back, braced, and waited.

The fourth slam blew open the crack all the way to the hinges. With his remaining strength, Michael kicked at the lid with both feet—once, twice, three times, and then, bang. The lid opened and he raised his head just as the box hit the rocks for the fifth time. Icy water poured in. He spun to his knees with the outward ebb, pushed off the lid, and grasped the sides, squinting into the gray mist.

A beach lay to the left. A wall of rock and crazy surf to the right. Rain poured from the hoary sky. Opening his mouth,

Michael tasted and swallowed, sucking in its freshness, reviving his wilted flesh. He straightened up and stretched his cramped muscles.

And then the coffin lurched forward and slammed into the jagged rocks. *"Fuck."* He wrenched back his hand. *"Stupid. Stupid."* The rock had shattered bone and flesh.

The coffin was busting apart, the wood splintering. Another crash, and he cradled his crushed fingers against his ribs. No time to wrap it. No time for anything. He had to jump in the sea and clear the surf, or it would catch him and hurl him into the rocks and his whole body would end up as mangled as his hand.

Sucking in one last breath, he jumped.

57

Wracked by conflicting emotions, Dylan perched on the edge of a wooden bench. He was relieved to be going free, but at what cost? His lawyer had come first thing that morning with the news. Kelly Mackeras had written a letter confessing to the murder of Alastair Steele and then hung himself.

Hung himself.

He hadn't even waited for his mother's funeral. *Kelly.* His mate. How had *he* got mixed up with Steele? Surely, it was self-defense. Kelly didn't have a violent bone in his body.

To make matters worse, the last few days Zeke had blathered on about how much Dylan reminded him of Jerry. Dylan had plugged some hole in his heart. But now Dylan was leaving, and Zeke would be alone again. Losing his brother for a second time. When the guards came to take Dylan away the big man wept. *Bittersweet.* That was the word.

Now, dressed in khakis and a navy-blue T-shirt, Dylan was about to walk out the door. The guard opened it, and Dylan stepped out. And that's when he saw her.

He recognized her face from a photograph. *Zeke's mum.* She trudged up the sidewalk, a sad abstracted scowl on her face. He had to stop her. He had to say something.

"Excuse me, Missus." He felt the awkward pause. He didn't know her name.

"Aye?" she said.

"I wanted to say . . ." Dylan stared at the sidewalk. He couldn't meet her eyes. He cleared his throat. "Your son, Zeke. He and I—"

"Ach, you're Dylan McBride. I saw you on the telly. I heard you was being released. You must be thrilled."

Dylan bit his lip, and when he finally spoke his voice quavered. "I-uh-I want you to know that Zeke watched out for me in here. I don't know what would have happened if . . . if he hadn't."

"Ezekiel has good and bad bits like the rest of us. I'm glad you saw the good."

Dylan relaxed. She was lovely. Just like Zeke.

"He remembered me from a piping competition years ago."

She furrowed her brow. "Ezekiel dinnae ever go to a piping competition. His younger brother, ach now, he could play the pipes."

"It was the National Championships in Glasgow, six years ago."

"He's dreaming, laddie." She shook her head. "Now that I look at you, though, I remember you."

Dylan surveyed her quizzically, the bleached blond hair and sad brown eyes. Wrinkles creased her pale neck and thin lips. Her crooked teeth were stained with nicotine. The stink of cigarette smoke wafted from her skin. She was maybe forty-five and looked sixty.

"You do?" he asked.

"Aye. You played your heart out and took first. But Zeke? He wasnae there." She shook her head. "I remember because he was here, doing two years for armed robbery and assault."

"But he said . . ."

"He must have imagined it. Ach, Ezekiel used to tell such tales when he was a wean." She opened her purse and fumbled for a cigarette. Blocked the breeze with her hand to light it, then smoked for a moment in silence.

Hearing Zeke's laughter in his head, Dylan thought of the Oak King and their ceremony that night at the Ballymeanoch Stones.

"I'm sorry about your boys," he said. "I hope they find Jerry's killer so Zeke can be exonerated. It happens. It happened to me."

"Don't be daft, lad. They know who killed Jerry. There were a dozen witnesses. A whole crowd who watched my son get beat to death by a gang of skinheads, and kept right on watching when Zeke ran up, pulled out a gun and shot them all dead. So many testified. Found their courage in the courtroom, after it was too late." Sniffing, she shook her head. "Ezekiel will ne'er be free. Not while I live at least."

"But—"

"The doctor says he blocked out the memory of killing those lads. It was guilt made him do it. He'd never been around for Jeremiah and seeing those boys beating on him just drove him mad." She puffed on her smoke. "He was a homosexual, my Jerry. Ach, I was proud of him. And I'm proud of Ezekiel too. All those people just standing there watching a gentle boy get beat to death and the bloody polis never there when you need 'em."

"I-I'm sorry." Dylan heard his own stammering voice. What else could he say? The poor woman lost both her boys that night.

"Zeke mentioned you. Said you reminded him of Jerry. I can see it, the resemblance."

"He looked out for me as if I were his brother."

She touched his arm. "Write to him sometimes, yeah?"

"Aye, sure. I can do that."

She crushed out her cigarette and walked on. Dylan stood and watched her enter the prison for the thousandth time. Then, he turned and walked away from Greenock and into the arms of his grinning granddad.

58

"No party. Not tonight," Dylan said. Estrada had parked the Harley in the lot across from Dunchraigaig Cairn. Dylan was antsy after an awkward meal where no one knew quite what to say. He needed to be on the move and Estrada was happy to oblige. Though he didn't quite understand why Dylan wanted to go back to the place he'd been apprehended.

"The party wasn't my idea. Sorcha thinks you need to celebrate your freedom."

Dylan yanked off the helmet and ran a hand through his hair. "I can't celebrate my freedom when it cost Kelly his life."

Estrada took the helmet and stashed it in the saddlebag along with his own.

"I just can't believe he killed a man or-or that he was a tranny all this time."

"It was self-defense. And as for being a crossdresser . . . People are masterminds at hiding who they are. It's how we survive."

Dylan shook his head. "I don't care what he was. I'm just shocked I didn't know. *Christ.* All the time we went to school together he was dressing up like a girl. He was my mate, and he never told me."

"He's happy now." Estrada remembered his vision of Kelly in the garden. It was the image he fought to keep.

Dylan squinted and cocked his head but didn't ask. "Come on, let's walk. I need to feel the wind on my face and the earth beneath my feet."

They crossed the highway and strolled up the path toward the cairn. Estrada thought Dylan was headed there, but he veered left to give it a wide berth, even avoided stepping on the stones. As if reading his mind, Dylan said, "They'll show me, and I can't handle seeing and feeling what went on in there that night."

Estrada nodded and walked on, wondering if Steele's spirit still haunted the cairn now that the truth was surfacing. His gut told him the ghost was hanging on, that justice had yet to be served.

They passed the bushy-headed trees, turned at the farmer's gate, and wandered down the fenced path between the fields. Glancing at the moss-crested stones, Estrada thought of Sensara for the first time in weeks—their forest walks and ceremonies at Buntzen Lake. It was almost August, and they'd be preparing for Lughnasadh. Was she training Yasu to take his place? He'd been terrified to lose his position as high priest but now it didn't really matter.

Once he'd rescued Rachel, he planned to propose. He squeezed the tiny black box in the pocket of his leather jacket and smiled. He'd found the three stone diamond ring in a jeweler's shop in Tarbert. Set in a white gold half moon, it was as radiant as his white goddess. He planned to take her with him to Vancouver so they could search for Michael together. The rest was still uncertain.

Dylan stopped suddenly and hunkered down on a stump.

Estrada stretched out on the soft grass pillowed his hands behind his head and stared at the flawless sky. This was Dylan's day, and he'd give him whatever he needed, including time and space.

"In jail . . ." Dylan began, and then his voice faded.

Estrada waited, wondering what his friend was about to disclose. This was as good a place as any to air confessions.

"In jail, I met a man. His name was Ezekiel, like the prophet. They called him Big Zeke. The thing is . . . Zeke saved me. If he hadn't, I don't know what would have happened. Wiley was . . ." Dylan ripped out a handful of grass and tossed it to the wind. "It was the magic, Estrada. It happened because of what you did here that night."

Estrada sat up. "So the ritual worked."

"Aye. It gave me Zeke and he was . . . he *is* my friend." Dylan rubbed his face with both hands. "Zeke's in prison because he shot a gang of skinheads after they beat his brother to death."

"*Jesus.*"

"His brother was gay and . . . Well, it was a hate crime. Jerry was just walking down the street and up comes a gang of thugs, and they beat him to death in front of a crowd of people. No one tried to stop them. And then along comes Zeke and catches them at it, and he goes mad. Shoots them all. They'd have killed him too if they'd had the chance, and yet *he* ends up having to live the rest of his life in prison." When Dylan shook his head, his whole body quivered. "I just can't reconcile it."

"Some things can't be reconciled."

"And, what about Kelly? He could have ended up as dead as Jerry and for the same reason. Kelly fights back and still ends up dead. I don't understand." Shrugging, he took a deep breath and exhaled loudly. "I mean, some people do terrible things, and nothing happens, and other people . . ."

"Kelly's dilemma left him with few choices. He didn't want to hurt his mum while she was sick, but he felt horrible for hurting you."

"That's just it. He didn't hurt me. Nothing happened to me and I'm not innocent."

"Come on Dylan, you're the most innocent guy I know."

"But you *don't* know. You don't know the *real* me. Just like I didn't know Kelly, and no one knew Zeke or his brother." Dylan stood and paced. "I'm not innocent." He was bursting from his skin.

Estrada joined him and the two men sauntered through the pasture side by side.

"When I was a kid in Nova Scotia, there were three boys who used to torment me something awful. It wasn't your regular kind of bullying. It was something else. Something I can't say aloud." Dylan sniffed back the words, and Estrada knew some perverse memory bubbled beneath his skin searching for a way out.

"I watched them all the time. Couldn't let my guard down for a second. I needed to know where they were and what they were doing every minute of the day and night. Then I discovered their hangout. They'd patched up an old beat-up fishing trawler so they could run it out in the bay."

He stared off to the west toward the ocean and rubbed his arms and Estrada waited.

"Well, one day, I stole a forty pounder of my mother's whiskey and left it down there by that boat in the cove. She hadn't even cracked it. I knew I'd get a thrashing later, but I didn't care. I hid in the rocks and waited. And I watched those three boys drink so much booze they could barely stand. I watched them pile into that boat, just like I knew they would, and head her out into the bay. They didn't get far because there was a submerged rock out there. I knew about that too. And, sure enough, they cranked her up and hit it dead on."

When he stopped to take a breath, Estrada could see the scene along with Dylan. The crashing. The splashing. The screaming.

"Two of them drowned right then. I sat on shore and watched them go down, and I didn't lift a finger. I just kept thinking that now I was safe." He scoffed. "The third one made it to shore and staggered home, but his dad put the boots to him so bad, he was never right in the head."

Estrada chewed his bottom lip. "That's heavy shit, man."

Dylan stared at Estrada, then sniffed and wiped his eyes. "So, how am I any different than Zeke or Kelly? I killed those boys just as sure as Zeke killed those skinheads and Kelly killed Steele."

"I can't answer that, Dylan."

"Neither can I, but I keep asking."

"Vigilante justice, vengeance, self-defense. I've dragged corpses too."

"I suspected so." Dylan winked, and they both snorted softly to break the tension.

"You know why they call it 'doing time' right? All you have in there is time to play judge to your own soul." He put his hand on Dylan's shoulder. "This thing with the boys . . . You've got to let it go."

"How can I? I set them up to die."

"Maybe, but they chose to drink that booze. And that father chose to beat his son when he could have hugged him and been happy his son survived. And Kelly . . . He made a choice too, though I can think of so many other ways that could've gone. And your man, Zeke? He chose to pack a gun and pull the trigger. The one thing I've learned from life is that it's all about making choices."

Dylan sighed. "So, what choice do I make now?"

"Let it go. Party and get wasted. Maybe lose that 'virgins rule' badge you've been wearing ever since I've known you." Dylan scoffed, but Estrada gestured across the pasture. "Now's your chance."

"Sorcha." Dylan wiped his face and sniffed, then took a couple of deep breaths, and rolled his shoulders.

"You still bit?"

"Ach, aye. She's all through me."

"Well, here's your choice. Kai's out of the picture. It's time to take your shot . . . if you think you can handle her."

"I love everything about her. She's spectacular."

In her tight khaki shorts and spilling out of a lime green halter, Sorcha was that. Her hair glowed like a stream of fire in the sun. Dylan knew he was in love and that was good. What he didn't know was that Estrada had texted Sorcha an hour ago pretending to be Dylan and asked her to meet him at Ballymeanoch. Sometimes, a man needed a little help to make the right choice.

"You know what to do."

"I've got the general idea." Dylan licked his lips. "Listen, thank you for everything, man. I couldn't have gotten through this without you."

"We're not through it yet. Enjoy today. We've got a Viking to crucify tomorrow."

59

T hank God the water was shallow. As Michael waded through the frigid waves, he was grateful for leather boots that saved his flesh from the cruelest rocks and barnacles.

On shore at last, he fell back against the sand, opened his mouth, and drank in the rain. If he hadn't been overcome by a fit of shivering that set his teeth jumping, he may have stayed that way, but the gale screeched and thrashed, slicing his flesh with steely blades.

When he pushed himself up, his left hand screamed. Crushed between coffin and rocks, it was bruised, swollen, bleeding, and most definitely broken. He couldn't bend the last three fingers. Fragments of bone protruded just above the knuckles. All three nails were crushed. His pinkie had taken the brunt of it. Open fractures. He'd need to clean it, splint it, and somehow wrap it. Make a sling if possible. No antibiotics, and all he had to work with was his belt and the shirt on his back.

He padded his trouser pockets. He still had his lighter and cigarettes. One soggy uncracked pack. Ten more in his gunmetal case. And *Lord have mercy*. Six fat joints.

He immediately stuffed one in his mouth, chewed, and swallowed. That should alleviate some of the pain.

As he stared at the damp cigarettes, he mulled about nicotine withdrawal. He wanted one now, but they were too wet to smoke. How long had it been? Hours? Days? Tobacco could dry if he could find somewhere to stash it out of the rain. Shelter. He must find shelter.

He stood and glanced around. The black sea churned before him but there was no sign of life. No boat. No lighthouse. He turned and surveyed the shoreline. The small sandy beach was mainly cobblestone, strewn with shells, driftwood, seaweed, and bits of plastic. Flotsam and jetsam, cast up by the sea, like him. It looked to be about thirty paces to the forest. Trees could provide shelter and if he was lucky, he might find a freshwater stream. Maybe someone lived here or had at one time.

How long had it been since he'd slept? Days? An extended party on the yacht, and then this crazy night of running and shaking and puking. His legs felt wooden. His back ached. His hand throbbed. It must be mid-morning, but he couldn't tell. In the great roiling mass of steely cloud, he could find no sun. He shuddered to think if Christophe had succeeded, this would have been his existence for eternity. Misery and shadow, devoid of sun. Death-in-Life. Or was it Life-in-Death? Some words about a mariner and a storm swept through his mind.

As he stumbled across the beach, he snagged a driftwood branch, hooked on one end, and knotted in the center. A staff. His first gift from the island. Crooking it under his armpit, he picked and wandered his way along the wooded shoreline searching for water.

An eagle's shrill cry drew his eyes skyward, and he noticed the tarnished cloudbank was lighter, the rain lessening, the storm burning out. Exhaling, he staggered on.

The rippling song of a stream beckoned, and he followed its melodious song. Engorged by the rain, it flooded its banks. He fell to his knees and dipped his aching hand in the frigid water. It had swollen to twice its size, and the open fractures, riddled with debris, were streaked red . . . like apples and plums and cherries. Why was he thinking of fruit? Oh, the weed. His empty stomach growled. The last time he remembered eating was that sunset dinner in Lund days ago. *Fucking Christophe.*

As he soaked his broken hand, he lowered his mouth to the stream. Sweet and cold, the water soothed his empty body and soul. Temporarily sated, he sat up and ripped the soaked T-shirt into strips as best he could using his teeth and one good hand. After rinsing off the worst of the mud, he hung the rags on branches to dry. Then, lying back, he cradled his head on a mossy log, and closed his eyes.

Fuck. His hand was screaming. He'd get no rest this way. Then he remembered the weed. Sitting up, he gently shook out the gunmetal case. He set the cigarettes and five of the joints on the flat rock beside his cell phone. The last, he ripped in half and ate, one piece at a time, washing it down with another swallow from the stream.

Then he opened the sealed pack of cigarettes. They were damp, but he slipped one between his lips and flicked his Zippo. Once. Twice. Three times. It burst into flame. Touching it to the end of his cigarette, he breathed in the precious tobacco and settled back against the moss. After smoking it down to the filter, he jammed it in the dirt and closed his eyes.

When he awoke the clouds had shifted and sun streaks were visible over the sea. He guessed it was perhaps six or seven o'clock. Had he slept the whole day? The weed had worked well to dull the pain. The joints felt almost dry, so he lit one using his lighter and inhaled the smoke slowly and deeply, cupping his hands to suck in every bit. Then, he ate the roach.

He sat a while staring at the shifting clouds, and then, grimacing, set about picking the worst of the debris from his injured fingers with an intense focus. Finally, he rinsed and wrapped his hand in the dried bandages. Fighting through the pain, he promised himself another cigarette when it was over. Finally, he tied the two sleeves together to fashion a sling and slipped his hand through. The falling temperature reminded him he must find shelter, a camp and a fire.

With his hand bound and secured by the sling, he stood and slipped the staff under his right armpit. He could leave his cigarettes drying on the rock, but he'd need to mark the spot. Taking one of the unused rags, he tied it to a branch beside the stream. At least, it was something to distinguish this place from others like it. He was finally taking control. Nature was harsh, but he could survive.

"All streams flow to the sea," he said aloud in a very British accent. Years ago, when he and Estrada first met, they'd spent the winter drinking brandy and smoking their version of pipe-weed, while reading *The Lord of the Rings* aloud in sundry accents. Estrada was charmed by Tolkien. Michael couldn't remember a time, he'd laughed more.

"Ah. Not even one day alone in the woods and already I've turned into Gandalf."

"Gandalf didn't say that."

Michael glanced around.

"And you're not alone, are you?"

"I thought I was." The husky male voice carried an odd accent. "Who are you? Show yourself."

When the branches parted, a tall creature emerged, his half-naked body tattooed in spirals. His deep brown eyes were lined in kohl, his chin finely bearded, his lips painted indigo, and his face . . . It was no ordinary face. The nose was long and angular, the ears pointed. A golden torque twisted around his neck like a coiled serpent, and from his long, braided russet hair sprung the velvety antlers of a stag.

"Ah, Narnia," Michael said. "This weed is fine. I've changed books."

"I am *not* a character from a book." The creature huffed, offended. "Neither a faun, nor a satyr, though they were fashioned from me."

"What are you, then?"

"Don't be impertinent." It thundered and swaggered a few steps closer. "I am not a what. I am a *god*."

Michael gasped, as the word echoed through the trees and he saw at the end of the hairy, muscular legs, two cloven hooves.

This statement was followed by another snort. "And I believe, Michael Stryker, that you fall under my purview."

"I fall what?" Michael sniffed and grimaced as a musky stench filled the air. "Under your *purview*?" He chuckled. "Alright, I'm game."

"Yes. You *are* game to that bloodsucker who hunts you."

"What're you talking about?"

"Now, he floats in the sea. But once he rises and realizes you're still alive, he'll come for you."

"Diego?" This was something Michael hadn't considered. *Would Diego pursue a vendetta?* "How do you know this?"

"Do you not listen? I am a god and, as I said, *you* fall under my purview. I've been tracking your activities since I was summoned."

"Summoned? By whom?"

"The shaman. The magic one."

"The magic one?"

"Must you repeat everything I say?"

"Do you mean Estrada?"

When the creature winked and smiled, light spread in shimmering waves through the forest. "The shaman and I made a good deal." With one twist of his pelvis an erection burst through the skins hanging from his hips.

"What the hell?"

"Have you never seen—?"

"Of course, I have, but . . . Wait a second. Did you and Estrada . . .?" Michael took a deep breath and exhaled loudly. This was getting stranger and stranger. "Or, is that for me."

Narrowing his eyes, the creature turned his head reflectively

"Really, really, good weed," Michael said.

"Follow me." The creature looked annoyed then, like sufficient homage had not been paid.

When it turned its back, a small yelp escaped Michael's lips.

"What is it now?"

Michael stiffened and stepped back. "It's just, your body is stunning. As perfect as a Greek statue."

The creature rolled its eyes and spit. "Bloody Greeks. So overrated."

"Well, if you're not Greek, what are you?"

"I am the Horned God. I am life. I am death." Its voice boomed and branches rattled in the trees.

Riddles. Michael disliked riddles. "Do you have a name?"

"Of course. How else could the shaman summon me?"

"Well, what is it?"

A scathing glare sent a shiver rippling through Michael's flesh. "A name is a power cache. It is not to be used casually or indiscriminately. Nor can it be demanded."

"Please tell me. What can I call you?"

The creature reached one hand back offering it, as if in introduction. Long and slender, the skin was like supple leather, the dark nails like talons.

For a moment, Michael hesitated, and then, remembering the vampire, he clasped the proffered hand. A devilish smile spread across those mulberry-stained lips and the creature pulled him close. Trembling, Michael breathed its musky scent and gazed into charcoal eyes that were much like Estrada's.

"Very well, Michael Stryker. You may call me Cernunnos. For I am here for you."

60

The moon was full to bursting that July night. Dylan remembered because it bathed the leafy valley in silvery shadow and merged with the fiery glow reflected in Sorcha's face to create perfection. He'd drunk just enough whiskey to feel its intoxicating effects without dulling his senses. Now, he was nursing a pale ale, so that later, when he'd taken Sorcha up on the offer she made him at Murphy's that night, he'd be feeling and remembering every moment.

One thing this chaos had taught Dylan was that life was short. Too short to be clinging to romantic notions of forever love. She'd reaffirmed her offer this afternoon by the stones, and Dylan had accepted with a long, slow kiss. He was admiring her now from across the circle, listening to her voice harmonize with the others, watching her body sway to the rhythm of the guitars. It was all the foreplay he needed.

"Party wasn't such a bad idea, eh?"

Estrada's question interrupted his reverie. Glancing up, Dylan noticed Estrada's eyes were as pink as his shirt. Bloodshot. He was wasted. Magus Dubh had acquired some weed and the pair of them had been off smoking. Estrada reeked of it.

"Pure dead brilliant," Dylan said, knowing it had been Sorcha's idea.

"Things worked out this afternoon then, between you and—"

"Aye. We went for a walk and talked."

"Talked? Is that all?"

"Aye."

"Sorcha's been a big help, you know. There were things I couldn't say while you were locked up. Things I didn't want the cops to know."

"I know."

"She introduced me to Dubh." Estrada gestured to the wee man who slouched beside her on the blanket, begging for attention like a dog. "She helped me save his life, and later, he saved mine."

Dylan nodded. "I heard."

"What's going on, man?"

"Nothing."

"You've barely spoken to me all night."

Dylan raised his shoulders and averted his gaze.

Estrada narrowed his eyes. "Oh, I get it. You think I slept with her. Is that what this is about? Listen, man. I did *not* sleep with her."

"You would have."

"She told you why Roskilde is so bent on ruining me, didn't she? Christ, Dylan. It was just a kiss."

"Just a kiss." Dylan drained his beer, then cracked open another and flicked the pull tab with a flourish. "If Kai hadn't barged into her tent, you would have—"

"No man, I wouldn't have. And for the record, *she* kissed me. You know what she's like. Sorcha kissed me, and I was thinking about *you* the whole time."

"Ach, don't make it worse. Stop talking."

"Come on, Dylan. You can't be mad at me for kissing her back."

Dylan smiled at last. "Relax, man. I'm just taking the piss. I don't mind that you kissed her. I just want you to know, that I know." He'd laid claim to Sorcha, and he intended to defend it.

"She's gorgeous, man. Look at her."

"Oh, I'm looking. I've been looking all night."

"Well, what are you waiting for? Get your ass over there."

"Ah, jeez, I can't. I don't know how."

"Just go over and kneel behind her on the blanket. Rub her neck and shoulders. Run your fingers through her hair and when she leans back against you, which I guarantee she will, kiss the side of her neck, right below the earlobe."

"Is that one of your moves?"

Estrada winked. "Come in from behind, man. Works every time. It's primal."

"Primal." Dylan stood and snorted. He sauntered around the outside of the circle, then knelt behind Sorcha and touched the tops of her shoulders. Immediately she turned.

"Finally. For a man who's been in prison for the past three weeks, you sure took your sweet time getting here." When Sorcha pulled him down on the blanket beside her and sat on top of him, all Dylan could do was grin.

Then, holding the whiskey bottle high in the air, she shouted. "To Kelly Mackeras. You'll be missed and always honored in this camp."

Sorcha took a haul on the open bottle, while the echo of her tribute reverberated around the fire. "To Kelly Mackeras."

"And to Dylan McBride, his friend and ours, who survived three weeks in Greenock."

Dylan heard his name chanted amidst the cheers.

"And who I plan to ravage mercilessly."

Whistles and whoops cut through Dylan's embarrassment. Clutching both sides of Sorcha's face, he pulled her down and kissed her—mostly just to shut her up. "Mercilessly?"

"Oh aye, McBride. I'll have you crying to the gods in no time."

"Me too." Dubh had suddenly appeared between them.

"Estrada's lonely," Dylan said, grinning. "He was just telling me how much he likes you, Magus Dubh. He said you saved his life, and he wants to show you just how much he cares."

Sorcha giggled. "Release the mighty dragon."

"Aye, go on. Creep up behind him and give him a peck on the back of the neck. Works every time. It's primal."

61

"How do you know Diego will come after me?" Michael asked. Cernunnos had led him to a small, isolated beach where stood the ruins of a cabin. In the wreckage of a stone hearth, the god helped him find enough dry wood and tinder to build a fire. Michael lounged on the sand with his back against a driftwood log and basked in its heat. Feeling the effects of another joint, he reveled in his hallucination, believing he'd created some strange apparition to allay his fears.

"The vampire lost something of value and holds you responsible."

"Something of value? The yacht?"

Cernunnos rolled his eyes. "It's no wonder your mundane world hovers on the edge of oblivion."

"If not the yacht, then what?"

"Use your mind for something other than obsessing over sensual pleasure."

"There's no need to insult me. I'm injured and starving and—"

"The human," he said, drawing out the words with his deep honeyed voice.

"You mean Christophe? What happened? Is he dead?"

Cernunnos nodded.

Michael hadn't thought about Christophe since he'd washed up on the beach. Now, the notion he was being hunted by a vampire because of an ex-lover revolted him.

"How is that *my* fault? Did I *ask* to be taken to a vampire? Did I *ask* to be locked in a coffin? Did *I* conjure a gale to sink that bloody yacht?"

Cernunnos reached over suddenly and slapped a steely hand over Michael's mouth. "You will need your strength when he comes. I will release you only if you remain calm. Do you understand?"

Michael nodded, and the creature released his grip. Feeling an increased need for tobacco, Michael swaggered to the fire, took out a cigarette, and lit it from a flaming twig.

"When the boy thought you were lost, he gave himself to the sea. The vampire knows this and will take his revenge."

"Suicide? *Jesus,* Christophe." Michael kicked the sand, and a small explosion of debris landed on the creature.

Dusting himself off, Cernunnos shook his head. "You are nothing like the shaman."

"What do you mean by that?"

"His magic is great. He knows not *how* great. He uses only a fraction of his power but endeavors to benefit others."

"Oh, I see. I'm narcissistic and Estrada's a fucking superhero."

"Would *you* give your life to save another? *He* will choose—" Cernunnos cocked his head slightly and sniffed as if he had picked up a scent on the wind. And then Diego descended.

Picking Michael up by the chin, the vampire hurled him against the stone hearth. He hung there confused, trying to remember what he was supposed to do. Finally, pulling a torch from the fire, he waved it in front of the vampire like a sword.

Diego laughed. "I thought to share my gift with you because *he* loved you, but you are nothing." Raising his lips, Diego revealed his fangs. "Insignificant. A mere aperitif."

"I could use a little backup here," Michael said. Turning, he scanned the beach but could see no sign of Cernunnos. Perhaps, he'd never been there at all, and yet, he was sure he'd just heard him say something about Estrada giving his life.

A vice-like grip on Michael's wrist forced him to drop the torch. With one kick, it flew and landed in the sea. Holding him by the shoulders, the vampire stared into his eyes.

Michael expected to see nothing but the cold eyes of a monster yet saw something else. Grief.

"Did you love him?" Diego asked.

Smelling the reeking carnivorous breath, Michael turned his face away and gagged. "No," he spat. There was something in that mesmerizing gaze that compelled him to tell the truth.

"I knew. I knew you did not love him." In his rage, the vampire squeezed.

Michael felt the keen claws dig into his biceps, saw the blood drip down. His right humerus cracked first, and pain shot up and into his head. Dazed, he felt bile rise into his mouth. He coughed and spit.

"Christophe was to be my next Salvador. You used and abandoned him."

As the vampire's hand slid up his arm and bit into his shoulder, Michael swayed with the pain.

"Ah, but what do you know of love? You've never loved anyone but yourself."

"That's not true. I love Estrada." If he was to die alone here on this beach, he would tell the truth.

"Estrada?" The cackle was deafening. "A Spaniard? You love a Spaniard?"

"Yes, and there's nothing you can do about it." He was ready to die, hoped to die before this filthy monster turned him into something vile and monstrous.

Diego leaned back and stroked his beard. "Ah, but there is, brainless boy."

A cuff to the side of the head sent Michael reeling. It was only the creature's grip that kept him on his feet.

"This Spaniard will become my progeny and then he will *drain you dry.*" Each of his final three words were punctuated by a stronger squeeze.

Michael felt himself losing consciousness. "Estrada would never do that."

"The Spaniard will do as I command. He will have no choice." Diego caught the soft flesh of Michael's neck with one of his fangs, ripped off a chunk of skin, and swallowed it. Then he licked the blood like a dog.

"I will not drain you now," he whispered in Michael's ear. "You will suffer as I suffer. Each time you see this scar, you will tremble to know that one night I will come for him. I will take this man you love, this *Estrada*, and he will be mine forever." With a quick turn, he flung Michael across the beach and his head hit the rocks.

62

Nothing much happened for several days as Estrada waited to hear from Kai Roskilde. If he'd harmed Rachel in any way, he'd repay every hurt in triplicate. That was three-fold Wiccan Law. Kelly may have confessed to killing Alastair Steele, but Roskilde was just as guilty, and once Rachel was safely back in his arms, Estrada meant to bring him to justice. Whatever that took.

While healing from both his physical injuries and his sorrow over Kelly's suicide, Estrada embraced village life. On long, quiet walks in the countryside he reveled in his heightened senses. The trees glimmered gold, wildflowers bursting with scented pollen attracted bees and butterflies, and animals of all kinds seemed drawn to him. Several afternoons, he sat on the sun-glazed hilltop beneath the ruin of Tarbert Castle and read *The White Goddess* in the company of the long-haired stray goat. He was intrigued by Graves' divinely inspired words and wondered if the Oak King himself had gifted the poet with his story. Dylan believed the Oak King had protected him in the guise of Big Zeke. The how of it was a mystery, but Estrada hoped his shield extended to

Rachel and Michael, and he continued to invoke both gods at nightly protection rituals.

All remained quiet until the following Thursday when two events occurred, one following the other.

Dermot shook him awake at dawn. "Did you nae hear the telephone, laddie?"

Estrada sat up feeling dazed and rubbed his eyes. He'd been so deeply asleep, for a moment, he didn't know where he was.

"It's a man for you, a Nigel Stryker from Vancouver." He handed Estrada the cordless. "He says it's urgent."

"Nigel?"

"Sandolino. Mowbray just called. They found him. They're flying him to VGH by Coast Guard helicopter."

"Is he hurt?"

"Minor injuries," he said, in a tone that told Estrada they were much worse. "Some kayakers discovered his camp on a small island off Johnson Strait, way the hell up the coast."

"Thank the gods," Estrada whispered.

"Thank *you*, Sandolino. You saved Michael's life. I don't know the whole story yet, but something happened out there on that yacht. It's a bloody miracle he survived. There was a battered coffin on the beach." Nigel paused, then cleared his throat. The idea of his grandson being locked inside a coffin during a storm at sea was too much to imagine. "I'll make sure he calls you."

After Estrada hung up the phone, he turned to Dermot and threw his arms around the old man. "My friend's safe. He was lost in a storm, but they found him."

"Oh, aye. Good." Dermot turned awkwardly. "I'll just go and put the coffee on."

But before he could leave, the phone rang again. It was Dylan calling from Kilmartin Glen, where he was shacked up with Sorcha. Dermot handed him the phone and went downstairs.

"I just got a text from Rachel's mobile. Kai wants to meet tonight at seven. He says to come alone. No cops or else. He sent coordinates."

"Coordinates? Like on a map?"

"Aye."

"Do you know where he is?"

"Scarba. It's an island in the Firth of Lorne."

"So, we'll need a boat."

"We? There's no we. I can't help you with this, Estrada. I wish I could, after all you've done for me. But boats . . . I can't, man."

"Look, Dylan. I've never driven a boat. Do you know someone who—?"

"I'll come," Sorcha yelled. "I can pilot a boat."

"I'll be right there." If Dylan was that freaked out by boats, he must have his reasons. But Estrada refused to involve the police, and boats were a mystery to him. He'd have to take Sorcha. He knew she could handle herself. That wasn't an issue. But she despised Rachel, and that was.

On the way to Kilmartin Glen, Estrada perseverated on Kai Roskilde. Why call him out to an island? There could be only one answer. He had murder on his mind. But why? Surely, his ego was not *so* fragile that one beating demanded death. The jackass had already beaten him, broken his nose, and shot him. Even by Viking standards that should suffice for payback.

He drove the Harley through the fields and parked close to the camp. He hadn't seen Dylan since Monday night when he'd left him there after the party. The two of them were sitting outside drinking coffee, along with a few others who worked the dig. Sorcha was mellower than he'd ever seen her, and Dylan looked different—like he'd been worked over by a wrestler but won the fight. He was wearing a sleeveless T-shirt, shit-kicking boots, and his blue and green plaid kilt.

That could only mean one thing. The last time he'd put on *that* kilt, they'd gone to rescue Dylan's girl. Now they were going to rescue his. Estrada wondered what had changed.

"Hey handsome," Sorcha said. "Angus here's done some serious kayaking out around Scarba. He's been regaling us with facts about the island." She poured Estrada a steaming mug of whiskey-spiked coffee and sat back in her battered lounge chair. "Better than feckin Google, aren't you Angus. Tell Estrada what you told us."

"Aye, sure. Scarba's part of a marine conservation area, so the folks you see out there are mainly kayakers, whale-watchers, photographers, eco-tourists, that lot. The island itself is in a treacherous location. The Strait of Gray Dogs at the north end is impassable, and the tides at the south end churn up some of the biggest, most hazardous whirlpools in the world."

"Okay." Estrada's voice rose in a question.

"Think of a funnel, but with tides rushing through simultaneously from both east and west. They smash against the Old Hag—that's an underwater basalt pillar—and she forces the water up to create a maelstrom. The currents can reach eight to ten knots. That, along with eddies, reefs, and shoals . . ."

"Right. What's the island like?"

"Rocky. Patched in heather. It's part of the Slate Islands and the coastline is riddled with caves. At one time, there were keepers. Kilmory Lodge still stands in the northeast corner, but the island's uninhabited now. Except for ghosts and faeries, of course."

"Ah, ghosts and faeries, is it? You've got a leg up there." Sorcha beamed. Apparently, maelstroms and whirlpools ramped her up.

"Anywhere to land a boat?" Estrada asked.

"Aye. There are plenty of sheltered bays with good anchorage, especially along the eastern shoreline. We sometimes put in at *Bagh Gleann a'Mhaoil*. There's a derelict cottage there."

"Right." Estrada let that one go since he couldn't pronounce it anyway.

"Just be sure you give the Corryvreckan whirlpools a wide berth."

Sorcha's eyes sparkled. "*Corryvreckan*. Even the name sounds treacherous."

"It comes from the Gaelic and means Bhreacain's Cauldron," Angus said. "Bhreacain was a Norse king intent on winning the princess of the isles. To prove his bravery, he attempted to anchor his boat in the whirlpool. We learned that story in school. Remember Dylan?"

"Aye, but King Bhreacain didn't win the princess. The poor man drowned."

"But his rope of virgin's hair lasted longer than the hemp or wool he tied to the anchor, which just goes to show you—"

"Where can we rent a boat?" Estrada had had enough of myth and was eager to get going. Rested and fully healed, he was hungry for blood.

"I know a place," Dylan said.

Estrada squinted, curious at this new development. "You're coming?"

"We need to talk."

"Ah, boys. Keep the broken bits to a minimum."

Estrada swallowed the dregs of his coffee and followed Dylan up a trail that led away from the main camp. As he watched the plaid pleats sway with each step, he wondered what was going on in Dylan's mind.

"I see you're wearing your traditional hero gear."

Turning, Dylan stood with his hands on his hips, as stern and solid as a standing stone. "Sorcha will no' be going on this caper. It's too dangerous and it'll only piss Kai off."

"Have you told her yet?"

"No, but I will."

"Listen. I don't know what you have against boats, but I don't want to force you, man. Perhaps Dubh."

"Don't be daft."

"Hey, the man's a Druid. He's powerful."

Dylan shook his head. "As I said before, there's things you don't know about me." He grasped the horizontal branch of a tree with both hands and did a few chin-ups. When he saw Estrada admiring his bulging muscles, he said, "I worked out in Greenock. I like how it feels."

"I'm glad it did you *some* good being in there." He certainly wasn't the same boy he'd met two years ago.

Dylan glanced away and refused to meet his eyes. "I'm going to say this once and then we'll never speak of it again. Agreed?"

"Alright."

"My dad was a fisherman, and he wanted me to be a fisherman too. He taught me everything he knew. He loved the sea, so I did too. Then, one morning, he sailed out early and the weather turned. They never found his body." He bit his lip to stop it's quivering. "I haven't been in a boat since that day. *Christ.* I haven't even eaten a fish."

"But you're coming with me."

"Aye. You came here to help me. It's only right."

Estrada clapped his hand on Dylan's shoulder. "I'm sorry about your dad, man." Lost fathers. That was one more thing the two men had in common.

"There's another reason I'm coming. This all started when Sorcha unearthed Meritaten's broad collar. Kelly might have stolen it, but who's got it now? Kai." He ground his teeth, his anger seething beneath the surface. "I want it back. I want it back for Sorcha."

"We'll get it back. But promise me one thing."

"What's that?" Dylan asked.

"I get Roskilde. I owe that Viking bastard for taking Rachel."

"Sorry, man. I can't promise you that. But we can take turns."

63

S pray flew from the propeller as Dylan cranked up the power boat and they headed southwest into the Firth of Lorne. Estrada cleaned and repositioned his shades. The late afternoon sun glinting off the teal water was near blinding. As they cleared the harbor, they passed a cluster of kayakers and several small pleasure craft. The place was a maze of rocky forested islands, much like the Pacific coast back home.

Sorcha had dropped them off without a fight, just a solemn promise to stay in contact. Estrada was relieved she'd be on the mainland with her cell phone just in case things got complicated. Angus said the Police Marine Unit patrolled the shoreline, but there were five thousand square miles of coastal waters and only a dozen of them. If the police didn't know their exact location, they'd never find them. The boat they'd rented was a Viking river cruiser, something Estrada found laughable considering who they were hunting. It was about thirty years old and built for canals, but it was peak season and the only craft available.

Estrada hunkered down beside Dylan on the flybridge in a cockpit decked out in faded blue vinyl. He wasn't much into boats either and his gut was on a slow roll like the engine. He pulled his new knife out of the sheath in his boot. It was a razor-sharp Bowie he'd just purchased at a rod and gun shop in Oban. He'd considered buying a pistol, but that required a Firearms Certificate, and there was no way he wanted his name attached to it—not with the police already on his case. Besides, knives were his go-to. He'd used them all his life, even incorporated impalement arts into his act.

Dylan glanced over as he hefted it. "What are you planning to do with that?"

"Whatever it takes. I've met clowns like Kai Roskilde before. He talks a big game but he's a buffoon."

"Aye, a fart in a windstorm."

"Too bad you haven't got one of these stashed up your kilt."

Flipping up a corner of his plaid, Dylan revealed a small sheath knife belted around his right thigh.

"Jesus, you're full of surprises. I assume you know how to use that."

"I know enough. Pull it out. Stick it in."

"Dylan, you—"

"Don't hesitate. Just do it."

"Only if you're cornered and—"

"That's Scarba." Dylan gestured with his chin to a distant rocky outcropping to the right. He'd outgrown Estrada's brotherly advice.

Estrada glanced at the waves as they hummed along in silence and prayed Rachel was safe. When he tried to pick up her energy, he got nothing, and that disturbed him. They'd only been together a few days, but he loved her. He should feel *something*. Unless, anxiety blocked him, or she was—

"We're close to those coordinates," Dylan said, interrupting his thoughts. He slowed the engine and unrolled a chart.

Estrada picked up a pair of binoculars and scanned all directions. "No boats. No one on shore either. Where's this whirlpool?"

"That way," Dylan said, pointing southwest. I'm sure the son-of-a-bitch is out there watching us."

"No doubt. Angus mentioned caves."

"Aye."

"Maybe he stashed the boat in one of those sheltered coves and he's holed up in a cave."

"Stalking us from behind some rock like the snake he is." Dylan scowled. "There's an easterly breeze and the tide's coming in fast. That's why he chose this time."

"I knew he wouldn't make it easy."

"We need to set an anchor. Have you ever done it?"

"Nope."

"There's a shallow bar off that point. I'll bring her in there."

"What should I do?"

"At the bow"—Dylan gestured to the front of the boat— "there's an anchor tied to a length of nylon rope. You'll need thirty yards, maybe more. Don't drop the anchor. Just ease it slowly over the side and keep it taut until you feel it hit bottom."

"Okay." Estrada stood. "I can do that."

"Once it's set, you'll need to tie off the line around the bow cleat. Nothing fancy, just make sure your knot holds. I'll do the rest." Dylan sniffed and rubbed his nose. "And watch you don't get caught up in the line."

64

"There," Estrada said. The name was painted in cobalt blue on the side of the sailboat. *Steele Away.* Rachel hadn't mentioned they owned a yacht. How the hell did it end up in the hands of Kai Roskilde? Had the bastard bullied her into signing it over to him?

"He said to come alone. You better go below. Update Sorcha and stay hidden."

Rachel stood on the flybridge swaying like a silver willow, caught between Kai and that son-of-a-bitch who'd cut him and Dubh. Estrada swallowed hard. He stood slightly behind her, had a gun jammed in her back.

Rachel called to him, then winced, as he pushed the muzzle deeper between her ribs. Her long platinum hair was flying free, her face healed. Draped in white, she was perfection.

My white goddess.

Estrada glanced at Kai and his adrenalin surged. *If they'd raped her . . .*

All three sauntered down from the flybridge and stood on the deck.

"I don't believe you two have met officially," Kai said. "May I introduce Héctor Hassan."

"What do you want, Roskilde?"

A corner of Kai's lip flickered. "Come aboard. We'll talk."

"I came for Rachel."

"My game. My rules." Roskilde rolled up his sleeves and bared his fists. Then hooking the gunwale of their craft, he drew them together and bound them.

Estrada had no choice. He crossed over as the two boats bounced and bumped in the current.

"Such heroic sacrifice. Like something from a myth. I never could understand why a man would get his head kicked in for a woman."

"Are you forgetting Sorcha? I seem to remember—"

"Sit." Kai shoved him down hard on a stool.

Estrada didn't protest. He even allowed Kai to bind his wrists and ankles. A few punches should do it, and he could take that if it meant Rachel would go free. Darkness had fallen and she stood beneath a light and glowed. He admired her beauty as he remembered those frantic days and nights they'd spent together.

Once bound, Kai yanked Estrada up and tied him to a pole so he couldn't move his torso, arms, or legs. He wasn't just a bully; he was a coward.

"You have me," Estrada said. "Now let her go."

"Rachel, darling. Are you ready to leave us?"

Rachel walked forward, grasped the back of Estrada's head, and kissed him. Then, the back of her hand caught his mouth so hard his teeth cut into his lip, and he tasted blood.

He spat and hung there gaping as she sashayed back and embraced Héctor.

"What the fuck?"

"Gosh, I'm afraid she's not," Kai said. "As you can see, Rachel and Héctor have *bonded*. Oh, it's not Stockholm syndrome. These two have been at it for months." Héctor cuddled up behind her and glared. "Keep watching. It gets better. An audience really gets our detective wound up."

Estrada's jaw clenched. He couldn't swallow.

"Ah, did you really think she *loved* you? A man of the world like you?"

"*Jesus,* Rachel." Estrada's eyes itched, yet he dared not cry. Not in front of them.

"I warned you not to get involved," Rachel said coldly.

"Why? Why all the talk about relationships? About love?"

"Oh, did you pledge your love?" Kai clutched his chest. "I think my heart is breaking."

"You wouldn't stop. I warned you. I threatened you."

"Was it all lies? The Swedish mother who left you? The cop father who died in the line of duty?"

Rachel strolled over and tried to kiss him again, but he pulled away and spat in her face.

She rolled her eyes and wiped it off with the back of her hand.

"It was three days, Estrada."

"Well, I hate to cut your reunion short kids, but we must go. Rachel darling, hoist their anchor. Héctor, pop over and have a look around, will you? I smell a rat in the hold."

The pair climbed aboard the river cruiser. "Perhaps, I can assist," Kai said, and taking out his cell phone, he keyed in a number. "Ah. The Proclaimers."

Dylan's ringtone. Estrada heard Héctor shout, and then he appeared on deck with Dylan in a headlock. With his other hand, he clutched his bleeding stomach. "Little prick stabbed me."

Kai climbed across and sucker-punched Dylan in the gut, then bound his hands and feet. Dylan cursed and struggled until the two of them disabled him. Estrada hoped he'd got through to Sorcha. It was the only way they were going to get out of this.

"You realize, you've left us with no alternative," Kai said.

Dylan stood up tall. "The polis are coming. They know exactly where we are."

"Héctor, I'll finish up here with McBride. I'm sure you have something to say to Estrada for spending so much time with your woman."

As Héctor's swift fist connected with his face, pain sliced through Estrada's head. The blood dripping from his broken nose spurred the man on. After the beating, Héctor cut the rope binding him to the pole, shoved him to the deck, and wound it around his legs. Then he tied it off with an anchor.

Estrada glanced over at Dylan. He too was trussed up and weighted down. The bastards were going to toss them both into the sea.

"He's done nothing," Estrada yelled. Blood dripped down the back of his throat. He coughed and spat on the deck.

"Oh, I disagree. Charlie informs me he's been spending nights with Sorcha, and *she* is mine."

"Charlie?"

"You boys really need to learn to keep your hands off women who don't belong to you."

Dylan was vibrating, but Estrada didn't know how to help him. And then, Roskilde let fly with a punch to Dylan's testicles that doubled him over in a heap. "That should do it." Hefting Dylan, he hurled him over the side of the boat.

"No!" Estrada shouted and watched him sink beneath the deep green waves.

"They should die together." Rachel's voice was ice. She'd crossed back over and stood beside Héctor.

"I'll fucking kill you all," Estrada promised. Launching himself at Héctor's legs, he battered him with his head and shoulders. They laughed, then the two of them hoisted him up and flung him into the sea.

The salt water stung his eyes, but he forced them open and searched frantically for Dylan. He remembered how he'd found Héctor that night in the alley. Heat imprints. Somehow, he had to do that again. Dylan's body would be warmer than the water. If he could find the trail, perhaps he could save him, or at the very least, not let him die alone.

When his vision adjusted, Estrada could see through the murky water. He searched for traces of color, as he worked at the ropes binding his hands. He'd never had a problem getting free of ropes. That was one of the first escapes he'd learned. But they didn't know that. He'd also performed Houdini's water escape several times. If he remained calm, he could hold his breath for three minutes.

Within the first minute, he'd freed his hands, and then his feet, taken the knife from his boot, and cut the weight tied to his legs. Clinging to the anchor, he continued to sink.

Glancing up, Estrada saw the two hulls of the boats drifting through the hazy water. Kai had used the anchor from the river cruiser to weight Dylan. Now they were towing it away. Even if the police were close, there'd be no sign of them by the time they arrived. What should he do? Release the weight, swim to the surface, and tread water until the police boat came? Or keep sinking and searching? The answer came in a burst of scarlet mist thirty feet below.

Estrada dove toward it, holding the weight out in front of him and using his feet to propel him through the frigid water. Dylan was caught on a shoal, face down, snagged on a jagged rock. Estrada turned him over. If he wasn't dead already, he was damn close. He tried to ventilate with what little air he held in his lungs, but it was useless. His face ached with broken bones, and he had no oxygen left to give. He cut Dylan free of the anchor and hauled him up. He wouldn't leave him to decompose in the sea like his father.

Up, up, through the frigid water Estrada struggled with Dylan's body. He was almost there. But the body grew heavier as he grew weaker. He could feel himself slipping into a place of darkness. Couldn't do this alone. Too tired.

And, then he glimpsed a man in the water. *Search and Rescue.* They'd come. Estrada pushed Dylan's body into the man's arms and let go, praying he was still alive.

65

This face. Dylan knew this face, adored this face. But why was he here now? "Dad, is it really you?"

"Aye, my boy. Cough up that water, now. Clear those lungs." Dylan felt his father's strong arms, holding him above the waves in the churning sea. His nose burned from the brine. Dylan wiped his mouth and sputtered.

"But you drowned, daddy. You drowned when I was just a kid." He stared into his father's deep brown eyes.

"Aye, laddie, but I never left. Always kept an eye on you. And I'm damn proud of the man you've become."

"Am I drowned too?"

"No lad. It's nae your time. That's why he saved you."

"Who?"

"Your mate."

"Where is he?" Dylan searched the waves frantically.

"There. Out in the channel."

At last, he saw Estrada's head bobbing in and out of the frothy waves where the tide poured into the strait.

"You've got to save him. He's caught in the current. It'll drag him into the whirlpool. He'll die."

"I cannae do it, son. I'm only here for you."

"Daddy. Please."

"He did his part. Saved your life. Brought you as far as he could and gave you to me."

Frantic tears streamed down Dylan's face. "No. Estrada doesn't deserve to die."

"I'm sorry, son."

"But we can't just—"

"You've got to let him go, boy."

"I can't let him die."

"Look now. Help is coming."

"Please, daddy. I beg you." His anguished sobs were drowned out by the oncoming motor.

"You'll be fine, son."

"No. I won't. Estrada's my best friend. He saved my life." Dylan closed his eyes in desperation and when he opened them again, his father had vanished. A hand clutched his arm. "Dad? Dad, please don't go."

With his ankles and wrists still bound by Kai's ropes, Dylan let them haul him into the boat. "You've got to go after Estrada. He's there, caught in the current and he's headed straight for Corryvreckan."

"The tide's peakin', lad. We cannae go in there. It's nae safe." The man smiled grimly. "I'm sorry."

"You can't just be sorry. It's your job to save people. You've gotta try." Dylan beat the officer on the chest, and then collapsed with his head in his hands, tears streaming down his face. "It's not fair. He saved my life. It's just not fair."

66

Over the next three days, Dylan stayed with Sorcha at the dig, while the police searched the island of Scarba and surrounding coastline. They found nothing. Estrada had simply vanished. Sucked into the maelstrom, they believed his battered body had been dragged out to sea with the current. Nor was there any sign of Kai Roskilde, Rachel Erskine-Steele, or Héctor Hassan. Dylan spent hours with the police repeating all he'd seen and heard. To no avail.

At first, the police prickled at the notion a detective could be involved, but then a DCI Lyon arrived from Glasgow and changed everything. The Detective Chief Inspector had been watching Rachel Erskine-Steele for months because of her romantic liaison with Héctor Hassan, a suspected drug smuggler. According to Lyon, seventy percent of the cocaine coming into the United Kingdom originated from Columbia, then traveled through West Africa and Barcelona. Lyon was convinced Hassan was the Spanish connection and they were using the yacht to smuggle it into Scotland.

Unfortunately, none of this helped assuage Dylan's grief over the loss of Estrada. And once the shock wore off, Sorcha was inconsolable. He'd never seen her so despondent.

"You're acting like you're somehow to blame for this and you're not," Dylan said.

"First Kelly. Now Estrada. You're forgetting this all started when I found the artifact. I thought it was a blessing, but it's a feckin curse."

"Ach, come on. You're a scientist. You don't believe in Egyptian curses. Besides, you didn't excavate a tomb and desecrate the dead. You only found her broad collar. Meritaten should be grateful."

"Dylan, it showed me things."

"What kind of things?"

"I saw herself. Meritaten. They hated her. The shaman tried to force her out. He ripped off her collar and threw it in the pit. That's how it ended up there. She's cursed it, she has. I feckin know it."

Dylan remembered the scene he'd envisioned that night as he laid among the stones, the woman's haughty demeanor and the shaman's chagrin. "Why didn't you say something before?"

"You'd have thought me mad."

"You're alright, Sorcha."

"I know that now. I've seen crazier things hanging around Estrada." She broke down then, and Dylan caught her in his arms.

"I have to call Michael Stryker," he said, once she'd calmed down. "I've been putting it off."

"Who's Michael Stryker?"

"Estrada's mate. I don't know how to reach him though. I'll have to call Club Pegasus. They'll know. And I should call Sensara and Sylvia and Daphne. God, I just can't believe he's gone. He saved my life. *Christ.* If he'd just let me drown."

67

Estrada awoke in a shadowy world of fractured rock and rumbling water. Had he sunk below the sea to some undiscovered Atlantean world? Or been cast up onto one of the islands surrounding the maelstrom. One thing was certain. The salt-stained grotto in which he lay flooded at regular intervals. His body had been placed—he knew not by what magical force—on a ledge projecting from the side of the striated rock wall, mere inches above the waterline. Whether to be grateful or not, remained to be seen. He was barely alive, after having survived a violent trouncing by the Old Hag, and his recollections were scant. Choking. Panic. Thrashing. Defeat. What chance had a man—even a man with an ounce of faerie blood—against a primeval basalt pillar?

He licked his lips and tasted blood in his parched mouth. His flesh shuddered from the cold and itched with dried salt. Battered and broken, his limbs were a mass of abrasions. He couldn't move them and feared paralysis. He dreaded to think the worst, that his back was fractured beyond pain. If that was the case, his prognosis was death. A slow, malingering death. Dehydration. Delirium. Kidney failure. Coma.

In a fit of exasperation, he screamed long and hard, the thunderous breaking waves outside his cell beating against his brain like Thor's hammer. If he had such a tool and could lift his hand, he'd use it to bash in his own skull. What was left but a lonely, agonizing time in which to reflect upon his folly? For he was nothing but a fool.

Again, he'd let himself fall in love, only to be duped by a psychopath. For like Hamlet, Rachel Erskine-Steele was mad in craft. She'd played him since that moment in the underground when she'd invited him to her flat—her true motive to assure Héctor Hassan's escape. Taunting him with liquor and that tight white slip of a dress, she'd seduced him. Stopping him the first time he tried to make love to her, so he'd ache to try again. And, when he didn't rush back fast enough, she came for him. He wasn't naïve enough to consider himself a victim. He was as much to blame as she was. He knew she was crazy but couldn't stop himself. Falling in love was like clasping a branch in an avalanche.

The engagement ring burned like a brand in his inside jacket pocket. If only he could move his hand, he'd hurl it far, far away.

But what did it matter now? His only hope was that Dylan had survived. He'd handed him off to a man in the water just before losing consciousness, and trusted he was safely home. He could at least die knowing he'd accomplished what he came to this country to do.

Hours or perhaps days later, Estrada awoke to the warm, rasping pressure of a tongue licking his face. The great pounding of Thor's hammer had lessened, though his head still ached incessantly. His weighted eyelids were swollen shut and it took a great deal of effort to force them open.

When he did, he was confronted by the close furry face of a handsome black dog with coffee-colored eyes. A word emerged from childhood. *Perro.*

As the dog stood staring, Estrada heard a voice. *Do not be afraid.*

Truthfully, Estrada was afraid. Not of this wolfish dog, with whom he felt an immediate bond, but of dying alone in a cave. Afraid kayakers would stumble upon his rancid remains months from now and wonder who and what and why. After some time, the dog laid down beside him and, though he smelled bad as wet dogs do, the warm familiarity of his body afforded some comfort. Again, Estrada slept.

Awakening some time later, he felt a heavy weight on his chest and opened his eyes to Perro's wolfish head. The dog rested; muzzle pillowed on his breast. Estrada lifted his hand from his side and stroked the damp black fur. It took several moments before he realized he'd moved his hand. His shoulder ached, and he cried with joy to feel the pain. He assumed it was dislocated again—he'd suffered that agony before—but if he could move his hand, soon he could move other parts of his body. That meant, he could reset his shoulder. He'd done that before too. In pain, there was hope. If he could endure long enough without water, he might eventually crawl out of this cave.

Sleeping and waking assumed a rhythm as natural as the tide that ebbed and flowed in the cave. Had Perro found him here or brought him here? Once during a slack tide, Estrada awoke in the pristine silence of a chapel and laid listening to a soothing swirl of water at his back. Perhaps, some freshwater stream fed into the cave from above. He determined to move his legs and, after some time, wiggled his toes.

Estrada laughed, astonished. "Perro, I can move."

The dog's answering whine reassured him he understood.

Not long after that, Estrada could move his hands and arms. In agony, he reached down, grasped his knee, and pulled until he felt his shoulder slip back in place. Perro couldn't stand the violent cursing that accompanied this wrenching, and vanished. Once his shoulder settled, Estrada pulled off his damp leather boots. Somehow, they'd remained on his feet, and he'd not lost them to the Old Hag. Even the knife remained. He drew it from its secret pocket and hefted it.

Shoving his hand into the inside pocket of his leather jacket, he pulled out the jeweler's box that contained the silver engagement ring. "Never again," he said aloud, and hurled it as far as he could. The box bounced off the far wall and opened, and the ring clattered among the rocks. Estrada felt immediately liberated, though no less foolish. "Perro," he yelled. "I'm free." The black dog loped toward him and laid down beside him.

Perro often arrived just before the flood and slept on the ledge beside him during high water, then left again during slack tide. Perhaps, he hunted or visited his family. A dog as friendly and healthy as Perro was no stray. Estrada wondered why he'd not brought his humans to meet him and discussed this with him. The dog didn't answer, but looked downcast, so he never mentioned it again.

If the tide ebbed and flowed twice a day, Estrada reckoned he'd been holed up in the cave for three days, when he investigated the source of the dripping. After easing his body off the ledge, he crawled on hands and knees into the dark recess of the cave. A tremendous headache prevented him from standing, but he knew time was running out. His heart beat rapidly and he was feverish. He must find fresh water or die.

Perro was absent when he began, but by the time he'd located the small slate crevasse at the base of a tiny waterfall, the dog was there beside him. They lapped up water together. Braced against the rock, Estrada drank for a very long time. When at last he felt satiated, he stuck his head under the icy waterfall and cleansed his salty skin. He discovered several gashes clotted with dried blood on his skull and determined that he'd likely suffered a concussion. If not for the faerie blood that flowed through his veins, he'd most surely not have survived the Hag. He'd like to have stayed lying on the cool smooth rocks by the waterfall, but he realized during high tide this part of the cave flooded. After bathing as best he could, he crept back to his ledge and slept, while the sea claimed the cave once again.

As his pain and fever lessened, Estrada obsessed about things, particularly food. Favorites paraded through his mind, especially the traditional foods his mother cooked when he was very young in Mexico—corn tortillas and guacamole, tamales, pig roasted in the ground for cochinita pibil, hot chocolate and cinnamon, scrambled eggs and peppers, fresh fruit, goat cheese, chilies, and aged wine.

After the food came the people. Faces he'd not seen in far too long—his abuela and abuelo, his mama and papa, y sus hermanas, Sofia and Maria. Laughing faces from photographs and long misplaced memories.

And Michael, green eyes and long honey hair, his face all angles and seductive shadows. Estrada touched the back of his hand to his chapped lips, closed his eyes, and kissed him. It was all he longed to do, and he slipped into sleep pressing his feverish mouth against Michael's.

Days later, after filling his empty belly with cold fresh water, Estrada pulled on his boots and limped to the opening of the cave. Sinking to his knees, he peered out at the sea. The cave mouth was small, adequate for Perro, and just big enough for a man to crawl through head down on hands and knees. He whispered a prayer of gratitude to the Earth who'd given him another chance at life, then looked up. Blinded momentarily by the harsh sunlight, he shielded his eyes. Corryvreckan lay before him, bounded by a rock-strewn beach.

Perro hadn't returned from his travels, but he knew the dog could track him if he chose to. He picked his way through the Hag's rubble—scattered shards of slate, slimy seaweed, and the shells of once sentient creatures—moving toward what appeared to be a climbable slope. Like some shipwrecked explorer, once at the top, Estrada could survey his kingdom.

68

"H e's coming." Dylan tucked his mobile back in his jacket pocket and managed a smile. They were huddled around the bonfire at Sorcha's rapidly diminishing camp. Charlie had been escorted out by two policemen early that afternoon. Dylan interrogated him until he admitted to being Kai's spy, but claimed he'd only done it because he'd been threatened. There seemed to be no end to the man's evil.

"Who?" Sorcha asked.

"Michael Stryker. He's furious the police gave up the search for Estrada after only three days. Apparently, Michael's granddad has connections here in the U.K. They're going to put the pressure on."

"Who is he, this Michael Stryker?"

"Estrada's best mate."

"As in . . ."

"As in what?" Dylan clenched his fingers tighter around his mug and sipped his tea.

"You know, Dylan. Are they just friends or something else?"

"Ach, I don't know. I don't ask things like that." He was embarrassed to even think about Estrada and Michael being together like that.

"You're lying, Dylan McBride."

"I'm not lying." But he felt the blood rush to his face.

"You're blushing and you scratched your ear."

"So?"

"So, that's what you do when you're lying."

Dylan scowled. He adored Sorcha but sometimes she drove him mad.

"Oh, don't get your thong in a twist. I'm curious, is all. I saw himself kiss Kelly once."

"You did?" There was another image he didn't want to conjure.

"Aye. Right on the mouth. It was beautiful and sexy."

"Estrada's a free spirit. Always has been. Do you think he and Kelly . . .?"

"Ach, I don't know. I don't ask things like that." Sorcha punched him in the arm. The punch turned into a wrestling match on the grass and ended in a long kiss. "Don't distract me with sex, McBride. Tell me about this Michael Stryker. I'm curious what kind of man Estrada would choose."

"Honestly. I've never met him."

"Well, what's the craic? Come on, you must have heard things."

"Just that he manages Club Pegasus. It's a gothic nightclub in Vancouver. People dress up in costumes, party and get wasted."

"Sounds cool."

"Estrada headlines there whenever he's in town."

"As a magician."

"Aye."

"He mentioned that. What sort of magic does he do?"

"Theatrics, I think. Illusions, hypnosis, escapes . . . that sort of thing. Jeremy used to call him Houdini."

"Did he now? So, Estrada's an escape artist, is he?"

"I know he's good with straitjackets," Dylan said, remembering their adventure last year.

"Suddenly, Sorcha bolted upright and clasped his arm. "He's not dead, Dylan."

"What?"

"Estrada is not dead. A man like that does not drown in the sea off the coast of Scotland. I was there when he conjured the old gods. I watched him hypnotize a man to save the life of Magus Dubh. And now, you tell me he's an escape artist. Estrada is not dead."

"I want to believe that."

"Believe it. The sooner this Michael Stryker gets here the better. We're chartering a yacht. One with a captain who knows his way around these islands. Estrada's out there and we're gonna find him."

Perhaps, he was still suffering the effects of dehydration or concussion, but anchored in a pale, aqua bay below him, Estrada spied a yacht that looked remarkably like the *Steele Away*. There was no sign of activity or the murdering trio though. Lying on his belly in the sun-warm grass, Estrada leaned over the cliff and scrutinized the craft. A white and blue Sea Saga, she flew the Union Jack. They'd audaciously changed the name to *La Escapada*—Héctor's influence, no doubt—but it was the very same yacht, right down to the ropes they'd used to bind and weight him before tossing him in the sea to die.

Gingerly, Estrada threaded his way down the rocky escarpment and around the bay, always keeping out of sight of the yacht. He intended a surprise reunion and, for once, he had the upper hand. They thought he was dead.

While passing a series of caves on his way to the beach, he heard a peal of familiar laughter. Slipping inside the cavernous mouth, he crouched behind a boulder and surveyed the scene below.

Rachel Erskine-Steele and Héctor Hassan were packing a mountain of white powder into dry bags. Suddenly, the ruse made sense. It had nothing to do with jealousy. That was all peripheral. A sleight concocted to divert his attention from the real trick.

Rachel was a dirty cop, involved in a drug smuggling operation with Héctor Hassan and Kai Roskilde. The cocaine—at least, Estrada assumed that's what it was—had been dumped, either on the island or in the ocean, and these three were collecting it for distribution.

Had Alastair Steele discovered his wife's liaison with the Spanish smuggler or her involvement in the operation? Kelly Mackeras assumed he'd murdered Steele, but what if he hadn't? What if Steele was only unconscious when he walked away from the cave that night? Kai Roskilde had been there. What if he'd returned to murder Steele as he lay unconscious in the cairn, after sending Kelly to get the artifact?

These two were likely armed. With this amount of dope to move, they'd have weapons to protect their investment, and all he had was the knife in his boot.

He was planning his approach when Rachel grew tired of the monotonous packing.

"This is boring." Pulling a small wooden box out of her pack, she slipped behind a rock.

"What are you up to, baby?"

Baby? Estrada wanted to strangle Héctor Hassan just on principle. He was a proponent of sexual freedom, but what kind of man encouraged his woman to whore herself for the cause?

Rachel sashayed from her hiding place. "Bow to your queen," she said.

Naked, but for a sheer sarong knotted at the hip, she wore what could only be Meritaten's broad collar. Shaped like a crescent moon, the piece lay flat around her neck and shoulders.

It was the first time Estrada had seen it, and, for a moment, it took his breath away. Though Sorcha had explained that faience was only molded and glazed ceramic created in the likeness of turquoise and lapis lazuli, the effect of the aqua interwoven with gold and precious jewels was startling. And there was the knowledge of its antiquity. And Rachel. Once, he'd imagined her thus—long, straight platinum hair falling across her cheeks, ornate jewels capping her creamy shoulders, and that swanlike neck. Now, all he wanted to do was wring it.

"Down on your knees, slave," she said.

Estrada wondered how far she'd take this narcissistic drama.

"Yes, my queen. For you, I will do anything."

"Will you, Héctor? Will you really do *anything*?"

Héctor, who'd dropped to his knees before her, loosened her sarong and let it fall to the ground. With hands and lips, he slowly explored the pale wasteland before him. "Oh yes, my queen."

"Would you die for me, Héctor?" she asked, gasping, as he found his mark.

He managed a moan.

"And would you kill for me?"

Héctor glanced up at her. "You know I would. I helped kill McBride and that interfering Mexican, and it's not my fault the dwarf survived." When he paused, his lips curled in, and his sharp chin jutted out. "I would have killed your husband too, if *you* hadn't beaten me to it."

"What?" The word escaped Estrada's lips before he could stop it.

Rachel shushed Héctor, and they paused in their play, listening.

Estrada held his breath and waited. *Rachel.* It was her all along. No wonder she didn't want him to solve Steele's murder. *She* was the killer. She must have been there that night too, hiding in the dark by the cairn, waiting for her chance. This was the woman Estrada had first laid eyes on in the café at Kilmartin Glen—the cold and callous queen.

"It was only the sea," Héctor said. He slipped out of his shorts and dropped them. Then, kneeling in front of Rachel, he kissed his way back down her belly. "I love how salty you taste after we swim, how the salt seeps into every crevasse."

It took everything Estrada had not to rush in and pummel them into the rocks. How many innocent people had to die for their pleasure? But he needed to know the whole truth, to hear it all.

"Can you imagine how perfect life would be if all of this were ours, Héctor? I mean, just yours and mine. We could buy an Egyptian palace, and with this collar we could start our own collection. Imagine it. We could *be* Nefertiti and Akhenaten."

For several moments, the cave resounded with her escalating murmurs as Héctor continued to worship his queen. Then he stood and scooped her up in his strong arms.

Taking advantage of the moment, Estrada slipped behind them unobserved. From this new vantage point, he scrutinized Héctor as a man does his enemy. His skin was slick with sweat, and he was much stronger than Estrada expected. Biceps bulging, he held Rachel airborne, exerting full control over each movement. His tall, sinewy body was lean and sculpted, and Estrada found himself impressed. Their cries crescendoed through the cave, until, at last, they collapsed on an empty dry bag.

"Consider it done, my love. Once we've loaded the yacht, I'll take care of Roskilde. I hate him. He's bossy, and he never shuts up."

"I couldn't agree more," Estrada said, sliding his knife against Héctor's warm, quivering throat. Rachel's scent on his skin was almost overpowering.

"Estrada. How did you—?"

"Live?"

"I saw you—"

"Yes, you saw me bound and weighted and cast into the sea to drown. But I didn't drown, did I?"

Rachel stood staring, momentarily stunned by his resurrection.

"I know you're planning your new empire, Rachel, but I want that collar. Take it off and set it on the ground."

"No. It's mine."

Estrada shook his head as he suddenly understood. "You told Héctor to kill Dubh just to ensure Kai wouldn't sell it."

"Don't say anything," Héctor said.

"Take it off, Rachel, or I'll cut your man. And I'll do it for real, not the way Kai cut you." He dragged the blade against Héctor's slick skin and watched the blood spurt.

"Stop." Reaching behind her neck, she unhooked the collar and held it out. "It *is* exquisite, isn't it?"

Estrada looked and in that instant Rachel tossed it into a crevasse.

Then Héctor jammed his elbow into Estrada's right leg, in precisely the place Kai had shot him. Simultaneously, the bastard struck his wrist with his left hand, snapping it back and extricating the knife, which clattered on the rocks. When his fist broke Estrada's nose for the third time in as many weeks, blood gushed.

"*Jesus.*" Estrada went for him.

The click of a pistol stopped them both.

Rachel's first shot was naturally aimed at Estrada but, at the last second, he dove behind Héctor. She shifted and the bullet ricocheted off a rock and caught Héctor in the kidney. Clutching his bleeding back, he crashed to the ground.

Still holding the gun, Rachel ran to him and stared at the wound in disbelief. "Héctor. Get up," she said, crouching beside him. "Get up now."

Héctor rolled his eyes and moaned. His blood was everywhere.

"I can help him," Estrada said. "Put the gun down and let me—"

"Stay away from him." She pointed the gun at Estrada.

"Do you remember how fast my shoulder healed?" Estrada ripped off his T-shirt. "Look. Not even a scar. And I survived the whirlpool. Rachel, I can save him."

"You ruined everything."

"He's bleeding out. If you shoot me now, he's gonna die."

"I hate you," she spat, and squeezed the trigger.

In that moment, Perro launched from the shadows and hit her broadside, a muscular force of teeth and fur. His thick growls echoed through the cave mingling with her screams as she kicked and punched, desperate to break free.

Estrada snatched the gun and held it on her, while Perro wedged her down against the rocks, mouth open, teeth against her neck.

"Get it off me," she yelled.

"Perro. Let her go." Estrada had her in his sights and there'd be no more trickery.

The black dog backed off and sat a few feet away watching. His slow growl resounded in the cave.

"We're running out of time," Estrada said, kneeling by Héctor's back. "I'm going to help your boyfriend, so just stay there." He turned toward the dog. "Perro, watch her. If she moves, rip her throat out."

Estrada considered the implications, then taking his knife, he sliced across his left palm. Dropping the knife, he picked up the gun, just in case she couldn't keep still. Then, holding his bleeding palm over the bullet hole in Hector's back he squeezed and watched the precious fey blood drip into the wound.

"Rachel." Héctor moaned.

"He's scared. Let me hold him, please."

"How stupid do you think I am?"

Like a silver snake, Rachel darted out, grabbed the knife from the rocks, and lunged at Héctor.

Estrada squeezed the trigger just as Perro attacked.

The bullet caught Rachel in the shoulder, where only minutes before the faience beads had rested. She cried out and as she fell back the knife slipped from her grasp.

"Man, Sorcha had it right. You're one crazy, selfish bitch. You'd kill him to save yourself." Estrada set the knife down beside the dog, then balled up her shirt and shoved it against the bullet wound in her shoulder. "Sit here and hold this and don't you fucking move."

Perro emitted a low, steady growl as he lay watching, muzzle to paws, and Estrada knew he wouldn't let either of them move again.

"You missed," Rachel said.

"I intended to."

"Don't you hate me enough to—"

"Kill a cop? I may be a fool but I'm not insane." Estrada shook his head. "Now, shut up and let me finish this."

Estrada turned to Héctor. "You have to stay alive, man, because you're going to tell the police what really happened to Alastair Steele." His nose was still gushing blood, so he took a handful and wiped it over the bullet hole. Then he folded Rachel's sarong and bound the wound tightly. He checked the man's pulse. It was barely beating. Héctor was in shock.

Taking the knife, Estrada made another cut in his palm beside the first and held it over Héctor's mouth.

The man licked his lips and grimaced. "What . . .?"

"This is the elixir of the gods and you're getting it just this once."

Placing both hands against his own broken nose, Estrada set the bones. "Christ, that hurts. If you ever break my nose again, I'll kill you."

Estrada wiped his bloody hands on his jeans and took a deep breath. "Now, where's your phone?"

Héctor eyed his shorts which lay in a heap beside the bags of cocaine.

"Don't pass out, man. You're gonna call Roskilde and tell him to get over here. Tell him you need help. Got it?"

The effect of the blood was startling. A miracle cure Estrada had no intention of sharing with Rachel.

Héctor made the call. He was still weak, but the shock lessened as he regained his strength.

"Now tell me where we are," Estrada said.

"Jura."

"Is that an island?"

Héctor nodded, sweat drizzling down his face.

"Where on Jura? What's this bay called?"

"Pigs. Bay of Pigs."

"Well, isn't that ironic." Estrada pressed 0 for the operator and asked for the police. He needed Héctor alive. He needed him to tell the police that it was Rachel who killed Alastair Steele. It shouldn't be much of a problem since she'd just tried to kill him.

Estrada wanted the memory of Kelly Mackeras vindicated and as much as he hated Rachel, he didn't want to be the one to take her life. He'd seen enough death, and he was tired. Tired of loving. Tired of fighting. Tired of playing games.

Still, he had one last son-of-a-bitch to reckon with before he slept. Estrada bound both Rachel and Héctor, and left

Perro to guard them. Then he walked outside into the sunshine.

On the beach, he chose a chunk of driftwood the size of a baseball bat and hunkered down inside the mouth of the cave to wait.

70

Sorcha's eyes widened. "Did you hear that?" They were huddled around the bridge of the chartered yacht.

"What?" Dylan asked. "What'd I miss?"'

"On the marine radio. The Coast Guard just issued a mayday."

"Aye," the young pilot said. "Someone's in need of police and emergency medical assistance at *Bagh Gleann nam Muc*."

"By-glan-nam-what?" Michael had been resting but hearing the excitement he suddenly appeared at the helm.

"*Muc*," the pilot said. "Pigs. It means Bay of Pigs. If we keep following this coastline, we'll be there in thirty minutes. Since, we're in the area, we're bound to respond."

"Do you think?" Sorcha asked. "Do you think it could be him?"

"It has to be." Michael was trembling.

There's no way he should be out of hospital, Sorcha thought, *let alone flying halfway across the feckin world. So, this is the kind of man Estrada would choose.*

Michael had arrived in Glasgow early that morning, looking frail, starved, and beaten. Dylan had picked him up at the airport. His left hand was in a cast, as was his right arm from shoulder to fingertips. His neck was bandaged, his skin cut and bruised.

"What about Corryvreckan? Aren't we heading straight for it?" Dylan's eyes widened.

"Aye, but it's slack tide," the pilot said. "I've cruised by the Hag a couple of dozen times at slack tide with no problem. Best to sit down though and stay clear of the side of the boat. I don't want you to bounce out if we get hit by a rogue wave. It could get rough."

Sorcha saw the blood drain from Michael's face.

71

Estrada felt Kai Roskilde's erratic energy before the man entered the cave. Hovering to the right of the entrance, he hoisted the driftwood bat and whacked him hard across both shins as he stepped inside.

Kai yelped, then went down gasping and gibbering, doubling over instinctively to protect his soft organs from further assault.

Estrada stood over him. "Look up, Kai. Look up."

His head tilted, and when the hazy, blue eyes connected, the blood drained from the man's face.

"Surprised to see me?" Estrada smirked. "Sometimes, dead men *do* rise."

Kai grimaced and spat. "Coward."

"Let's just say, I'm efficient. I don't usually break a man's legs before a fight, but I'm tired. And that was payback for shooting me in the thigh." Estrada rubbed his jaw. "This," he said, catching Kai underneath the chin with the bat and breaking the left side of his jaw, "is for the brass knuckles."

Kai fell forward holding his face and moaning.

"The pain is excruciating, isn't it? Shoots right up into your brain."

Kai's eyes burned with rage.

"The police are on their way. Maybe, they'll give you something for the pain. Maybe they won't. Better get used to it. This is just the beginning."

In his eyes, Estrada saw the terror the man had instilled in others his whole life.

"I owe you enough pain to last forever and I intend to settle that debt. And Dylan owes you too. In fact, we debated who would get to beat you first. I guess I won that one, because .. . Well, here we are."

Estrada paused, then cleared his throat and spit. "Now, you and your associates attempted to drown me, so I've been sitting here imagining how I could pay *that* back. Poetic justice, you know. I thought about dragging you down to the sea and holding your head under with my boot."

Kai cowered, eyes bulging from his head.

"And I thought about shooting you somewhere inconvenient with Rachel's Glock," Estrada said, pulling the gun from his pocket.

Snorting, he mumbled something incoherent.

"Broken jaw, and still talking?" Bringing up his right foot, Estrada balanced on his left. "I even thought about breaking your goddamn nose." Jamming the heel of his boot into Kai's face, Estrada listened to the bones crack. Tears welled up in the man's eyes. "Oh, come on, man, you can't blame me for that."

Estrada leaned back against the rock wall, fondled the gun, and ignored the cursing and moaning.

"Anyway, after all this reflection, I decided Dylan owes you more than I do. You're the bastard who planted that bloody hanky and got him sent to prison. You even cleaned Kelly's prints off that bloody rock and called the cops that morning to tell them the killer was sleeping by the Ballymeanoch Stones."

"No," Kai muttered through thin bloody lips.

"Héctor says you did." Estrada pulled a cell phone from his jacket pocket. "In fact, Héctor says you planned it all. Listen." Estrada hit play and a man's voice echoed through the cave.

"Kai Roskilde phoned us real late Friday night. It was almost morning. Rachel and I were asleep at my place in Ardfern. Steele had found out about the smuggling and wanted in. Kai said he had a way to get rid of Steele and get the Egyptian collar without getting us involved. He could blame a couple of kids. We drove to the cairn and found Steele unconscious just like Kai said he would be."

"I didn't kill him," Kai mumbled.

"Oh, I know. That was crazy Rachel. But you did use Kelly Mackeras to steal the artifact and then you framed Dylan for murdering Steele. Do you want to hear that part too?"

"No proof."

"Maybe not. But I'm willing to testify to what happened on that yacht and I'm sure there's still evidence there. Fingerprints, blood spatter . . ."

Kai's faced paled.

"Attempted murder. Two counts—me and Dylan. That'll get you into Greenock."

Estrada glanced at the sky, distracted by the thunder of an incoming chopper.

Kai's eyes closed. He was passing out.

"Wake up, man. Here's the part you don't want to miss."

Eyelids fluttering, Kai turned his head.

"Dylan made a great friend in Greenock Prison. A lifer, who's in there for shooting a whole gang of skinheads because they murdered his gay brother. They're practically family. Can you imagine that? Big guy. Tough. Crazy as shit. How's Big Zeke going to feel when he finds out it was you who set Dylan up for . . . what? That mountain of blow in there?

And then, you tied him to an anchor and tossed him in the sea? And Dylan hates the sea."

The police helicopter landed nimbly on the cliff above the cave whipping up wind and dust.

"Anything else you want to say, Kai, because I'm about done, and the cops are here."

"Fuck off."

"Yeah, that's what I thought you'd say.

72

When the police arrived, Estrada gave them Rachel's Glock and Héctor's phone. Then, he went outside and leaned back against a rock. Closing his eyes, he took a moment to breathe and to ground. The violence had taken its toll. Now, all he wanted was peace.

"Excuse me. Is your name Estrada?"

He opened his eyes to an inquisitive young officer.

"It is."

"We've been looking for you. Heard you went down in the whirlpool. How'd you survive all this time?"

"What do you mean *all* this time? How long's it been?"

"Seven days."

"Seven days?"

"Aye. After three days, they called off the search, and then yesterday, it was on again. Someone cares enough about you not to give up."

"Aye, but not just someone. Everyone."

Estrada turned and scrambled up when he heard Dylan's voice. "Hey man. You *are* alive. I prayed that wasn't a dream. They got you out."

"*You* got me out," Dylan said, and the two men embraced.

"Estrada!" Sorcha screamed and grappled them both.

"Easy now," Dylan said. "He's likely broken."

"On the mend. But how did you—?" Estrada stopped in mid-thought when he saw who was standing behind them. "Michael?" Shivers raced up and down Estrada's arms.

Michael's right arm was in a cast from shoulder to fingertips. His neck bandaged. His left hand in a cast. He wore a baseball cap and sunglasses and tears dripped down his cheeks.

"What are you doing here?"

"I knew we'd find you," Michael said, falling against Estrada's chest.

"Are you crying, man?"

"I thought I'd lost you, compadre. Christ, I thought I'd lost me."

Estrada held Michael, feeling things he couldn't put into words. And then, he too, was crying . . . holding Michael and sobbing into his shoulder.

73

Later that night, after hours spent conversing with the police, they huddled around the bonfire at Sorcha's camp, swapping wine and stories. It was July twenty-fifth—exactly one month since Estrada flew to Scotland. When he got to the part about Perro, Dylan burst out laughing and snorting, grasping his belly while tears rolled down his cheeks.

"What's so funny?" Estrada said.

"Jeez, man. A thing like that could only happen to you."

"What do you mean?"

"Do you remember the story of Bhreachan, the Norwegian King who tried to conquer the whirlpool so he could win the hand of the island princess?"

"Yeah, the fool drowned."

"Aye, but we didn't tell you the end. Bhreachan's body was pulled from the whirlpool by his faithful black dog and deposited in a cave on the north end of Jura."

"No way." Estrada skin rippled with goose bumps.

"Aye, it's true. The cave is called *Uamb Bhreacain* and it's right where you woke up."

"Holy Christ, Estrada. Dylan's right. Only you could be rescued by a ghost dog," Sorcha said.

Had the dog pulled his body from the whirlpool and dragged him to that ledge? But he couldn't have been a ghost. Rachel and Héctor had seen him too. When she tried to shoot him, the dog had knocked her down.

"Perro saved my life," Estrada said. "Twice."

"What happened to him?" Sorcha asked.

"He disappeared. I guess he knew I didn't need him anymore."

"I hope they're locked away for life," Dylan said, suddenly serious. "All three of them."

"Hey, I almost forgot." Estrada pulled a box from his jacket pocket. "I have a gift for you, Ms. O'Hallorhan."

When she opened it, Sorcha's eyes widened. "Hah. You found it. I thought herself had hidden it where no one ever would."

"She tried. She wanted to use it to build her empire." Estrada scoffed. "But it came home. It belongs here with you."

"Ah, you're wrong there. Meritaten's collar belongs to the Lord's Remembrancer; at least for the moment." Sorcha took the collar from the box, closed her eyes, and touched it to her heart.

"What the hell is that, anyway? The Lord's Remembrancer?"

"Ach, it's Scotland," Dylan said. "Tradition and all that."

"But it's probably worth millions. Dubh could broker it. With that kind of money, you could do anything."

"True enough," Sorcha said. "But this collar is both blessed and cursed. I'm sure you've heard of Egyptian curses."

"It's not cursed," Dylan said. "It came back to you, didn't it? And the murdering thieves are behind bars."

"Where *is* Dubh?" Estrada asked. "He should be here tonight."

Sorcha shrugged. "No idea."

"Magus Dubh is someone you really should meet," Estrada said to Michael. "He's extraordinary in the truest sense of the word."

Dylan stood and touched Estrada's arm. "Got a minute?"

"Sure." Estrada rubbed Michael's uninjured shoulder. "I'll be right back."

Michael had been quietly popping painkillers, but Estrada didn't think chemicals could touch what he was going through. Locked in a coffin, floating in the sea during a gale. That was traumatic enough, but Estrada suspected something else had happened out there on the coast. Something unspeakable. He'd tried to find the old Michael, but he'd vanished. This new man was a stranger, so tightly bound, if he pulled the wrong thread, he might unravel. Still, after the ordeal he'd suffered, Michael had come all this way to find him, and that meant the world.

Estrada followed Dylan out into the shadowy field. When they stopped at last, Dylan looked deadly serious and he felt a shiver of apprehension, wondering what was coming next.

Dylan took a deep breath. "I need to tell you something."

"I'm listening."

"After three days the police called off the search. They told us . . . They thought you were dead, and I thought you were dead. I saw you caught in the current."

"It's okay, man. I thought I was dead too."

"Aye." Dylan paused and gnawed at his lip.

"What is it?"

"Well, I felt it was my duty to call home and tell them. I called Club Pegasus, and they put me in touch with Michael."

"Yeah, man. Thanks for doing that. I'm glad he's here."

Dylan paced back and forth along the grassy patch. "Then, I called Sylvia. I thought the coven should know."

"Absolutely." Estrada couldn't imagine what tragic news Dylan was building to. Had someone been hurt back home? Was Yasu now High Priest? Had he and Sensara got married?

"Sylvia told me something . . . something you should know."

"Just fuckin' say it, Dylan."

"It's about Sensara."

Estrada held his breath but moved his hands to urge him on.

"She's pregnant."

Estrada choked and coughed. "Pregnant?" Of all the things, he expected to hear, that was the furthest from his thoughts.

"Aye. Sensara's having a baby."

"Wow. I . . . Wow."

"Sylvia said, she's due the beginning of August."

"What? That's next week." Estrada's eyes narrowed in confusion.

"Aye."

"How? How did we not know something like that?" He'd seen her a month ago at their solstice ceremony and she didn't look pregnant. Then he remembered she was wearing that flowing saffron gown and had strings of flowers dangling from her neck. Had he been so distracted by Yasu he hadn't noticed the bump?

"She's been hiding it all this time. She told the girls a few months back but swore them to secrecy."

"Who's the father? Yasu?"

Dylan shook his head and grinned. "Count back, man." Dylan held up nine fingers. "Remember Samhain? The baby's yours."

"Mine?" Estrada shook his head. "No, that's not possible. Sensara always made me . . ."

His mind raced back to the previous fall, their brief affair, the last night they'd made love in the hallway outside

Michael's place. Sensara had been so desperate, she hadn't cared about protection.

Dylan smiled. "You're going to be a father."

"A father." Somehow, Estrada just couldn't imagine it. And yet, he knew in his heart, it was something he wanted. He remembered his time with Primrose in the forest at Taynish. *You'll be a father and a grand one,* she'd said. Could faeries prophesy the future?

"Jesus, Dylan. I'm just . . . I'm amazed."

"There's not a man I know would make a better dad than you, man. You saved my life, and I'll never forget that, but you also made me a better person. And that's what dads do. That's what you'll do for your child."

"My child," Estrada said.

He was going to be a father, and life would never be the same.

74

Things had been quiet around Sorcha's camp since the sensation died down, the paparazzi disappeared, and most of her crew returned to their respective jobs and universities. That included Dylan McBride, who'd just completed another year of study in Vancouver. Sorcha was ready to pull up stakes. It was time.

She'd written and published her paper on Meritaten—the Egyptian Princess who'd visited the Hebrides and left behind her broad collar in 1350 BCE—and lectured at several universities. But her mind kept returning to that night, last July, when she'd stood naked by the standing stones and promised herself to the Horned God.

It seemed like a dream, and yet, on moonlit nights she wandered the fields, calling his name. *Cernunnos.* It was derived from the Greek word *carn* meaning horn. He was as old as humanity, the spirit of the hunt. *Christ,* he'd inspired the word *horny.* After his image was painted on a cave wall at Caverne de Trois-Frères in France, during the Paleolithic, he'd drifted through time, surviving until Christians turned him into Satan.

Sorcha had traced the appearance of the Horned God through a myriad of cultures, times, and locales beginning with Pashupati from the Indus Valley, into Minoan Crete and what was once Thrace; through the Danube Valley, Northern Italy, and into Gaul, where his name and image were etched on a pillar beneath Notre Dame Cathedral in Paris.

She'd even traveled to the British Museum to see the original Gundestrup Cauldron. Crafted by multiple silversmiths and gilded in gold during the Iron Age, this ritual cauldron depicts the Horned God seated as a yogi. He holds a Celtic torque and a serpent, and is surrounded by lions, deer, and gryphons. The cauldron's origins were debated, yet Sorcha knew if she could only touch it, she'd know the truth.

And Sorcha wanted to know, needed to know.

Cernunnos. With those primordial hands, he'd touched her and left her longing to be touched again.

It was the first of May. Beltane. Sorcha was sleeping when his scent wafted over her, infused with everything in nature she relished most. The odor of fecund earth after a spring rain, musky wild horses, and puppy's ears, ripe peaches soaked in honeyed spices, and something else, some pheromone that awakened her desire.

Sitting up, she turned on the torch beside her bed and shone it around the carpeted walls of her tent. Seeing nothing, she emerged, and opened the partition, feeling her pulse quicken as the scent intensified. He was near, but where? She poured herself a large shot of whiskey and downed it, then drew a soft white cotton robe around her naked body and slipped outside barefoot. It was around three in the morning, so the few volunteers left in her sparse camp were asleep. She followed a sheep trail through the damp grass, down through the meadow, toward the stream.

When Cernunnos touched the back of her neck, she gasped, lost her balance, and fell to the ground. Reaching down, he offered his hand, and his touch made her weep.

"I don't know why I'm crying."

"To find that which you seek can be overwhelming." Sweeping her into his arms, he held her against his chest. "Do you fear me, Sorcha O'Hallorhan?"

"Certainly not."

"Good. I will not hurt or force you, though my desire for you is immense."

"Aye," she said. "I can feel it."

"It has been a very long time since I coupled with a woman on Beltane. Over two millennia."

"Really? But, why now? Why me?"

"The shaman summoned me, and you . . . you offered, and you believe. How could I not accept such an offer?"

The touch of his dark lips against her neck sent a shiver spiraling down her spine, and she gasped again.

"I know you, Sorcha O'Hallorhan. I know your desires and your dreams, and I can give you the answers you seek."

"What do you mean?"

"You long to live in the past, to experience that which exists no more."

"That's true."

"Then I shall take you there." His dark eyes, so mesmerizing, caught and held her. Laying his palm against her cheek, he touched her warm lips with his thumb. "Anywhere in this world, to any time or culture you desire. It is your choice."

Impulses flooded her body, fantastic sensations, building like the force of a sensual current when the cavern walls close in. "I can't think. I can't . . ."

"Close your eyes."

As his mouth opened to hers, their breath and flesh merged, sensations deepened, rippling through every cell of her body and culminating, at last, in an orgasmic peak.

"*Holy Mother of God.* Did we just . . .?"

"You did."

"From a kiss?"

When he smiled, a torch burned in his dark eyes. "It was needed to balance your equilibrium."

"Cernunnos." Reaching up, she touched his horn. "I'm still feeling a little unbalanced."

Smiling, he brushed her lips with his. "Have you decided?"

"How can I? There are so many cultures, so many moments in time I've studied and dreamed of experiencing."

"Close your eyes, breathe, and envision this place of your dreams."

Nestled in his arms, her mind drifted through a theater of stars and came at last to rest on a jewel that felt like home. "It's incredible. But I don't know where I am."

"I do, Sorcha O'Hallorhan. For I am here for you."

My Dear Readers,

The germ of this story was a McGuffin—an object that drives the plot and motivates the characters but isn't terribly important in its own right. At least, it's not as crucial as the journey itself. From the outset, I wanted to focus on Dylan, and since he's an archaeology student and I'm a huge fan of archaeological movies, an artifact seemed to be the perfect McGuffin. But what artifact?

When I ran into a rather obscure book (big breath) *Kingdom of the Ark: The Startling Story of how the Ancient British Race is Descended from the Pharaohs,* I knew it would be Egyptian. Written by Egyptologist Lorraine Evans, it came to me as a battered paperback in a thrift store, whispering stories of Meritaten.

Egyptians in Scotland. I already knew that Dylan McBride had a unique ability to speak with stones, since he'd revealed that in Book 1, when he mentioned spending his teen years in Argyll, an area rich in megaliths. Later, I traveled to Scotland with my friend Jackie. Naturally, we went to Tarbert where Dylan spent his teen years. We also explored Kilmartin Glen and wandered through Ballymeanoch, where Dylan sleeps with the stones and Estrada conjures the gods.

A shout out to Andrew MacDiarmid, proprietor of The Moorings Bed and Breakfast in Tarbert, Scotland who had one room left "obviously meant for us" the night we rolled into town. And to Marina at the Archives in Lochgilphead for her answers to my email inquiries regarding police and legal proceedings in Argyll, Scotland. Errors are my own. I've taken liberties and apologize to Police Scotland, who I'm sure are a sensitive, respectful, and dedicated force. Thank you to Scottish and Irish friends who helped me with language, especially Kenny Turner, whose witty emails always made me laugh.

I must acknowledge Rachel Butter's book, *Kilmartin: An Introduction and Guide*, with photography by David Lyons (Kilmartin House Trust, 1999), and poet Robert Graves, who authored *The White Goddess: A Historical Grammar of Poetic Myth.* (UK: Faber and Faber, 1999). Without Graves' intuitive insights, I fear neither Estrada nor I would have properly understood the Oak King.

Most settings in Scotland exist, including Dunchraigaig Cairn in Kilmartin Glen, and Her Majesty's Prison Greenock. If you're curious about the Corryvreckan Whirlpool, you can find more information at Whirlpool Scotland and watch a fantastic video of this unique landscape. Scotland is a beautiful and magical land; a place to be explored time and again.

Michael Stryker's meeting with Christophe and Don Diego was a natural evolution to his obsession with Vampire. When I traveled as a relief lighthouse keeper, I fell in love with the scenery of the Northwest Pacific Coast. A secluded island in the Broughton Archipelago seemed the perfect place for an exotic vampire lair. Michael's confrontation with Don Diego inspired two more books, and Sorcha's bargain with Cernunnos, yet another. When characters become real, you never know where they'll lead you.

Because I don't write with an outline, I didn't know where this story was going until I reached the end. Christophe and Kelly, both casualties of love, broke my heart, and I cried as I watched and listened and wrote. I agonized with Dylan, Big Zeke, Michael, and Estrada. What began as a murder mystery morphed into something else as I witnessed and documented how lives can be affected by ignorance, hatred, and fear.

Stay strong, dear readers. A magical black dog waits in the shadows who knows the ultimate gift is love.

Thank you for reading my stories. If you'd like to help a writer write more, please leave a review on Goodreads and with your favorite retailer.

You can sign up to receive my six-week seasonal newsletter at https://harpercarr.substack.com/and follow me on social media.

g goodreads.com/user/show/183384153-harper-carr

instagram.com/harpers_books/#

tiktok.com/@harperwrites1003

blessings and all good wishes,
Harper
xo

PRAISE FOR THE VAMPIRE'S GAME

"An intoxicating mix of magic and mystery that will keep you turning pages"

—EILEEN COOK, AWARD-WINNING AUTHOR AND EDITOR

"A magical thrill ride packed with action, beautiful imagery, and imaginative lore . . . complex queer characters and realistic emotional situations."

—SIONNACH WINTERGREEN, QUEER CRIME/FANTASY AUTHOR

"The sense of conflict is exemplified—love, jealousy, revenge. Characters are elaborately written and believable. I enjoyed the fluidity in the prose, the superior storytelling, and the unrelenting tension. A page-turning narrative that will have fans of the genre enthralled."

—THE SERIAL READER

"Harrowing, engaging, and captivating . . . heartbreaking twists and turns"

—ANTHONY AVINA

"The true draw is the intricate psychology of the characters, who are complex, nuanced, sympathetic, and occasionally, deeply irritating—a sign of just how invested I've become. A highly recommended read."

—JUNIPER GREER-ASHE

"This fantasy/murder story deftly weaves Wiccan ritual and magic in the beautiful and somewhat haunting setting of British Columbia's coastline. The characters are memorable, and I especially love the author's fresh take on vampirism."

—DEBRA PURDY KONG, URBAN FANTASY/CRIME AUTHOR

THE MAN IN BLACK SERIES

The Witch Killer

The Conjurer

The Vampire's Game

The Tortured King

The Druid's Tune